THE MEN OF
HALFWAY HOUSE
Series

A MENDED Man

JAIME REESE

Published by Romandeavor, Inc.

ISBN: 978-0-9907786-0-8 (Kindle)
ISBN: 978-0-9907786-1-5 (ePUB)
ISBN: 978-0-9907786-2-2 (Paperback)

First Edition, April 2016
Printed in the United States of America

Edited by Jae Ashley
Cover art and formatting by Reese Dante
Cover Photographer: wagnerLA Photography
Licensed material is being used for illustrative purposes only and any person depicted in the licensed material is a model.

This book is intended for adult audiences due to language, sexual content, and other subject matters some readers may find distressing.

Message to Readers

Although Aidan and Jessie are not residents of Halfway House, the house is the reason their paths crossed. Hopefully, in the end, you'll understand why these guys took so long to finally reach their happily ever after and why they'll fight like hell to keep it.

* * * *

Creative license was taken with this story and may slightly stray from factual medical or police procedure. It is a work of fiction.

Trademark Acknowledgements

The author acknowledges the trademarked status and owners of the following trademarks mentioned in this work of fiction:

Dr. Phil: Peteski Productions, Inc.

Google: Google, Inc.

iPod: Apple, Inc.

Marines: US Marine Corps, a component of the US Department of the Navy

Miss Universe: IMG Universe, LLC

Olympics: United States Olympic Committee

Skype: Skype Corporation

Superman: DC Comics General Partnership

Velcro: Velcro Industries B.V.

For Aidan.
You win.

"Every man has his secret sorrows which the world knows not; and often times we call a man cold when he is only sad."

— *Henry Wadsworth Longfellow (1807-1882)*

Prologue

He woke with a start and stilled, trying to focus on the faint sound on the other side of the door. He could have sworn he heard something. He tried to hold his breath to quiet the sound of each intake of air.

Someone was there.

He slowly climbed out of bed, his movements light and cautious. The cold tile floor against his bare feet sent a chill through his body. His small bedroom offered no escape except for the doorway between him and whoever was out there. There was also the single window behind the bed, two stories up. He cursed under his breath, realizing he had left his phone charging in the living room. He scanned the room for a weapon, something, anything that would provide protection. Times like these he wished he knew how to use a gun, a knife, or had the strength to swing a stick at anything other than a dog to play fetch.

He grabbed a cardboard shipping tube resting along the wall. It probably wouldn't offer much of a beating, but hopefully it would, at least, slow someone down and give way to an escape. He leaned against the wall, holding the tube like a baseball bat ready to swing. Who was he kidding? He didn't know how to handle a damn bat. He screwed his eyes shut and listened closely.

His arms and neck tingled as if a swarm of insects crawled under his skin. His heart raced faster; his breath came at a clipped pace. His eyes snapped open when a thought struck him. A shiver traveled his body and his hands began to shake. *Please no.*

Somehow…he just knew. *Oh God.*

A split second later, the bedroom door flew open and slammed against the wall. A dark shadow appeared, backlit by the faint streetlight coming from the living room window. He couldn't see the face but recognized the man and the familiar fear his large body commanded. No cardboard tube could fight off the man twice his size, and bigger and broader…and infinitely stronger.

The shadow's thick, meaty hand grabbed him and threw him on the bed, momentarily numbing him. The shadow pushed its large, muscular frame over his, suffocating him and pressing him into the mattress. He pushed back against the broad shoulders, trying to break free from the power holding him down.

"I missed those baby blue eyes of yours," the shadow said as he licked up the side of his neck. "Keep fighting me. You know I like it rough."

His stomach roiled and that night's dinner bitterly rose in his throat. He looked up at the small ceramic vase on the windowsill and his glass angel figurine. The T-shirt was yanked off and over his head harshly. The rush of cold air skated across his chest followed by a hot, wet mouth.

He tried to move higher on the bed, hoping to gain those precious inches of distance he needed. He reached up, his fingers barely grazing the vase's rough ceramic exterior. He pushed off the broad shoulders and grunted with the force to stretch. He reached up with one hand and finally wrapped his fingers around the ceramic vase, slamming it against the shadow's head.

The looming silhouette sat up and raised a hand to the side of his own face. "You son of a bitch!"

He took advantage of the momentary distraction and pulled his knees up to his chest and kicked outward with as much force as he could.

His father would be so proud.

The shadow reared back on the bed and he managed to get out from under him. He tried to run for the door, but a thick, strong hand grabbed him by the back of the neck and threw him against the dresser in the corner. The hard wooden edge rammed into his side, shooting bolts of pain through his limbs, weakening his legs and robbing him of the breath in his lungs. He gasped for air and tried to stand straight, holding the dresser to keep his balance. A powerful force grabbed him by the waist and slammed his back against the wall, off the ground. One large fist landed squarely on the side of his head with minimal effort, like someone shooing away a gnat on a typical hot Miami summer day. Pain instantly bloomed across his face, numbing everything above the neck, and his eyes watered.

He pushed against the shadow's face, clawing at his features, knowing exactly where the eyes were and the slight bend of the already broken nose he was all too familiar with.

Wetness covered his hand. He had drawn blood from the monster.

"You're going to regret that, Runt!"

Another punch followed and another. He fell to the floor, the squares and streaks of light in the darkness became blurry and his stomach churned from the pain. More kicks and punches landed in rapid succession. He lost count. He gasped, rolling his body into a fetal position, needing to protect himself as sharp ripples of pain shot throughout every inch of his body.

I don't want to die.

His eyes burned from the tears he tried to hold back.

I won't cry. I won't cry. Men don't cry.

He yelled, unable to control the pain any longer, when the monster pulled him by the leg. He heard a pop, a sound he prayed he'd never hear again, then another blinding pain in his hand, arm, he wasn't even sure anymore. Everything felt loose, broken...not connected at all. His vision blurred. He was roughly thrown on the bed again, no longer able to control the sob that escaped.

He hated being helpless.

He tried to pull away the fingers from around his neck. His head fell back as he gasped for air, feeling the life leaving his body. His blurred vision now inked with black spots, disguising the few specks of light that still lingered.

Oh, God...please. I don't want to die.

Through his fuzzy vision, a glint of light reflected on the glass angel on the windowsill, like a beacon answering his plea for help. His protector. As if the one who'd given him the figurine commanded him to fight.

A surge of adrenaline jolted his body. He reached up with his good hand and firmly gripped the glass angel. With a warrior yell, he summoned every ounce of strength in his shattered body and jammed the glass figurine into the monster.

part one
SURVIVING

Chapter ONE

Detective Aidan Calloway signed off on the last document, closed the file, and sighed. He hadn't discharged his weapon and no one had gotten hurt. Less paperwork for him and a better day for everyone in his proximity. A win all around. He could finally call it a night and head home after another painfully long day.

He threw the pen on the desk and caught his reflection in the screen of his propped up phone. He ran his fingers through his hair and scratched his chin, cringing at the growing stubble and his now disheveled dark hair. It was getting too long and he found himself brushing it out of his eyes more often than not. Maybe he should go back to the high and tight look he used to wear in the Marines. He wasn't a vain man, but he looked a bit worn, even to his own eyes. And he couldn't do this whole metrosexual-gel-hair shit to keep it all in place.

"You look fine, pretty boy. Stop fussing."

Aidan scowled. Sunny, his partner of six months, had more balls than most of the men he'd been paired with since he'd joined the force roughly six years ago. Growing up with a flower child name like Sunshine Mooney definitely forced a kid to develop one hell of a thick skin rather quickly. And good luck to the person who called her by her given name. He wouldn't openly admit it, but he had mad respect for the woman who never turned away from a challenge and never took shit from anyone. Including him. They were a perfect match and could dish out comebacks until the end of days.

"You're a real fucking comedian," he said, glaring into her chocolate-brown eyes.

She quirked a dark eyebrow. "You know, that evil, hazel-eyed glare of yours has zero effect on me."

"Calloway," Captain Harry Jameson yelled from his office across the department floor.

"Oooh, you're going to the principal's office," Sunny whispered from her desk.

"Cut it out, Sunshine," he growled, emphasizing her given name. She straightened in her seat with a smirk, having figured out early on when not to push. He stood from his corner cubicle and grabbed the file and his sport coat, hoping to quickly wrap up whatever the captain wanted and head out of the station without much delay.

Sunny opened the drawer and grabbed her keys. "I'm outta here before he decides to do a group think meeting or something."

"Don't get into too much trouble on your own this weekend." Finally, they had the weekend off after working consecutively for the last three weeks.

She cackled.

"That's attractive."

"Mock me all you want. You're the one headed into a meeting while my ass heads home into a nice, warm, comfy tub." She turned and dramatically flipped her bleached hair then waved over her shoulder as she walked away. "See you Monday!"

He dropped the folder off at the processing table and shrugged into his jacket as he headed over to his captain's office. All he wanted right now was his couch and some white noise from the TV until he passed out. He made his way down the hallway and caught another glimpse of himself in the glass of the picture hanging on the wall. It seemed reflective surfaces were on a mission to showcase just how badly he wore his exhaustion. He straightened the collar of his shirt under the jacket and finger-brushed his hair. He added another item to his weekend checklist: get a haircut.

Aidan entered the captain's office and cleared his throat.

"Shut the door," Harry said, not bothering to turn around from his perch by the window.

Aidan closed the door to his boss's office then walked over to stand behind the chair opposite his desk.

The captain finally turned around. "I wish you'd actually wear a tie to work and follow our dress code."

"I'm not wearing a fashion noose," he said, tugging the cuffs of his shirt while he maintained his spot behind the chair.

Harry shook his head and groaned. "It makes it a bit tough to enforce the code with the other detectives when you refuse to follow it."

"When they close as many cases as I do, then I think it's fair to extend them the same courtesy."

Harry grunted and sat in his chair, gesturing toward the vacant seat. "Please sit."

Aidan internally cringed with the dimming promise of a quick escape. He pulled out the chair and crossed his legs, hoping the captain would skip the chitchat about his kids, the wife, or dog. Whatever. He just wanted to wind down and disconnect.

"I'm putting you in a group."

"Like therapy?" he said with a lopsided grin.

"Smartass. No. Although I'm sure you could benefit from that."

"What kind of group?"

"A team of detectives."

Aidan threw his head back and spread his arms dramatically. "C'mon, Harry. You know that shit never works well with me. I'm surprised Sunny's lasted this long." He looked back at his captain and lowered his brow.

Harry rubbed his temples. "That's why she's going in with you. For some reason, she doesn't want to strangle you at the end of the day so I'm not messing with that formula. I'll call her and tell her tomorrow. I figured it was easier to break it to you individually rather than have the both of you gang up on me."

"Captain—"

Harry raised a halting hand. "They're trying something new. You guys will help with potential serial cases that have a local connection. That includes current and cold cases. Assess the situation and whether it may be linked to other jurisdictional files…work them, find leads.

The team will work with the federal agencies, have access to their resources if needed and determine when the agencies need to step in. The case will get handed off or you all will close them as the intermediary working between jurisdictions."

Aidan mulled it over. Locals always bitched and moaned when the FBI came in and snatched a case from them. Ego, glory...there were tons of reasons as to why, so having a team as the go-between seemed like a viable solution to soften that transition. "I'm fine with Sunny, but you can't stick me with a group."

"Think of it as a hybrid task force. We're gathering a group of people from different divisions. You and Mooney are the two coming from homicide. It's a small group and no one's a paper-pusher. I think you'll fit right in."

"Why me?"

The captain raised a gray eyebrow. "You really have to ask me that? You're working on taking down one of the largest crime and drug rings the city has seen in over a decade, and six months ago you cracked down on a country-wide counterfeit auto parts dealer and an exotic car theft export network. You've helped contribute to the highest arrest record in the state. You've already worked with several government agencies. With your contacts and this team, I think the group can be quite effective."

"I'm quite effective without a group."

"You are. But this will make everyone better."

"Yay team," he mumbled.

"I know this isn't your ideal situation, but I need you to play nice with others. We both know Mooney will jump at the chance. She fights the glass ceiling at every opportunity so she's not going to sit on the sideline to pacify you. I've held them off as long as I can with every kind of excuse I could think of. They don't care."

"Who's *they*?" Aidan asked, crossing his arms.

"Way above my pay grade and yours. They asked me to assemble the task force from various departments. Your name was specifically mentioned...I'm guessing because of your existing work with the agencies on our other cases. There will be certain liberties with this group and the reach is far more than the tri-county area."

Aidan uncrossed his legs and leaned forward, resting his forearms on his thighs. He glanced over to his right and spotted himself in the reflection of the silver pen holder. He reluctantly admitted his stare was a little angrier than the norm. He reached out and repositioned the cup-like object out of his line of sight. Even he couldn't stand himself sometimes.

"Manny Reyes is going to head up the task force."

Aidan shook his head and raised his hands. Manny was the most pigheaded, self-centered son of a bitch he knew—excluding, of course, the man who seemed to stare back at him from every reflective surface that day. He often served as his department's mouthpiece when the press needed a statement. When things went badly, Manny zeroed in on people's weaknesses and went in for the attack like a ravenous pit bull. No one ever knew where they stood with the man, and it was that unexpectedness that made one question their loyalty to him.

"No way. We're like oil and water. Besides, his focus is special victims. You and I agreed that's one area not up for negotiation."

The captain stacked a few folders on his desk then crossed his arms. "You're in it. Stop arguing with me on this."

"It's not going to work."

"You have that third eye and usually see things differently in cases. It's multi-jurisdictional, so the fact that you occasionally liaise with the FBI makes you a logical addition to the team. I think the team synergy will work well."

"Third eye? Team synergy? Wow, Harry. You're reaching."

The older man rubbed his balding head and winced. "I need you to bend a little here. You're the best detective I've got and I need to keep you in the field working cases. The higher-ups want you on the team. It's bad enough I have to deal with the FBI trying to steal you away from me. If you don't agree to this, you'll be relegated to desk duty."

Aidan frowned. Paperwork all day every day would be a slow death. Then again, working with Manny could be a close second.

"Try it and see how it goes. If Manny's a prick about it, we'll figure something out. Just give me a heads-up if you think you're getting close to putting a bullet in him," Harry said with a hint of a smile. "Deal?"

Aidan blew out an exasperated breath. People. They always pried too much into his business, asking questions and invading his space. Why the hell did everyone always feel the need to interfere in someone else's life? As if that wasn't enough, there was the issue of trust. Trust didn't magically appear upon assignment of a team.

He sighed heavily. "I'll give it a shot."

"No shooting, please. Just promise you'll try."

Aidan chuckled. His captain knew him well. If Aidan didn't want to do something, no one could force him. Period. He held his right fist up to his chest. "I am your humble servant, my captain."

Harry laughed. "Bullshit. Now get out of here and have a great weekend. I need you to come in all bright-eyed and bushy-tailed first thing Monday morning."

Aidan stood and made his way toward the door. "By the way," he began, looking over his shoulder before exiting, "I wouldn't leave you for the FBI. They'd *demand* the tie." He wouldn't leave his job or his captain. Not only did the man put up with his shit, he took Aidan at his word and let him do his job with the least amount of meddling possible. The captain had *earned* his trust over the years.

"Glad to know that's the only reason," Harry responded with a knowing grin.

Aidan quickly turned and exited, hiding the hint of a smile that tugged at his lips. He had a reputation to protect and quickly steeled his features. He'd try the task force. Besides, he didn't have much of a choice. Pushing papers all day was not an option. A paper cut would be certain death.

* * * *

Aidan turned on the couch and rolled onto his side, ignoring the vibrating cell phone dancing across his small living room table.

Persistent son of a bitch.

The constant vibrating wreaked havoc on the peaceful white noise of the television station. He cracked open an eye and raised his arm to look at his wristwatch. Two in the morning. Someone was going to suffer for this.

He reached over and grabbed his cell phone, instinctively catching the picture frame before it slid off his chest and onto the floor. He held the frame protectively in one hand and looked at the phone's caller ID in the other. *No way.* His first weekend off in weeks. Why the hell was someone calling him from the precinct?

He swiped his finger across the screen. "Yeah," he croaked, incredibly thankful he had bypassed the beer the night before and opted to crash on the couch naturally.

"Detective Calloway, I'm patching through a call from the field," the dispatcher said, the line clicking then silencing.

Aidan waited—not so patiently—while the call connected.

"Detective Calloway?" the male voice said on the other end of the line.

"Who's this?" Aidan asked, needing to know exactly whose ass had to be kicked.

"This is Detective Jason Palmer. I contacted Detective Manny Reyes and briefed him on the crime scene and he urged me to contact you directly."

Of course he had. Manny knew better than to be the one placing the call to Aidan on his weekend off.

"I'm responding to a call that is potentially connected to one of the cases the task force will be handling."

Aidan sat up on the couch and carefully set the picture frame on the table. He ran his fingers through his hair as he sighed. Jason was a newly hired detective transferred from the southern region. Definitely green and probably going through some major culture shock trying to settle into the Miami pace. Working the streets for a month did not prepare the southern gentleman for the revolving door of criminal cases at their Miami precinct. Manny was probably sitting back at home laughing his ass off knowing he had sent Jason to the big bad wolf. Screw Manny. Aidan could do nice…if he tried really, really hard.

"Hi, Jason. Call me Aidan. I'm scheduled to start on the task force on Monday so I'm not familiar with any existing cases in their workload."

"Yes, sir. But…I think you need to be here."

Aidan sighed. Mr. Southern Charm was probably on his own and overwhelmed handling the crime scene. Rather than be a prick, Aidan opted to grin and bear it. He was awake anyway. He reached over to pull the pen out of his jacket hanging on the back of the chair. He snatched the magazine from the coffee table and flipped it over. "Give me the address." He jotted down the information and disconnected the call with a promise to be there within fifteen minutes.

He lowered his head and took a deep breath. He'd managed to steal a few hours' sleep, but it still didn't seem like enough. He reached out and grabbed the framed photograph. A hint of a smile tugged at the corner of his mouth at the sight of the three familiar faces, two of which always seemed to give him a sense of peace. On one end of the pictured trio was Hunter Donovan, former assistant state attorney and Aidan's best friend of more than a decade. Not only had they served together in the Marines, Hunter was his mentor, best friend, and close enough to consider a brother. He hadn't seen him in well over a year since he'd entered the WITSEC program with his partner, Cameron Pierce.

On the other end of the trio was Aidan with one of his rare smiles. The Three Amigos, Hunter had called them. He huffed his amusement at the memory of that moment when Hunter had come up with the name while they were burning the midnight oil every night for weeks working Cam's case in this very same house—Hunter's former house, which he had left to Aidan when he'd entered the program.

Between Hunter's commanding six-foot-four stature and Aidan's lean but broad six-foot-one frame stood the man who always seemed to trigger that smile in Aidan. Jessie Vega. At barely five foot eight inches tall and a trim physique, he seemed even smaller bookended by the two figures in the photo, but his smile radiated a vibrant energy larger than life.

Jessie.

Aidan ghosted his finger over the picture, outlining the familiar features of the man who always made his heart beat a little faster—his dark hair, those bright blue eyes, and that huge smile. There Jessie stood between them in one of his sharp, dark suits, polished and professional as always. He sighed. *Jessie.* The man he had fallen in love with more than a year ago as they continued their work on taking down the drug and organized crime ring linked to Cameron's case. The one man who seemed to bring a glimmer of light into his dark life. The only person in the last six years who'd managed to draw Aidan in and awaken a desire to see the positive in the world with his ever-present smile and gentle nature.

He'd fallen hopelessly in love, even though he had fought it every step of the way.

He took a deep breath and exhaled slowly. They had started with random texts and phone calls or the occasional visit at the precinct to discuss potential leads. Somehow, during the last six months, that had transitioned to spending every available weekend moment together, even if only for a few hours at a time, with the excuse of working together to close out the cases. He sensed a mutual attraction—like an unspoken current between them, always present, always alluring. During their moments together, he enjoyed every casual brush and the easy laughter that escaped Jessie from some comment Aidan made over a working lunch or dinner. And when Jessie unconsciously touched his arm to draw his attention, a spark always ignited at the point of contact. Jessie's magical touch somehow stilled Aidan's inner storm.

It was the tiny things. The private things. The things most people took for granted with the people they loved.

Aidan didn't take *anything* for granted. There'd never be anything more between them than friendship so he cherished every microscopic gesture, comment, word, and smile. Memorizing every subtle nuance in the things Jessie said and did, engraving them in his mind and storing them away to recall at some later time when the darkness became suffocating and he needed a memory that would serve as a beacon to pull him from the abyss.

He ran a hand down his face, willing his mind to focus on the present. He rose from the couch and entered his bedroom, carefully returning the picture frame to its place on his desk. He grabbed a crisp white shirt from his closet, buttoning up and tucking the shirt into his worn jeans, and headed into the living room. He slid on his shoulder holster and reached for his badge and sport coat on the way out the door, sneaking a peek at his watch and giving himself a pat on the back for making it out of the house quicker than anticipated. Nice *and* punctual. That was a surefire way to shock the night crew and keep them on their toes.

Aidan drove along the highway, enjoying the Miami skyline. He loved his city and the way the lights flickered in the evening, accenting each peak of the graceful man-made landscape. The city, in all her seductive elegance, dared both tourist and city natives to venture and explore what she offered. But he wasn't fooled. Behind the stunning skyline, vivid nightlife, and two-hundred-foot-tall dancing silhouette illuminating the cityscape, a darkness lay within the beautifully colored buildings. A darkness that was all too familiar. Dealing with homicide cases on a daily basis was enough to taint the facade of beauty. And working as a liaison with the FBI on Cameron's case and discovering the dirty line of politicians, officials, corporations, and other random arrests yanked the color right out of his high-definition world.

He arrived at the address, immediately greeted with the typical crime scene staff parked outside the building. Even though there were familiar uniformed officers working the curious crowd of onlookers, something...seemed off. An ambulance instead of a coroner's vehicle? Why the hell were EMTs at a homicide? He flashed his badge at the officers blocking off the public with crime scene tape. He spotted Officer Max Banks, one of the seasoned night-shift patrolmen, and saluted him in greeting.

"I thought you had the weekend off?" Max asked, walking over to him.

"I did."

Max snickered. "Jason must have called you then."

Aidan nodded and ducked under the crime scene tape.

"Poor guy is struggling up there."

"Calloway to the rescue," he said sardonically. Aidan clipped his badge on his belt and headed up the stairs, spotting Jason flipping pages on his small notebook in the doorway of the second floor apartment. "Hi, Jason."

Detective Palmer looked up, an obvious wave of relief passing over his features. "Detective Calloway, thank you for coming so quickly."

"Tell me why I'm here."

"I believe you know the victim."

Aidan stilled.

"He's in the bedroom and won't let anyone near him."

Aidan lowered his brow. *Won't let anyone near him?* Corpses didn't put up much of a fight. And they weren't fighting a zombie apocalypse the last time he checked. He shook his head, obviously having heard the wrong words. He must be more tired than he had originally thought. He followed Jason into the small apartment, trying to make sense of the situation. He sharply turned at the muffled voices coming from the end of the hall. *I believe you know the victim.* He took a deep breath. If the victim *was* still alive and kicking, he damn sure needed to get in the right headspace or risk making an ass of himself.

No fucking way would he crack in front of anyone.

He looked around, hoping to find something—anything—that would help him make the connection to this supposed person he knew.

"He's in the bedroom, sir," Jason repeated.

Aidan turned and gave Jason a pointed glare. He didn't need the same information repeated. "You said I knew the victim?"

"Yes, I believe you might."

Aidan sighed. Why the hell did Jason need so much prompting? *Tick tock.* Just fork over the information and move on. He scanned the room, not spotting much of anything in the spartan living room—no pictures on the solid-colored walls, nothing but a couch, a corner table, and small television. Unless you counted the framed photo on the end table as clutter, this place was devoid of anything personal and barer than his own place…and he was the Webster definition of minimalist. "What's the crime and what's the vic's name?"

"He was attacked—"

Aidan stopped him with a raised hand then planted both hands on his hips and sighed. He closed his eyes and willed his temper to take a backseat. *Nice…be fucking nice.* "Jason, I'm trying here. I'm really trying. I don't work assault cases and Detective Reyes knows that. But you asked me to come, so I'm here."

"Yes, sir. But you may know this victim."

"Jason," he said as calmly as he could muster, looking over his shoulder at another rise in the voices from the room, sensing the urgency of the scene. His focus snapped back to the officer. "I need you to stop repeating everything and just give me information so I know what I'm dealing with before I set foot in that room. So give me a very quick rundown. I need the vic's name, anything relevant you've gathered in statements from the neighbors. Quickly." He added the latter with emphasis. "Something new. And I swear, if you waste any more time and repeat anything you've said again, you're going to understand why Reyes had *you* call me rather than him picking up the phone."

Jason's eyes rounded. "Yes, sir." He flipped through the pages of his notebook, back and forth. "Reyes said the task force was going to handle a case with a series of attacks crossing over into Florida in the last two weeks. He's not sure if the cases are related, but he thought you would be best to call since you know the victim."

Repeater Jason irked him. He walked over to the end table in the bare living room, hoping to learn something from the only personal item he could see in the room. He couldn't deny needing a few more precious seconds to mentally prepare for walking into a scene with an assault victim holding center stage. Especially someone he supposedly knew.

"I found your business card held up with magnets on the refrigerator. That's why I think you might know the victim. Sorry, I've already said that," Jason said, flipping the pages back and forth. "The building manager came by. According to the lease, the victim's name is…um." More page flipping back and forth.

Aidan picked up the picture frame from the table—a copy of the same photograph that sat on the desk in his bedroom.

The same one he had held to his chest less than thirty minutes ago.

His heart jackhammered in his chest.

The picture frame shook in his hand.

"His name is Jessiah Vargas."

"Jessie *Vega*?" He gripped the frame tightly and screwed his eyes shut, trying to swallow past the knot that seemed to suddenly choke him. He couldn't breathe and the fingers wrapped around the edge of the picture frame started to numb.

"Sir, it's possible. I was writing down the notes rather quickly. The building manager should be back at any moment with a copy of the lease if you need to see it. The lock on the entry door is damaged and someone called 9-1-1 when they heard yelling. We arrived a few minutes before I called you, but he won't let the EMTs near him."

A garbled yell came from down the hall. Aidan jerked the frame back onto the table, the adrenaline pumping through his veins pushing him down the narrow hallway to the cluster of people in a few long strides. The blood drained from his body and weakened him at the sight.

He'd walked into tons of crime scenes before. He had walked through minefields, jumped out of planes and landed smack dab in the middle of enemy territory with bullets flying. He'd seen and experienced more than his share of brutality, violence, and death. But this? Nothing could have prepared him for this.

Or the sudden, breath-stealing pain that speared his heart.

There, in the middle of the bed, sat Jessie, battered, riddled with bruises all over his body. His face beaten—his cheek, lips, and one eye already swollen shut. His leg was oddly bent, obviously broken in several places with the bones pushing his skin taut. Blood was smeared on his body and bedding. Arcs of blood spattered the otherwise plain, solid-colored walls. He firmly held out what appeared to be broken glass, on guard in front of him, while his other arm hung at his side like a broken wing, with the wrist at an odd angle. A steady trickle of blood dripped from his outstretched hand and down along his arm.

"Sir, we need to get you to the hospital," the EMT standing to Jessie's right said.

Jessie swung his hand to his right, ready to attack. He tried to move on the bed, but his broken leg restricted his movement.

"Sir, please," the EMT to his left said in the same coaxing tone.

Jessie swung his arm to his opposite side and winced, but still held the broken glass in his hand.

The voices of the EMTs sounded distant and everything slowed around Aidan. His heartbeat thumped in his ears, muffling every other sound in the room. He couldn't rip his eyes away from the swollen cheeks and the bruises scattered along Jessie's body. Each mark, bruise, and blood smear against Jessie's pale skin seemed to have a life of its own, darkening and swelling from one moment to the next as if one was trying to outdo the other to stand out more. Every second that passed seemed to reveal and birth another bruise. Another mark marring his usually perfect and polished skin.

This had to be a nightmare. It *had* to be. He must have fallen into a deep sleep on his couch. No way was *his* Jessie sitting in the middle of this bed in this state.

This is not real.

This isn't happening.

Snap out of it.

Wake.

The.

Fuck.

Up.

"Leave me alone!" Jessie yelled in a panicked tone, jolting Aidan back to the present. Jessie swung the broken glass toward the EMTs, forcing them to take a step back.

Aidan fisted the collar of the closest EMT and dragged him near. "What do you need to happen here to help him?"

The EMT stood a breath away. "If we don't splint the broken arm and leg, he could lose a limb due to compromised blood vessels. And I think he has a broken rib or two based on his breathing, so we need to brace him to avoid a possible puncture to a lung or organ if that's the case. And that's only what we can see. Bottom line, we need to stabilize him to avoid further damage, but he won't let us anywhere near him. His adrenaline level is probably the only reason he's conscious right now. He's going to crash. And it's best we're at the hospital where we're more prepared to handle that."

Aidan nodded curtly, releasing the EMT. "Clear the room." The other EMT in the room looked up at him. "Now!"

They gaped at his tone but stepped just outside the doorway, leaving him alone with Jessie.

Jessie swung the broken glass item to the left then right in quick shifts, panting each rapid, shallow breath.

"Jessie," he said, forcing the words past the tightness in his throat.

"Aidan?" Jessie said, his voice broken and trembling as he slowly relaxed his outstretched arm. "I can't see you."

Aidan's brow lowered when he looked upward at the brightly lit room. He walked over to the side of the bed, to Jessie's right. "I'm right here," he whispered, unable to use his full voice for some reason.

Jessie's lip quivered. "I can't see you," he repeated.

"I'm here," he said, reaching out and gently placing his hand on Jessie's bruised and swollen cheek. "It's just the two of us here."

Jessie sniffled.

Aidan grabbed one of the evidence bags lying on top of the bed. "Jess, you're holding glass in your hand and you're bleeding. I need you to let that go." He inverted the bag and grabbed the broken glass Jessie held. Jessie immediately released the item and Aidan pulled the edges of the plastic upward to seal the broken glass inside the bag. He spotted Officer Max Banks—who had obviously made his way upstairs—standing by the doorway and motioned for him to come over, handing him the evidence bag then shooing him back out of the room.

"I can't see," Jessie whispered through his swollen, split lips. "I…I don't…want anyone to touch me."

"Do you know who did this to you?" Aidan asked.

Jessie nodded.

"Tell me." Aidan glanced up at Max, giving him a chin-up gesture. The officer immediately handed Jason the evidence bag and pulled his own notebook out of his pocket, ready to jot down whatever Jessie said. He returned his focus back to Jessie, trying to keep the worry and panic in check.

"It was dark, but I believe it was a guy I knew a few years ago. Michael," Jessie responded, a shiver visibly rippling through his body.

"I need a last name." Aidan clenched his fist, trying to stave off the boiling rage, unable to pull his stare away from the blood-matted hair at Jessie's temple.

Jessie remained silent, panting each breath. He closed his eyes and a tear escaped, turning pink as it mixed with the smeared blood down his swollen cheek. "John…Johnson." He started to gasp each breath.

"Jess, I need you to let the EMTs here do their thing."

"Don't leave!" He reached out in a panic with his bloodied hand, searching for Aidan, finally finding his shirt and fisting the material. "Please," he said, in a voice Aidan barely recognized as Jessie's.

"I'm not going anywhere."

The EMTs immediately shuffled around them, rolling the gurney into the narrow space between the bed and the wall. They worked in concert, bringing in supplies to begin prepping.

Jessie gasped each breath, turning his head from side to side at the ruckus surrounding him, clutching Aidan's shirt more tightly.

"Jess, I'm here, so are the EMTs. You need to let them work. Focus on me. Tell me about Michael Johnson. Just keep talking. I'll need more information. Age, height, where he lives. Anything you can tell me." He glanced over to the officer, thankful the man stood stoic, waiting with his notebook still in hand.

The EMT leaned over, nearing Aidan to whisper. "We need you to leave the room. We need the space."

Aidan turned to face him. "Work around me," he said slowly, leaving zero room for argument or misinterpretation of his intent to stay planted at Jessie's side.

The EMT stepped away, returning his focus back to Jessie. "Mr. Vega, I need you to keep your arm still so I can start an IV."

Jessie flinched at the touch then winced from the obvious pain when the other EMT stretched an oxygen mask over his face.

"Jess, tell me about Michael Johnson. Is he tall?" Aidan asked, hoping to shift Jessie's attention to the line of questioning.

"Yes, he's tall and big," Jessie said, the mask slightly muffling his words.

"Like me?"

Jessie closed his almost-swollen-shut eye and winced again when the EMTs braced his neck and splinted his leg and arm. "No," he said, panting each breath and fogging up the oxygen mask. "He's taller. And broader. Broad like Hunter. Dark blond hair. Blue eyes. He should be in his late forties now…I think. He…he lived in Central Florida. At least…he did years ago. But I don't know where he lives now." He quieted, panting each breath more heavily.

Aidan's heart slammed against his chest repeatedly. He looked over to the officer with the notebook in hand. "Put an APB out on Michael Johnson. Dark blond, blue-eyed, over six feet tall, thick-muscled frame and he's in his forties or early fifties. Prior known residence was Central Florida. Got it?"

The officer nodded and immediately turned, pulling a too-confused Jason along with him.

"We need to move you, Mr. Vega." The EMTs shoved Aidan out of the way and slid a board under Jessie, pulling him and the board onto the gurney and securing Jessie in place. Aidan numbly stepped aside as they worked then rolled the gurney out of the room, pushing through the crowd of officers and techs in the hallway.

"Aidan!" Jessie yelled on a panicked gasp, extending his bloodied hand and waving it from side to side searching for him.

"You need to lay still, Mr. Vega. You're going to pull out the IV," one of the EMTs said as they rolled the gurney out of the apartment.

Aidan pushed his way through the crowd of officers in the hallway and reached out to grab Jessie's hand. "I'm right here," he said, forcing the words through the suffocating knot wedged in his throat, thankful the contact seemed to calm Jessie a little. "Talk to me, Jess. I don't care if you recite the ABCs or count. I just need to hear your voice."

They jerked the gurney into the small elevator when the doors slid open.

"I fought back," Jessie said, slowly gasping each breath.

"I know you did."

"I…I hit him…with the angel."

"The angel?" Aidan brushed his thumb along Jessie's hand, not sure if Jessie could even feel the caress with all his injuries.

Jessie closed his swollen eye, his breath slowing. "The one…you gave me," he said, his voice growing fainter with each passing breath. "The one…you said…would watch over me…after Hunter went away and I started working on my own."

Aidan leaned over to whisper in Jessie's ear. "Please, Jess...I need you to keep fighting," he said, battling with the tightness in his throat and the pain in his chest.

"Aidan..."

"Yeah?"

"My head...it...hurts...and my...left..." Jessie said, each syllable more faint and slurred as he spoke.

One of the EMTs grabbed a stethoscope just as the elevator doors opened and they rolled the gurney to the ambulance. "He's got a pulse. It's thready but there. We need to get to the hospital. Now."

They all climbed into the back of the ambulance—fuck 'em if they thought he was staying behind. He sat on the bench seat, still holding Jessie's hand, refusing to release him as the EMTs continued to check and work on Jessie's injured body. In a matter of seconds, Jessie had tubes, wires, and entirely too many things connecting him to a series of bags, bottles, and machines.

Aidan tried to level his breathing and stave off the emotions choking him. In the midst of the frenzy surrounding him, he closed his eyes and took a deep breath, letting all the sounds fade around him. He leaned forward and buried his face into Jessie's hair, then did something he hadn't done in years.

He prayed.

Chapter TWO

Aidan paced the waiting room, cursing and mumbling under his breath with his cell phone pressed against his ear. "Ty?" he immediately said when the ringing stopped on the open line. He screwed his eyes shut, finally taking his first semi-deep breath after handing Jessie over to the doctors at the hospital emergency room.

"No, it's Cole. Ty's doing an interview. What's going on?" Cole Renzo, his brother's partner, asked, his voice alert and direct.

Aidan ran his hand through his hair. There was no way in hell he could put up with Cole's crass sarcasm or twisted humor right now. What the hell had possessed him to call them knowing they were in Orlando doing an annual auto show? "Never mind," he said, his voice strained.

"Fuck you. What's going on? Are you okay?"

Aidan's throat tightened. Okay? He was far from okay. He felt as if someone had ripped out his heart and lungs and left him on his own to figure out how to breathe.

"Is it Jessie?" Cole cautiously asked.

Aidan nodded then realized Cole was on the phone and couldn't see him. He cursed under his breath. "Hospital. It's bad," he managed to say in a tone he hoped sounded somewhat steady.

"Which one?"

After a few more seconds and even fewer words, they finally disconnected the call.

He paced the waiting room, repeatedly cursing, bartering with anything he could think of in hopes of changing the shitty hand of fate he always seemed to be dealt. He mumbled under his breath to himself, avoiding the odd stares from the people sitting in the hard plastic chairs in the room. What the hell was taking so long? He finally sat on one of the plastic chairs, crossing and uncrossing his legs. The TV mounted up in the corner of the room aired some stupid late-night rerun of some crap show that had ended years ago. They should have let it fade away in the sitcom graveyard. He stood and paced again, taking a deep breath and shoving his hands into his pockets. He looked toward the floor, trying to avoid the worried faces of the strangers in the waiting room.

He stopped when he saw the blood on his shirt. Jessie's blood. He clenched his jaw, looked straight ahead, and continued pacing. Fuck, he hated this place. The smell made him twitch. He wasn't sure if it was the smell of Jessie's blood on his shirt or the chemical stench inherent in the sterile setting he hated so much.

Why the hell couldn't someone give him an update? Something.

He paced, over and over, watching the clock tick away the seconds, minutes, an hour. The walls seemed as if they had shifted, somehow closing in on him. He shook his head and crossed his arms again. His pulse sped and his heart pounded against his chest, urging him to escape. Fucking hospital. Spending six months by Ty's side while he lay in a coma after the accident was enough hospital time to last a lifetime. How he had managed to stay sane while waiting for his brother to wake, he still didn't know.

A scream from the television snapped him back to the here and now with jarring speed. Damn, he hated that stupid show. He wrapped his arms around himself, hoping to hide some of Jessie's drying blood on his crisp white shirt. He just needed peace and quiet right now. Silence. No, he needed senseless white noise to set his mind right. Anything other than the screams from the TV or the worried faces cycling through the waiting room.

And he needed a fucking update.

He was going to go insane.

Julian Capeletti walked in through the sliding glass doors of the emergency room, towering over the night-shift nurses. Aidan sighed and his body sagged. Finally, a familiar face. He'd never been happier to see the prickly man. Julian quickly scanned the room and his pale green gaze locked with Aidan's, sending Julian on a beeline path toward him. He reached Aidan, grabbed him behind the neck, and pulled him into a hug without saying a word.

"I swear, if you tell me everything happens for a reason, I'll fucking rip you apart," Aidan said, his words muffled against Julian's muscled shoulder. He screwed his eyes shut as he took each strangled breath, trying to hold back the emotions that shook his body.

After a few seconds, they finally separated from the embrace, clearing their throats.

"Did Cole call you?" Aidan asked.

Julian nodded. "He told me to get my ass over here right now because you needed me to sit with you and be quiet until you told me to leave."

"Where's Matt?"

Julian sat in one of the waiting room chairs. "He's at home. I figured you didn't want a crowd. I'll text him updates."

"Thanks," Aidan muttered, sitting next to Julian, grateful he hadn't asked for details. Aidan wasn't sure he could handle retelling what he'd seen with the storm of emotions twisting his gut. And somehow, the quiet presence of Julian at his side did ease his mind.

During the last year, he had managed to build a slow friendship with Julian and his partner, Matthew Doner. They both owned and ran a halfway house, aptly named Halfway House, in the business district. He had first met the couple when his brother-in-arms and best friend, Hunter Donovan, had needed help with his new partner and then resident of HH, Cameron Pierce. That first encounter started a domino effect in Aidan's life. He'd finally been able to do something to repay Hunter for a debt he could never really settle, and through the course of working the case, he had met Jessie, Hunter's assistant at the state attorney's office at the time.

Seemed Julian and Matt had also played a role in returning some balance to Aidan's personal life with another one of their residents, Ty's current partner, Cole—his self-proclaimed future brother-in-law. How Cole had managed to pull Ty from his shell was still a mystery. But Cole had single-handedly restored Aidan's brother's inner strength and the laughter Aidan had missed after the accident that stole their parents from them and nearly claimed his brother's life. That house and these men had all played a role in guiding Aidan's life to the point where he was at that very moment. If it weren't for these men and that house, he never would have reconnected with his brother, helped his friend who was more of a brother to him, and he wouldn't have met Jessie.

Jessie. The one man who seemed to calm his inner storm.

Sometime later, Julian stood and looked toward the hallway. Aidan followed Julian's line of sight, spotting Cole's older sister wearing hospital scrubs walking toward them alongside another woman with rich brown skin, high cheek bones and closely-cropped, curly hair.

"Hi, J," Carmen said to Julian with a hint of mischief that immediately faded once she shifted her green-eyed gaze to Aidan. "Cole called me and said you were here with Jessie. This is one of my affiliated hospitals so I came right over to find out what was going on."

Aidan nodded, for once, happy to see a bossy Renzo steamroll their way into a situation. "Thanks."

"He's in surgery. Ryan Green's an excellent surgeon so he's in good hands." She placed her hand behind the other woman's back. "Emma will provide you with periodic updates. I'm heading back in there just in case Ryan needs a secondary, but trust me when I say he won't need me."

Aidan nodded. "Thanks."

"Emma will give you the details and an update," Carmen said, squeezing Aidan's shoulder and giving Julian a quick peck on the cheek before racing back down the hallway.

"I'm Emma Sinclair," the nurse said, extending her hand. "The trauma to Mr. Vega's spleen was so severe surgery was the only option. It's taking a little longer because we had to remove the organ."

Aidan inhaled sharply and swayed, suddenly unsteady on his feet. Julian immediately took a step closer to his side, silently offering support.

"He has several bone fractures. His two fractured ribs will have to heal naturally, but other than that, we'll be able to set most of the bones with casts in a few days after we've confirmed any necessary surgical sites and incisions are healing properly. His wrist and leg require the most attention. He'll need the aid of screws and plates to set the bones, but it'll heal faster. Right now, we're most concerned with the injury he sustained to the head."

Aidan tried to focus on the words and not jump ahead and speculate, hoping to keep himself centered and steady, but he couldn't stop the room from warping in and out of his vision.

"Aidan, ask what you need to know while she's here," Julian said.

He mentally ran through the list of injuries again, matching each with what he remembered from the scene, trying to determine if anything hadn't been mentioned. He ran his hand through his hair, forcing his mind to focus on the list and not the visual of an injured Jessie. *Shit.* What had the nurse said? *Injury to his head.* "Is that why he had trouble seeing?"

Emma nodded then reached out and placed her hand on Aidan's arm. "He woke before we administered the anesthesia. First word out of his mouth was your name. He said we were to treat you as his next of kin."

"Emma, you're killing him," Julian said.

Aidan closed his eyes and took a deep breath, trying with every ounce of strength he had to remain standing. He reached up and rubbed the hollow ache that tightened his chest.

"He wanted to make sure we kept you updated. He was…insistent. He said you would storm in there waving a gun at us if we didn't," she said, slowly raising a thinly tweezed, judgmental eyebrow. "He'll need some support to get through this and the recovery. I'll make sure to keep you updated once he's out of surgery." She squeezed Aidan's arm in a comforting gesture then smiled before finally walking away.

Aidan blew out a deep breath and plopped himself on one of the stiff plastic chairs, resting his head back against the wall and stretching out his legs.

He closed his eyes and sat there as the time passed, hyper-aware of each voice and step in the room, hoping the pain in his chest would lessen.

Aidan sat in the hard plastic chair with his arms crossed, staring at the closed doors, waiting for Emma to return with an update. Over three hours and he hadn't heard a peep from the staff.

"You can go." At the brink of losing his shit, he didn't need an audience to witness his inevitable shutdown.

He sensed it—the helplessness creeping through and weakening his protective shell.

Julian rubbed his shaved head. "Not if you need me to stay."

"Really, please go."

Julian watched him closely then nodded. "Keep me updated. If you need me back here, just text me. Okay?"

"Thanks. And please thank Matt for letting me steal you in the middle of the night."

Julian half smiled and stood. He touched the tip of his fingers to his temple and gave a two-fingered salute before he turned and exited the hospital through the sliding glass doors.

Aidan leaned his head back against the wall and stretched out in the hard chair, anxiously awaiting the next update. He closed his eyes, the exhaustion and stress starting to wear him down. He needed to *see* for himself that Jessie was fine. What the hell was taking so long?

"I received a call about a patient who came in via emergency," a man's voice echoed to his left.

Aidan opened his eyes, casually observing the older man with the dark hair graying at the temples, fidgeting with a pen at the nurse's counter. There was something about him, something familiar yet different. He stood tall, Aidan guessed at just under six feet in height with broad shoulders.

"The patient's name is Jessiah Vega," the man said.

"And you are?" the nurse asked.

The man cleared his throat. "I'm his...father." He withdrew his wallet from his back pocket and presented his identification. "Why was I instructed to come here?"

The nurse tore her focus from the computer monitor. "All our satellite hospitals share the same database and are networked and updated real-time throughout the state. We have you on file as a parent. He's in surgery and we may require a decision to be made if he's unable."

"I would appreciate it if the records were updated, unlinked, or whatever you need to do. I refuse to have a say-so in a decision affecting him."

"Yes, sir," the nurse quietly commented. "We'll need you to fill out this form." She handed him a clipboard then resumed tapping away at her computer.

Aidan bit back the surge of anger boiling his blood. He didn't need to hear anything more to know this was the reason Jessie never spoke of his father. He once mentioned his mother and that she had passed away when he was barely a teen but never his father other than a passing comment of "we don't stay in touch."

He stood and paced the room, needing to let off some of the simmering rage rising inside him. *Son of a bitch.*

The older man handed over the clipboard. "Can I go now?"

"Yes, sir," the nurse said, in a tone much more polite than the bastard merited.

The man turned to walk out the door but hesitated, instead making his way to the restroom.

Aidan shoved his hands into his pockets, fighting the urge to race into the bathroom and beat the shit out of that son of a bitch.

The man exited the restroom a few moments later, and Aidan stood in his path, blocking his exit. The man startled and inched his gaze up at Aidan. "Can I help you?"

Aidan took a deep breath and focused on leveling his tone. "You're Jessie's father?" There was an unquestionable similarity in his eyes. The shade of crystal blue, bright and unmistakably familiar but everything else was off. Jessie's nose was thin and smooth while this man's was wider and slightly askew from an obvious break. Jessie's eyes were bright with life and mirth while this man's held a darker undercurrent. Even the shapes of their faces were different.

The older man cocked his head and observed Aidan with the same scrutiny a biologist would inspect a specimen. "And you are?"

"I'm the detective who brought him in."

The man raised his chin. "Did he cry?"

"What did you say?" Aidan asked, planting his hands on his hips.

"I imagine someone hit him. Did he cry?"

Hit him? Hit. Him. Aidan bit down so hard his molars began to hurt. "How about we play what-if?"

"Excuse me?"

Aidan took a deep breath and tried to keep his rage in check. "What if it was the middle of the night and you were awakened by someone who attacked you, breaking bones in your body and hitting you so fucking hard your vision blurred..." Aidan stopped and clenched his jaw, taking a step closer to the man who threatened his ability to stay in control. "What. Would. You. Do?"

The man looked at Aidan firmly. "I'd fight back like a man."

Aidan straightened to his full height, taking advantage of the few inches he had over the man. He took a deep breath and exhaled slowly. "Then I guess the two of you are more similar than you think."

The older man raised his head slightly as his lips twitched into a sneer. "He is nothing like me. The only reason I'm here is because the hospital was on my way home from work and I received the annoying call to come over. I have no interest in being here or what happens to him." He withdrew the keys from his pocket, turned, and walked away. "The world's probably a better place without him and his whining."

Aidan stood stock-still, observing the older man as he walked past the reception desk and exited the hospital through the sliding glass doors just as Cole ran inside. Cole stopped for a moment and turned to look at the man as he exited, then glanced back at Aidan, scowling as he walked over to him.

"Shit. Was that Jessie's dad? He looks like Jessie doped up on some serious steroid and fertilizer."

"No. Just some fucking asshole."

"Those were his same ice blue eyes, man," Cole said, but didn't push the point further. "You look like you need to get off your feet." He steered Aidan back to the plastic chairs in the waiting room. He pulled his cell phone from his back pocket and pressed a few keys. "Is that Jessie's blood on your shirt?"

Aidan nodded, not wanting to think about it or look down. "What are you doing here? I thought you guys had a show up in Orlando?" He absently looked at his watch. He was due a damn update already and how the hell... "How did you get here so damn fast?"

"Your badge earns me some respect," Cole said, waggling his eyebrows. "It's like a get out of jail free card. Totally awesome."

Aidan sighed and blew out a breath.

"I'm kidding. We were careful driving. Traffic was light and we drove straight here."

"Where's Ty?"

"He's parking the car. I texted him to bring you a shop shirt from the show swag we brought back. So give him a couple of minutes, he needs to sift through the trunk."

He stared at the emergency room's sliding glass doors, waiting for his brother to enter. "Thanks for calling your sister and Julian."

"Did anyone else call you?" Cole asked.

Aidan turned to face Cole slowly. "Who else did you call?"

"I didn't *call* anyone else," Cole said with a shrug. "How's Jessie doing?"

Aidan shook his head, too exhausted to deal with anything other than the stress of Jessie's current situation. "I'm waiting for an update."

Ty entered through the sliding glass doors, quickly walked over to them, and handed Aidan a black T-shirt before pulling him into an embrace. "We got here as quick as we could."

Aidan screwed his eyes shut and tightened his hold on his brother. "Thanks," he whispered. "Give me a sec." He escaped into the restroom and emerged seconds later with a fresh *Calloway's* T-shirt on, thankful to finally be able to take a semi-deep breath without getting a whiff of the metallic scent of Jessie's blood.

"Now how about you tell us what the hell happened?" Cole said.

He tugged on the new shirt and took a few more breaths, trying to assemble the right string of words to provide just enough information without causing another fissure in his already beaten state of mind. "He was...attacked. It's...bad...it's..." *Fuck.* He didn't know what else to say.

When Cole sprang forward, Aidan turned to see Carmen coming down the hallway toward them.

"He's out of surgery and in recovery," Carmen said, then paused with the collective sigh from her audience. "So far, we were able to do everything we could on the operating table. However, he sustained blunt trauma to the head and he has some cerebral contusions that seem to have caused cortical blindness. Right now, that's our greatest concern."

Cole was fidgeting. "Fucking. English. Please."

"His brain is bruised."

"How bad?" Aidan asked.

Carmen turned to Aidan and her brows knit together. "There's a lot of swelling but, thankfully, minimal bleeding. His pupils are responsive, so it's not an injury to his eyes. It's the swelling that's causing him to have trouble with his vision. We need the swelling to resolve or we'll need to step in and relieve some of the pressure in his head."

Aidan took a deep breath and clenched his hands to stop the shaking. "Can I see him?"

"We're closely monitoring him for the next few hours in the recovery area so you need to give us a little time first. I'll sneak you in when I can, but he's going to be sedated."

Aidan ran his hand through his hair. "I just…need to see him." He managed to squeeze the words through the suffocating tightness in his throat.

Carmen reached out and grabbed his shoulder. "I know. I've got to get back in there." She hugged her brother quickly and gave Ty a chaste kiss on the cheek before jogging back down the hallway.

They sat for another hour before Emma appeared and stole Aidan away from an overly anxious Cole and Ty. "I'll try to get you a minute with him, but that's about it until we can move him to the Intensive Care Unit," she whispered.

Aidan nodded, thankful for the chance to see Jessie. All the reassurances in the world hadn't been enough. He just needed a glance. Emma ushered him down a series of hallways and pushed through the doors leading to the recovery area. He stepped in and obediently stayed by the door, anxiously waiting as Emma walked over to the half-moon nurses' station to the right to speak to the sole nurse on duty. Two rows of patients in various stages of recovery lay in beds—

no walls between them, and a consistent beep and series of chirps echoed in the otherwise silent space. Everything was white and freakishly sterile, except for the faces of each patient lying in bed or the hand resting at the patient's side that hadn't been covered by the white bedsheet.

He scanned the room and crossed his arms, fighting a sudden chill. Jessie didn't belong here. He had entirely too much life and fire within him to be in a place so cold and colorless. Emma continued her exchange with the nurse at the station, her arms animated yet her volume hushed enough where he could only catch a few random words—detective, kin, friend, partner. At this point, he'd say and do anything to be near Jessie. He switched his weight from one foot to the other, his breath catching in his throat when he spotted Jessie's bed in the second row.

The nurse nodded at Emma then turned toward Aidan. "We have a strict no-visitor policy while patients are in this recovery area." She looked over to Emma then back to Aidan. "But I'll give you a moment with him." She directed him toward Jessie's bed then walked away with Emma to check on the other patients in the room.

He rubbed his palms on his thighs and blew out a deep breath. He walked to Jessie's bed and leaned over, reaching out and hesitantly brushing his thumb along Jessie's cheek. Bruises had bloomed across his entire face and the swelling had worsened. His arms and legs were held in soft splints and he was heavily bandaged all over. Tubes and wires ran from his body to machines that beeped in tandem.

Steady and strong. Just like Jessie.

Aidan ran his fingers through Jessie's dark hair—a stolen caress he craved, hoping the contact would calm his nerves. He swallowed heavily and gasped a few shallow breaths, battling the emotions that tried to claw their way to the surface. He couldn't stand this. His instinct was to hurt and maim the bastard who had done this. He leaned over and placed a gentle kiss on Jessie's forehead. He closed his eyes as his trembling lips pressed against Jessie's fair, bruised skin.

"Please don't leave me," he whispered in Jessie's ear before stepping away and finally exiting the room.

Chapter THREE

"Have you gone home?" Cole asked.

"No," Aidan responded, still sitting in the waiting room, with arms crossed, in those stupid connected plastic chairs that numbed his ass. Jessie had been in recovery for a few hours before finally being transferred to ICU. After almost a full day there, the machines started going apeshit and in the midst of the chaos, they sent him back to the waiting room until they stabilized Jessie.

Twice.

He took a deep breath, trying to control all his circling thoughts and avoid spiraling into the abyss. He had to focus on Jessie and the strength Jessie used to always seek the positive in the world. Jessie was strong, far stronger than most people could imagine. Aidan somehow needed to put himself in that same mindset and think positively.

God, please.

He needed something to keep him going. Aidan called headquarters for an update on whether they had caught the Michael Johnson bastard. Nothing. He struggled. He wanted to be at the precinct to work the case and ensure they caught the son of a bitch, but there was no way in hell he could will his body to leave Jessie. The bastard could wait. Jessie was his priority.

His body hummed, and not in a good way. The urge to snap at someone tickled his senses.

"It's been almost two days. You need to shower," Cole said.

Maybe his self-proclaimed future-brother-in-law would be a convenient target. He sat and stared at the closed doors, waiting for Emma or Carmen—or anyone at this point—to emerge with any new bit of information. He'd only received a sprinkling of vague updates during the last forty-eight fucking hours.

We're monitoring him.

We're keeping an eye on him.

He's still the same.

Blah blah blah.

"And you need a shave. You're starting to wolf it."

Cole was begging for it now. Aidan had already managed to block out all the panicked families cycling through the waiting room, he could certainly tune out Cole and his attempt to bait him.

"Aidan, you need to take a break."

He turned to face Cole, ready to attack, stopping only when the worry in those mismatched eyes stared back at him. "No," he said through clenched teeth, returning his focus to the doors. "I'm not leaving him."

"At least eat something."

He heard a rustling beside him. "If you don't want the sandwich I brought you, at least have one of the candy bars."

He closed his eyes and leaned his head back against the wall.

"If you take the candy bar, I'll shut up and won't nag you for a bit."

Aidan sighed. Cole's tone carried the same concern Ty's had before he'd left a few hours ago for a doctor's appointment.

"Please."

He pivoted his head toward Cole. If eating something gave him a little silence while he waited, he'd eat a fucking candy bar as long as he wasn't expected to leave the room for more than the time it took to take a piss. "What have you got?"

Cole immediately withdrew three candy bars from the bag and two protein bars. "Pick two. One for now and another for later so you don't have to go to the vending machine downstairs."

Aidan held out his hand to Cole, palm up. His mind was so focused on an update he couldn't decide what to eat. And quite frankly, he didn't care.

Cole grabbed one of the protein bars, opened it, and shoved it into Aidan's hand. "Eat this one now. You need the boost." He opened Aidan's jacket and slid the chocolate bar into his pocket. "Save this one for later."

Aidan took a bite then scowled. "This tastes like shit."

"I'm not a connoisseur of fecal matter, but you're eating that for the energy boost not the taste."

Aidan chewed the crappy excuse for sustenance, refusing to comment further on Cole's special brand of humor.

"Have you heard anything?" Cole asked.

"I thought you were shutting up?"

Cole shrugged. "I was quiet for a whole minute before I asked."

Aidan took the last bite. Cole snatched the wrapper from his hand and shoved it into the bag before withdrawing a bottled water and handing it over to Aidan without another word.

He uncapped the bottle and threw his head back to chug down the contents.

"Aidan..." Cole whispered.

He followed Cole's line of sight, straightening when Carmen pushed through the doors. He launched forward and met Cole's sister in two strides. "How is he?"

Carmen crossed her arms and lowered her brow. "He's not improving and we're worried about the swelling in his brain. We're going to have to medically induce—"

Aidan swayed. He didn't need to hear the next all-too-familiar word. A strong hand grabbed his bicep, holding him steady and returning his focus to the conversation.

"Why do you have to put him in a coma if he's not in one? You're supposed to make him better, not worse," Cole said.

"It *will* make him better." She looked at Aidan. "I need you to trust me. This is not like Ty's situation. This is us putting him in this state with sedatives to help him. It's not his body giving out on him. This will allow him to recover from all the fractures and internal damage without the sensation of pain. But most importantly, it will relax him and not force his brain to do more than it needs to so it can work on healing itself. And right now, that's what we need to happen to get the swelling down. We're going to closely monitor him for the next few hours. Once he's stable, we'll move him from ICU to the special care floor in the new hospital wing. It's similar to ICU but for rehabilitation and long term care. It's more private than ICU and he'll have a room. The nurse to patient ratio is small so he'll have both the privacy you'll want and the close monitoring he needs."

"Sis, I love you, but I'm not liking you very much right now."

Carmen turned to her brother. "You can hate me now, but this is the only way we can get him healthier without running the risk of him getting worse."

Aidan rubbed the pain in his chest that just didn't seem to go away. "Can I sit with him when you move him to his room?"

"Yes. I'll make sure to get a note added to his chart so none of the shift nurses give you a hard time. Either for round-the-clock protection because of what happened or something else with equal weight so there's no issue with the visiting hours. I'll take care of that. Don't worry."

"Thanks. Let me know when he's moved." Aidan turned away and returned to the plastic chair in the corner of the waiting room. He crossed his arms and leaned his head back against the wall, closing his eyes, trying to block out the emotional storm swirling within. He counted backward, needing to center himself and calm his nerves. There was a shift next to him and the rustling of that fucking paper bag Cole had carried around for the last hour. Thankfully, Cole didn't open his mouth to utter another word for the next hour.

Seemed his future brother-in-law was smart after all.

* * * *

Aidan pitched the paper cup in the trash can and walked over to the elevators, pressing the up button to return to Jessie's room. He'd stepped away for about fifteen minutes, just enough time to grab a stale doughnut from the skeleton crew manning the cafeteria and the piece of crap coffee he'd barely been able to swallow. He'd needed a sanity break.

The elevator dinged and he slid through the open doors, pressing the number to Jessie's floor then letting his arms fall at his sides. He closed his eyes and stretched his neck, rolling his head on his shoulders until he heard a pop. After only one day at Jessie's bedside in his new room, the wear on his body and sanity were uncontrollable. It was all too much. The exhaustion from work and lack of sleep coupled with the stress of knowing he was helpless in the hunt for the son of a bitch attacker and seeing Jessie lying in bed... His breaking point inched closer with each passing hour. He couldn't stop the shaking of his hands. "Shit," he said, under his breath.

The ding sounded and the doors slid open. He exited and quickly scanned the hospital floor. Two men in dark suits he didn't know had hauled away Jessie's guard to a spot halfway down the hallway. His hackles rose and he withdrew his sidearm. He slowly stepped toward Jessie's door and carefully pulled the handle, trying to avoid any sound before stepping into the room.

A large figure hovered over Jessie in the dark room. His heart pounded in his chest and pulsated in his ears as he straightened his arm, ready to shoot.

"I taught you to have more stealth than that," a familiar voice said in a steady, firm tone.

Aidan slowly lowered his gun. Great, now he was hallucinating.

"Hunter?"

His friend looked over his shoulder and smiled before turning to face him, straightening to his full height. He looked different, still tall and broad with a commanding presence, but his dark hair was trimmed short and an equally short-trimmed beard now covered part of his face. He had abandoned the usual suit and now donned casual jeans and a long-sleeved henley pulled up to his elbows. Hunter's silver-gray gaze cut through the dim room, squarely aimed at Aidan. He was older than Aidan by five years, but there, standing before him, his older friend looked younger, happier, and stronger than Aidan's own thirty-six.

Aidan reached over and pressed the secondary light switch,

illuminating the room with a soft glow.

"How are you holding up?" Hunter asked.

"What are you doing here?" Aidan shook his head. Was he seeing things? *Fuck.* He really did need to get some sleep.

"Cam told me what happened."

"Cam? How did he…" The one question that hadn't made sense at the time. *Did anyone else call?* "That fucking, little, meddling prick—"

"Stop it."

The anger swelled his body and forced him to grit his teeth. "If that little shit put you guys in danger—"

Hunter stepped forward. "I said stop it. Apparently Cole's got a tech friend who set them up to communicate on some anonymous forum or some shit like that. In some weird, twisted, loudmouthed way that kid champions you more than you know and was panicked enough to worry Cam and that's what got me here."

Aidan sighed. "Did Cam come with you?"

"Absolutely not and he's fucking pissed about that."

Aidan took a deep breath. "How the hell did you get here?"

"I assume you saw the marshals outside. Now answer my damn question. How are you holding up?" Hunter asked again.

"Barely," he whispered. No sense lying to his closest friend, he'd see right through whatever bullshit he attempted to dish out.

Hunter pulled him from the back of the neck into an embrace. "I'll stay for a couple of days until I know you're steady."

"You can't. It's not safe."

Hunter pulled back from the embrace, still keeping a firm grip on the back of Aidan's neck. "Then I guess it's a good thing we've got a guard and two marshals outside and two guys in this room who are far more dangerous with their bare hands than the average guy with a weapon. Now stop fighting me on this."

Aidan stepped away, walking over to Jessie's bedside to grip the railing. He screwed his eyes shut and took a few deep breaths, shaking his head. His thoughts were jumbled and the slightest thing kept setting him off. He listened to the rhythmic click and whoosh of the ventilator as it breathed for Jessie, and the steady hum of the oxygen running through the machine. His eyes burned and his throat tightened as the rage bubbled within. The helplessness...the feelings of uselessness, it was too much. Not being able to capture the son of a bitch who did this to Jessie during those critical first forty-eight hours and now, standing here, watching Jessie's bandaged and bruised body with an endotracheal tube in his mouth braced around his head and not being able to do a motherfucking thing to help was just... He gasped a breath, then another, tightening his fists around the bed railing.

"Aidan. Talk to me."

He turned to face his friend and ran his shaky fingers through his hair, unable to voice a single word.

Hunter stood next to Aidan for a few moments, watching him closely. He sighed and retreated to the corner table, grabbing one of the wooden chairs and flipping it around, straddling the back of the seat. "Sit down," he said, pulling the other chair next to him.

Aidan obediently sat. He wasn't sure if it was a brotherly thing, a mentor thing, or a former sergeant thing, but he always listened to his long-time friend.

"We haven't really talked about what happened. I can't imagine what you went through, but shutting everyone out is not the answer."

Aidan sat still, his internal shield fully erect and trying to deflect Hunter's concern about the topic at hand.

"You can't be in a relationship with him and keep this under wraps."

He turned to face his friend and delivered his most serious death glare. "I'm not in a relationship with him."

"But you want to be. Don't deny it."

Aidan turned to Jessie lying motionless on the bed. He wouldn't deny it. He *couldn't* deny it.

"You two... I don't know what the hell it is, but he calms you and gives you some weird balance I hadn't seen in you since before everything happened. You need that. You're too wound up and always on guard, pushing everyone away. And that's going to wear you down." Hunter shook his head and scoffed. "I remember those long nights working on Cam's case. I saw it then, the way you two looked at each other. But I didn't think it would take you guys this long to do something about it."

Aidan's focus snapped back to Hunter. "It's not easy for me."

Hunter rested his chin on his crossed arms lying on the back of the chair. "I know. But shutting everyone out is not the answer. Take it one step at a time and start with him. You need to talk to someone about it."

Aidan frowned. "You know I can't."

"You can't disclose the classified information from the mission, but you can talk about what happened to you so you can work through that. You need to. You're putting up one hell of a front and you're functional. But you keep everyone at a guarded distance and you're sacrificing any chance at happiness because of it."

Aidan let his friend's words sink in. He needed help, even his stubborn mind acknowledged that. He'd somehow managed to survive the series of clusterfucks in his life, but that last epic failure, he couldn't deal with. Shutting down and locking it away was the easiest alternative. Retelling what had happened six years ago would bring it to the surface again, far worse than the occasional flashback or nightmare. He looked up at Hunter's intense gaze on him. His internal sirens wailed and a clear message to abort the conversation blared in his head. "You know, you're not supposed to be calling him Cam."

"He hates the WITSEC names and he refuses to sleep with me if I use them. So we use nicknames."

"Do I want to know the nicknames?" Aidan asked with a tired smile.

"No." Hunter groaned and gripped the back of his own neck. "How long before you think you can get everything wrapped up with the drug and crime ring case and gauge if Cam's linked to any other potential arrests?"

"I don't know." His focus absently shifted to Jessie and the monitors still displaying the same steady peaks and numbers before returning his attention to his friend. "Jessie's been helping me, but we're not moving along as quickly as we'd hoped. Maybe Cam is only linked to Rick's case, but I don't know for sure. After all, he did essentially cut off the head of the snake, so to speak, when he took him down. I could grill Rick, but that slippery son of a bitch is still running things from within the prison walls. He's actually requested to see me."

Hunter's brow lowered. "You need to be careful with him. He's a smart, dangerous, manipulative prick who managed to head up a crime and drug ring for over a decade without getting caught."

"I know," Aidan said with a sigh. "How's Cam holding up?"

Hunter quieted, staring off to the side as if lost in thought. "He built up his business and it all disappeared when they moved us to the next location. From one day to the next, it all went away." He remained quiet for a few moments, no doubt reliving those few days again and the toll it had taken on his partner. "Constantly moving and changing names... It's been tough. Three times in the last year. Hell, they moved us twice in eight weeks. Me and Dad, we manage, but Cam can't seem to get his footing again." He ran his hand through his closely cropped hair and exhaled a heavily weighted breath. "He begs me to call him by his real name when we're alone." He rubbed his bearded face and stared at Aidan as if ready to drop another bomb on his lap. "I need to get us out of the program."

"Fuck, Hunter." Aidan groaned and buried his head in his hands. "I know it's voluntary, but you can't leave the program until I know it's safe. The moment you walk away they won't protect you guys."

"I know there's a risk, but *this* is his home," Hunter said, jabbing his finger toward the ground to emphasize the point. His silver-gray eyes burned with a fire Aidan hadn't seen since their shared time in the battlefield. "Whatever I need to do to get him back here, consider it done. If I need to be his personal bodyguard, I will, but I need him to be happy. Besides, he refuses to marry me with a fake name. He says it won't feel real."

Great. Let's turn the pressure cooker up a notch. Aidan looked over his shoulder, timing the rise and fall of Jessie's chest, matching it to the steady whoosh and click of the machine. "You need to go."

"And you need to get some sleep. Don't think for a moment I didn't pick up on your subject-change tactic. But I'll let it slide because you look like you're going to pass out from exhaustion. I'll watch over Jessie and you. Go sit over there and get some sleep."

Aidan returned his focus to his friend. He was too damn tired. He needed Jessie's light to guide him through his murky, dark internal abyss. "I'm not winning this argument, am I?"

Hunter arched an eyebrow. "What do you think?"

Resigned, Aidan rose from his seat and walked over to the more comfortable chair at Jessie's bedside, suddenly feeling the weight of all the sleepless nights bearing down on every muscle in his body. He sat and stretched, turning to look over at Jessie's still body in the bed. He tentatively reached out and carefully laid his hand on Jessie's, thankful for the contact that seemed to instantly soothe his inner turmoil.

"Good night," he said, maybe to Hunter who sat in the room or to Jessie who lay in bed in his line of sight. Too tired to decipher the jumble of thoughts filling his mind, he finally surrendered as sleep came barreling in, commanding his attention.

* * * *

Aidan stretched his arms and yawned, feeling far more rested than he had in the last few weeks. He immediately turned to Jessie, his still body in the exact same position as the night before. He reached behind his neck and tried to squeeze the kink out of his muscles, straightening in the chair at the sound of muffled voices. Hunter and Cole spoke softly, quieted, then turned to face him. Aidan slowly stood and Cole took a step back. In a split second, Aidan sprinted toward Cole, ready to attack, stopping only with the force of Hunter grabbing him by the waist.

"Calm the hell down. He was worried about you," Hunter said.

Aidan jabbed his finger toward Cole who stood with his back against the door. "You could have put them in danger, you son of a bitch! Do you have any idea—"

"I'm not stupid," Cole said from a distance. "Geek hooked us up with a VPN and an IP anonymizer that triple-encrypts everything. We were careful as hell and only communicate with code on a message board. And I was worried about you, dumbass."

Aidan breathed heavily, fighting the hold on him as he tried to balance the anger and now the confusion from Cole's words. He'd met Geek during a sting more than six months ago. The guy from Cole's old crew stored more tech details in that impressive brain than Aidan could ever possibly learn in a lifetime. If anyone could implement the tech needed to keep any sort of remote communication safe, Geek was the guy to do that.

Cole took a cautious step forward, nearing Aidan and Hunter. "You're tough, but everyone breaks. I know you've got Ty, but he tells me no one gets through to you the way Hunter does." He stopped and tugged on his beanie cap. He crossed his arms and took another daring step forward. "I figured you'd need Hunter here for support."

Aidan didn't say a word. He loathed himself and his inability to keep his emotions in check.

"You can hate me all you want, but you need to be here for Jessie so you need to get through this. I'll be here for him too, but you're the support rock. I'm the comic relief."

Aidan finally pulled out of Hunter's hold. Cole hesitated, obviously debating if he should take a step back, but decided to stand his ground. Aidan walked over to his self-proclaimed future-brother-in-law and wrapped a single arm around his stocky, broad shoulders. "Thanks," he whispered then quickly released Cole before stepping away.

Cole looked at him, blinking in stunned silence.

"Now that we're all playing nice...Cole, I need you to take Aidan to his house and make sure he packs a bag and gets whatever else he needs. I'm guessing that once I leave, the man is going to sprout roots in this room until Jessie wakes."

Cole quickly nodded, and Aidan turned toward Hunter, narrowing his eyes.

"Don't look at me like that. You're the one who wants me to leave. I refuse to go unless I know you have what you need in this room to get you through the day." He looked over to Cole. "I'm assuming you drove here, right?"

Cole nodded again then gave him a wicked grin. "I've got a badass ride someone left me."

Hunter snorted on a chuckle.

"And...just an FYI. You're not getting it back."

Hunter's laugh echoed in the room.

The corners of Aidan's mouth twitched, imagining Jessie's laughter with their conversation. He glanced over to Jessie and the hint of his smile quickly faded and the pain in his chest throbbed.

"Aidan?"

He numbly turned to face Hunter.

"Go with Cole. Get your things. Talk to your boss. Pick up your car from Jessie's apartment. Get your shit in order so you can come back here. Understand?"

Right now, all his thoughts focused on the lean frame resting on the hospital bed and nothing else made sense. Commands from his former sergeant? That he could do.

Cole shifted his weight from one foot to the other. "Aidan, the sooner we leave the sooner you get back here."

He nodded. Back here quickly, yeah, that was the priority. He turned toward Hunter. "Did you bring a gun?"

"I'm a teacher now. You think I stash that shit under my lesson plans?"

Aidan raised his boot onto the chair, removed the smaller gun from the hidden holster, then handed it over to his friend. "Not your usual, but it'll work in a pinch just in case this asshole tries to get into Jessie's room. I'll be back as soon as I can." He walked over to Cole who still watched him with extreme caution.

"Cole?" Hunter said.

Cole's focus shifted to Hunter. "Yeah?"

"If he was going to attack, he would have done it by now. He has no patience. So you're safe."

Cole nodded and blew out a relieved breath.

"For now," Hunter added with a smirk.

Aidan felt the tug at his lips again and walked toward the door, pulling Cole by a grip behind the neck. He had to talk to his captain, pack a bag, and fuck if he could think past two steps on a list when all his thoughts focused on Jessie and returning to his bedside. Whatever the hell he needed to do, he needed to get it all wrapped up quickly. He stole another glance back at Jessie lying in bed, trying to ignore the pain that tightened his chest.

He didn't know where he would draw the strength he needed to get through this, but he had to. He needed to be Jessie's rock of support when he woke.

Chapter FOUR

"You can't do that!"

Everything was crumbling around him.

"I just did," Captain Jameson said with a sigh. "You stay the hell away from Vega's case. It's not your department, so you need to back away and let them do their job. You're lucky I notified the officers to keep you updated, but you're hands off, so stop calling them every hour. *You* work homicides. That's your focus. It's bad enough you get pulled into the other divisions and agency work with all these other cases you handle. Besides, I don't care how good you are, you'll get myopic and miss something. It's human nature."

"That's fucking bullshit," Aidan thundered, pacing the room like a caged animal and running his hand through his hair. "No one's going to work Jessie's case the way I would."

The captain rolled a pen between his fingers, watching Aidan intently. "I don't know what kind of relationship you have with this man, but—"

Aidan stopped pacing and returned the captain's stare with equal intensity. "What the hell does that have to do with anything?"

The captain tossed the pen into the cup holder and leaned forward, resting his forearms on his desk. "What aren't you telling me, Calloway?"

He didn't hide his sexuality, he refused to broadcast it. It was no one's fucking business and it didn't affect his work. Besides, nothing good ever came out of him being honest in the *personal* department.

"You can stare me down all you want, but I know there's something more there. People talk."

"And?"

The captain rubbed his balding head. "You know some gossip spreads faster than others, especially where cops are concerned."

"And?"

Harry stood and looked off to some random spot on the floor and shook his head. He finally met Aidan's eyes and his lips thinned. "You should have told me."

Maybe his silence would be a clear indication this subject was... Off. The. Fucking. Table.

The captain shook his head again. "You freaked people out during the call. Those guys have seen you a million times over the years and not once...*not once*"—he emphasized with a raised index finger— "have they *ever* seen you anything but steady and hard." He leaned forward, resting his palms on his desk. "You have them all talking, Aidan."

Great. The captain used the *first name* card. Lovely. His subtle way of begging Aidan to bend. Bend to what exactly? Who knew. If he remained silent long enough, maybe his captain would lose steam and drop the subject.

"They saw you crack. The ones who were there got a better picture and know the scene was a fucking mess and even tougher to swallow with a friend front and center. But the only thing people are hearing is that you cracked over a friend. A male friend. One who is obviously...gay."

Aidan straightened. Fuck being silent. "*Obviously* gay? How do you figure that?"

Harry squared his shoulders.

"You weren't there, so how do you know what did or didn't happen and what is and isn't obvious?"

"Aidan, don't—"

"Jessie is not as tall as we are. He's not as broad as we are. That doesn't mean he's *obviously* gay. It just means he's not as tall or as broad as we are. Period. Anything else anyone is deciding based on those bits of info is on them." Aidan scoffed and resumed his pacing, trying to determine what he should say. He could have a conversation with Harry and it would remain within these four walls, but how much exactly could he…or did he want to say? "This is exactly the kind of shit that creates all this other bullshit."

"You shouldn't have lied to me. I can head things off—"

"Oh, I'm sorry, Captain. At what point did we crack open a beer and shoot the shit about whether I liked dick or not?" Yeah, he said that. Fuck it. He'd had enough of this bullshit.

Harry cringed.

"I didn't lie to *anyone.* People have the common sense not to ask me. Because it's no one's fucking business."

"You should have told *me!*"

"What would that have done?" Aidan leaned forward, gripping the back of the chair opposite the captain's desk until his knuckles whitened. "I get it. You're offering support here. But it's no one's fucking business. I hate labels, but now it seems everyone out there wants to brand me because of one thing. Maybe I should get a T-shirt—*I like dick, just not yours.* Maybe that'll get them to mind their own fucking business and get back to solving cases."

"You're overreacting."

"Overreacting? You have no idea what it's like. Everything changes and everything is that much more difficult. People talk about fairness and shit, but they don't want it in their backyard. It's no wonder my brother makes it a point of surrounding himself with people who don't care about his orientation. Just so he doesn't have to deal with all this shit and can focus on his work. I didn't choose it," Aidan said, slapping his chest with his fist. "It chose me. I've got to be tougher, stronger, harder than everyone else all because I'm fighting a fucking stereotype that's bigger than me. So excuse me if I need a reprieve and want to keep it to myself so I can just be me."

Harry pulled out his chair and sat. He pointed to the chair across from his desk. "Sit."

Aidan bit back a complaint, biting down so hard he thought his jaw would crack. He didn't need this headache right now. Any of it. He just wanted…*needed* to get back to the hospital and be with Jessie, not fighting off the wolves because of what he felt for him.

"Sit," his captain insisted. "Please."

Aidan sat and leaned forward, resting his forearms on his thighs.

"You're starting with the task force today."

Aidan shook his head. "I'm here to take time off not—"

Harry raised a halting hand. "Let me finish."

Aidan quieted.

"You're starting the task force today. I've already requested to have the case files copied so you can take a set with you so you're on the same page with the team. Do you have your laptop with you?"

Aidan nodded.

"Make sure you have Skype installed. You're going to use that as your virtual connection to them when you all pow-wow on a case."

"Harry—"

"I'm not finished."

Aidan leaned back in the chair and waited.

"I know you well enough to know you need to work right now. Because if you don't, you're going to snap. More than you already have. You're barely hanging on, and you look as if you haven't slept in weeks. You need to talk to someone. You keep putting it off and all this is building and it's going to explode when you least expect it." His captain quieted, lowering his brow. "You're good, Calloway. The best damn detective I've got here. And I'll gladly keep you while you talk to someone *if* it's voluntary and doesn't affect you in the field. But the moment it starts to affect your work and I *demand* you get help, you're off until you get the all-clear to return. And I don't want to see that happen because I need you here. So don't you dare argue with me on this because I will fight you tooth and nail. Understand?"

Aidan sighed. He hated when someone used logic against him.

"You'll meet with the group online on a daily basis, contribute. Once a week, you're coming in to the precinct for a one-hour sit-down meeting at the round table with them. That'll give you face time with them and a break from the hospital. Knowing you, I imagine you're going to pitch a tent and take up residence there until Vega is discharged. You'll need the break whether you're too stubborn to realize it or not. You'll work the case files until I feel you can focus in the field. I won't let you put yourself in harm's way until I know, with one-hundred-percent assurance, that your head is in the game again. Understand?"

Aidan reluctantly nodded. *Logical bastard.*

"And if someone gives you shit, report it."

"I don't snitch out—"

"You report it. Understand?"

Aidan frowned but finally nodded. He'd agree to anything right about now to end this conversation and return to Jessie's side.

"Now get your ass up off my chair and come with me so I can introduce you to the team." The captain stood and made his way to his office door.

"I want to work Jessie's case."

Harry turned and crossed his arms. "I already told you, I can't do that. I'll make sure you're updated on anything we find out."

Aidan shoved his hands in his jean pockets. "What else have you found out?"

"Not much. We have the description Vega provided. When CSI processed the scene, they pulled DNA from the blood on the broken glass and the wall as well as some strands of hair they found. They all match the same suspect, but there's no match in CODIS for comparison."

Aidan ran his hands through his hair. "How can someone who's done this not have a damn record for something? Have you checked—"

The captain reached out and grabbed Aidan's shoulder. "We're not sitting on this, I promise you. We'll keep a guard posted at his door in the hospital until I can't justify it anymore. Okay?"

He hesitated but eventually nodded. He could grant his captain a little wiggle room while he got his head straight. His captain was a rock-solid guy and sure as hell wouldn't twiddle his thumbs waiting for something to happen. But damn it all to hell if they thought *he* was going to sit on the sidelines and go strictly on a play-by-play recap. There had to be some way he could be involved.

"Good, now let's meet your new best friends."

Aidan followed with a groan. More people. More curious, meddling people who probably didn't want to be anywhere near him.

Lovely. Just fucking lovely.

* * * *

"How'd it go?" Hunter asked when Aidan entered Jessie's room.

"I don't want to talk about it." He walked over to the corner and set his laptop and stack of files on the small round table.

"That bad?"

Aidan tossed his duffle bag on the chair and flipped open his laptop, powered it on and launched Skype. He sat in the chair and leaned back, absently glancing over at Jessie lying on the bed. "Any change?"

Hunter stood and walked over to him, leaning on the small round table that didn't seem as if it could hold the weight of much more. "You know he won't wake until they wean him off the meds. In the last hour while you were away, the doctor came in twice and three nurses have circled. They're watching him so you just need to sit back and give it time."

Sit back.

Wait.

Give it time.

Bend.

The exhaustion of hearing the same shit, over and over like a scratched record wore him down. Why the hell did things need to change? Why did fate need to come in and screw around with his semi-perfect world? Correction. It was a mainly fucked-up world, but whatever, he'd been able to dog paddle in that cesspool and survive. Why did something have to happen to Jessie? He could handle just about anything thrown at him... But why Jessie? He was always nice, always helpful, always—

"Stop it. Whatever is running through your mind, stop it the fuck right now."

Aidan looked up, blinking to focus on his friend's face. "Why did this have to happen to him?" Hunter was all-knowing in that odd paternal way, always righting the star alignments and making sense of things that didn't seem to balance in the world.

"Why does anything happen?"

Aidan grunted. "Don't get philosophical on my ass, please. I'm just trying to make sense of this."

Hunter took a seat in one of the neighboring chairs. "Sometimes, shit happens that doesn't make sense. If you try to find reason in an unreasonable situation, you'll drive yourself crazy. Focus on your work. Focus on being there for him. That's all you can do right now."

"I hate it when you use logic."

Hunter half smiled. "It's my secret weapon against you and Cam. You two always seem to think the world is out to punish you."

"Can you blame us for thinking that with everything you know?"

"No. I can't. But I also know the two of you well enough to know that neither of you could have done anything in this lifetime or the next to deserve what happened to either of you. So stop it. Karma works on debits and credits, and I'd say the both of you have had plenty of debits pulled out of your accounts. The credits are due. So give it a little time and stop fighting it. Just roll with it the best you can and reach out if you need a steady hand until it balances."

"Are you sure you're teaching law? Sounds like you're teaching higher world philosophy or some other metaphysical shit."

"Smartass. Focus on work and Jessie, but don't lose yourself in the process. Okay?"

Aidan nodded. Through all the bullshit and the crap pushing upstream lately, he was lucky enough to not have pushed away those around him who obviously cared enough to stand by his pissy personality through all this. He was thankful and had no way of repaying them for their support other than doing what everyone was telling him to do.

Focus, but don't lose focus.

Easier said than done.

Chapter FIVE

Two weeks later

Aidan closed his eyes as he placed a gentle kiss to Jessie's forehead. Today was his forehead, but he'd mix it up with each cheek as well. Sanity commanded he maintain a routine. Each morning he'd wake, read Jessie the news from the morning paper, and then take a quick shower in the hospital bathroom to start his day.

Two weeks, he had watched the man he loved lie motionless on the hospital bed. The swelling had significantly gone down on his face and the bruises had transitioned from rich maroons and purples to browns and yellows. He had a thin scar cutting through one of his eyebrows and another he would be able to easily hide under his hair at his temple, but overall, the doctors had been right. The swelling in his brain had receded and his body was healing. The two broken ribs were mending on their own and the incision from the splenectomy was, thankfully, free of infection. Jessie now had a small titanium plate with screws for his broken wrist and a few plates and screws in his leg. All the surgical points were healing well so they were able to restrict any movement with full casts on his arm and leg. He would end up with a scar on both his leg and wrist from the plate implants, but supposedly, all the hardware would help him mend faster and better than a traditional cast alone. At least that was what they kept telling him.

Over and over.

They awaited the umpteenth round of medical results. If all went well, they'd finally ease Jessie out of the medical coma. Anxious didn't begin to summarize the jumble of nerves twisting his stomach on a daily basis, more so lately while he waited for the last set of results so they could finally test his breathing and get him off the ventilator. He was tired of hearing the rhythmic swooshing sound of that fucking machine and the consistent hum of oxygen flowing through it.

But *not* hearing those sounds would be far worse. Even he recognized the logic in that.

He hung the used towel back in the hospital bathroom then sat at the small round table that he'd repositioned next to Jessie's hospital bed. Hunter had kept him steady and grounded, but Aidan had to send him away after a few days. There was no way he could risk Hunter's safety any longer. He was more determined now than ever to wrap up Cam's case and get them back home. He flipped open his laptop and checked his email. He busied himself with work, either another file in Cam's case, a cold case requiring more research than the task force cared to contribute, or he'd Skype with the team to brainstorm on leads with current cases. His captain was right, he needed to work, anything to keep his focus off the what-ifs that plagued his mind—especially knowing they hadn't been able to find and arrest Michael Johnson. He had yelled at the detectives and had again been reprimanded by his captain. Harry had been understanding, far more than he would have ever imagined, but Aidan had to work to control his anger.

The anger that nearly boiled over to the point of no return when the captain informed him they had to pull the uniformed officer from Jessie's door after that first week. They could no longer justify taxpayer dollars for a guard. Aidan had nodded, then exited his captain's office, refusing to utter another word. He then contacted an old Marine friend of his and hired him to stand guard at Jessie's door. Someone who didn't need a weapon to do some damage.

Seeing Jessie slowly improving, at least…put his mind at ease. Jessie was his priority. And making sure he was safe while he recovered was imperative. But he needed to work. Work had played a critical role in maintaining his sanity in the last two weeks. Seemed his captain did know him well after all. He wouldn't admit it openly, but he loved the Skype chats and agreed the team had made great strides. Except for Manny. The guy was just a fucking prick who took too much pleasure in delivering an occasional homophobic jab.

"Good morning, Aidan," the nurse said when she entered the room.

"Morning, Nancy."

He knew them all by name—all the nurses, doctors, techs, and random staff who entered the room. Regardless of the guard posted at the door, no one neared Jessie unless they were cleared by him. Hunter had been right. Aidan had planted virtual roots in the room during the last two weeks and refused to leave for more than an hour or two at a time but only if Cole swore to stand by Jessie's bed until he returned just in case there was any change.

He scanned his emails and responded to the most critical ones.

"Did you read him the news already?"

Aidan nodded. "I even managed to sneak in a little of the entertainment section."

"I'm sure he liked that."

"Has Dr. Green arrived yet?"

The nurse shook her head as she checked the monitors and jotted notes in Jessie's chart. "Not yet, but we're all on alert for when he does," she said, looking over her shoulder as she swapped out the IV bag from the pole.

Aidan returned his focus to an email from his captain. Another conference call today with the team in—he looked at the wall clock—fifteen minutes. He quickly responded, acknowledging the call, and downloaded the attachments to review. He responded to another message from his friend at the bureau with an update on Cameron's case. He absently glanced up to look at Jessie, closely watching Nancy adjust the pillows under Jessie's head then straightening the collar of his hospital gown. A soft smile tugged at his lips. Jessie would like that detail; a crooked collar would drive him nuts. He identified the two new markers he'd use until someone moved Jessie again. Markers that would let him know if Jessie shifted in the slightest. The tip of the "S" of the logo on the headboard just above his left ear and half of the "R" just past his right ear. He nodded to himself with the mental note and resumed typing his email reply.

"Have you had your coffee yet?" Nancy asked.

"Not yet," he responded, pecking away at the laptop keyboard. "Chad was in here earlier, and I haven't had a chance to grab it yet." He still didn't feel comfortable leaving anyone alone with Jessie. Even though the physical therapist who came in several times a day for a few minutes at a time to work Jessie's limbs was helpful, he had major trust issues until the attacker was officially caught.

Nancy pressed the call button. "Amy, can you bring in the cup for Mr. Calloway."

"Be right there," the perky speaker voice responded.

"That's not necessary, Nancy. You already do so much for him. I'll grab a cup from the vending machine as soon as I finish responding to my email."

Nancy crossed her arms. "Nonsense. Besides, Amy made a coffee run this morning and she brought you a cup. But she knows better than to sneak in here until after you've finished your shower."

"Will she ever forgive me?" That was the last time Aidan took a shower in the hospital room without taking a change of clothes with him into the bathroom. Emerging from the bathroom with a sliver of a towel that barely covered his bits in one hand and a cocked gun in the other was enough to initially terrify the nurse and subsequently trigger a wave of giggles that still lingered in his wake when he walked down the hallway.

Nancy waved her hand, shooing away his comment. "The nurses love to gossip about you. They think you're the sweetest man to walk the face of the earth the way you watch over him."

"I've been called a lot of things, sweet isn't one of them."

"Maybe no one dares call you that to your face."

"Maybe." Aidan looked up from the laptop screen with a half smile. He liked Nancy. Jessie was always the first patient she checked in on at the start of her shift and the last one before she left the hospital. That scored her some major points in his book.

A soft knock sounded at the door. Amy entered and walked over to Aidan's table, handing him a super-sized cup. "Extra hot, quad shot, white chocolate mocha. Just the way you like it."

He took the cup and sipped from the opening in the lid. He'd downed enough of the liquid caffeine fuel in all varieties throughout his life—from the plain, bitter, tasteless tar to the gourmet homegrown beans that shot a jolt of adrenaline straight into a vein. He didn't care if it was straight up caffeine or some fancy-pants blend of java, but for some far-off and silly reason, drinking a blended coffee always reminded him of those days when Jessie would bring him one of Cam's latte art drinks from the diner so long ago. It was silly, but anything to keep that connection with something Jessie-related was all that mattered. "Mmm. Perfect." He reached over to his wallet.

Amy waved him off. "Gift from the nurses. We're all anxiously waiting for Dr. Green's news because we all want to meet Jessie," she finished with a blush then turned to leave the room.

Aidan took a sip of the liquid heaven and moaned, sneaking a glance at Nancy who watched him with a smile.

"See, you're sweet."

"Only because I'll be on a sugar and caffeine high after this," he said with a quiet laugh.

Nancy finished making her notations in Jessie's chart then exited the room.

He stole another glance at Jessie, making a mental note of the unchanged place markers. He blew out an exasperated breath. Soon, hopefully soon. He could only keep his shit together for so long before something would give. He glanced up at the wall clock and still had a few minutes to spare before the scheduled call. He pulled out the files for the two cases they were ready to discuss and made a few notes. Maybe things would be timed perfectly. Maybe he'd wrap up the call and the doctor would arrive with the test results and finally give him the news he'd been anxiously waiting to hear for two weeks. He could hope. After all, without hope to tether him to his sanity, he would have lost it long ago.

* * * *

Aidan jerked his head upward after having nodded off. He rubbed his face and leaned forward, digging his elbow into the bed again and resting his head in his hand. He willed Jessie to move. Something.

Anything. He laid the palm of his other hand against Jessie's fingers and tucked his thumb under Jessie's palm, hoping to detect the slightest movement if Jessie's fingers twitched at all.

Dr. Green had stopped by for his visit and delivered the news they had anxiously awaited. Finally, they were weaning Jessie off the meds. They'd tested his breathing and all went well enough to finally remove the breathing tube. Now, here they were, days later, and still nothing other than the unnerving silence now that the whooshing and rhythmic clicking of the ventilator was gone.

He cleared the sleep from his throat. "Do you remember the first time we met?" he asked, not expecting to hear an answer but still not losing hope that Jessie would jump into the conversation.

He hated the way his voice echoed in the solitary room. He usually couldn't handle the heart monitor beeps reminding him of how much time he took to compose himself between bouts of his one-sided conversations. He'd silence the beep while awake then switch it back on when his eyelids weighed too much and demanded he steal a few hours' sleep to recharge. Only then could he handle the rhythmic sound that would alert him if anything changed in Jessie's heartbeat. Talking to Jessie seemed to soothe him and keep his emotions in check, even if having one-sided conversations were the first outward sign of his deteriorating sanity.

He absently stroked Jessie's hair as he spoke. "I remember as if it were yesterday. I couldn't take my eyes off you. And the funny thing is, I don't even remember what you were wearing." He huffed out a weak laugh. "Me, a detective, unable to remember what the hell you wore. I'm guessing a suit, but I can't remember which one." He continued to softly stroke the hair away from Jessie's forehead. His hair was longer than Aidan ever remembered it being in all the time he'd known him, or maybe it was the absence of any hair product that usually kept everything neatly in place. The uneven hair growth now shadowing Jessie's face would probably result in a gasp or scowl, but he didn't want to risk shaving him until all the swelling was down and most of the bruises faded. No way would Jessie be out in public unpolished. He smiled to himself, gently stroking the soft, dark hair against Jessie's temple, watching the peacefulness in his expression. The tousled, messy look suited him well.

"I couldn't tear my eyes away from your face." *I still can't.* "You were talking with Hunter at that storage unit where you guys had just sorted through Lydia's files, and you had this huge smile that brightened your entire face. Then, something changed. The smile evaporated and your eyes were different when you heard my truck pulling up. The way you looked at my truck, your eyes, they were…haunted. As if you were weary….scared and guarded about something. I remember wanting to hurt whoever or whatever had caused that. Just as much as I want to hurt the man who did this to you, who put that haunted look back in your eyes when I saw you sitting on your bed with that broken angel in your hand." He rhythmically stroked his fingers through Jessie's dark hair as he continued to talk. "You didn't take your eyes off my truck, probably wondering who the hell was in that dark SUV. I noticed you took a step closer to Hunter, inching behind him for cover. But when I stepped out, and you saw me, you…relaxed and that haunted look in your eyes disappeared. Almost instantly. Then you smiled."

He looked down and ran his thumb along Jessie's cheek. "I want to do that for you…always." He reached down and placed a soft, gentle kiss against Jessie's forehead. "Please, wake up. I miss your smile."

* * * *

Darkness. Nothing but an endless void and…

Beep. Beep.

That sound. That annoying, consistently aggravating sound that pierced every nerve ending. He wanted to run. He needed to escape. He needed to hear the other sound instead. The voice. The steady deep ebb and flow of that tone he loved.

Beep. Beep.

He looked over his shoulder, trying to avoid the monster that haunted him. The one that hovered just around the corner, waiting for him to let his guard down. He tried to straighten his arms to feel his way in the darkness, but it was useless. His arms refused to lift when his mind commanded. The panic started to escalate and his heart pounded madly.

He couldn't hear the voice that accompanied him in the darkness. The voice of the man who watched over him and would protect him with every ounce of power in that lean-muscled, strong body.

Aidan.

His guardian angel.

There was always a sound, either the voice he craved or the steady beeping that offered no comfort. Never both at the same time. Sometimes, the voice accompanied a soothing, protective warmth in the air that surrounded him. Heat on his hands and against his cheek, forehead, or neck. A small current would start at the point of contact and travel throughout his body, shooting a bolt of determination to continue to seek the light in this abyss, where the voice sounded clearer. He needed that voice, the one that had become his tether to sanity in the darkness. The smooth, quiet tone of Aidan's voice always lingered in the air like a steady melodic song guiding him in the dark. Even if some of the words were whispered and indistinct, they were there, making him aware of his presence and keeping the monster at bay.

Beep. Beep.

He would give anything to hear that voice right now. At least he felt the warmth around his hand. That always seemed to soothe him a tiny bit in the uncertainty of the blackness that enveloped him.

He pushed toward the faint hint of light ahead. The beeping became louder. His legs weighed heavily as if stepping in quicksand, almost too much to bear, requiring more force than his body could handle. He willed his mind to push forward and place each foot in front of the other, fighting his body's need to stand still. His breathing slowed as his heartbeat sped. It was odd. His body seemed to be fighting its own war while he seemed to trudge along the dark path to the flickering light.

He gasped when he heard the low, haunting laugh of the monster. He glanced over his shoulder and saw nothing but darkness. But he was there. Waiting. As he always was.

He turned and looked ahead, willing himself to reach the flickering light that called to him. He fought the exhaustion racking his body, pushing ahead with determination and fighting the need to take a break.

The light flickered a little more.

The haunting laugh echoed in the blackness again, taunting him.

He needed to hear the voice. His mind and body struggled, weighing him down and tying him to that spot in the darkness as he watched the teasing flicker of light ahead. He couldn't coordinate his limbs and frustration bloomed. He yelled for Aidan, begging for him, but his voice wasn't working. He closed his eyes and wanted to give in. He needed the strength that voice fueled within him.

Beep. Beep. Beep.

* * * *

Aidan jolted upright in the chair and inhaled sharply. He'd swear he felt it. He looked at Jessie's still body lying in bed. The virtual place markers around him showed Jessie hadn't shifted a millimeter. He looked up at the monitor and there was the single, subtle spike in the graph.

His own heartbeat sped.

The steady rhythm had changed. Easy-to-miss, but something was different. He leaned forward, reached out, and ran his fingers through Jessie's hair. "I'm right here, waiting for you. You know how impatient I am. Just open your eyes or move your hand." He swallowed heavily and tried to keep the hope at bay. "C'mon, Jess. Don't try to do everything at once. Just do one thing."

He looked up at the monitor when he heard a break in the rhythm again. He smiled as hope began to spark. He gently ran his thumb back and forth along Jessie's cheek. He looked down at his other hand solidly planted above Jessie's.

Nothing.

Yet.

"Jess, wake up. Even if only for a second. Just—"

He held his breath when Jessie's eyelids moved back and forth quickly as if in a deep REM sleep state. He waited until finally, he released his breath when a hint of crystal blue peeked through a tiny sliver.

"Hey there," he said, smiling as Jessie's eyelids barely fluttered open. He reached out and slapped the nurse's call button, not shifting his focus from the blue eyes staring back at him. He ran his fingers along the front of Jessie's hair. The beeping spiked again.

Repeatedly.

"Calm down. You're safe here." Through the drug-filled gaze staring back at him, there was recognition, but also confusion, fear, and something else he couldn't quite peg. Maybe frustration? "You're in the hospital. You've been out of it for a while. So you need to give your mind and body a chance to sync. Don't push it."

The tension seemed to ease in the stare.

A hint of pressure pushed against the thumb of his other hand. The corners of Aidan's lips curled into a smile and a flutter replaced the ache that had lingered for the last two weeks in his chest. He laid one hand under Jessie's—palm to palm—and continued to stroke Jessie's cheek with the other.

"Yes, Mr. Calloway?" the nurse's voice echoed through the speaker.

"He woke up!" he excitedly yelled, loud enough to probably wake the other patients on the floor, unable to control the emotions twisting his stomach.

He took a deep, steadying breath. "I'm right here and I'm not going anywhere," he said, ignoring the crack in his voice. He half-stood from the seat and reached over, silencing the beep of the monitor. He sat again and resumed the slow stroke of Jessie's cheek. "Go back to sleep. I'll be right here waiting for you to wake up again."

Jessie's eyelids slowly closed again and the graph on the monitor steadied to its usual pattern. Aidan took a few, slow, calming deep breaths to steady his own heartbeat. For the first time in the past few weeks, an inner strength returned and hope resurrected. The silence of the room didn't unsettle him. In fact, it seemed to calm him as he focused on the sound of each breath passing Jessie's lips.

Those perfect lips he hadn't been able to see for two weeks, hidden under the strap holding the breathing tube. He wanted to reach out and touch them, kiss them…taste them.

He took a few deep breaths to calm the swirl of emotions warring within. Jessie would come back to him, and he was going to be right there by his side when he opened his eyes. *That* had to be his focus, not a hopeless daydream. Aidan glanced up when he heard a noise by the door, smiling when he spotted four of the night-shift nurses huddled in the corner.

"The doctor's on his way," Nancy whispered, shooing the nurses out of the room.

He nodded, eyeing the steady peaks on the monitor before returning his focus to Jessie. With one last, centering deep breath, he calmed his nerves before doing what had become another ritual in the last few weeks. "Did I ever tell you about the case with that guy who kept leaving a polka dot scarf at the scene of each crime?"

He'd ramble on about silly cases, inept criminals who missed their calling in life as hosts of idiot bloopers. Those random cases that made everyone laugh at the precinct because there was just no way a criminal could lack that much common sense. Those were the cases he shared with Jessie when his insomnia was in full force. The ones that were rare but would make Jessie laugh if he were awake and mentally present in the room. Nothing negative, no homicide cases, nothing with trauma, gore, or heartbreak. He hoped the funny stories and tone of his voice would provide some comfort to Jessie in his drug-induced state.

He smiled, not sure if it was a result of the story he'd told or of the hope that continued to bubble to the surface. He didn't care. He'd talk about anything and everything silly, funny, with pixie dust and unicorns if he had to. Jessie was coming back to him, and that was all that mattered.

part two
RECOVERING

Chapter SIX

Jessie tugged the edge of the bedsheet, waiting for the doctor's final evaluation. His reflexes and motor skills were a little slow, but the doctor assured him they would improve. And once the drugs were completely flushed from his system, his sometimes-fuzzy mind would clear up as well.

He remembered Cole herding their mob of friends into the room the day he'd come out of the coma, two weeks ago, and the collective sigh of relief from the standing-room-only audience as they waited for him to react to the pen running down the flat of his foot. Of course, that was the most inopportune time to release a giggle. A grown man giggling. The only thing that prevented him from dying of embarrassment at that very moment was the huge smile that split Aidan's face. The most stunning, breathtaking smile he had ever seen.

Aidan. His stoic, bulldog bodyguard ready to fight off anyone who didn't treat Jessie as if he were a king perched on his throne rather than a recently awakened coma patient. He didn't think it was possible to love the man any more than he already did.

He was so wrong.

For almost a year and a half, he had worked alongside Aidan during any spare moment they could share on weekends or between their work schedules. They'd go through every detail of each case— sometimes more often than needed just to spend extra time together. When they worked weekends, those times were spent at Aidan's house, but Jessie would find an excuse to visit the precinct or text him if a new idea or approach came to mind. They worked effortlessly together, sometimes over lunch or dinner. But he wouldn't deny he wanted far more than friendship with the one man who seemed to always take the time to listen to anything and everything he said. The one man who always respected him and made him feel like an equal. Every moment together added another drop into his already overflowing love bucket for Aidan.

"Everything seems to be healing well," Dr. Green said, writing notes in his chart, pulling Jessie from his thoughts. "Your blood levels are coming back normal so there are no complications from the splenectomy. But it's always best to not take that for granted, especially if you catch a cold or run a fever."

Jessie nodded.

"And it's my understanding you didn't go with our recommended trauma therapist, but you are speaking with a...Dr. Engel. So everything seems to be in order."

"When can I go home?" Jessie croaked then cleared his throat, still battling with the random slight hoarseness of his voice after the removal of the breathing tube. Aidan instinctively reached over, pouring a cup of water for him. Jessie smiled as he took the cup and a small sip.

"Not until you're able to walk and handle the basics on your own, so it'll be a few weeks. We can discharge you and set you up with home visits with a nurse, but I would prefer knowing you can walk down the hallway here without help. Okay?"

Jessie nodded.

"Any other questions?"

He tugged on the edge of the bedsheet again.

"Jess, tell him about the nightmares," Aidan said.

He looked up at Aidan, his cheeks heating as a flood of memories of the last few nights took center stage in his mind. The nightmares seemed to haunt him and only lessened if Aidan held his hand while he slept. Something about Aidan's strong, firm, yet gentle touch seemed to give him the support he needed to guard himself against the monster that always came to him in the darkness.

Dr. Green crossed his arms. "Nightmares or hallucinations?"

"Only happens when I'm sleeping so I'm guessing nightmares."

"Is that common?" Aidan asked.

"Some patients have reported similar issues. It's a possible side effect from the sedatives we administered during the coma, but they'll lessen with time. Have you mentioned it to your trauma therapist?"

He nodded.

"Okay, so we're covering it on both fronts. We need to monitor the change there as well."

Jessie sighed. *Wonderful.* Until then he'd have to deal with that damn monster laughing and reaching for him when he tried to get some sleep, even though the demon wasn't really there.

The doctor proceeded to make additional notes in the chart. "I'm adding more time to your physical therapy schedule so we can work on building your muscle strength back up. But I don't want you pushing things too quickly and risking your recovery. It's important you take your pain meds if your ribs cause any discomfort with your therapy. That's why they're there."

Jessie nodded again.

Dr. Green silently watched him, probably gauging how much his nodding was an actual agreement or dismissal. The doctor finally turned away and deposited the chart in the holder on his way out the door, leaving him alone in the room with Aidan.

Aidan pulled the chair closer to Jessie's bed. "Cole sent a text. He's coming over in a bit. Did you want me to sneak something up from the cafeteria before he gets here?"

He smiled at the mischievous glint in Aidan's eyes. "Nancy said I should stick with the diet until I start walking around a bit, but I would totally steal fries if you get that burger from downstairs again today."

"I know, right? I think they lace those things with something. They're addictive as hell," Aidan said with a smile. "I was going to grab that tonight for dinner. I've got a forensics cleaning crew going by your apartment today, so I want to be there while they do their thing so I can lock up afterward."

"Can you bring me a change of clothes so I have something when I finally get out of here?"

Aidan lowered his head and his jaw clenched.

Jessie reached out and placed his hand on Aidan's forearm, hoping to ease the sudden tension. "What's wrong?"

"I'm going over to your apartment to make sure it's cleaned up. I don't want you going back to the way we left it. But I don't want to go through your things. That's…" Aidan reached up and rubbed the back of his neck.

"Personal?"

Aidan nodded. "I know how you are about your space."

"And I know how you respect that. So I'm not worried about it because it's you. Okay?"

Aidan nodded again, a hint of a smile washed over his features.

"Shorts are in the drawer in the dresser. I'm guessing that'll be easier with the leg cast. That one's not coming off anytime soon."

"Okay. Anything else?"

"My phone and charger…and my laptop with the portable external hard drive. They should be in my office, either on the desk or the top drawer on the left hand side. I need to check my emails and I need to touch base with a few of my clients so they know I'm not available for any consulting work for a while. Damn," he said, rubbing his eyes. "And I need my mail so I can check the bills that have come in."

"I…um, took care of your rent for the month."

Jessie's gaze snapped up to Aidan. "Why did you do that?"

Aidan looked…uncomfortable. "After the investigators released your apartment I had the locks replaced and the building maintenance guy was there. I didn't want there to be an issue with your lease so I paid the rent and monthly fee."

He reached out for Aidan's hand, hoping to settle the discomfort between them. "Thank you. I appreciate that. But I've got that covered. I promise."

Aidan nodded. "I'm paying for the cleaning crew."

A smile tugged at his lips. "Thank you."

Aidan nodded again. "Anything else?"

"I…I want to shave before Cole gets here. My face doesn't feel swollen anymore, so, I…I want to shave." The facial hair was really getting to him, especially knowing he couldn't grow out an even beard. Everyone had been so keen on keeping any mirror away that he wasn't sure what he'd see staring back at him.

"Okay." Aidan helped shift him into a sitting position, moving the pillows to help secure him in place. He hated feeling dependent, but the cast on his arm didn't grant him enough balance to do certain things on his own yet. Aidan disappeared into the bathroom and returned moments later with a small plastic kidney-shaped container with water and a shaving kit.

"I want a mirror," Jessie said, trying to control the slight tremble in his voice. Others had acted as if he hadn't spoken when he'd requested to see his reflection, but he hoped Aidan wouldn't balk as well.

Aidan's brow lowered. He hesitated for a moment, stepped away, then returned with a mirror in hand.

Jessie took a deep breath before finally looking at his reflection. He inhaled sharply at the faint, lingering bruises yellowing his skin. A slight scar cut through his eyebrow and one of the whites of his eyes was still red, making the light blue of his eyes stand out even more. His hair was a mess, sticking up in all directions and the patchy beard just added to the unkempt appearance that made him cringe.

"Shit," he cursed under his breath. He grabbed the shaving cream and held it in the casted hand and unsuccessfully tried to dispense some into his good hand to start the process. Aidan took the bottle from his hand and squeezed out enough foam into Jessie's hand to silence the groan of frustration. Jessie lathered his face then wiped his hand on the towel, snatching the razor in one hand and the mirror in the hand with the cast. Another groan escaped when he couldn't lift the mirror high enough to see his reflection to guide the razor.

"Jess, I know you want to do this on your own, but please let me help you."

He set the mirror down and wet the razor in the water, knowing the planes of his face enough to shave without that unfamiliar reflection staring back at him. He reached up and swiped the razor down the side of his face then rinsed the blade in the water, repeating the process. He angled his hand to swipe under his neck and stopped when Aidan firmly held his good wrist.

"Your hand is shaking, and you're trying to shave with your non-dominant hand."

Jessie pulled away, angry at himself more than anything. He had to be in control. He had to be independent. There was no other option. He held the razor again at an awkward angle and brushed the edge against his jawline. He winced when the now cut skin burned. "Dammit."

Aidan stood and carefully took the razor from his hand, then rinsed the blade. He grabbed the towel and dipped the edge into the water then patted the blood away as he spoke in that soothing, gentle tone he used that always made Jessie cave to whatever he requested. "You're going to have plenty of time to do this on your own. Until then, let me help you. If you don't want anyone else helping you, that's fine. But let me."

Jessie swallowed heavily, fighting the need to rebel for independence. Without waiting for his permission, Aidan leaned over and held his chin, guiding Jessie's head upward as he shaved his neck. He closed his eyes as those rough fingers gripped his chin and gently caressed his cheek, guiding his face as the cool blade ran against his skin. He couldn't control his hands enough to shave, and now, it seemed he couldn't control other parts of his body either. His blood heated and his dick slightly hardened. How the hell his prick didn't get the drug-numbing memo was beyond him. The splash of water drew his focus as another swipe along his face and brush of fingers against his jawline comforted him. It didn't take much effort to will his body to calm with all the painkillers coursing through his veins. Relief didn't quite sum up how thankful he was to confirm that not all parts of his anatomy had suffered from the attack.

"There." Aidan pressed the towel to Jessie's cheeks and neck.

"Thanks."

Aidan gathered the items and retreated to the bathroom, returning with a hairbrush that seemed like a gift from the gods. Jessie quickly grabbed the brush and stroked his hair, taming the mess he wished he could wipe from his memory.

"Anything else before Cole steamrolls in here?"

He smiled. "I'm good. Are you taking a break when he gets here?"

"You're getting all polished up for him and now you want some alone time with him, too?"

Jessie's cheeks heated again. "Smartass."

Aidan chuckled and returned the brush to the bathroom. "I've got a benchmark meeting at the precinct, and I've got to get some fresh clothes before I stop by your apartment. I'm sure he'll talk your ear off long enough until I get back."

"You can take a break, you know. You don't have to stay here all day and night." He looked up and tried to steel his features, hoping he hadn't revealed how much he wanted Aidan, especially when the nightmares were in full force.

"People say I'm stubborn." Aidan sighed as he sat in the chair at the small round table in the corner. "I've already told you, it's not a problem."

"But your work—"

"Is totally under control. They've got me chained to my laptop and this chair at their beck and call whenever they want to ring me in or pick my brain. It's fine."

Jessie exhaled, relief pouring through his aching body.

"Now, if you want me to go because I'm annoying the shit out of you—"

"You're not. I just don't…"

"Don't what?"

Jessie's focus snapped to Aidan. The concern staring back at him made his heart beat faster. "I don't want to be a bother," he said, looking away. A bother, a burden, it was all the same thing. He hated feeling this way.

"You're not."

"You spoil me."

"I want to."

Jessie looked up and his lips parted on a quiet gasp at the intensity in those hazel eyes before Aidan turned away, busying himself with the folders on the table.

Two quick, hard knocks sounded at the door, signaling Cole's arrival.

"Come in," Aidan called out, rising from the chair and stuffing a stack of folders into his bag.

Jessie bit back a grin. Aidan couldn't escape fast enough when Cole was in the same space.

"Wow…look at you. Aren't you all polished up, little man!"

"Don't call me that," Jessie grumbled through a smile, happy as hell to see Cole's smiling face.

Cole grabbed the chair next to Jessie's bed and flipped it around, leaning his crossed arms along the back. He looked over to Aidan. "Are you hanging around or are you working on your escape?"

Aidan peered up as he dug into his duffle bag. "Escaping from you. How long are you staying?"

"Until Jessie gets tired of hearing me yak away. When are you coming back?"

"I need at least two and a half hours," Aidan said, slinging the bag over his shoulder. "If you can't stay that long, let my guard at the door know."

"I can easily talk a hell of a lot longer than that. Now get the hell out of here so we can talk shit about you."

Aidan sighed. "Jess, anything else before I go?"

"I'm good."

Aidan stared down at Cole and pointed a finger at him. "Don't give him a hard time."

"I'll behave," Cole said with a huff of amusement.

Aidan exited the room, grumbling something that sounded remotely like a curse.

Jessie flattened the sheet on his thighs again, trying to busy himself with anything to do while lying in bed. "You enjoy driving him crazy."

"It's the only way I can get him to show any sort of emotion. He's a tough nut to crack."

"I want to crack that nut," Jessie mumbled before realizing he'd said that out loud.

"I bet you do," Cole said with a chuckle.

Jessie's cheeks burned as he ducked his head.

Cole rested his chin on his crossed arms. "I'm glad to see you're not shying away from him anymore. I think he needs that."

"Why's that?"

Cole shrugged. "He's standoffish, but I think it's part of that whole *fuck-off-and-leave-me-alone-so-you-don't-know-the-real-me* type of thing. These Calloway men are guarded and keep to themselves. But when you get them to open up…"

"Yeah?"

"It's a beautiful thing."

"You're very poetic. I think Ty's rubbing off on you."

"He rubs off on me, but that makes me horny not poetic." Cole finished with a guffaw.

Jessie shook his head. "You're impossible."

Cole quieted, leaning forward and focusing his mismatched eyes with intensity. "And you're crazy in love with Aidan and horny as hell. Go crack that nut already."

"He's… I don't know…"

"Tough. Stubborn. I can do this all day."

Jessie sighed.

"He's been here every day. He didn't even trust me to stay with you at first, only Hunter. You didn't see him those first few days." Cole straightened in the seat and lowered his brow. "Or hear his voice that first night. He sounded…broken somehow. I don't know how else to explain it. But fuck me, I didn't know what to do so I contacted everyone I could think of to help him. But he's calmer now."

Jessie tugged the sheet and shifted in the bed. "I think it's a defense mechanism. He distances himself. Sometimes, I feel as if we're getting close, but…who knows for sure. He keeps me just outside that line and I can't seem to cross it. And when I get a little close, he shuts down. All those weekends working together, he never once came over to my apartment to work on Cam's case. Not once. It was always from his house because that's where it all started with Hunter when he lived there. It was as if changing things would have crossed some line or made it personal. It's probably why he didn't know it was my place when he got the call that night to come over. I'm guessing he never looked up my address because he would have seen it as an invasion of privacy or something." He shook his head and blew out a deep breath. "I don't know how to get through to him. But I want to…more than anything."

"You guys are like two turtles. You both move slow as hell and you have these hard shells." Cole quieted then snorted a chuckle.

"What's so funny?"

Cole bit his lip. "Turtles fucking. They make funny noises. Google that shit."

Jessie ducked his head again and held back a smile.

They chatted about hospital food, the auto shop, the nurses—small talk to pass the time. The nurses filed in in small clusters when they heard Cole was visiting, seemed no one could resist his larger than life laugh or smile. They finally left when the overhead speaker announced a code, beckoning their attention. Jessie leaned back in the pillow as their conversation segued to a discussion of Cole's huge family.

"Your dad was here."

Jessie sat up, his mood sobering. "What?" he whispered.

Cole rested his chin on his crossed arms and spoke softly. "Your dad. He was here that first night. I'm pretty sure he was your dad. He had your eyes, but he was bigger, broader. Looked like a mean son of a bitch."

Jessie looked down, pulling, folding, and flattening the top of the sheet. "It couldn't have been him." After everything that had happened between them, he didn't have a clue what he would say if his father visited. He tried to dismiss the thought, but he wouldn't deny a tiny glimmer of hope flickered at the idea of his father wanting to know what had happened or how he was doing. Anything.

Cole continued to talk, jumping into another discussion about Ty's latest restoration project. But all Jessie could think about was why his father had come by and if there was even the slightest chance he could have cared about his son at all.

* * * *

Aidan planted his hands on his hips to avoid picking something up and throwing it across the room. "What do you mean you don't have any leads?"

The captain rubbed his balding head. "I told you, they've checked everything. There's no video surveillance in a mile radius they can reference. The building didn't have security cameras. The neighbors didn't see anything or anyone, they only heard the yelling. We've matched the DNA from the blood and fingerprints to the same person. But without some checkpoint to compare that information with a face and record in our database we've got nothing."

"So he just gets away with it? That's bullshit."

"They're sending another detective over to talk to Vega again. Maybe he's a little clearer now and there's something that was missed from the initial interview when he first woke."

Aidan vehemently shook his head. "No. I'll talk to him about it and relay relevant info." He remembered how distant Jessie had become after the initial recounting of the attack, and there was no way in hell he was going to subject Jessie to that again.

"Calloway, it doesn't work that way. It's not your case. You're not supposed to be anywhere near it."

Aidan stepped forward, each angry, frustrated breath heaving his chest. "And they've gotten nowhere." He'd normally be the one to get the answers, find the suspect, and catch the criminal, not be the guy sitting at the sidelines waiting for an update. "Get me on the case. Make it official."

"I can't do that."

"Sure you can. It's been over a month and a half, and it's going to drop on the list of priorities. I'll work it on off time, I don't care. But grant me access, so I don't have to drive anyone crazy and I have the resources on this without raising any red flags or stepping on anyone's toes."

The captain squared his shoulders. "One condition."

Aidan straightened and crossed his arms.

"*You're* not on the case. However, I can assign it to the task force. It's the only way I can allow you to be anywhere near it." He held up a stopping hand before Aidan had a chance to interrupt him. "But you are *not* working it. You are there, you get your info real-time, and you can even offer suggestions and review the case. But that's it. Detective Reyes is lead since it's his specialty. That's my condition. Accept or decline?"

At this point, he'd be willing to agree to anything just to have some involvement in the case. "Accept. But, I have a...request."

Harry nodded, encouraging him to continue.

"*I* talk to Jessie about this guy. I'm not going to subject him to any Reyes bullshit during his recovery. I don't want Jessie under the team's scrutiny until I get a take on their position."

"There's no position to take. This is another case they're going to work."

Aidan raised an eyebrow. "Do you really believe that?"

The captain sighed and ran his hand down his face. "Fine. You're going to give me an ulcer with all this shit."

They exited the captain's office and silently walked down the corridor to the task force's secure area. After a thumbprint identification and passcode, they entered the gated area and walked down the hallway to the small conference room where the team members met and were probably already a few minutes into the weekly recap meeting.

"Morning. You guys are now on the Vega case."

No one commented other than Manny's groan.

"Is there a problem, Detective Reyes?" the captain immediately asked.

Aidan hid a smile. Just one of the reasons he liked his captain. He didn't take shit from people and rarely ever backed down.

"No, sir," Manny forced through a tight grin.

"I didn't think so. As you were," Harry said before exiting the private room and closing the door behind him.

"Now where were we," Manny said before resuming the weekly recap of cases and lead progress.

Aidan walked over and pulled out the chair next to Sunny.

"How's Vega doing?" she said, bumping his shoulder.

"Hanging in there. Pushing himself too much sometimes. He's stubborn."

"He's obviously been around you too long," she said with a teasing grin.

Aidan scoffed. He peered up at Manny, pointing to one of the three large bulletin boards with papers, photos, and notes haphazardly pinned and taped. The boards were constantly updated and discussed so everyone could cross-contribute with a fresh perspective when an epiphany hit. They split the cases up within the team and reported updates and leads, either real-time if critical, or during the weekly benchmark meetings. They reviewed the leads and planned the next steps, delegating responsibilities along the way.

He humored Manny and his need to lead; after all, everyone had their quirks in the group and most preferred to not have the spotlight shone on them for the dog and pony show. But Manny, that man loved to be the central focus. He was the mouthpiece. Sure, he was a great detective as well, but it was tough to see past that aura of superiority he loved to flaunt. He worked with the Special Victims Bureau. Regardless of all the arrogance that surrounded him and his craptastic attitude, Aidan did respect the jerk. It took a special type of personality to handle so many assault-related cases and stay sane without hitting the bottle as so many others had in that position.

Every now and then, Travis would jump in with a question or comment about one of the updates. Travis Keller came to the team from the Organized Crime Section. Aidan had known Travis for a while before actually working with him, tackling some of Cam's related cases in his division. He was a *by-the-book* type. That book had one line in it—*get the bad guy, one way or another*. Period. End of story. He wasn't a dirty cop by any means and his clean-cut boyish looks often fooled everyone, but the guy must have taken a crash course at the *whatever-means-necessary* school of thought while acing the *cover-your-ass* workshop. He was unconventional but always legit and loved to push the boundaries.

And his classmate at the school of hard knocks must have been Wall. Not short for Wally, Wallace or anything sweet or posh like that. He came to the group from the Special Response Team, and SRT had given him that nickname because they all felt talking to him was the equivalent of talking to a brick wall. The guy rarely spoke and had most people guessing if he'd had his vocal cords removed. Most of his responses were a random head shake or nod. Occasionally, people heard a mumble or a grunt, but that was the extent of his communication. Aidan liked him best. Wall always minded his own business. Out in the field, he was stealthy silence, and pure, brute force. He could take down a man twice his size with ease, and had done so in several instances. While others did the talking during interrogations, he stood in the corner, arms crossed and watched. That stare would make anyone piss in their pants and sing like a bird when they needed a confession.

Manny finished his soapbox speech and reached out for Jessie's case file, thumbing through the pages. His thick, wavy, perfectly-styled dark hair matched his dark brown eyes. His tall, broad physique always seemed to be polished and his tan skin freshly shaved, ready for an impromptu television statement appearance. His attire of choice was a three-piece suit, and the son of a bitch looked sharp and ready to campaign for a political position. He closed the file and pitched it to the center of the table. "I thought it might have been linked to the serial attacks trickling into the state, but it looks more like a pissed off ex."

Aidan's hands curled into fists, pushing through the red haze clouding his focus, resisting the urge to pummel the man. "You're making assumptions. You don't know any details."

Manny opened his arms and raised his palms. "Do tell. I'm curious, how do two guys—"

"Does your fiancée prefer missionary or good ol' fashion doggie—"

Manny launched from his seat, stopped only by the force of Wall, holding him back. "Where the hell do you get off talking about her? What she and I do is none of your fucking—"

"Exactly," Aidan said, slowly rising from his seat and leaning forward toward Manny. "You can hate me all you want, but show Jessie and his case some fucking respect. The captain thinks you guys can help. If he's wrong, then maybe you should tell him."

Manny quieted but refused to back away.

"Reyes, calm down," Travis said. "You know if shit went south, you'd want Calloway behind you all the way."

Manny yanked himself out of Wall's hold, maintaining his laser focus on Aidan. "I don't want you behind me at all."

Aidan rolled his eyes. "I'll fight the urge to suck your precious dick or lick your ass. Can we focus on work? I need to get back to the hospital."

The team members coughed to cover their laughter but still held their smiles while Manny gave each of them a menacing glare. "Fine," he said, tugging the edges of his vest and pulling his cuffs before returning to his seat to address the group. "Now that we're all up to speed, we need to decide who's following up on which leads."

They switched into work mode with the standoff forgotten. Aidan had done everything in his power to keep his life private. That cat was now out of the bag and hissing and clawing at every dog that challenged it. He hated losing control, but there was no way in hell he was going to let anyone disrespect Jessie or their friendship, even if that was all it was ever meant to be.

Chapter SEVEN

Aidan stared at the metal elevator doors, waiting for them to slide open to Jessie's floor. He tightened the grip on his heavier than usual duffle bag. Aside from the few items he had picked up from Jessie's now sparkling clean apartment, he had packed most of his remaining clean clothes, not planning on returning to his house anytime soon. He stared at the elevator buttons as each dimmed and lit the next. He stepped out and breathed a sigh of relief when he saw the guard standing by Jessie's door.

"Hi, Bull," he said, greeting his Marine friend. The man was built like a lineman—big, broad, and thick—with enough power to have earned his nickname. "Everything cool?"

"Yeah. Your brother-in-law is still in there and only the nurses have gone in and out."

He nodded, thankful his friend was always alert, so he decided to ignore the wrong assessment of his relationship with Cole. After all, Cole told everyone who'd listen about his plans with Ty. The man bragged about *his My-Ty* more than his love for cars. That loud-mouth brat drove him up the wall, but his deep love for Ty offset his need to wring the little shit's neck.

Barely.

He knocked and pushed open Jessie's door, quickly scanning the room until his focus landed on Cole and his worried expression. *Great.* What trouble had his mouth gotten him into now? He tried to hide it, but the crease between his brows couldn't be hidden, regardless of how low he tugged that beanie over his forehead.

"Aidan's back, so I'm going to bail. I'll call you tomorrow." Cole stood and returned the chair to its place against the side wall.

Jessie's demeanor was different, silent, as if his mind had taken a vacation to la-la land. Aidan dropped his duffle bag in the chair and the dinner bag on the table.

Cole fidgeted in the corner, chewing his lip as if he wanted to say something. He tugged on his beanie again then walked out the door.

"I'll be right back," Aidan said to Jessie then followed Cole out. In a few quick strides, he reached Cole bouncing on his feet by the elevator. "What the hell happened?"

Cole shoved his hands in his pockets, his arms straight as a board. "I think I fucked up. I'm sorry."

"Why is he shut down like that?"

Cole looked at him and squirmed, the concern screaming from those mismatched eyes.

"I swear, if you don't start talking—"

"I don't know, okay! We were talking then he got all quiet. I talked about everything I could think of, but it's like he checked out somewhere along the way."

"Backtrack. What were you guys talking about before he spaced out?"

Cole cycled through topics of what they discussed like checking off items from a grocery list. Obviously, Cole could talk, but the randomness of the conversation was jarring. How the hell could someone go from talking about rusting parts of a car to gourmet ingredients in a recipe, then jump to such random facts like horses couldn't vomit? No wonder Jessie sat numbly in bed, and it was an outright miracle Cole's head didn't explode on a daily basis. Something did manage to break through in the middle of Cole's verbal diarrhea.

"Wait…you told him his father came by?"

Cole nodded quickly. "I know you said it wasn't him, but shit, man, those eyes. That same pale blue."

Aidan shut his eyes and lowered his head. "Get out of here."

"I'm sorry. I didn't—"

He looked up and, for some reason he couldn't understand, felt the need to console him. Cole may be a lot of things, but he would never do anything to intentionally hurt anyone. But that damn mouth of his didn't know when to stop. "I know you didn't. But there's a reason people don't talk about certain things. Remember that the next time."

Cole ducked his head. "I fucked up. I'm so sorry. I'd never hurt him."

And that right there was another reason Cole remained on Aidan's good side, regardless of all his twisted shit. "I know. Thanks for staying with him while I was out."

Cole nodded before entering the elevator and apologized again before the doors closed between them.

Aidan stood with his head down and his hands planted on his waist. He didn't know what exactly had happened between Jessie and his father, but the pained look in those crystal blue eyes when the subject had come up once before had sliced through his heart. It had been enough to never speak of it again. But now, he felt as if he didn't have a choice but to broach the subject.

He returned to Jessie's room and grabbed the bag from the table with the burger and fries he had picked up from the cafeteria. He pulled the chair closer to Jessie's bed and noticed the tray of untouched food. *Dammit*. Jessie needed to eat to remain strong with all the pain meds and physical therapy. "How about you join me and eat something so I don't feel like a greedy pig?"

Nothing.

"Jess?"

Jessie finally made eye contact and forced a smile. "I'm sorry. What did you say?"

"You haven't eaten."

"I'm not hungry."

"Not even for one of these?" Aidan teased, holding up one of the fries Jessie couldn't resist.

"Thanks," Jessie said, taking the fry and biting into it. He closed his eyes as he took another bite. "I swear, I think they inject something highly addictive into these things. Fries just don't taste this good on their own."

Aidan smiled and made a mental note about the power of drug-laced fries and their ability to break down Jessie's walls. He reached into the bag and gave Jessie another while he rolled the tray of hospital food within reach and handed him the fork. Jessie gave in and ate his dinner while Aidan shared more wall-crushing fries along the way. When they finally finished, Aidan repositioned the pillows behind Jessie and set the now empty tray on the small counter area by the door. He filled a cup with a little water and set it on the table within Jessie's reach, finally settling in his usual chair to Jessie's right, where he had a clear line of sight to the door.

"Can we try walking later?" Jessie asked.

"Only a few steps," Aidan said. "I don't want to overstress your good leg." That was putting it mildly. A few weeks of inactivity coupled with all the broken parts and surgery had weakened Jessie's body and he was too hard-headed to pace himself. "Something's on your mind and I want to get that out in the open first, then I need to ask you a few questions."

"Ask me about what?"

"Your attacker. Michael. We don't have much to go on so I'm hoping you can...tell me about him to see if there's anything we can maybe use to find him." The last thing he wanted to hear about was Jessie's prior relationship with the asshole attacker, but better him than another detective who wouldn't be able to pick up on the minor nuances when something struck a nerve.

Jessie nodded, more an absent reaction than a response.

"Jess?"

He looked up, a hint of sadness in his eyes. "Is it true? Was my father here?"

Aidan swallowed heavily, thinking of how best to steer around the metaphorical elephant in the room. Fuck, he hated knowing he would hurt Jessie, because he couldn't imagine the conversation ending on a positive note. "Yes."

Jessie did that subtle, slow nod thing again, as if digesting bits of information at a time. "It was a mistake...him being here. It's not something he wanted to do. Right?"

Aidan's chest ached at the sadness in Jessie's eyes. He wanted to kill that bastard who had caused this much pain to haze the otherwise bright, crystal blue. "I don't think he's coming back."

Jessie took a deep breath and his expression softened. *Acceptance.* As if he had known what Aidan would say, but finally hearing it released a huge weight off his shoulders. He remained quiet for a few, never-ending seconds, until he finally spoke. "I didn't think so." His focus shifted again to the bedsheet and the routine of flattening it when he tried to gather his thoughts. "I've told you about my mom and how close we were when I was growing up, but I guess I've never told you anything about my father, huh?"

Aidan's throat tightened. "No. I know your mom died when you were twelve and you told me she was like a buffer between you and your father, but we haven't talked about it. I know it's...not a good subject." After hearing Jessie's father's words straight from the asshole's mouth, yeah, understatement of the year.

Jessie reached out for Aidan's hand, clasping it tightly as if it would give him strength before he spoke. "There was always friction. He was very old school. He believed men should be big and strong and women should be at their husband's beck and call. My mom... She was my best friend. She took me everywhere. I think part of that might have been that my father didn't really care for her to have any friends of her own. I don't know. But I know we went shopping together, grocery stores, anywhere she needed to go. I remember watching her one time in the kitchen, cooking dinner. My father came home that day and he lost it. Told me it was not my responsibility to know my way around the kitchen."

. He paused for a moment as if trying to choose the right words. "A few months after my mom died, he said he was tired of trying. He said he couldn't understand me or why I couldn't throw a football straight or hit a baseball farther than the baseline. He didn't understand why I loved our neighbor's shih tzu and would play with her whenever she dug her way out of her yard into ours to spend some time with me when I came home from school. He said it was a little girl's dog and that young men wouldn't play with dogs like that."

He spoke distantly, as if reading a detached script, trying to avoid any emotion. He took a deep breath and straightened his shoulders. "He made his feelings about me very clear when he threw me head first into the grass and I landed inches away from one of the presents she'd left in our yard I hadn't had a chance to clean up yet. He laughed and called it ironic considering *I was a shitty excuse for a son*," he said in a mocking deep voice. He paused again and swallowed heavily before looking over to Aidan. "He gave up on me and told me to leave. If I'm going to be honest with you, I didn't want to stay. I was terrified of becoming him."

Aidan gripped Jessie's hand almost as much as the hold that twisted his stomach and threatened to cause his dinner to come back up. Although he had never really felt a connection with his father the way Ty had, his dad would never, ever have treated him that way.

"You are nothing like him."

"You spoke to him?"

Aidan nodded curtly, unable to formulate a somewhat decent sentence with the anger turning his stomach.

"I wish you hadn't," Jessie said quietly. "He's toxic. And I don't want him to infect you in any way." He absently rubbed his thumb along Aidan's hand, moving his fingers and watching the way their hands mingled. "When my dad kicked me out, I didn't have any family to turn to. School had ended for the year so it was summer. I had a couple of friends whose parents let me sleep on their couch for a few nights. They knew my father and…I guess they weren't surprised we had a fight and he was pissed off at me. They were nice, maybe they figured things would blow over. I never really asked, I was happy to finally be able to be in a place where I wasn't getting yelled at. The neighbors started talking after about a week and my friends started getting teased about having a gay friend living with them. They didn't deserve that; they were just trying to help me. I couldn't go back home so I packed up my backpack and went for a walk and never turned back. I saw a few kids who slept under an overpass close to the highway, so I worked my way over there. I barely survived three weeks when I met a man. I didn't have a lot of choices," he finished quietly.

Aidan wondered if Jess had tried a shelter, a youth home, anything before taking refuge in the arms of a stranger. But there was no way he'd ask and risk Jessie feeling as if he were trying to place blame or imply there was some other, better option than what he had considered.

"I know what you're thinking."

"What's that?"

"Yes, I did try finding a place to stay. People think it's easy to walk into a shelter. I was barely thirteen. There weren't many in the area and even fewer for kids my age. I'd heard horror stories during those few weeks about child services and how they would take me back home. My father didn't want me, so I didn't think anyone else would want me either."

Aidan watched as Jessie trailed off, lost in thought with a hint of anger he didn't often see. "This man you met..."

Jessie looked back at Aidan, his focus obviously elsewhere until it snapped back to the present. "Don't hate me."

"I could never hate you."

Jessie swallowed heavily and lowered his head, his voice faint and barely audible when he finally spoke. "It was Michael."

Aidan stilled, trying to control the storm of emotions churning his stomach. Rage, hatred, a need to maim the bastard, then more rage. "You were young and had no one else. You were trying to survive and accepted the only hand that reached out to you."

"Please don't hate me," he whispered again.

Aidan dared to reach out, placing his hand against Jessie's cheek. Jessie's touch was magical, always calming his inner chaos. He hoped he could offer the same. "I could never hate you."

Jessie leaned into Aidan's palm and closed his eyes as a single tear escaped his lashes and ran down his cheek.

Aidan's breath hitched and somehow got stuck in his chest. He wasn't sure how long he held his breath as he watched Jessie stay still, pressing the cool of his cheek against his palm, seeking comfort until he finally spoke.

"He used to call me Runt. He'd tease me with the nickname, almost as if he thought it was an endearment. And he told me to call him Sire. I'd keep the house clean in exchange for living there. He hadn't asked for anything more. He said he was tired of being in a house by himself and just wanted some company. He was really nice at first, cordial, thoughtful. I had a roof over my head and a hot shower each day." His voice became distant and lowered. "I was a stupid, naive kid," he said in a whispered tone.

Aidan could barely breathe and now couldn't swallow past the tightness in his throat. The pain and sadness vibrating off Jessie radiated straight to Aidan's core and made him raw. He blocked all thoughts and wayward flashes from his mind, focusing only on Jessie's precise words. He couldn't let his mind embellish or fill in the blanks. That would break him. His leg bounced repeatedly, trying to burn off some of the tension surging through his body. But the not knowing was killing him. "Did he…"

Jessie remained still and his eyes pooled with more tears.

Aidan slowly exhaled and tried to focus on the present. "Don't think about that part."

Jessie nodded and took a deep breath. He pulled Aidan's hand away from his cheek and held it in his lap, stroking his fingers. He slowly blew out his breath as if centering himself before continuing. "His house was very private and all the windows and doors bolted shut. No phone. Windows were blacked out. I asked him once, what if the house was on fire, how would I get out?" He finally looked at Aidan, his eyes filled with a terror Aidan had never seen. "He told me to make sure that never happened. So I was really careful when I tried to cook something. I screwed up most of the stuff I tried to make. I wish I had paid more attention to my mom in the kitchen."

He rubbed Aidan's hand, running his fingertips along Aidan's fingers and palm while he gathered his thoughts. "One night, he came home drunk then passed out. He never did that. Usually, it's as if the alcohol would heighten his senses…and his temper. But that night, it was different. It was the only chance I had and I took it. I built up the courage to grab his keys from his pocket and I unlocked the bolts on the door. I ran. I didn't care if that meant I had to be on the street and take the risk. I didn't have any money. I was barefoot, wearing nothing but the big shirt I had on and the jogging pants I had to wash at the end of each day so I could have them ready for the morning." He finally straightened and his jaw muscles tensed and relaxed. "I hated those damn pants, but that's all he let me have. Those pants and one of his shirts so I…wouldn't forget him throughout the day."

Jessie closed his eyes and took a deep breath as if steeling himself again. "I lived in that hell for four hundred and fifty-six days."

After a few more breaths, he finally opened his eyes. "The only reason I know his name is because he left a magazine out one day. He never even carried a wallet in his pocket. I imagine he did that deliberately and was careful so I wouldn't know his name. I guess he hadn't noticed the mailing label on the magazine. So I went over it in my head all day to make sure I memorized it, then I set it back in the exact same spot before he returned home. A few minutes after he arrived that day, the magazine disappeared from the table."

"Did the label include an address?"

Jessie nodded. "I drove by one time about five years later and the house was no longer there, just the land. But that's where the house was. The same train still passed by at the same time in the day. When I mentioned that to the other detectives, I think they might have disregarded it. I don't know. But I'll give you the address if you think it'll help with anything. I still remember it."

Aidan nodded, thankful they had some bit of information that might be helpful in tracking this son of a bitch down. Regardless of any Reyes drama, he was grateful the task force now had the case. Disregarding an address, even if the house was no longer standing, was a stupid error and could potentially have caused this asshole to slip through their fingers. "Did anyone ever go by the house? Call him? Anything?"

Jessie shook his head. "No. And he never mentioned any family." He closed his eyes and shook his head. "More than fifteen years later, why the hell would he come looking for me? He didn't even want to know my name. He said it didn't matter." He finally opened his eyes and looked up at Aidan, the pain and sadness spearing through Aidan's heart.

He wanted to comfort Jessie in some way but didn't have a clue how. He pulled his hand away and clasped his hands together, squeezing tightly as if it were Michael's neck. He hated this. Sometimes, he wished he could connect better with people. "He was trying to strip your identity. It's what kidnappers do. They typically don't want to know your name to avoid personalizing things. When we find the bastard, I'll ask him why he came back. Don't think about that right now. What did you do after you left the house?"

Jessie fidgeted with the bedsheet again. Aidan finally reached out and held Jessie's hand, knowing he seemed to talk more openly with the connection, or maybe it was for his own comfort to settle the tornado of emotions swirling inside. He didn't want to overthink it and welcomed the contact.

"I was on my own for a while. For almost two years after that—"

"Did you make any friends, talk to anyone—"

"There's nothing more about Michael." He looked exhausted as if the haunting memories had somehow weakened his body further.

Aidan looked away, knowing he was pushing the point and going into personal territory. He wanted to know everything about Jessie but didn't want to push him to the brink of discomfort, especially after everything he had just shared. But he wouldn't deny his craving to know every minute detail about Jessie and how he came to be the man he was today.

"But if you want to know more, I'll tell you."

Aidan nodded once in acknowledgment, ignoring the now rapid heartbeat in his chest. He cherished any little nugget of personal information Jessie shared. It all helped to put the pieces together to solve the Jessie mystery in his mind.

"I didn't go back to that same place. I was worried he'd go by there again and see me. I hitched a few rides and worked my way a little farther south. There was a group of people who lived in this fenced-in place. It was safer there for the most part. I talked to someone a few times. A girl I met. Her name was Lucky." He huffed out an almost-quick laugh. "She called herself that because she thought that if she had enough people call her by that nickname, then maybe she'd start to believe it and things would turn around. She was nice. She found me a pair of shoes I could wear and an old pair of pants. They were a size or two too big, but I didn't care. Anything but those stupid jogging pants and shirt. She tried to teach me how to pick pockets, but honestly, I sucked at it. I usually ended up asking people for food instead. I figured that would be easier than asking for money. And most people thought I was too skinny so I did have people who'd sometimes buy me a burger or something." Jessie looked off to the side, lost in some thought. "One day, when I went back to look for her at the spot she normally slept, they told me she had left with someone. I never saw her again and don't know what happened to her."

Aidan stilled his bouncing leg, steeling himself to offer support he imagined Jessie needed. "What happened after that?"

Jessie's focus darted back to him. He shook his head as if dispelling a memory. "Sorry?"

Aidan leaned in, holding Jessie's hand in both of his own, mimicking the same thing Jessie had done moments before. "What happened after that?"

Jessie looked down at their hands and a small smile tugged on his lips. "I was sitting against a wall in an alley. I remember being buried under a layer of flattened cardboard boxes I had set up like a tent, trying to fight off that rare chill in the air we get in late December on a few random days. I could hear the Christmas music playing from the speakers of the shops. And I remember…"

"Remember what?"

"It's stupid," he whispered. "I remember wishing for a Christmas miracle. How cheesy is that?"

Aidan squeezed Jessie's hand. "It's not."

"For those two years, I'd see people running in and out of the stores, fighting over the presents to buy their kids. I didn't need the fancy bikes or toys." He quieted and continued to stare down at their hands. "But I was jealous."

Aidan ran his thumb along Jessie's skin, thankful for the contact, but not trusting himself to voice a single word.

"I felt so alone. When Lucky wasn't around anymore, I just… I almost gave up." He stopped and took a deep breath. His Adam's apple bobbed, and he withdrew his hand from between Aidan's, reaching for the cup of water to take a sip. He returned the cup to the table and shifted it until it was perfectly positioned again before continuing. "Then this man comes walking down the sidewalk. He came over to me and said I shouldn't be sitting there all alone." He ducked his head, tugging the bedsheet, flattening it again. "I know what you're thinking."

"What is it you think I'm thinking?"

Jessie glanced up at him. "You're wondering why I would ever put myself at risk of a repeat situation after what happened."

Aidan couldn't lie. The thought had crossed his mind. So he chose to remain quiet.

"That man was my Christmas miracle," Jessie finished with a sad smile. "He took me in." The tears slowly began to fill his blue eyes like a dam releasing the clear water into a stream. "He extended his hand to me and swore he wasn't some twisted old man who picked up kids on the street."

"Was he?" Aidan managed to ask past the emotions choking him.

Jessie shook his head. "He was a good man. An amazing man with kind eyes. You learn quickly how to look into someone's eyes and see inside of them. It's true what they say, about the eyes being the window to one's soul. Once you've seen evil and cruelty, you can tell when it's not there if you pay attention."

Aidan squeezed his own clasped hands so tight his knuckles began to whiten.

"His eyes were honest…and sad. He asked me one question. 'Are you planning on spending Christmas in that box?' I nodded and he extended his hand to me."

He quieted and Aidan wondered if Jessie had gone back in time to relive that moment.

"Steven. That was his name," he said with profound respect. "He didn't want to spend another Christmas alone. He gave me some clothes he had from his son who had passed away a few years before. His son was younger than me, but his clothes still fit me fine. He said he never wanted to see me helpless and dirty again. He's the one who taught me how to cook. He said I needed to learn how to stand on my own. He's the one who taught me to not let all that other stuff get to me. He told me that, every day, you wake up and need to make a decision to be happy." He smiled fondly. "He had me take some tests to get credit in school and try to skip some classes. He then enrolled me in night school to finish my requirements and helped me with my homework. By that time, I was almost seventeen years old and working on finishing up my senior year in night school. It's as if I hadn't missed the time out of school." He looked over to Aidan and smiled. "He said I was smart and that's why I was able to do that even though I had missed those years in school."

He looked down and reached for Aidan's hand. "He didn't want me working while I was in school until I was sure I could do both without sacrificing my progress. So he paid me to do things around the house. Cut the grass, fix leaks. Stuff like that. He thought I didn't realize he was teaching me to be independent, to do all these things on my own." Jessie suddenly laughed. "Then he'd take half of what he paid me and told me it was to pay for rent and expenses." He looked up with a lingering smile on his face. "He said having money required discipline. He had me open a bank account and taught me how to manage my expenses. He said I had to put some away so I'd never have to worry about a roof over my head again."

Jessie's love, respect, and admiration for this father-figure screamed from every pore of his body. Aidan stroked his thumb along Jessie's hand as he slowly exhaled, thankful there had been someone there during those tough, defining years that had helped lessen the tarnish of his family and the domino effect of events that'd followed. "What happened to him?"

Jessie looked away and sighed. "He died a little over a year after he rescued me." He took a deep breath and bit his lower lip. "Fourteen months and sixteen days to be exact. I didn't know he was dying the day he found me."

"I'm sorry you went through that."

"I'm not," Jessie said, shaking his head, fighting the tears that reflected the light in his eyes. "He's the reason I do a lot of things the way I do them. He was more of a father to me in that short time than my father was in all the years before. So I don't regret anything that happened that led me to that alley that day where he found me. Because of him, I know what it was like to have a real father. He told me he had been so sad since his son had passed away, and that I had been the only blessing in his life to ease some of that pain. When Steven died, I felt more alone than I had since my father kicked me out. But this time, I had money in an account and clothes to wear for at least a full two weeks without a wash and enough common sense and confidence to not be terrified about being on my own. And that was *all* because of him," he said fiercely.

Jessie took a few deep breaths and absently stroked his thumb along Aidan's hand. "He had two mortgages he took out years before to pay for his son's medical bills. So as soon as he passed away, the bank came to take the house…but I wasn't scared. I packed my things and went to the bank to withdraw money from the account he made me set up. That's when the bank manager called me over." He quieted, the energy escaping his body. "Steven had set up a second account with all the rent money I had paid him all those months." He inhaled a shaky breath. "I didn't know. He was even taking care of me after he had passed away." He blew out a deep breath, trying to fight the tears. "That's why I love Cole and Hunter and Matt so much. I see bits of Steven in them. And Sam." Jessie shook his head and smiled. "Have you met Sam? The reintegration officer who works with Matt to bring the guys to Halfway House?"

Aidan nodded.

"He reminds me so much of Steven. The always big smile and the undercover lessons he teaches. I don't know if he realizes how wonderful he is and how he changes the lives of those men." Jessie sighed and leaned back against the pillows. "Can I ask you something?"

Aidan nodded again.

"Do you..." Jessie looked away. He fidgeted with the bedsheet again and hesitantly looked at Aidan. "Now knowing what you know about...what happened. Does that change anything...between us?"

"No." *Just makes me realize how strong you really are.*

Jessie smiled weakly. "Thank you." He looked exhausted, as if he had relived all the experiences he'd recalled and now couldn't even seem to keep his eyes open. "I'm too tired. Can we do a little walking tomorrow?"

Aidan nodded and stood, thankful Jessie wasn't going to attempt to push himself any more for one day. He pulled up the sheet once Jessie settled into a comfortable spot. He walked over and noted the address Jessie gave him then sat at his laptop to shoot a quick email with the update to the team. He peeked over the laptop as he worked, watching Jessie turn to his side and switch off the overhead light shining down on the bed.

"Maybe someday you'll tell me about you. I know there's a lot you hide away," Jessie said, snuggling into the pillow.

He didn't have a response for that, but there was no way he would poison Jessie with any bit of info from his past. He did everything in his power to lock that shit up tight and throw away the key. "Good night, Jess."

He finished going through his emails and unpacked a few items from his bag before settling in his chair to the right of Jessie's bed. He stared up at the ceiling tiles, going through everything Jessie had said, trying to compartmentalize Jessie's experience from his own. He turned to face Jessie and reached out with a shaky hand, ghosting his fingers along Jessie's fair cheek—a stolen, reverent caress he would only dare when Jessie was in a deep, peaceful sleep. He didn't know how someone could go through all that and still have a strong spirit and a smile brighter than the sun. How could someone not let something so negative break them? How could they manage to move forward and not let something so horrible color every action, decision, and relationship from that point forward?

Somehow, Jessie had found a way.

He brushed the loose strands of hair away from Jessie's face and wished that someday, maybe he could be strong enough to find a way to do the same.

Chapter EIGHT

"So your physical therapist tells me you're making great strides," Dr. Green said, scribbling notes in Jessie's chart.

"Yup," Jessie said, sneaking a glance at Aidan out of the corner of his eye. He bit his lip to hide the laugh that almost escaped at the scowl on Aidan's face. His "progress" could be attributed to his midnight rendezvous down the hall a few steps more each night with a skeleton crew of nurses at the edge of their seats or cheering him on. And Aidan right there by his side, supporting him as he hobbled each step down the hallway. He had been awake now for five weeks and he definitely felt stronger and a little closer to his usual self. They had replaced the full arm cast with a shorter, temporary forearm cast that extended to his wrist, and he was thankful to not have that extra weight to lug around.

"Considering your rapid progress, we've got a present for you." The doctor closed the chart and smiled.

"Do I get to go home?"

"We had a deal. When you make it to the end of the hallway and can handle the basics on your own, yes, you can go home."

Jessie deflated and crossed his arms then winced, regretting the action as soon as the cast jabbed into his ribs. He looked up, hoping the doctor had missed his reaction.

He hadn't. *Damn.*

"You've got the pain meds, and I've got a standing order if you need something to help you sleep with the nightmares. Don't push yourself so much."

Aidan shook his head, obviously echoing the same reprimand he voiced each night they walked a little farther down the hallway. He busied himself, typing away on his laptop, but most likely still listening to each word of the exchange. How that man managed to not go stir crazy keeping him company was a wonder. He could have easily escaped to the precinct, his house, anywhere outside of these sterile, white walls. But no, Aidan *chose* to be by his side—all day, every day.

He loved the stubborn man more with each passing day.

He had grown accustomed to Aidan's company, his protective, watchful eye, and those tentative, gentle caresses at night against his cheek. So much so that he'd often close his eyes and fake a deep slumber, craving the warm graze of that touch against his face. But most of all, a cloak of love and safety enveloped him, warming him to the core and motivating his recovery. Aidan always offered an awe-inspiring secret smile that made him feel seven-feet tall. He needed to feel independent and that had been the requirement that drove most of his actions since he was finally on his own as a teen. But he wouldn't deny that the look of admiration in those watchful hazel eyes was his greatest motivator, pushing his progress along.

The doctor walked to the door and returned with a single crutch in hand.

Jessie beamed and Aidan groaned.

"This should help you meet your goal. But I don't want you trying to walk on your own. Even with the crutch, you need to make sure someone is always with you."

"Okay." Jessie set his rubber-soled, hospital-socked foot on the floor and steadied himself with the weight of the leg cast and support boot.

The clicking of the laptop keys stopped.

The doctor tucked the crutch under Jessie's good arm then removed the crutch to adjust the height, repeating the process until it fit perfectly.

"You've created a monster, Doc," Aidan mumbled from the corner round table, watching them closely.

Jessie laughed and the doctor smiled. Dr. Green turned to walk out then paused before opening the door. "Just remember, having a crutch doesn't mean you go at it alone until your step is more confident. Understand?"

"Okay," Jessie agreed, holding his balance as he stood with the crutch.

"That includes your midnight walks," the doctor added before exiting and closing the door behind him, leaving them alone in the room.

Jessie's focus snapped to Aidan. "Did you—"

Aidan raised his hands in surrender. "I don't snitch," he said with a chuckle. "Aren't you sitting back down?"

Jessie slowly shook his head, his focus never leaving Aidan's intense stare. "I'm going to walk over to you and sit next to you at that table."

Aidan stood, ignoring Jessie's plea to remain seated. "I'll let you walk on your own, but I'm not going to watch you fall on your ass to prove a point and risk canceling out all your progress."

"Fine," he grumbled, balancing himself on the crutch as Aidan stood like a guard dog at his side. He wobbled once, but Aidan instantly extended his hand to offer that additional support to stay righted. He finally reached the chair and eased himself into the seat. "So what are we working on?"

Aidan raised an eyebrow, but a subtle smile curled his lips. "*You're* working on getting better. *I'm* working on cases."

"*You're* no fun."

Aidan chuckled.

Jessie reached over and opened one of the files then looked over at Aidan. "This is one of the case files related to Cam. Right?"

Aidan glanced at the file and nodded. "I've been trying to tie up the loose ends." He looked off at a distance and his lips thinned. "Cam's having a hard time with all the changes and moving around, so Hunter wants to come back home." He shook his head, battling some inner argument. "I can't risk their safety until we figure out how Cam is linked to any other potential arrest in that crime ring. I just need a little more time."

"It must be difficult. Cam felt as if he had finally settled into things when he was here, but then had it all stripped away. Aside from that, names are an important part of your identity. Makes things personal. Someone really smart told me that a couple weeks ago," he said, gently bumping Aidan's shoulder. "So give me one of the case files and let me take a look."

Aidan looked at him then reached into his bag and withdrew a few more files. "These are the new ones I've got since we last worked on it. Maybe you can make some progress on these."

He took the folders and craned his neck to peek at the file Aidan held in his hand. He missed working—being in bed was entirely too overrated, at least, under these circumstances. He craved spending time researching, helping to solve a puzzle, and finally closing a case. He rested his cast arm on the table and thumbed through the file with his good hand. Aidan laid out the photos from a different case and stared at each image with an intensity that could have easily burned through each picture. There was something exciting and intriguing about Aidan when he worked, channeling his focus so every millimeter of his being concentrated on the case at hand. That intensity, that commitment, that drive. It was in everything he did—nothing Aidan did was ever half-assed.

"Fuck me," Aidan mumbled with a faint whisper, reaching for his cell phone after cursing the team's offline status on chat.

Jessie closed his eyes when Aidan's arm brushed against him, that subtle graze shooting a bolt of need through his body. He took a deep breath and opened his eyes, trying to focus on the papers before him. He heard Aidan tell the team to pull the photos and to look at the tattoo work of each of the victims. All of the victims had inked their skin at some point in time. However, they all shared one tiny addition—the small butterfly tattoo incorporated into one of their designs.

"It's there. Look at the photos of the hooded skeleton tattoo. The nose is the butterfly. And the other victim's tattoo of the fairy. The little pixie is wearing a necklace with the same small butterfly design as a pendant. Even the damn snake on victim number fifteen has it hidden in the scales. Find who did the ink work, and we might have something to go on." He finished the call and stacked the images, shifting his focus to a new file.

"Speaking of ink," Jessie said, shifting his position in the chair to face Aidan. "I heard you have some."

For the first time in almost a year and a half since they had known each other, a flush of color tinted Aidan's cheeks.

"Are you embarrassed I know about the ink?"

Aidan shook his head and fidgeted with the edges of the papers on the table, refusing to make eye contact with him. "No. I'm bothered by how you found out."

Jessie leaned in, enjoying this unhinged version of Aidan he hadn't seen before. "Did you think walking out of the bathroom, still wet after a shower, sporting a half torso of ink wasn't going to get talked about?"

"The nurses gossip too much," he mumbled with a scowl.

"Can I see?"

Aidan shook his head.

"I thought you said you didn't mind that I knew?"

Aidan sighed. "I don't mind. But expecting me to strip down to put a spotlight on it isn't going to happen."

"Why not?" Jessie said with a smile, loving the way Aidan squirmed in discomfort with the conversation. Aidan kept his personal stuff locked away in a very closely guarded private vault, but dammit, Jessie needed to know.

"Can we drop this?"

"No. I want to see."

Aidan sighed.

"How far down does it go?"

"What?"

Jessie inched closer. "You said 'strip down.' That's more than lifting a sleeve or a shirt. How far down does it go?"

Aidan's jaw muscles twitched.

"Aidan, I know it bothers you that Amy saw it. She told *me* about it because she thought I had already seen it. I asked her not to tell another soul. She swears she hasn't. She was too embarrassed that day and quickly turned around to avoid seeing more than her hormones could handle. She knows you're inked but couldn't even tell me what it was. And she didn't even bother to tell the nurses about the tattoo because she said she felt silly teasing about seeing something and not being able to back it up with details."

"So she's a gossiper with a need for fact-finding. That's a first." Aidan leaned back in the chair, crossing his arms.

"I get it. It's personal and it's private and who knows who else has seen it other than the artist who did it. I'm guessing, only a handful. I want… I'd like to be one of those few lucky people you let see it," he finished in a rush of words before he lost his nerve.

Aidan pushed out each exhale heavily while his jaw muscle repeatedly twitched. He was obviously having one major internal argument and he was fighting the end result.

Jessie knew how to make him cave. "Please."

Aidan closed his eyes and sighed. He hesitated, then pulled the edge of the T-shirt out of the left side of his jeans and looked away.

A carnal need began to bubble within Jessie with the sight of the tight, lean, tan muscles flexing with each labored breath. The tattoo covered the entire left side of Aidan's torso. The ink had no sharp black lines, rather, the design used shadowing to shape the image. A long scroll dipped below the waistline of his jeans and spread upward just past the middle of his torso. The words "what doesn't kill you makes you stronger," etched in an elegant font, flowed with the curves of the scroll that framed them. Jessie reached over and grabbed the edge of Aidan's shirt but glanced up at his face, requesting permission before he dared move.

Aidan turned his face to the side, like a wolf baring his throat in submission. Submission wasn't something he imagined was part of Aidan's personal code, but the permission granted in that subtle gesture was unmistakable. Jessie pulled the shirt up slowly, guiding Aidan's hand upward to reveal more. He released the fabric and let his eyes follow the design of the angel with wings spread wide, inked with heavy shadows almost appearing three-dimensional and ready to leap off his skin, holding up the flag of victory in one hand, and a fighting dagger in the other. The design looked like a classic Roman painting, a piece of art that must have taken hours to complete and the message a clear reminder of strength and resilience. He was a survivor. A fighter. Jessie reached out and ghosted his fingers along the words permanently inked into Aidan's skin. The current of electricity passed between them and followed his finger like a plasma lamp from a novelty store, prickling his fingertip with the contact.

"That's enough," Aidan said in a hoarse voice. He pulled down his shirt and backed away a few inches. He cleared his throat and crossed his legs and arms, punctuating the end with both his words and body.

Jessie refused to let him lock this up in his private vault. "It's beautiful," he whispered.

Aidan swallowed heavily and closed his eyes.

"Can I ask you a question?"

Aidan opened his eyes and took a deep breath. He turned to face Jessie, a mix of emotions playing in his expression. "One."

Jessie smiled warmly, seeing Aidan more vulnerable than ever. "Why did you get the tattoo?"

Aidan's throat worked as if fighting which words to spill out in response. "I…needed to feel something."

He imagined Aidan might hint at the message of strength staring back at him when he faced a mirror. How empowering it was or something of that nature. But to *feel* something? Pain squeezed Jessie's heart, not sure what else to say, and he refused to push Aidan with this level of vulnerability on display. He inched closer, hesitant and unsure how Aidan would feel about more than just a touch on his arm or holding his hand. He rested his head against Aidan's shoulder and sighed, reveling in the warmth and comfort that emanated from his strong body. "Thank you for showing me."

Aidan didn't say a word, but his chest heaved with each deep breath.

Jessie closed his eyes when fingers tentatively combed through his hair. He slowly straightened, his eyes still closed, unable to focus on anything other than calming his frantically beating heart and the surge of emotions welling within. He finally opened his eyes and connected with Aidan's hazel gaze. The insecurity and love staring back at him stole his breath. He wanted to reach out, he wanted to touch the tan skin of his chest again, or his arm, or feel the scrape of that persistent stubble…but he couldn't will his body to do anything but stare into those eyes as if he could see into Aidan's soul. Mesmerized, he leaned in toward that beautifully perfect mouth he wanted to taste. He parted his lips on an inhale and moved closer when

Aidan did the same.

Two quick knocks at the door broke the spell.

Aidan's body jerked back, straight against the chair, his inner protective shield slicing through their connection like a guillotine.

"Hey, guys!" Cole announced with Ty at his side and Matt and Julian following closely behind.

Aidan shot up from his seat, slammed his laptop closed, and grabbed his keys. "I'll give you all some time," he said in a thick tone.

Jessie reached out and placed a stopping hand on his forearm. "Promise me you'll be back later."

Aidan looked to the mob that now wore perplexed expressions then back to Jessie and that hand resting on his arm.

"Promise me," Jessie insisted, ignoring everyone else in the room. Nothing mattered at that moment but Aidan and knowing he would come back to him rather than finding some excuse to stay away.

Aidan nodded once, but that was enough. He was a man of his word—spoken or not—and if he agreed to return, then he would…when ready. That reassurance eased the tension in Jessie's body.

Aidan mumbled something and waved to the group on his way out the door, quickly making his exit without looking back.

"Did we interrupt…something?" Matt asked.

Jessie waved his hand in the air. "No, we were looking at something with one of his cases and he got a break."

Ty started to walk toward the door but stopped when Cole grabbed his arm and subtly shook his head. Cole glanced back at Jessie with obvious concern.

His poor excuse seemed to satisfy the others, and they each found chairs from within the room or pulled from the nurses' station. Jessie enjoyed their visit, but his mind wandered back to Aidan. The insecurity and love visible through the window to his soul made Jessie's heart ache. He wanted to comfort him and ease that worry, but Aidan had undoubtedly escaped to bury it all again and hit his reset button.

Long after everyone left, he pushed his dinner around on the plate as he absently looked up at the door. Waiting. Aidan had been gone for hours. He'd come back. But Jessie wondered how tough that inner shield would be upon his return, and if there was any way he'd be able to break through again.

* * * *

Aidan finally arrived home and shut the door behind him, leaning back and breathing heavily. Even after spending hours at the precinct then going for a run at full speed for several miles, he still couldn't seem to shake the warring emotions unsettling him. He was attracted to Jessie. He hadn't denied that to himself since the first moment he saw him. But he had forced his mind and body to disconnect years ago. Yet something had shifted between him and Jessie earlier. There, in that moment back at the hospital table, strong tendrils twisted and knotted around his heart, braiding with the tether that always lingered between them, pulling him toward Jessie, daring him to take a chance.

And it fucking scared the shit out of him.

His chest heaved with each rapid breath. He'd never felt so vulnerable, so open, so willing to do anything to inch closer and take what was offered. He screwed his eyes shut and swallowed past the lump in his throat. His mind had weakened, going blank with all thoughts but one. *Jessie.* His body had betrayed him, syncing with his mind…and heart. The way Jessie had looked at him and that tentative touch along his skin had almost broken his resolve. He lowered his head and tried to annihilate the thoughts that fueled his betraying body.

Nothing worked to dispel the want.

The need.

Not just to relieve a physical craving but to satisfy the desire for intimacy.

To connect.

His mind returned to visions of those lips. Those perfectly defined, equally full lips which he'd never tasted but almost had. And most likely, never would. High, sharp cheekbones centered by the slope of his perfectly straight nose which led upward to those incredibly piercing eyes beneath those thick dark eyebrows. His eyes. He could lose himself in those crystal blue pools.

He steeled himself and finally stepped away from the door, hoping to reset the carefully crafted facade that had taken years to build. He swore he wouldn't go there ever again. What was the point? Pain was the only outcome…in more ways than he had imagined. And he was tired of having life bitch-slap him and make him beg for mercy. He couldn't subject himself—or others—to that again. He took a deep breath and made his way to the shower, hoping to wash away the seed of hope that had tried to plant itself in his heart.

He turned on the water then stepped into the steaming shower a few moments later, letting the warm water sluice the planes of his body. The rivulets traveled along his torso, reminding him of Jessie's fingers tracing his ink, instantly driving a bolt of want and need through his body. His breathing sped and he planted his palm against the tiled wall. He dipped his head under the spray and closed his eyes, trying to calm the battling thoughts waging war in his mind. He wanted Jessie—he wanted to touch him, hold him, and be inside him. But most of all, he *wanted* to feel the tug of that tether between them, the one that reminded him he was in the land of the living, feeling, and with someone who thought he was worthy enough to stay with. He willed his body to calm down, to remember the promise he had made so many years ago. Maybe this time would be different? Maybe it didn't always end the same. Maybe?

He couldn't.

He wouldn't.

There was no way he'd ever hurt Jessie. Aidan's heart would shatter if Jessie ever walked away.

The water pelted his body, unable to wash away the haunting memories or cool the desire coursing through his veins. He reached down and wrapped his fingers around his hardened shaft, instantly groaning at the contact. He pushed his hips into his fist, quickening his pace with each harsh tug. He snarled and grunted like a feral animal, seeking friction, forcefully yanking his dick, desperately reaching for that elusive precipice. His fingers clawed at the tile wall as he pulled and pulled, jerking his hips forward into his tightly clenched hand, battling his warring thoughts and the flashback worming its way into his mind, threatening to derail his path to release. He closed his eyes and parted his lips when an image of Jessie immediately flooded his consciousness.

Jessie's fingers tracing his skin.

Crystal blue eyes. Soft, dark hair. Full lips.

Those full lips wrapped around him… The warmth of Jessie's mouth sucking and pulling until his cheeks hollowed.

A roar ripped through Aidan's body as he coated the tile wall with his release.

He leaned into the spray, chest heaving as he tried to settle his breathing. *That wasn't real. That won't happen.* He turned the dial to the hottest tolerable setting, angry at his life, fate, and the weight of the memories that haunted him. Under the spray of the steaming hot water, he scrubbed his skin until it was almost raw. Regret flooded his weakened limbs at the realization that he'd washed off Jessie's touch from his skin—both the real and the imaginary. He flattened his hands against the tile shower wall and let the hot water beat against his back. He looked upward, begging for the heavens to give him strength to continue, to carry out his solemn vow to remain on the path he had chosen to take years ago.

He dried off and looked at himself in the mirror, his vision following the lines of the tattoo. He took a deep breath as phantom fingers tentatively grazed his skin—Jessie's fingers, tracing each shadowed line of his angel and scroll.

He grabbed his shaving cream and razor. He lathered up and swiped the stubble off his face. *Fucking persistent shit.* It didn't matter how often he shaved, the damn thing would sprout up within an hour after he'd managed to scrape it all off. Finally finished, with his face burning more than the norm, he walked into his room and reached into his almost empty closet. He flattened his palm against the wall for balance and sighed. Most of his clothes either needed a wash or were at the hospital. He turned and leaned his back against the wall, gasping for air, suddenly feeling a suffocating grip at his throat, constricting each labored breath as everything closed in on him. He slid down along the wall, stopping only when his towel-wrapped ass hit the floor. He huddled against the wall of the large room, resting his chin on his knees. He looked around and couldn't see anything in the blackness of the room.

Darkness and loneliness was all that accompanied him.

His chest tightened as he willed his mind to focus on the nothingness of the space rather than the series of snapshots that had transitioned into a full-fledged, high-definition multimedia presentation only he could experience from a time he wished he could permanently wipe from his mind. A private showing that was quick to castrate any hope that dared take root in his heart. He reached up and fisted the sides of his hair as a scream ripped through his body, hoping to drown out the sounds and the pictures and smells that accompanied them. He needed to be strong. He needed to be the safe haven Jessie sought during his recovery.

He didn't know if he could. He wasn't sure he deserved it. Was it punishment for his past crimes or just a shit hand of luck in life? He wasn't attracted to women, why the fuck would he think Lady Luck would give a shit about him? He wanted to be Jessie's pillar of strength. The one Jessie would turn to when he needed someone.

He couldn't...

He began to shudder, and he could no longer contain the sobs that racked his body in the darkness. He resented himself, his decisions, his life. But most of all, he hated hope and how that bitch teased him just when he thought he could manage things on his own. He was cursed to a life of solitude and it was a burden he had accepted years ago.

But now, with Jessie, he realized one thing far worse than any torture he thought he had survived.

He hated being alone.

Chapter NINE

"Here you go," Nancy said, handing Jessie the discharge papers. "Do you want me to call anyone?"

Jessie shook his head.

"I can call Aidan."

"I already called a cab."

Aidan had returned that night two weeks ago, but he had closed himself off more than ever. Every now and then, the expression in Aidan's eyes softened, but almost immediately, that damn iron wall would erect in full force. Each day, a little more of Aidan's clothes emptied out of the small hospital closet until nothing remained. More work meetings resulted in less hours during the day at the hospital. Work became the official excuse. It was clear in Aidan's eyes. Something had spooked him and forced him to keep his distance. Jessie swore if he had another chance to break down that damn barrier of Aidan's, he'd take it and wouldn't back down. He'd do anything to avoid the unbearable ache that pained him in Aidan's absence.

"Does he know you're being discharged today?"

He reached for his jacket and winced when a shock of pain traveled the length of his arm. *Dammit*. He hadn't known being so dependent on using a crutch would resurrect his need for pain meds when he pushed too much. He refused to risk stressing his wrist so he overcompensated, which only seemed to aggravate his shoulder and good arm from holding the crutch so damn hard. At least his ribs didn't hurt as much, assuming, of course, he didn't tighten his midsection when lugging around the extra weight of the leg cast. He was still a mess, but dammit, he was getting discharged today. Period. He steadied himself and tried again, finally grasping the material.

"Jessie?"

He tried to ignore the concern in Nancy's eyes and tone. "He was here when the doctor mentioned I would be discharged soon."

"Soon is rather vague. He may not have expected you to be discharged this *soon*."

He shrugged and hissed when a jolt traveled across his shoulders. "He's been here too long. He needs to get back to work. Can you please help me with the backpack?"

Nancy scowled but guided his arms through the shoulder straps.

"Thanks," he said, balancing the weight of the laptop in his backpack. He adjusted the strap on the new sling that had replaced the temporary forearm cast, fidgeting, busying himself to avoid the topic. He wanted Aidan with him, and if he had asked, Aidan would be there in a heartbeat, regardless of the distance he tried to place between them. And if he tagged on a "please," Aidan would cave if there had been any resistance. That was what kept Aidan by his bedside each night. Even though the drug-lingering nightmares were less frequent, having Aidan's presence to keep the nightmares at bay was a far better alternative than the body-numbing sleeping pills that would put him at the monster's mercy in the abyss until he could move again.

Was he silly to want Aidan to come back of his own accord? He was starting to think he'd missed his chance that one day when they came so close he could feel the link between them. But it had snapped, almost quicker than the time it had taken to build.

Hope bloomed when he reached for his vibrating phone but quickly dissipated once he caught sight of the display. "Cab's here."

Nancy sighed. "I'll get the chair."

"I can walk."

"You know it's policy." She exited the room and returned a few moments later with the wheelchair.

He slowly rose from the bed and steadied himself, extending a hand to stop Nancy who immediately jumped to help. He needed to take the pain pill, but getting out of the hospital was the priority. He reached for the crutch and eased it under his good arm then carefully walked the few steps to reach the chair. One step at a time, just as he'd done for the last few weeks. He tried to reach for the wheelchair armrest but couldn't reach down far enough with the crutch limiting his movement. He took another deep breath and tried to shift his weight. He reached again for the armrest and let his body drop into the seat, ignoring the clank of the crutch hitting the floor.

"Sorry."

Nancy reached down and retrieved the crutch, slipping it into a makeshift sleeve in the back of the chair. "No worries." She grabbed the bag of prescriptions and placed them in his lap. "Don't forget. You're due for your pain meds as soon as you get home."

He nodded. How could he forget? When he walked for more than ten or fifteen minutes, each current of pain rippling through his body was a constant reminder, not to mention that stupid crutch was bruising his armpit as well. He was better and able to walk short distances without help, but he hadn't mastered the *don't-push-yourself* philosophy everyone kept jamming down his throat.

She unlocked the wheels and pushed the chair out the door and down the hallway.

He waved goodbye to the staff and rolled through the hospital hallways until he finally exited the doors and was greeted by the waiting cab. He settled in with minimal help then waved goodbye, finally on his way back home. He leaned back in the seat and closed his eyes, anxious to settle into the space he had called home for the last few years. Twenty minutes later, he shimmied out of the backseat and balanced himself with the single crutch, fumbling with the plastic bag of medication. The driver reached out and tied the bag to the crutch.

"Thanks," he mumbled and reached into his back pocket for his wallet to pay for the cab fare and tip. He stood and waited as the car pulled away then steeled himself for the next few moments. He would finally be on his own for the first time in months since that night. He gripped the crutch and turned to enter his building. He balanced himself and held back a flinch of pain that jolted through his body with each forward shift of the heavy leg cast. Times like these he wished for more bulk and strength. He didn't know what hurt more—

the bruise under his armpit from the crutch, his biceps from overcompensating and holding the crutch too tightly, or the pain shooting across his shoulders from the combination of it all.

A few steps later, he wiped his brow of the beads of sweat that had surfaced and pressed the elevator button.

"It's busted," someone said as they passed him and started heading upstairs.

"Excuse me?" Jessie bit back the arc of fire that shot between his shoulders when he turned.

The man stopped on the third step. "The elevator. It's been busted for two days. Building manager posted a memo. It's supposed to get fixed tomorrow. Something about parts getting ordered," the man finished with a shrug and continued his trek upstairs.

Jessie walked over and made his way to the base of the stairs. Somehow, the half dozen steps to the first landing seemed as if they had multiplied. *"Don't-push-yourself" my ass.* He was glad he had ignored everyone's suggestion to pace himself, otherwise, he wouldn't dare take another step. He squared his shoulders the best he could and focused on one step at a time.

* * * *

Aidan darted out of the hospital elevator toward Jessie's room, finally releasing the breath he had held since receiving the short text from Bull.

Jessie's discharged.

Why the hell had he found out about Jessie's release through a third party? *He* should have known Jessie was leaving today. Why the hell hadn't Jess called him?

He swallowed heavily and stood stock-still after he stepped into the hospital room.

Empty.

He exited the room and sped out to the nurses' station, visually scanning the new day staff for a familiar face. He spotted Nancy down the hallway and beelined to her.

"He was discharged a while ago," she said with her usual smile.

"When?"

She looked at her watch. "About an hour and a half ago."

"He didn't call me," he said, absently.

Nancy reached out and placed her hand on his shoulder. "He called a cab to take him home and he told the guard you had at his door to leave."

He lowered his head, processing the information. *He* wanted to be the one Jessie called. The one who would come to mind first if Jessie needed a ride home or…anything. "He could have called me," he said, trying to bite back the words after they had escaped. This was all his fault. He was the one who'd driven the wedge between them, the one who'd taken time away with the bullshit excuses. All because he was too chickenshit to take a chance.

He met Nancy's gaze and tried to ignore the sympathetic expression on her face.

"Thanks."

She gave him a sad smile and squeezed his arm before walking away.

Aidan grabbed his phone and dialed a number, speaking before giving his friend a chance to respond after answering the call. "Tell me you're with him."

Bull's laugh echoed through the line. "He's as stubborn as you are. He can tell me to go away all he wants, but that's not his call. I'm at his apartment building now. I can monitor the main entrance and parking garage from my location."

"Thanks," he said before disconnecting the call. Aidan rubbed his chest to fight off the sudden ache. He couldn't be angry at anyone but himself for the distance he'd shoved between them. Jessie was simply granting him the space he had—in not so many words—demanded. He shoved his hands into the pockets of his slacks to stop fidgeting. He surveyed the staff as they ran through the hallway, oblivious to anything around them other than the clipboards in their hands. So much had changed in the last two weeks. The staff shifts had adjusted and so had most of the familiar faces. He felt out of place. He took a deep breath and fisted the hands in his pockets. He looked upward and blew out a deep breath, hoping for some sign or guidance on what he should do next.

He thought of Jessie and the look in his steady, warm, caring blue eyes. Always strong, always supportive…always patient. There was nothing he wanted more in the world than to be with Jessie, but the fear, the pain, and all the other crap that circled in his mind kept his walls firmly in place. *Fuck it.* He withdrew his hands from his pockets and tugged on the cuffs of his shirt. He worked his way out of the hospital and jumped in his SUV. He turned the key and made his way onto the expressway, absently passing each exit without a second thought before finally taking an exit. He shook his head and scoffed at himself for being so stubborn. Even though he sat behind the wheel, a fundamental need to be near Jessie drove his actions.

* * * *

"You can't just lock me out," Jessie said, still trying to take in enough air to settle his breathing. The two flights of stairs had seemed like a climb up Mount Everest. His good arm was numb from firmly holding the crutch and the ache under his armpit a clear sign the crutch had left its mark. Hobbling around was bad enough, but climbing the steps with the cast on his lower leg felt like lugging around an iron weight wrapped around his muscles. He couldn't seem to catch his breath or settle the current of pain radiating in his shoulders and arm.

"Mr. Vargas, I don't have a choice," the building maintenance man said. "I was asked to change the locks. I put the personal stuff I found in the apartment in the box and stored it in my office for you so I could give it to you when you arrived."

Jessie leaned against the wall for balance and tried to steady his shaking hands. "I've lived here for years and you still don't know my name? It's Vega. And you can't just pack my things in a box and kick me out. I've been current with the rent and you have no legal justification for evicting me." He looked down at the medium-sized box holding his belongings. How had his life been reduced to a box no bigger than one of the banker's boxes he used for case files?

"I'm sorry, sir. It wasn't my decision," the pudgy man said in a broken accent.

"Who decided?"

"The board made that decision," a new man said as he walked up the stairs.

Jessie glanced over to the man in the suit as he stood alongside the shorter, stockier maintenance man. "And you are?"

"I'm the building manager, and I asked Mr. Gonzalez to call me when you returned. You have a safety hazard clause in your lease agreement that has been violated so we executed remedies we've been granted in such instances."

"The board is kicking me out?" Jessie absently asked, trying to mentally recall the term from his lease. "Safety hazard?"

"We haven't had a break-in or crime reported in this building. Your…situation has caused a great deal of safety concerns among the other tenants. And to be quite candid, they voiced their opinions during our last meeting. We were left with no choice but to remedy the situation."

"You think the person who did this to me is going to wreak havoc on *all* your tenants or suddenly lead to a rise in your precious building crime statistics? That's ridiculous. Your elevator is broken, and I had to climb up the stairs and risk falling. Now *that's* a safety hazard that can affect your tenants!" He clenched his fists and instantly winced at the spark of pain in his hand.

"Sir," the suited man said, not caring to hide his distaste. "The board met this month and formally made the decision. I instructed Mr. Gonzalez to change the locks and to contact me when you arrived. I did not, however, ask him to put your items in a box." He turned to the smaller man and delivered a chastising look.

The shorter man reddened.

Jessie closed his eyes and took a deep breath. He could legally fight this, but that wouldn't resolve the problem right now. Besides, he certainly didn't want to live where he wasn't wanted. He had already done that in life and it never ended well.

"What's going on?"

Jessie turned at the familiar voice, trying to avoid making eye contact with Aidan as he walked up the stairs, but nothing could keep his focus from shifting back to those piercing hazel eyes.

Aidan reached the top of the stairs and stood next to Jessie. "Are you okay? You should have called me," he whispered.

He should have. He'd wanted to. But he was trying to respect the distance Aidan obviously needed. He looked into his box and his breath hitched when he saw the photo of them with the glass cracked. He closed his eyes as the tightness in his throat suffocated him. "I'm sorry," he whispered. *I'm sorry I didn't call you. I'm sorry I couldn't take care of this on my own. I'm sorry—*

"Don't apologize. None of this is your fault."

In the midst of the pleading expression in Aidan's hazel eyes, there was regret, frustration and…a slight openness that hadn't been there in the last two weeks.

"Tell me what's going on," Aidan said.

"They're evicting me."

Aidan's focus snapped to the two men. "If you want to evict him, you need to follow the law."

The suited man straightened. "The board agreed—"

Aidan took a step closer to the building manager. "I don't care what the *board* agreed to. You can't strong-arm him out onto the street. He's been paying his rent so—"

Jessie reached out and placed his hand on Aidan's arm. "I'm not staying."

Aidan turned to Jessie, the questioning expression in his eyes transitioned to understanding. No doubt Aidan would suspect he wouldn't want to be where he wasn't welcomed. "Do you have a place to go?"

Did he? Not really, he hadn't thought that far ahead yet. Maybe Cole would take him in, but he wasn't sure being in Cole's domain was a good decision. Who knew what Cole with his beanie and superhero undies, or lack thereof, would do under his own roof.

He turned to the two men. "Is my car still in the parking garage?"

Mr. Gonzalez winced. "It was impounded after the board

decision."

"Jess?" Aidan prompted.

He closed his eyes and took a deep breath. Screw it. He'd call another cab. He couldn't let all this beat him down. "I'll call the hotel on—"

"You're staying with me."

"I can't," he whispered. If Aidan wanted distance between them, there was no way this would work. Aidan was a protector by nature. He'd offer his home even if that meant pitching a cot at the precinct to avoid him.

Aidan leaned in and forced Jessie to make eye contact. "Please."

Now he understood the power of that little word. *Dammit.* It was no wonder Aidan always caved when he used it. There was nothing he wanted more than to be near Aidan, in his personal space, to hear his voice and see that rare smile that brightened his entire being. He met Aidan's gaze. He would never deny Aidan anything. Ever. He cocked his head slightly. He could swear the openness had returned and stared back at him, not the coldness that had recently dulled the life in Aidan's eyes. If that slight gap was in his iron wall, then dammit, Jessie was going to take that chance and squeeze through that tiny opening.

He nodded.

"Good," Aidan said. He pointed to the box on the floor between them. "What about the rest of your stuff?"

Jessie faced the building manager again. "What did you do with my clothes?"

The building manager turned to Mr. Gonzalez.

"I left them there." The paunchy man shrugged.

Aidan took a deep breath, obviously trying to control his temper. He turned to Jessie. "What about furniture, appliances, anything else?"

Jessie shook his head. "The apartment was furnished, so that stays. The bedroom set was mine but...I don't want it anymore after what happened. I've only got the microwave and my office desk, but I don't care. Leave it. I want my clothes. In my closet and in the dresser drawers. I just...want to go," he finished quietly, looking down, hoping to avoid Aidan's piercing gaze.

"You're going to open that door and let me in there to grab anything that he's mentioned is his property. You'll pitch whatever the hell Jessie didn't want to keep considering you've already taken certain liberties. And you're going to refund the rent he's paid since he's left."

"We're not refunding the rent. We haven't been able to rent the apartment and he's still committed to the term of his lease."

Jessie took a deep breath trying to calm his frustration.

Aidan reached into his jacket and withdrew his badge, holding it up to the suited man's face. "Care to repeat that?"

The man's Adam's apple bobbed. "I…" He cleared his throat and tugged his suit jacket. "I can ensure the last payment is refunded considering that's when the board reached their decision. And…and we can officially release Mr. Vega from the financial responsibility for the remaining months."

"And you're going to prepare a letter to that effect officially terminating the lease. You're also going to include the parking and maintenance fees he's paid from the date the board reached their decision. And you're going to pay the fees from impounding his vehicle. Now nod your head in agreement before I haul you and your sidekick in for unlawful eviction, harassment, breaking and entering, and anything else I can think of on the way to the precinct."

The building manager nodded and withdrew his phone from his suit pocket to make a call. Mr. Gonzalez jerked forward, his hands shaking as he unlocked the door.

Jessie loved this side of Aidan, the protective, caring one, the layer that peeked through when he wasn't so preoccupied with maintaining his hard-shelled facade.

Aidan entered the apartment and returned a few moments later with a duffle in hand and a stack of suits folded over his arm. "I found the duffle in your closet. What about any client stuff in your office?"

Jessie shook his head and hooked his thumb in his backpack's shoulder strap. "It's all digital. I've got it with my drive and laptop."

"Are we done here?" Aidan asked, staring down the man in the suit.

"Yes. I'm having the letter prepared and can have a cashier's check issued."

"Have them sent to the precinct to my attention." Aidan withdrew a card from his jacket and handed it over to the man. "I expect to have them by the end of day. And add on to the cashier's check the cost of a new picture frame to replace the one you broke when you carelessly tossed his items in the box."

The man nodded and Mr. Gonzalez locked the apartment again, both competing to see who could escape the fastest.

Aidan turned to Jessie and sighed. "I'm sorry you had to go through that."

"I'm…used to it."

"That stops today."

Jessie's pulse sped at the intensity staring back at him. Another drop into his love bucket for Aidan.

"My truck's parked out front. I need a minute to put these things away then I'll come back to help you down the stairs." Aidan picked up the box from the floor and balanced all the items in his arms, sprinting down the stairs. He returned a few moments later and stood by Jessie with a mix of emotions in his expression. "How bad does the leg and arm hurt after dealing with the stairs?"

He could lie to Aidan and say it was fine, but going down the same two flights of stairs and risking tumbling definitely wasn't on his bucket list. "Kinda bad," he whispered. "I can walk, but the crutch hurts."

Aidan gave him a quick nod of acknowledgement and eased the backpack off his shoulders. "Lean on me as we step down. Forget the crutch. It's probably bruised your arm already after coming up."

Aidan fished his hand through the prescription bag handle and grabbed the crutch, wrapping his other arm around Jessie's waist. "C'mon. I'm taking you home."

His lips parted on a breath when their eyes met. There, clear as day, a crack in Aidan's iron wall made an appearance. He reached up and wrapped his arm around Aidan's neck for balance, closing his eyes for a moment and reveling in the welcoming warmth and comfort that supported him.

This was right. This was the way a home *should* feel. He let Aidan lead him slowly down the stairs and didn't bother looking back again.

Chapter TEN

Aidan turned into his driveway and parked his SUV before switching off the engine. Bull pulled up behind them just as Aidan stole a glance out the corner of his eye at Jessie unlocking the passenger side door and exiting the truck. They'd driven for thirty minutes in traffic and hadn't spoken a word. Jessie was familiar with Aidan's home after working together there so many weekends. He hoped the familiarity might make Jessie feel welcomed and at home. But he wasn't kidding himself. He was to blame for the silence. He'd put enough distance between them these last two weeks, so he had to be the one to take the initiative and break the tension.

He exited his truck and unlocked his home. "Here we are," Aidan said, opening the door and switching off the alarm. "You know where the second bedroom is."

Jessie carefully took each step into the living room. He nodded then hobbled his way down the hallway without a word.

Aidan fought every urge in his body to stalk up to Jessie and carry him into the bedroom. The crutch must have bruised Jessie's arm by now, but he was too damn stubborn to mutter a complaint.

He jogged back to Bull's truck. "Can you stay?" he asked his friend as soon as he lowered the driver's side window.

"Yeah. You want me out here or in there?"

Aidan sighed, struggling between making sure Jessie was safe while also granting him some form of privacy. He tapped his thumb on the driver's side door as he raced through a few variables. "Inside until I get back, but give him his space."

His friend switched off the engine and exited the truck. "He won't even know I'm there."

Aidan huffed out a laugh. Bull couldn't hide if he tried. "We'll figure out what he's most comfortable with. Then we'll go from there."

"I'm going to sweep the perimeter, then I'll head inside before you leave."

Aidan nodded then returned to his SUV. He grabbed the stack of suits and flung them over his arm, finally reaching for the box of belongings. He scowled and made a mental note to buy a replacement frame for the broken glass sometime today. The one personal item from Jessie's apartment and it had gotten damaged by those careless, heartless bastards. He might suck at decoding all of Jessie's moods, but it was clear how upset Jessie was when he'd seen the discarded photo. He made his way back into the house and headed toward Jessie's new room.

"I'm coming in," he announced through the slightly ajar door before pushing it open with his foot. He entered and found Jessie sitting on the bed with his head down, taking a few deep breaths, wiping his brow of the beads of sweat that shimmered in the light. He looked flustered and downright exhausted.

Aidan set the box on the dresser and walked over to the closet to hang the armful of suits. He turned and shoved his hands in his pockets. "Are you hungry?"

Jessie shook his head.

Fuck, he hated this. "Talk to me. I'm not a mind reader."

Jessie shifted his leg and winced.

"When was the last time you took your pain meds?"

"Yesterday. The hospital pharmacy filled the prescription for me. That's the small bag you had with the crutch."

"Okay. Stay here," he said, making his way toward the kitchen. He grabbed the bag of bread and sniffed the contents to make sure it was still good. He didn't know how to cook much, but he could toast bread and butter it to make sure Jessie had something in his stomach with the strong meds.

He returned to the room a few minutes later with semi-decent buttered toast and a glass of water instead of the long-expired juice that had somehow taken residence at the back corner of his fridge.

Jessie reached into the prescription bag and pulled out a bottle of pills. He held the bottle in one hand but couldn't undo the top.

Aidan set the plate aside and reached for the bottle to open it. "One or two?"

"Two," Jessie quietly responded. He took the pills from Aidan's hand and accepted the glass of water.

Jessie looked up and those clear blue eyes stared back at him as if reading every private entry he'd ever thought of in his twisted, fucked-up mental journal. *Shit.* He picked up the plate and placed it on Jessie's lap. "Eat. I slaved over lunch, so you need to eat."

A small smile tugged at the corners of Jessie's lips. "Thank you." He took a bite of the toast.

"I need to go back to the precinct for a while. Bull will be here until I get back. Then we'll all talk about what works best and what you're comfortable with. I don't want him suffocating you, but I want to make sure you're safe. I'll pick up some Chinese food on the way back. I'll get you a chicken lo mein, unless you want to change it up."

Jessie looked up at him. "You remember what I like?" Jessie stared, blinking.

He shrugged. "You like chicken lo mein, anything Italian, you don't like pickles, you hate zucchini or peppers in your salads." Aidan could easily rattle off a list of preferences, quirks, and habits. He finally sat next to him, carefully trying not to move the bed. "A few conditions."

"Conditions?" Jessie asked, still looking at him with a puzzled expression.

"Of living together."

"Okay," Jessie said, absently nodding and taking another bite of the toast.

"First. Don't push yourself too much and don't be shy if you need some help with anything. As far as you staying here…" He paused, unsure of how exactly to finish his thought. He rubbed his palms against his thighs, trying to think of the best way to get the words just right. "You're here because I asked you to be here and I *want* you to be here. I'm not going to apologize for that. Understand?"

Jessie nodded and took another bite of the toast.

He turned to face Jessie. "Second. While you're here, this is your home. You can do whatever you want, whenever you want, and however you want. Understand?"

Jessie nodded again and took the last bite of the toast. He pressed his lips tightly together as if trying to hide the smile that clearly played across his face as he watched Aidan in that *I-know-what-you're-doing* sorta way.

He was so fucked.

"Good. Any questions? I think you know where everything is. I didn't really move anything from when you were here the last time."

"Last time? You haven't changed anything at all since you moved in," Jessie said, taking a sip of water.

"Yeah. Decorating's not my forte. I figured I'd leave it alone rather than fuck it up. You can change anything if you'd like."

Jessie nodded. "Thanks."

"You're welcome."

Jessie turned slightly to face Aidan. "I have conditions, too."

"Shoot."

"I'm helping. I know I can't do much right now, but we'll have to figure something out. I can do the cooking."

"I won't fight you there. I'm surprised I was able to handle the toast without burning the house down."

Jessie smiled again.

That smile. *Fuck.* He'd do anything to just have Jessie smiling all the time again.

"And when I start taking clients again, I'll cover half the expenses—"

"It's not a problem—"

"You have your conditions, Aidan. I have mine. It seems silly, but it's important to me."

Aidan clasped his hands in his lap. "It's not silly. You need to be independent. I get it. I know what that means to you."

"You're taking that check you're getting today from those assholes and you're applying it to my half of things."

"It's too much. I already know what you paid in rent."

"Then apply it to the following months as well."

Aidan nodded. He'd learned to not stand in Jessie's way when he was this determined about something. "I'm here and will help you with anything. I need you to know that."

"I do know that." Jessie nodded and lowered his head again. "I will need something from you, after I'm healed up." He fidgeted with his sling, before continuing. "I want you to show me how to fight."

"There are some self-defense basics we can run through. But you need full medical clearance before we even think about that."

"And shoot a gun."

Aidan straightened.

"Don't flip out and go all mother hen on me. I just want to be able to defend myself. I don't plan on going out there and becoming a vigilante. I just…I don't want to be a victim."

"I'd say you did a damn good job at fighting him off."

Jessie smiled. "Thanks."

"I'm not a mother hen," Aidan said with a frown.

"You so are." Jessie looked up and smiled again. That smile was going to kill him. "One more thing."

"Anything," Aidan said. *And isn't that the truth.*

"Stop pushing me away. Just be honest with me. If I do or say something that makes you uncomfortable or sets off one of your internal red-alerts to erect another layer of that shell you've got, please, just…talk to me. The last two weeks were…tough," he finished quietly and lowered his head.

"I promise to try," he said solemnly. *Be honest, talk, don't shut him out.* He took a deep breath then another, hoping to steady himself before his next few words. "The last two weeks were tough for me too."

Jessie glanced up, hesitated, then reached over and gave Aidan a peck on the cheek.

Aidan stilled and swallowed heavily. All the *while-you-were-*

sleeping kisses he'd placed on Jessie's forehead or cheek while he was in a coma had been stolen. This…this was real, although somewhat *sur*real at the moment. And Jessie-initiated. He was thankful as hell he was sitting down when it happened because he couldn't feel his legs at the moment. He stared at Jessie, not knowing what to say, but he hoped whatever had triggered that action would just rinse and repeat. Something kept fluttering inside his chest and stomach.

It was stupid. It was ridiculous how excited he was over such a tiny thing…and he didn't give a shit. His heartbeat raced. He was happy for the first time in a long damn time to have some form of personal contact. And the fact that it was Jessie? *Hell yeah.*

Jessie watched him carefully then tightened his lips as if holding back a smile as a flush of heat colored his cheeks.

"What was that for?" Aidan asked hoarsely.

"You said I could do whatever I wanted. Right now, I wanted to kiss you. Was that okay?"

Aidan nodded. "Um, you can"—he cleared his throat and rubbed his palms against his thighs again—"do that whenever you want," he mumbled, unable to think of anything else semi-coherent to say to fill the silence. And shit, had he just said that out loud?

Jessie leaned over and rested his head on Aidan's shoulder. "Thank you. For always being there for me."

He closed his eyes and turned his head, inhaling a breath as his lips brushed against Jessie's soft hair.

"I think the pain meds are kicking in," Jessie said, slurring his words.

Aidan stood and took the crutch, placing it against the nightstand. He closed the blinds and pulled back the sheet as Jessie slowly positioned himself in the bed. He stepped forward to raise Jessie's casted leg and removed his shoe, helping him settle into the bed before pulling up the sheet again. Aidan walked out of the room and returned with one of the cordless phones, dialing his cell number then hanging up the line. "If you need me, just hit redial. Otherwise, just call out for Bull who'll probably be in the living room."

"Okay," Jessie said, snuggling into the pillow and yawning.

"I'm going to set the house alarm before I leave so don't pop a window. And don't worry about your car. I'll get that taken care of."

"Thanks, Aidan."

He looked at Jessie's semi-sleepy, smiling face and nodded before walking out of the room and leaving the house.

He was wrong about one thing.

Jessie's smile wasn't going to kill him. Waiting for another kiss would.

part three
MENDING

Chapter ELEVEN

Four months later

Aidan held up the punch mitts toward Jessie, bouncing on his feet and circling the matted floor, forcing Jessie to follow his path. Aidan loved sparring with him, knowing he had played a role in Jessie's recovery.

"Again."

Jessie wiped the sweat from his brow and immediately reset his stance—hands up, blocking his face like a boxer. He'd managed to avoid a punch by ducking then retaliated with a swing. Textbook perfect. Just like everything he did.

"Don't be afraid to hit me," Aidan teased. "But that would mean you'd have to catch me first."

Jessie scowled, tightening his stance and unconsciously flexing his arm muscles. The taunt had obviously hit its mark.

They'd been working out together for the last few months, mainly on weekends or on those evenings when Aidan needed to work off some steam. Sometimes, they'd work out before he had to head in to work. They began with walks in the neighboring park and had worked up to cardio workouts to build up endurance. Jessie wanted to quickly move on to physical sparring sessions, but Aidan fought the urge to cave into those pleading, crystal blue puppy-dog eyes. He had never denied Jessie anything, but no way would Aidan put him at risk of injury.

He took a step forward then backed away just as abruptly, smiling when Jessie's body tensed in anticipation. "Your attacker won't announce an attack and won't stand still and wait for you to hit them. You need to be ready for the unexpected," he said, lowering his hands and pacing back and forth, keeping eye contact with Jessie's unwavering gaze. He loved it when Jessie was all intense and no nonsense. And damn, all the working out suited him well. His overall lean physique was now defined, and his biceps curved and dipped to exhibit each firm muscle. His stride held a confidence that hadn't been there before. His now tight abs, and his taut shoulders and neck, showcased every muscle and bone in his upper body to pure perfection. And the way Jessie's Adam's apple moved up and down his neck always threw Aidan into a fantasy world where Jess did more with his throat than just swallow spit and breathe in air.

Beautiful. Breathtaking. The thing of wet dreams that triggered a perpetual hard-on, keeping Aidan in an eternal state of frustration and bliss.

"So come at me already," Jessie said, dipping his head and raising his gloved fists, readying himself, blowing a wayward strand of hair out of his eyes.

As if the body changes weren't lickable enough, Jessie had kept his hair slightly longer in the front, and it now brushed his forehead during their workouts when he bypassed the gel products.

Aidan wanted to run his damn fingers through that soft hair. He wanted to grip that shit and pull Jessie's head back and lick and bite that fucking sexy as hell Adam's apple.

He finally stopped pacing and placed his hands on his hips. "I think we're done for the day." He removed his mitts and reached for the towel on the side table, patting the sweat off his face.

Jessie frowned, dropping his arms to his side. "You're no fun." He ripped off the Velcro strap with his teeth and tucked his hand under his opposite arm to remove the glove. He bent and reached for his towel then walked over to the corner to turn off the music streaming from his iPod.

Aidan turned his back to Jessie, hiding a smile. He loved having Jessie around. Evenings at home were better than he could have ever imagined. Not only was the man a beast in the kitchen, but he'd grown incredibly comfortable around Aidan and they teased each other endlessly. They'd become best friends, and Aidan enjoyed every second in his presence.

A yank on his shoulder pulled him out of his thoughts. He raised his hands to prepare for a punch but hadn't anticipated the leg sweep that knocked him flat on his ass...or the accidental jab to his groin with Jessie's knee on his way down to the mat. Aidan's eyes teared up and he immediately cupped his balls and bent his knees. He'd been shot at, stabbed, and hit with more weapons than he cared to remember. But his family jewels...they were sacred and very delicate. And very much in severe pain at the moment.

"Oh shit, I'm sorry." Jessie knelt on the floor at his side.

Fuck. Fuck. Fuck. "Don't apologize," Aidan hissed through clenched teeth. "Cheap shot, Jess. But a damn good one I might add."

A laugh bubbled from Jessie, and he quickly slapped a hand to his mouth to cover the smile. "I'm sorry. I don't mean to laugh. I just meant to drop you. I sure as hell didn't mean to hurt you."

Aidan scowled. "Go away. I'd like to keep my other parts intact."

"Aww, the big strong man got taken down by his smaller pupil," Jessie said, poking Aidan's side with his index finger and speaking in a mocking tone.

"Shut up," he said, laughing, then ending on a groan. Aidan uncupped his balls and test-stretched a leg, grimacing at the shock of pain and the churning in his stomach. He lay on his back and closed his eyes.

"Damn, I'm really sorry."

"I fucking deserved it. I shouldn't have taunted you."

"When are you going to show me more of those self-defense moves you talked about?"

"When I get a pair of iron balls."

"Mmm."

"I swear you're obsessed with balls." For some reason, any mention of balls, nuts, globes, or anything remotely suggestive and spherical always made Jessie perk up and stand at attention. He had a bona fide ball fetish he didn't even bother denying.

Jessie softly laughed. "You give me an Aidanism even when you're in pain. I keep telling you, it's a gift."

A smile spread across his face. Jessie had coined the phrase after Aidan's repeated comebacks and snarky comments during their conversations. He fucking loved that silly little word and knowing Jess actually liked his occasional sarcasm enough to give it a nickname. "You did good. Just give me a little bit to recover." After a few minutes, he slowly sat up then stood before bending forward and resting his hands on his thighs, breathing heavily to steady himself.

Jessie stood alongside him and reached over, rubbing his hand up and down Aidan's arm.

He took a deep breath, enjoying the heat of the comforting touch. "It's not my arm that hurts."

"Want me to rub your balls?"

Aidan straightened. "Smartass. I don't want you anywhere near my balls."

"Shame," Jessie whispered with a smirk.

They often teased, but Aidan always nipped it in the bud before it went too far. He enjoyed living under the same roof with Jessie and refused to do anything to make their relationship awkward again. The occasional smooch on the cheek with good news or a goodnight hug held him over just fine—far more than any contact he'd had with anyone else in quite some time. He looked up at the wall clock. "I'm going to grab a quick shower."

"I'm going to run on the treadmill for a few minutes. Meet you for breakfast in the kitchen in twenty?"

Aidan nodded, finally straightening and walking out—oh so slowly—from their workout room and into the bedroom to get ready for work.

About twenty minutes later, he stood in the kitchen—leaning forward, resting his elbows on the countertop and his chin on his fists—staring at the bread, waiting for that perfect shade of gold.

"Wait a minute. Do I smell what I think I'm smelling?" Jessie said with a gasp, entering the kitchen, trailing a faint hint of lemon soap in the air.

Aidan looked over his shoulder with a half smile, before

refocusing on the bread. He had quickly pinpointed Jessie's weakness: croissants, fresh from the oven, warm enough to melt the butter. "That depends on what you're smelling."

"I can sniff out a croissant a mile away." He inched closer, resting his chin on Aidan's shoulder. "Why are you staring at them?"

He turned his head, barely an inch between them. "I don't want them to burn." Even though Jessie had attempted to teach him how to work his way around in the kitchen, anything above and beyond boiling water or toasting a piece of bread—under close supervision—was a crap shoot. His toaster oven had a mind of its own and never cooperated. No way in hell would he deprive Jessie of his one weakness.

That would be worse than a double kick to the balls.

Jessie smiled and leaned in, his still-wet hair brushing against the side of Aidan's neck. He then placed a kiss on Aidan's cheek before stepping away and reaching into the refrigerator for the juice.

He smiled at Jessie then returned his focus to the evil toaster. He refused to chance it further and pulled out the warm breads from the small oven.

"Mmm, that smells good." That moan shot a bolt of heat right down to his aching balls as he walked over to the table with the plate full of warm croissants.

Jessie needed no further prompting before ripping apart a croissant and buttering it up. Aidan drank his juice, trying to ignore the sounds of pure ecstasy coming from Jessie. *I wonder if he makes those same sounds...* He squashed the random thought before it had a chance to plant roots and drive him mad. He wouldn't go there, *couldn't* go there.

They finally finished up breakfast and cleared the table. Aidan grabbed his wallet and keys then abruptly turned to face Jessie. "If you want me to pick something up, just text me." He smiled as Jessie walked over to the sofa and straightened the cushions, stepped back, then repeated the process until everything was picture perfect.

"I've got a stack of case files I need to research by the end of the week," Jessie absently said, inspecting his work. "So if you don't hear from me, feel free to nudge me. I'm always worried I'm going to text you at the worst possible moment."

Jessie worked from home as a legal research consultant and often lost track of time. Aidan missed seeing him dressed in his sharp suits, but he was definitely happier knowing Jessie was safe at home. *Home.* Aidan sighed inwardly. He liked the sound of that. Not *his* home and no need to clarify *their* home; just home. Plain and simple. And he couldn't have asked for anything more. Living with Jessie was easy, comfortable, and he craved the evenings when he could just spend time with him.

"You're never a bother. If I'm busy, I'll respond as soon as I get a chance." He looked away before he revealed more than he should and made his way toward the door.

"Have a nice day at the office." Jessie shoved him out the house with a pat on the ass.

Aidan stumbled out the door with a silly grin plastered on his face. Yeah, he totally loved this living together thing.

* * * *

"I hate this Michael Johnson asshole," Manny mumbled.

Aidan looked up from the case file. "Finally, Reyes, we agree on something."

Manny frowned, the crease between his brows deepening with each passing second. "How the hell is it possible for someone to vanish off the face of the earth like that?"

"He came back for him after fifteen years. That's a big span of time, so he's careful and meticulous."

"And patient," Manny added. "That's a big problem."

"Make that two things we agree on."

Every lead they had on Jessie's attacker had gone ice cold. Manny had demanded Jessie come in two months ago to answer more follow-up questions. Aidan feared the pushy prick had planned to take advantage of the interrogation to dish out a lengthy list of stupid homophobic jabs…but he couldn't have been more wrong.

Manny had approached each question with uncharacteristic gentleness which Aidan suspected mirrored the manner he usually handled cases within his department. But Manny's irritation was tangible and the extent of his questions, however delicately phrased, still punctuated the epic proportions of his frustration at not being able to solve the case that would have landed in his own department, regardless of his appointed team status.

He had asked hundreds of questions about Michael, trying to pinpoint anything that would shine some light on how to find him—what type of magazines Jessie had seen, what types of items decorated the house, any logos on store bags, the man's schedule, whether it remained the same on weekends, what did he usually wear, the length of his hair, and on and on. What the fuck did Aidan care if this bastard kept his nails clean or if he had calloused hands? But apparently, Manny said it might be an indicator of the line of work he did.

Logical bastard. Hell, those were clues Aidan spotted in homicide cases. But somehow, when it came to Michael Johnson, he had a hard time focusing or using anything remotely resembling common sense. He hated to admit his captain was right...he had become myopic. He had been given a very strict *hands-off* ultimatum from his captain on anything related to Jessie's case. If he interfered in any way, the case would be pulled from the team and delegated to a different department, probably buried under the pile of unsolved, pending casework since they'd hit the six-month mark.

He granted his team the space they needed but still managed to linger close enough to keep his finger on the pulse of progress. They kept him updated on every tiny detail they encountered, regardless of how small. And each of them worked the case from different angles.

One thing kept his mind at ease, Jessie had managed to effortlessly win over the team with his quiet demeanor and soft-spoken nature, which seemed to motivate them to work the case more diligently.

The thought of that bastard out there grated on every protective nerve ending in Aidan's body. He just wanted the asshole caught and everything done so they could move on. How Jessie managed to not let it get to him was a wonder. He'd simply stated, "It took him more than fifteen years to come after me. I'm not going to sit around and panic for another fifteen."

Aidan shook his head, hoping to dispel the thoughts racing through his mind and focus on the case file in his hands.

Manny continued to flip each sheet within the file as if some new information would appear just as quickly as Michael had vanished. "It's ridiculous. I contacted every damn agency who's tapped us to help on a case to see if they could poke around in their system…just in case the guy had decided to go global. Nothing. I can't even attempt to sweet-talk one of them to use their facial rec system because I don't have a damn face to go with this asshole. He's. Pissing. Me. Off."

He definitely liked this version of Detective Manny Reyes far more than the jab-delivering prick he had become accustomed to. "What do you suggest?"

Manny tapped his pen against the folder. "Not sure yet. But I'll be damned if I let that jerk best me in my own field. I've got a profiler coming to discuss another case, and I'm going to pick his brain on a few things regarding this asshole." He pushed back his chair and stalked out of the room with determination, barely missing Sunny and Travis as they walked into the team conference room.

"What bug crawled up his ass?" Travis asked.

"Michael-Fucking-Johnson."

His team members groaned. "The part that gets me…" Travis began, pulling out the chair across from Aidan. He lowered his brow and clasped his hands on the table. "What he did back then to Vega, it's…not the kind of thing someone does once and that's it. The attack that night, that was different. Horrible, yes, but different. You piss anyone off enough, and they can lose their shit. But kidnapping someone and holding them in those conditions for that length of time…that's the part that drives me crazy and the thing that's driving Reyes nuts. Someone like that does it more than once. And we've got no other victims, nothing else to show any pattern to guide us or anything to point us in any particular direction."

"Jessie's not lying."

"He didn't say that," Sunny jumped in, sitting next to Aidan.

Aidan raked his fingers through his hair. "I know." Everything regarding this case had him on edge. "Jessie did try to report it back then, but the moment he approached a cop, they were more concerned about having a guardian with him because he was a minor. And where

Jessie was concerned, that wasn't an option so he didn't file a formal charge."

Travis's jaw muscles twitched. "That's the problem. We think it's not the first time and we think the victims have always been in the same age group and circumstances. That's why we're looking into unsolved cases that might share some detail to what happened to Vega. Just in case he's done this before and slipped up somewhere."

"And Reyes has me looking into missing persons that fit the same physical traits as Jessie. Just in case we spot a trend for that region. We're all looking into different areas. Hopefully something will hit," Sunny said.

Aidan exhaled slowly, trying to control the simmering rage that threatened to break free, underscoring why he hated working assault cases. He wanted to catch this monster and exercise any one of the million kill options he'd noted on his mental list in the last six months. Cuffing the bastard and letting him serve prison time on the taxpayer's dollar…nope, definitely not on that list.

"Thanks, guys. I really appreciate it. I don't know how Jessie handles this so well, but I just want this done."

Travis leaned back in his chair and lowered his brow. "Is he being careful or has he let his guard down?"

"We sent Bull away two months ago because he felt suffocated with a bodyguard and always being watched. Jessie's careful and aware. He works from home and all his work is through his corporation, so his personal info is shielded for the most part. He's got access to all my accounts, so anything he needs goes through my name. He doesn't go out alone unless he's got a business meeting with a client. And when he does, he makes it a point of letting me know when he leaves and returns home. He's cautious but not obsessed about it."

"But?" Travis prompted.

Aidan sighed and hung his head. "He's still pushing me to show him how to use a gun."

"So show him," Sunny said. "Who better to teach him how to use a gun than Mr. I Don't Miss. You can use the range here. There's absolutely nothing wrong with knowing how to use a gun."

"Said the *homicide detective*." Aidan glared at his partner.

Sunny rolled her eyes. "There's a difference between having peace of mind knowing you're comfortable with how to use one if the situation arises and being pushed into a situation where your life depends on it but don't know what to do."

Fucking logic again. He hated that shit. Aidan rubbed his eyes then ran his hand harshly against his face. Jessie had mentioned wanting to know how to use a gun but never mentioned wanting to carry one or get a permit. Then again, Aidan kept a small arsenal stashed in different corners throughout their house. It made sense for Jessie to know how to use one of the weapons to defend himself if needed. "I'll think about it."

Travis chuckled. "You're such a momma bear."

Sunny covered her mouth but snorted in amusement.

Mother hen now momma bear? Being castrated to fit some bullshit stereotype pissed him the hell off.

"Just show the guy how to use a gun. Look at it this way. Do you want him to learn from you or take some class and learn from someone else?" Travis asked.

Damn Travis and *his* fucking logic. He sighed and crossed his arms. Mixing Jessie with anything aggressive or violent didn't sit well with him and forced all his protective instincts into overdrive.

Wall entered the room carrying a handful of files, sparing Aidan the need to respond. Another group of potential cases to review and leads to follow. Over the course of the last six months, their small team had exponentially closed more cases than their individual departments combined. They'd proven their effectiveness and the other government agencies were anxious to include them in more multi-jurisdictional cases.

They were successful.

They were problem solvers.

Except for the one case that seemed to nag them all the most.

* * * *

"You've got to be kidding me?" Cole said, leaning back in the side chair and propping his boots on the coffee table.

"Get your feet off the table," Jessie said, walking over to the living room and shoving Cole's boots off the wooden edge. "I asked you to send me that recipe for that stuffed chicken breast thing Aidan likes so I can make it next week, I didn't expect you to show up and give me a hard time. You could have emailed it." He sat on the couch and leaned his head back, blowing out an exasperated breath.

"That's no fun. You know I love to shoot the shit with you for a while. Besides, with that mountain of file crap on the table, you need a break."

"Did you bring the recipe or do you need something to write it down?"

"Don't change the subject. You're not getting off that easy," Cole said. "Come to think of it, you're not getting off at all," he finished with a guffaw.

"Real proud of yourself, aren't you?" He wouldn't deny he could use a break from all the casework, but he didn't need Cole to highlight his frustration.

"This whole 'just friends' shit is getting old," Cole said with an eye roll and air quotes. "You guys have been puppy dogging each other for almost two years. Why the hell doesn't he make a move?"

"Fuck if I know why." Jessie straightened in his seat and pursed his lips, crossing his arms, asking himself the same question for the millionth time.

A slow smile spread across Cole's face. That look never meant anything good.

"What?" Jessie rolled his eyes and inwardly cringed.

"You've been hanging around him too much. You've turned into a potty mouth."

Jessie narrowed his eyes.

"Ooh, you're picking up the glare too."

"Fuck you."

Cole scowled then scrunched his face after a moment. "Nah. That doesn't sound right coming from you. Tell me to go 'shove it where the sun don't shine' or something like that. That would fit better with you."

Jessie sighed. He and Aidan teased one another, but it never went further than a chaste kiss on the cheek or a random gesture like the morning pat on the ass. And certainly nothing Aidan initiated. While in the hospital, he was always there and didn't hesitate to help or sit bedside each night. And if Jessie had a restless night, Aidan would hold his hand to keep the monsters at bay. Since his discharge, the nightmares had subsided, so had the bedside watch. Jessie was left with the occasional brush of fingers in his hair when they sat on the couch, a gesture he suspected Aidan didn't even realize he did as they watched television.

"Maybe I'm wrong. Maybe Aidan's not gay," Jessie finally mumbled.

"My gaydar is finely tuned, little man. Trust me, he's gay and has the hots for you."

"He's close with his partner," he said with a sigh. Damn, he hated feeling self-conscious.

"There's no way he's into 'flowers' or whatever PC term is being used today to describe the vajayjay."

Jessie rolled his eyes again. "I'm being serious."

"I am too. He's into you…well, not literally, but you know what I mean. He's got a thing for you. You've changed in the last few months but—"

"I haven't changed," Jessie said, his eyebrows arching upward, worried he had done something unconsciously to stall any minute progress between him and Aidan.

"You've got biceps you can flex now." Cole leaned forward and yanked up Jessie's shirt. "And you've got abs too."

Jessie pushed away Cole's hands and pulled his shirt back down, scowling at his always meddling friend.

"You can arm wrestle Carmen and totally kick her ass."

"That's…flattering."

"Carmen was the only girl out of six of us. She's an undercover badass. And what's up with you? It's like I'm talking to a little version of Aidan. You're even picking up his sarcasm."

"Shut up," Jessie mumbled. "And stop calling me little. I'm only an inch shorter than you."

Cole leaned forward in the chair, resting his forearms on his thighs. "Do you ever ask him?"

Jessie cocked his head. "Ask him what?"

"There's something about him I can't figure out. I know the man's crazy about you—that's a given. You can see it in his eyes. His body vibrates when you're in the room."

"Stop being so dramatic. I'm trying to have a serious conversation here."

"How do you not see it?" Cole asked and shook his head. "I totally get that he's private. But he takes it to a whole other top-secret level. You're going to have to make the first move. Just jump the man."

Jessie grabbed one of the small cushions and hugged the soft material. Being so close to Aidan each day was torturous—they were close in proximity but, somehow, still light years away. "I'm not pushing him. That's a surefire way to get him to shut down."

"You can't go at him like a regular person. You need to take a crack at him in an unexpected way. If he doesn't see you coming and lets his guard down, you might be able to break through. Maybe you can sneak up on him, dig underneath that barrier he has around him."

"You make it sound like a prison break," Jessie said, raising an eyebrow.

Cole shrugged. "Well, technically. Isn't that what it is for him?"

Jessie chewed his bottom lip as his mind wandered.

"It's like... I don't know," Cole said, tugging his beanie. "It's as if he wants to be with you, but he doesn't know how. I doubt it's a lack of sexual experience. I mean, seriously, look at him. The guy's super-hot."

Jessie's focus snapped back to Cole. He tightened his grip on the cushion in his arms, fisting the material to control the bubbling jealousy.

Cole immediately raised his hands in surrender. "Whoa there, Vega. He's not the Calloway I want." He then scowled and waggled his finger at Jessie. "And if you tell him I said he was hot, I swear, I'm totally unfriending you."

Jessie bit his lip. Cole always seemed to make him smile

regardless of his mood.

"He's different." Cole's mood sobered, leaning back in the chair again with a frown. "When you were in the hospital, Aidan freaked out...but not like regular freaking out. It's as if he was numb or something. It wasn't like him. He's usually in control and has a plan, but he seemed...lost. He even had me worried so I tried to see if Ty could get through to him, but Ty was scared out of his mind. He'd just tell me that *that* guy wasn't his brother so he didn't know how to get through to him." Cole shook his head and crossed one booted foot over his knee. He tugged on his laces, lost in thought for a few moments before he spoke. "I didn't know what he meant at first and I kinda shrugged it off."

"But?" Jessie prompted.

"Then I saw an old video."

Jessie tossed the cushion to the side and leaned forward. "Of what?"

"A home video. Ty totally looks like his dad. And man, Aidan looks like his mom. It's funny, because they kinda look alike but still different and you know that thing—"

"Cole, focus please." Sometimes, he could easily understand why Aidan wanted to strangle him.

Cole stared at him and blinked a few times. "Oh! Yeah! The video. He was different. Not like the Aidan I know and love to piss off."

Jessie threw his head back against the couch. Sometimes, even *his* patience ran a little thin. Especially when he was so...frustrated. "You already said he was different. Different how?"

"Everything. He was smiling, laughing, and he and Ty were roughhousing the way I used to with my brother. It's like he's a pod person now. Totally weird."

Jessie fidgeted, tugging on the seam of his jeans. He had to admit, the shift in Aidan's personality from lighthearted to all-serious piqued his interest. What had hurt Aidan badly enough to warrant that iron fortress around his heart? Jessie took a deep breath. That answer would have to wait for now; he had a few pressing deadlines. "Believe it or not, I'd love to have you hang out, but I have a ton of work I need to wrap up today."

Cole nodded and stood from the chair, walking over to the folders and papers Jessie had spread out on the table. "Can I grab a sheet from this notebook?"

Jessie nodded and walked over to him. If Cole was going to write down that recipe, Jessie needed to make sure he could understand the handwriting which was usually as erratic as the man himself or the quirky Renzo-shortcode for abbreviations he assumed the world could decipher on their own.

While Jessie questioned each random squiggle he couldn't understand, his mind wandered elsewhere, to the one mystery man who increased his frustration yet still managed to ease his mind. A mystery he couldn't wait to solve.

Chapter TWELVE

Aidan sat in the rickety chair and leaned forward with his forearms against his thighs. He hated waiting. He peered up at the walls and the high ceilings at the peeling paint and broken windows of the abandoned building. Definitely not the standard interrogation room, but it would work all the same. Especially under these circumstances.

He swiped at the sweat trickling down his temple. *Fucking Miami heat.* The musty scent of concrete mixed with the all-too-familiar humidity definitely didn't help cool his temper. He pulled out his phone to send a text message.

Probably going to be late.

Jessie immediately responded. *Want me to save you dinner?*

Aidan smiled and something fluttered in his chest. Jessie always seemed to do that to him. *I'll grab something.*

OK. Be safe.

He pocketed his phone and watched his equally impatient team members. Travis paced the room with his hands shoved in his pockets, and Wall stood with arms crossed, leaning against the concrete wall. *Wall against a wall.* For some reason, that always made him chuckle.

"If he doesn't talk here, and we take him to the station, he'll be out within the hour and we'll lose the only fucking lead we've got." Travis continued to pace.

Aidan crossed his arms and scowled, staring at the closed door of the neighboring room. It shouldn't take fifteen minutes to extract information. Not unless Manny was offering the perp a drink and a smile and trying to charm the information out of him. *Any means necessary.* The rules handed down for this case were clear: there weren't any. They had finally found a lead in the Traveling Matador case, the FBI-nicknamed serial killer responsible for three dozen deaths over a span of five years across six states—the most recent, two nights ago in South Florida. The link: the discarded victims were each wrapped in a red cape and speared with a decorative dagger. Their one lead sat in that room—the man who'd decorated the daggers had decided to start signing his work. He had picked the worst time to showcase his vanity.

The barely-hanging-on door of the room swung open and Manny stormed out with Sunny close on his heels.

Manny planted his hands at his hips and his nostrils flared with each angry huff of breath. "Son of a bitch won't give us the name. I texted our contact at the FBI to come here and pick him up. Maybe they can get something from him."

Aidan looked over at a too-quiet Sunny with her arms tightly crossed. Even he could detect something was off. He walked over to her. "Are you okay?"

She nodded quickly. Too quickly.

Aidan glanced over his shoulder to Manny. "What the hell happened in there?"

Manny turned sharply, then stilled when he saw Sunny, her arms wrapped even tighter around herself. Manny's features softened and hardened at the same time. She pointedly glanced at Aidan before exiting the building.

She was anything but *fine* and she'd never let anyone else in on the whys.

Aidan walked up to Manny, invading his space. "What did he say?"

Manny glanced at the door of the neighboring room and sneered. "The son of a bitch said he was working with someone, but we'd never catch him. He described what the guy would do to her." He turned to face Aidan, the anger evident with each controlled breath. "In detail. She wasn't fazed at all in there. I didn't think she'd let it sink in."

Of course he didn't. No one ever did. Sunny was as much a wall as Wall was to most people, especially when it came to anything emotional or personal. In her mind, she had to be. Just as Aidan fought a stereotype regarding who he preferred in bed, Sunny constantly kicked and punched that glass ceiling every chance she had and refused to show any form of weakness or fit anyone's version of a damsel in distress.

But one homicide case they had worked together some time ago had revealed a hint of vulnerability she couldn't hide from Aidan's questioning stare. She'd finally confessed that her driving force to join the police had also been the one thing that ate away at her core. As a child, she had witnessed a violent attack against her older sister and had locked it away as best she could in her mind. But Aidan had seen that same vulnerability a few times since joining the team—handling Jessie's case and all these other serial assaults the team tackled affected her. Unfortunately, he could sympathize far more than he wanted to admit.

Aidan tried to control the building rage vibrating throughout his body. "Give me five minutes."

"He won't talk."

"Five. Fucking. Minutes. Reyes."

Manny raised his hands in exasperation. "Fine. You've got a few minutes before they get here to take him."

Aidan looked at Wall and tilted his head, signaling him to follow. Wall pushed off his perch and silently fell in line behind him as they walked into the room. The scrawny man with closely cropped hair sat on the wooden chair with his hands bound in his lap. Wall found a spot in the corner and waited with crossed arms.

"What the hell do you want? I already told that other guy I wasn't saying shit," the man spat.

Aidan clasped his hands behind his back and slowly paced in front of the perp. He generally wasn't patient, but he knew enough about head games to wait out a suspect during an interrogation. Especially one where a little more...*encouragement* was needed to get the end result. He walked the length of the room, not saying a word, his gait slow, without a hurry in the world. A simple power play so the jerk thought he had the upper hand. He expected Aidan to speak, to ask the same questions as Manny, to be on edge and asking nicely for answers the suspect would not willingly give. The man was too confident and had already rattled Sunny's cage. The smug look on his face, a clear indication he thought he had won this battle.

Not on his watch and sure as hell not against his team.

The man stayed focused on Aidan's pacing as the seconds ticked by. Aidan had played this game many times before. A basic power play rule: first man to speak was the first to crack.

More seconds ticked by and not a word was spoken.

The man began to shift his bound hands as Aidan continued to walk across the run-down room. Aidan stopped for a moment and took a deep breath, looking off at a spot in the corner of the room.

The man stilled.

Aidan resumed pacing, and the man started fidgeting again, squirming in the seat.

"I'm not sayin' shit to you!"

Aidan stopped directly in front of the man before he spoke in a level tone. "I think you need better motivation."

"What the hell does that mean?"

In a split second, Aidan had pulled the wooden chair from under the man and knocked him to the floor on his ass. He flipped the chair over and planted the spindle stretcher between the back legs of the chair flush against the man's neck. The perp's eyes widened when Aidan put his weight on the seat of the angled chair, pressing the wood against the man's throat.

The man gasped a breath. "You're fucking crazy! You can't…can't do this." He tried to look past Aidan at Wall in the corner.

Aidan pressed the chair. "You're shit out of luck if you think he's going to snitch me out. Tick tock. I need an address and a name."

The man's focus snapped back to Aidan. "He'll kill me."

Aidan slowly raised an eyebrow. "You're assuming I wouldn't."

The man stilled. "You…you can't. You're supposed to…"

"Serve and protect. I'm here to *protect* future victims. And if you ask me to serve you, I'll rip your dick off and *serve* it to you down your fucking throat. Talk. I won't ask again nicely."

"I…I…I don't know his name," the man finally said.

"Where can I find him?"

"He's…he's finished here. He's leaving. He might already be gone."

"Address?" Aidan asked, leaning into the chair again.

"I have rights!"

"So did his thirty-six victims." He leaned more into the chair and glared at the man with the sheen of sweat across his forehead. "I hate repeating myself."

"I…have money. A big stash. You let me go and I'll give you—"

Aidan fought back the fury that roared like a beast within. "My loyalty is *not* for sale."

The scrawny man's eyes rounded. "If…if I tell you…you…you need to hide me. If he finds me…he'll—"

"Kill you like the others?"

The man nodded quickly.

"I'm heartbroken."

Images of all the victims flashed in succession in Aidan's mind. The savage brutality of each visual lit a fire in the pit of his stomach and began to twist his gut. All he cared about was the information ready to spill from the perp's lips.

Any means necessary.

He leaned forward and zeroed in on the man beneath him, staring back at Aidan with rounded eyes filled with fear.

"Address? And I'm not asking again."

Four minutes and twenty-seven seconds later, he and Wall left the room with the man sitting in the chair, uninjured and once again upright.

Manny spun on his heel the moment they swung the door open. "Did you get anything?"

Aidan nodded curtly. "Address. And we need to get there ASAP."

They all turned toward Sunny standing by the exit door at the sound of a car pulling up outside. "They're here," she called out.

Two suited agents entered the building and Travis immediately joined them, briefing them as they headed over to collect the suspect. They emerged from the room moments later with the handcuffed perp. The second the scrawny man saw Aidan, he tried to pull away from the agents, wildly yelling to keep the "psycho cop" away from him.

I've been called worse. Aidan shrugged off the questioning glances and ignored the chuckle coming from Wall.

"Reyes, you're lead on the takedown plan," he said, trying to shift the focus off the perp's crazy mutterings as the agents dragged him out of the building, still kicking and screaming.

Manny looked a little surprised, probably shocked Aidan hadn't tried to take over since he'd managed to extract the address. Regardless of how they acquired the lead, he wouldn't step on his team member's toes, same way Manny wouldn't step on his. Aidan may have a reputation for being an asshole, but he damn sure extended professional courtesy to his coworkers who put their lives on the line on a daily basis to protect others.

"We need to get aerials and building schematics so we know all possible entry and exit points," Manny finally said to the team.

They made their way out of the building and to their cars, itching to plan a strategy to finally catch the serial bastard.

* * * *

"Something's wrong," Aidan whispered.

"Ditto," Sunny said, her voice echoing faintly through the earpiece.

Within less than an hour of securing the address, they had arrived to find the Traveling Matador still in town. One team member stationed at each entry and exit point—easy in and out plan. He peeked around the right corner of the south side of the one-story building, trying to catch a glimpse of his partner guarding the west end, finally spotting Sunny craning her neck to observe Wall stationed on the north side of the same building. Aidan looked to his left and took a deep breath, anxious as Travis stood guard in the southeast corner.

"Travis, can you see Reyes from your vantage point?"

"Negative," Travis said, inching forward.

Fucking Manny Reyes tried to be ballsier than the other team members. His ego had taken an obvious hit. He refused to remain stationed in his spot. Rather, he wanted to fly solo and nail the guy himself to make up for not having stellar interrogation skills to pull an address from the suspect. The team agreed, more than anything, to get him to shut the hell up and stop complaining. But now, as they waited for their team member to come out of the building, they all probably shared the same regrets as Aidan for caving in to Manny's ego.

"Shit!" Manny's voice boomed through the earpiece followed by a door slam and rapid footsteps. "We've got a runner!"

"He's headed east," Travis added, sprinting after them.

Aidan motioned Sunny over as he spoke into his mic. "Wall, come around to the south side. You and I are going to pair up," Aidan directed, quickly formulating a mental plan. "Sunny, pick up the car and get on the laptop to track us and call in for backup." With Sunny's speed, she could easily reach the parked car several blocks away in less than a minute. She nodded and sprinted west toward Douglas Road.

They each wore GPS trackers during a takedown to avoid any surprises and only Sunny and Travis could decipher which blinking green dot was who on the screen. Without questioning who took the reins, they each broke free with their orders. Wall ran alongside Aidan, effortlessly matching each stride as they headed east at a full-paced run to catch up to Manny and Travis.

With each stomp of his booted feet on the pavement, a new scenario and quick solution arose in Aidan's mind. Within seconds, he had a plan and mentally sorted through potential backup plans as well. If the perp entered a populated area, if he held someone hostage in their home, if—

Sunny's voice over the radio pierced his thoughts. "I've got each of you pinged. Reyes and Trav cut through the park and are heading east down Oak Ave. Calloway and Wall, keep cutting through the way you're going. I'm going to drive down Grand."

They ran at a full speed, hyperaware of their surroundings as they raced along the rear periphery of Coco Walk. The beautiful street-side and social gathering hot spot was elegant and often ideal for photo shoots and artistic street vendors. But just outside the shops and restaurants vibrating with nightlife bordered a less than glamorous part of town. Empty, rundown buildings on the outskirts created a visual marker, clearly defining a boundary—a warning to tourists that they could have that spot to live in their dreamy, ritzy street-side cafe or restaurant, but everything else was off limits.

They raced down the street, ignoring the drug transaction on the corner. They had bigger problems on their hands if this asshole escaped. They vaulted over a chain link fence like synchronized, seasoned gymnasts, the bulk of the tactical gear no match for the adrenaline injecting power through every muscle. Aidan ducked to avoid losing an eye to the branches of the overgrown black olive tree he hurtled past then scurried through a backyard to cut through and make up some ground, never breaking rhythm as a Rottweiler jumped toward them, held back *only* by the chain leash wrapped around its neck. They picked up their pace, both in stride like a single runner with his reflection against a mirrored wall.

"They're heading toward Tigertail," Sunny said through the earpiece.

"Shit," Aidan cursed under his breath.

Too many residences along that road and too many trees to provide cover in the faint evening light or the randomly working streetlights, most intentionally shot out by the dealers who preferred the cover of night for their transactions. And if they managed to still have sights on the perp through the residential area, they ran the risk of the suspect complicating things if he hit the business district a few blocks down.

"Trav stopped. Reyes is still going. Wait, he's backtracking. Shit, I think he might have lost the guy."

With all the overgrown trees, it was too easy to lose the runner. Especially if the suspect was familiar with the area. "Let's split up," Aidan said to Wall. They went their separate ways with swift, practiced ease, never missing a step—Wall to the right and Aidan heading left.

After a few moments, Sunny's voice radioed through. "Wall, cut back around and circle from behind. Aidan, you're coming up on Trav. He's going to be on your left in about fifty yards around the corner."

The message sent a bolt of energy racing through Aidan's body. He turned the corner and spotted Travis on the ground with his hand pressed against his head. Aidan hit the ground and slid on his knees the few inches to reach his team member. "You okay?"

Travis nodded, removing his hand to inspect his blood smeared palm before returning it to his temple. "Fucking Good Samaritans thought they were helping him. I'm fine. Go!"

Aidan curtly nodded, his body instinctively darting forward at a dead run. "Sunny, pick up Trav."

"On it." The faint sound of screeching tires making an obvious sharp turn a few streets down immediately followed her response.

Aidan charged forward, his heart pounding and the sweat on his brow chilling his skin with each speedy stride down the residential streets as he headed toward the edge of The Grove's business district. A prickling behind his neck alerted him, flashing warning lights in his head. He slowed his pace to a trot and stealthily worked his way around the darkness, taking advantage of the cover offered by the trees.

"Wall's here. We've got Trav. You're coming up to Reyes. He's not moving."

A grunt and clanking of metal echoed in the silence of the night, guiding him to the next corner. He withdrew his sidearm and inched forward, turning the corner to find Reyes about fifty yards away on the ground up against the building in the dark alley. His body slumped at an odd angle against the large, metal garbage bins and his chest heaved with each labored breath.

The large, thick man loomed over him with a gun aimed squarely at Manny's head.

Aidan straightened his arms and an instant stillness overtook his entire body, steeling his pounding heart and cementing his muscles to his position, demanding precision. Without hesitation, he aimed at the monster's heart and pulled the trigger. The sound of the bullet pierced through the silence of the night and jerked the huge figure back onto the ground.

Manny abruptly turned his head, looking over to him. Aidan marched down the alley toward him as tires screeched behind moments later and car doors swung open.

Aidan kicked away the gun on the ground then extended his hand to Manny to help him stand. His focus snapped to the large figure on the ground, alarmed by the sound of a sudden grunt.

Sunny and Wall lunged forward, holding the large man down to the pavement.

Manny clasped Aidan's hand to stand. Finally upright, he swayed slightly, stopping only when Aidan braced his arm with his other hand to steady him. Manny repeatedly blinked as blood oozed from a gash at the side of his head. Without further prompting, Manny silently acknowledged he was fine with a slow nod.

Sunny yanked open the Traveling Matador's shirt. "What the fuck?" She looked over her shoulder at Aidan. "Did you know he was wearing a vest?"

Aidan holstered his weapon and his jaw muscles twitched with new tension. "No."

He turned toward the car to check on Travis who sat in the back with a bloody towel against his head. Aidan took a few deep breaths to calm the rage clawing away at him as a series of photos flickered through his mind in rapid succession.

Images of the victims who had suffered at this monster's hand.

Snapshots of Jessie sitting in the middle of a blood-smeared bed.

His bloodied and injured teammates…from now and from a time he wanted to forget.

Everything. All at once. Sorted and dog-eared in his memory bank for future reference.

One last thought crossed his mind as sirens wailed in the stillness of the night: he should have aimed for the bastard's head.

Chapter THIRTEEN

He hated the fucking darkness and the musty smell of damp mud. He tried opening his eyes, but the blindfold made the attempt pointless.

He waited. Listening. He couldn't see, but didn't need to. He had memorized every corner of the mud-brick structure. The walls were the same tone as the boring, brown, desert dirt. Open squares in the uneven walls served as windows, and a stained piece of fabric draped from the rooftop covered the large rectangular opening that served as the doorway.

Regardless of how they bound him, they always kept him in the main room while at least one man remained in the smaller side room—the main headquarters where the cell team coordinated their invasions. Times like these he wished he had a tracking chip implanted so the higher-ups could come in and raid the handmade mud structure.

He waited for the silence to confirm his solitude in the space as he lay on his back—held down with braided material that seemed stronger than traditional rope. Fuckers had figured out braiding made it tougher to tear.

He took a slow, shallow breath, hoping to mask the rise and fall of his chest. He lay as still as possible, filtering out the sound of each scrape of nature rubbing against the fabric door, waiting to hear a voice.

He'd counted up to six distinct male voices. Occasionally absent for some stretch of time, but always the same six. Their leader was the worst and took great pleasure in overseeing every ounce of pain dispensed by his clan, urging his disciples to show no mercy. They yelled and spurred each other on in a foreign language they thought he couldn't understand.

He understood everything. Every. Fucking. Word.

He and his team had been trained to know the language of the lands they invaded.

"Break the man, so he speaks." The sick bastards chanted their mantra over every member of his unit as they all lay naked on a bed, or bound, waiting for their turn in the beating queue. Tied and naked made it damn near impossible to hide anything that could double as a weapon. Days, weeks, months...he'd lost count without the rare gift of the rise and set of the sun. After several escape attempts, his team had been punished and forced into the helpless darkness. Blindfolds their captors only removed so each man in his unit could serve as witness to the torture of the others. They thought that would encourage someone in his crew to betray their country.

Morons. He and his unit were patriots to the core.

The captors had become creative with their household items, learning quickly how a simple battery cable against wet or sweat-slicked skin could cause a body to arch in agony or how a simple twist of an arm or a bound limb in just the right position for the perfect length of time could result in a lingering taste of pain.

He and his men were trained to withstand torture and how to ignore the bite of pain.

But he hadn't been trained for the full spectrum of possible torture while captive or the soul-piercing ache each time he watched the bastards slowly and calculatingly murder every member of his unit, until only he remained. With nothing further to witness, the blindfold had become a permanent reminder of his lack of control...or so they'd hoped.

Finally, the sound he sought. One muffled voice.

He steeled himself, ready to act. He couldn't stand this anymore. This helplessness. Not sure why this time would be different, but he had to try to free himself again. Death was the inevitable endgame.

The question was...when? And he sure as hell wasn't known for his patience.

One man far enough away meant he had a small window of time. He quickly tried to loosen himself from the leg and hand restraints. The restraints seemed different than usual. Odd. The voice came closer. He gnashed his teeth as he fought the braided fabric that bound him, pulling and pushing, hoping for an inch of give in the binding.

That voice again. It sounded different, but he wasn't going to chance quieting to distinguish the tone of which captor neared him. It didn't matter which one.

They all deserved to die.

His jaw muscles hurt from the pressure of each muffled grunt as he twisted and straightened his wrists and feet, hoping the fabric would loosen just enough to allow him to slip through the restraint. His heart jackhammered in his chest as the voice sounded closer. He didn't have much time. He struggled, arching his body and channeling his strength into his limbs, fighting with every ounce of power for a chance to escape.

In an instant, the restraints dissolved from his hands just as a touch grazed his now magically freed ankles. He didn't question how it happened. Fuck it, freedom was all that mattered.

An ingrained instinct charged him toward his captor.

"Aidan."

That voice, the tone familiar but nothing he associated with the darkness or the evil that suffocated him.

"Aidan."

* * * *

The power outage from the blown transformer had been loud enough to wake Jessie with a start. He rose from bed and stretched as he walked over to the window, yawning and taking a peek out into the still of the night. An endless sea of darkness except for the hint of moonlight that brightened the top layer of leaves of the large black olive trees.

Pained, strangled grunts came from the living room. *Aidan.* He grabbed the flashlight from the nightstand and quietly took the familiar steps in the darkness down the hallway into the open space. "Aidan, are you okay?"

The pitch black stole the living room of the usual glow from the television and the steady whisper of white noise Aidan always seemed to play during the night to lull himself to sleep. A hint of moonlight filtered through the living room window, just barely enough to show Aidan thrashing on the couch in distress with the sheet pushed off his body and onto the ground. For some reason, Aidan preferred to sleep on the old, worn-out couch in the living room rather than in the comfort of a bed or in the large, almost-empty master bedroom he used as an office.

"Aidan?"

He continued to thrash on the couch, grunting and shifting, snarling like a wild animal. Jessie reached out to touch Aidan's ankle, hoping to soothe him and wake him from the nightmare. In a move faster than he thought humanly possible, Aidan launched forward, pushing Jessie's body against the wall, and locking his forearm across Jessie's upper chest. Even in the blackness of the room, Aidan's hazel eyes appeared vacant and crazed.

The sweat on Aidan's brow multiplied and his body heaved with each labored breath. He screwed his eyes shut, his hold loosening a fraction. He shook his head as if dispelling a thought and mumbled something Jessie couldn't quite decipher.

"Aidan." For some odd reason, Jessie wasn't scared and had an unusual sense of calmness take over every inch of his body. Without question, he sensed he should remain as still as possible to let Aidan know he wasn't a threat, but the need to comfort him took center stage. "It's me. Jessie." Aidan had served several tours in the Marines. Jessie had researched enough court cases to know flashbacks or intense nightmares were common after serving. Deep down in his soul, the thought that Aidan would never hurt him gave him peace.

Assuming, of course, Aidan was aware it was him and not an illusion of something or someone else.

Realization came crashing in, an odd time to have a major

breakthrough—this must have been a reaction to the large explosion and blackness of night. Was this why Aidan slept with the white noise from the television each night? To have the noise and the light from the TV? To avoid a trigger?

"Aidan. It's me. Jessie," he repeated in his most calming voice. The sweat glistened on Aidan's brow and his jaw muscles twitched. He repeatedly mumbled again, barely a whisper. Whatever thought had overtaken his mind had a firm grip on Aidan's entire being. The man before him wasn't the Aidan who protected him and warded off the monster that threatened him.

This was a man possessed by his *own* demons.

"It's me. Jessie."

Aidan screwed his eyes shut and shook his head again, struggling with something internal. The pressure of the forearm across Jessie's chest loosened further as Aidan continued to repeatedly mumble the same stream of words he now clearly understood. "It's not real. It's not real."

"Aidan. You're home. You're safe here," Jessie softly coaxed. He kept his arms as still as possible and moved his thumb to press the button on the flashlight, shooting a beam of light upward to the ceiling and bouncing off the side walls. "You're safe, at home, with me."

Aidan's eyes sprung open, and he blinked repeatedly, staring at the beam of light.

"Aidan. It's Jessie. You're in the living room. You're home. You're safe." He didn't know if it was useless to chant the same words, but he had to comfort Aidan in some way. If not by touch, then by his voice. He remembered the comfort Aidan's tone offered him when stuck in that drug-induced darkness. He hoped the sound of his voice could do the same and somehow reel Aidan back into the here and now.

The haunted cloud in Aidan's eyes began to recede and the familiar hazel expression made an appearance. He stared at Jessie and slowly blinked.

"Shit, shit, shit..." Aidan immediately pulled his arm away, stumbling backward.

"It's okay."

Aidan ran his trembling fingers through his hair and exhaled a strangled breath, shaking his head madly back and forth. "Oh my God."

"It's okay."

Aidan turned to him, a crazed, wild look still in his eyes, but the hazel stare was clearly *his* Aidan. "It's *not* fucking okay! I could have killed you!"

"You didn't. You wouldn't hurt me."

Aidan shook his head and gripped his hair in both hands. He clenched his jaw shut as a slow, pained groan escaped. He slumped on the couch as if all the energy had drained from his body just as quickly as it had surged, then buried his head in his hands and let out a strangled moan that mirrored the cry of a pained animal.

"Look at me."

The sound of Aidan's shaky breathing echoed in the quiet room.

"Look. At. Me."

Reluctantly, Aidan turned his head upward, hesitant to make eye contact.

"I'm okay. I need to make sure you are." He stepped forward, and Aidan inched away on the couch, trying to retain the distance between them. This wasn't a rejection, the worry and pain in his eyes made that clear. Jessie took another step forward then another until he stood in front of Aidan. He reached out and ignored the wince just before his fingers made contact with Aidan's chin. "Look at me."

"I'm sorry," Aidan said faintly in a broken voice. "I'm so sorry. I'd never..." He yanked his head out of Jessie's hold and looked away.

It was a chance, but something within directed Jessie's next move. He raised Aidan's legs, positioning him back onto the couch to lie down. Aidan stared at him, his body tense but still willingly letting Jessie guide his limbs as if unable to move his body of his own accord. Jessie picked up the sheet from the floor and hesitated for a moment then sat on the couch next to him, laying out the sheet to re-cover Aidan's body. He set the still-turned-on flashlight on the coffee table, pointing upward to fill the room with a faint blue glow. "You're tired and you need to get some sleep before you go in tomorrow." He stretched his legs under the sheet along the length of the couch, lying down parallel to Aidan's stiff body, and pulled the sheet up over them. "Go to sleep," he said, snuggling into the single pillow, barricading

Aidan between him and the couch.

"I'm sorry," Aidan brokenly whispered.

Jessie looked over his shoulder. "That wasn't you. I know that." He turned to face forward then reached behind him to grab Aidan's trembling hand and tugged it against his chest. "Try and go back to sleep."

"You shouldn't be here," Aidan said, just barely above a whisper.

"I'm exactly where I need to be." He pulled Aidan's hand upward and kissed his fingers then rested his cheek against Aidan's palm. "Go to sleep."

After a few moments, the stiffness in Aidan's body eased slightly as he shifted on the couch. He slid his arm under Jessie's head offering his bicep as a pillow, then pulled Jessie closer, caging him tightly in his still-shaking arms.

Jessie nuzzled into the warmth that enveloped him, kissing Aidan's hand whenever he heard another whispered apology or when the muscular cage surrounding him would quiver again. Jessie finally eased into sleep when a comforting weight rested against his head and a rhythmic brush of air danced across his shoulder like a gentle caress.

* * * *

Aidan reluctantly opened his eyes to face the morning. On the couch, with Jessie in his arms, he could no longer deny last night had been a nightmare, literally. Not just the memory itself, but the thought that he could have hurt Jessie—he couldn't wrap his brain around that. How could he have let that happen? How could he have risked the one person—

"Stop it," Jessie mumbled, snuggling into Aidan's embrace.

He scowled and looked over Jessie's shoulder. How long had he been awake?

"Stop it."

Aidan leaned forward and pushed his nose into Jessie's hair. How could he have been so careless to put Jessie's life at risk like that? The one person who had kept him more steady than he had been since that time. The one person who…

Jessie shifted on the couch, turning himself around to face Aidan, his crystal blue eyes piercing into him with an odd mix of anger and affection. "I said, stop it. I can feel you kicking yourself."

Aidan looked away. "I could have hurt you."

"But you didn't. I know you wouldn't."

"You don't *know*. I wasn't in complete control." He rarely had flashbacks, and when they came, they were manageable—exhausting and sometimes startling but always manageable. But all bets were off with the nightmares. He refused to sleep with a gun under his pillow or anywhere within reach to avoid exactly this type of situation. And hitting the bottle to ease a memory and risk his defenses waning—a definite *hell no*. He refused to lose control and risk compromising his ability to distinguish the reality from a memory. Exactly why he took such effort in controlling the damn triggers, especially at night. In his mind, easy math. Reduced triggers equaled reduced memories. Why deal with a damn bed that would remind him of that shitty, hard, musty mattress where they'd tied him down sometimes? He always had the TV on at night for the steady light to avoid any déjà vu of being blindfolded and vulnerable. Fuck anyone who thought he was afraid of the dark. He'd much rather have the TV on at night to some stupid, annoying white noise than the worry of doing something to hurt someone he cared about.

Like last night.

If he hadn't snapped out of it and had hurt Jessie…no way could he have recovered from that. No. Fucking. Way.

"Damn, you're stubborn."

Aidan scowled. Stubborn or not, he had a solution. Distance. No way…

Jessie reached up and placed his hand at the side of Aidan's face, brushing his thumb along the stubble and completely cutting off Aidan's train of thought. "You want me to come to you when I need something. You want me to feel at home here and comfortable around you. But you need to do the same with me." He withdrew his hand then snaked his arm around Aidan's waist, resting his head against his chest. "You know how I feel, Aidan. At least…I think you do. You keep your heart locked away in a steel box within an iron wall with triple combination locks and a biometric security system. When you shut down, you are completely closed off. Don't shut me out. Please. I want there to be an *us*."

Aidan closed his eyes and sighed. *Us.* After all these months together, every day, the teasing, the smiles, the quiet times… He wanted nothing more than to be with Jessie, but he couldn't. Now he just needed to get his damn body to get with the program and unwrap his arms from around him. "It's probably easier if we keep things the way they are."

"Easier for who?"

He bit back the anger that began to simmer. *Dammit.* He hated doing the right thing. He wasn't fucking noble or a damn gentleman. He had a chance to be with Jessie. To have something more than just a friendship. Where waking up with him wrapped up around him was totally okay. But he…couldn't. "I can't give you what you want."

Jessie inched back and looked up into Aidan's eyes. "What is it…exactly…you *think* I want?"

Aidan exhaled a shuddered breath, holding back a frustrated yell. *This sucks. Wanting something so badly, having it right there, handed to you on a silver platter, but having to turn it away because you know that's the best thing to do to stay sane. Fuck. My. Life.*

"How about I tell you what *I* want so there's no misunderstanding."

Aidan shook his head and closed his eyes, pulling Jessie closer and pressing their foreheads together. He could barely breathe through the tightness in his throat. He held Jessie close, ignoring the screaming voice in his mind demanding he retreat.

"I want you," Jessie whispered, combing his fingers through Aidan's hair. "Any way I can have you, as long as it's the real you. Do you hear me? I want the *real* you. With all your soft and hard edges. With all your truths, regardless of how dark they may be."

"I'm sorry." Aidan swallowed heavily, unable to force another word past the knot in his throat and the twist in his gut from the war raging between his mind and body. He should back away, cut off this connection between them before it went too far. But his damn arms couldn't release the warmth and safety of the body pressed against him.

Jessie pulled away from the embrace and sat up on the couch. He ran his fingers through his hair to tame his bed-head then clasped his hands together between his legs, sitting quietly as if gathering his thoughts. His lean, tightly-muscled square shoulders slowly rose and fell with each deep breath.

"Do you remember what you told me when you went to my place after I was discharged from the hospital?" Jessie asked. He looked up, straight ahead toward the turned-off television as he spoke, meeting Aidan's gaze in the reflection of the dark glass screen. "You told me to stop apologizing. You said nothing was my fault. Do you remember that?"

Aidan nodded.

"It was your way of telling me to move forward. To not let what happened weigh on me."

Sometimes, Aidan wished his words were far less philosophical.

Jessie glanced over his shoulder at Aidan. "I'm asking you to do the same. Don't let the guilt or blame or whatever weigh you down. Whatever it is that happened that causes you to shut down like this, it does not define who you are. Don't you dare let whatever this monster is that's always hovering over you win the war." Jessie straightened and rubbed his hands on his thighs, taking a few deep breaths as if thinking carefully of his next words. "That day, you also told me I was here because you wanted me to be here and that you liked having me around. Do you remember that?"

"I remember everything."

Jessie turned his body and sat sideways to face him, a sudden determination sizzling in the air around them. "Good. Then you also remember you said you wouldn't apologize for that. Well, guess what? Neither am I. I *want* to be here, I *want* to be with you. But I can't be with you in here," he said, reaching out and resting his palm against Aidan's chest, "if you don't let me in."

Aidan pushed his head back into the pillow, slinging his arm over his face, covering his eyes. "I'm going to fuck this up." He paused and took a deep breath, puffing his cheeks out with an equally heavy exhale. "You ground me, Jess, and...I really need that." He quieted for a moment, trying to control the surge of emotions threatening to surface. "I know what it's like not having you around and I can't risk going there again."

"Well, here's the thing." Jessie ran his fingers along Aidan's stubble. "I feel as if I'm already losing you. And that's killing me."

Aidan took comfort in knowing his eyes were hidden with his forearm, not really sure what to say. The chirping of the alarm forced Aidan to sit up. He reached for the phone and stopped the repetitive chime, tossing the phone back on the table. Shit, he needed coffee. It was too rough of a night and too early in the morning for deep conversation without enough caffeine to erect his protective shield. He scrubbed his face with his hand then ran his fingers through his hair.

"You're like a dam, Aidan."

Okay, yeah, he definitely needed some coffee. *Pronto*.

"You're too busy guarding and protecting everything around you and you don't take the time to see you're slowly wearing away. You barely get through the day, guarding that water from hitting the town you love."

That's one way of putting it, he thought with a frown. Even he could understand that through his caffeine-deprived mind. "What's wrong with that?"

Jessie shook his head. "You don't realize…you're not guarding a stream, you're trying to hold back every body of water on the planet…at once. No one can do that on their own. But you're too stubborn to see that. You're so busy taking care of everyone else, who's going to take care of you? You're going to crack and I won't stand idly by and let that happen."

No one's ever wanted to take care of me. Aidan looked over to his reflection in the dark television screen and inwardly cringed at the visual train wreck. He ran his fingers through his hair and tugged his T-shirt to straighten it out. He didn't have the energy to fight Jessie when the man was this wound up and tenacious about something. "You don't give up, do you?"

"Not when it comes to you. No."

"Jess, I'm not easy. I have more baggage than the underbelly of a cargo plane."

"Then I'll set my bags right next to yours."

He shook his head. No one had ever been this relentless to be with his miserable ass.

"I've got one last question for you," Jessie said.

Aidan turned his head slightly toward him but refused to make eye contact.

"Do you…" Jessie hesitated and rubbed his hands on his thighs again, revealing a hint of that introverted, vulnerable side others usually saw when they looked at him. "Do you *want* to be with me?"

Point-blank. That was the million-dollar question that determined how this conversation would end. Even if he did have enough energy to erect his shield, he couldn't lie to Jessie. He exhaled heavily. "More than anything."

"Then that settles it."

"Jess…it's not that easy."

"Don't make it harder."

Aidan sighed. "I'm not used to this," he said, gesturing between them with his hand.

"Talking or having a relationship?"

"Either. Both. Fuck if I know."

"Okay. Well, you've never had a problem talking to me before, so we'll work up to the big stuff. One detail a week. I'm not going to stress you out with a one-a-day quota. One detail we wouldn't share with anyone else."

One a week. Aidan forcefully rubbed his hands together. He could handle that. Maybe. Sorta.

"And as far as the whole relationship thing, I'm not an expert. But, we kinda already have something. Don't you think?" Jessie looked over to him with a hint of a smile playing in his expression, cocking his head.

He definitely wasn't an expert in relationships, but if Jessie thought this defined a relationship, then maybe he could totally handle this.

Jessie bumped his shoulder. "We're just missing out on all the fun stuff."

Aidan groaned. It drove him nuts when Jessie teased him.

"I'm not saying it'll be easy. I know..." Jessie hesitated and rubbed his thighs again. "I know we're both very different from each other and from what other people usually see when they look at us. But...I see *you*, not the guy you want everyone else to see. And you're worth it, Aidan. It bothers me that you don't recognize how amazing you are, but I'm willing to give this a shot. I just...I hope you think the same of me." He quieted for a few moments then subtly nodded, concluding some internal conversation. "You work at things so you can appreciate the success at the end."

Aidan shook his head and scoffed. Jessie and his inspirational poster lines...too fucking cute to deny. His ability to take a mountain and turn it into a few pellets of dust always amazed Aidan. Jessie was bossier than people could imagine and far more of a control freak than anyone suspected.

"Jess."

"Yeah?"

"You're totally worth it."

A hint of a shy smile tugged at the corner of Jessie's mouth. "We'll make it work. Now stop with the guilt trip and give me a hug so you can get ready for work."

Aidan reached out and wrapped his arm around Jessie's waist, tugging him into an embrace. He held him close and rubbed his cheek against the smooth, dark hair. How the hell did Jessie wake up smelling this good and looking so damn polished? Aidan peeked back at the reflection in the television screen, amazed at how different they seemed. But somehow, so damn perfect.

"We'll make this work," Jessie repeated, running his hands up and down Aidan's back.

Aidan leaned into the embrace, closing his eyes and not letting the what-ifs ruin the moment. He wanted this—this closeness, this peace, this ability to surrender to everything else around him with Jessie's nearness. He didn't have a clue how to make this work, but he refused to burst Jessie's bubble or risk another inspirational poster speech. He could take a leap of faith and take things one step at a time.

Baby steps.

Jessie had a plan—he always did. If anyone could make this

work, Jessie would make it happen. Aidan pushed his nose into Jessie's hair, reveling in the comforting scent that always calmed him with Jessie's presence. His mouth parted as he breathed Jessie in, enjoying the sensation of the silky strands tickling his lips.

He remembered his solemn vow, to spare others of all his bullshit and to not subject them to the pain that always followed him like a dark dust cloud. A promise he had held sacred for years and swore he'd keep to his dying day. But there, holding Jessie in his arms with his defenses still broken from the night before, he realized this was one promise he could no longer keep.

* * * *

A crumbled ball of paper drew his attention as it bounced off the folder and hit him in the chest. He slowly looked up from the file, hoping his glare captured how peeved he was by Sunny's childish actions.

His partner gave him a lopsided grin. "If you hadn't zoned out, I wouldn't have had to resort to a primitive means of communication."

Aidan grabbed the paper ball and threw it right back at her, popping her in the forehead. "I wasn't zoned out."

"You so were."

He focused on the notes from his phone interview with a case lead. Definitely *not* thinking about waking up that morning with Jessie in his arms. *Nope. Not for a second.*

"You want to grab some lunch? We've got about forty minutes before we need to head out."

"Nah. I'll grab something from the street vendor in a bit. I want to wrap up my notes while it's still fresh in my head."

"'Kay." She grabbed her keys and headed out, finally giving Aidan some much needed space.

About ten minutes later, he finished the last of his notes then fished the business card out of his pocket. He flicked the edge of the card stock, debating if he should pick up the phone. Jessie didn't push, well, at least not directly. He had this slick way of setting up a situation that led to Aidan making the decision. He never really steered Aidan one way or another, but he seemed to lay out the options then he'd sit back and wait. And he'd *so* fallen for it that morning. *I'm such a sucker.*

He had arrived at the kitchen, ready to head out to work, greeted with a fresh cup of coffee and a still-warm, buttered croissant.

"Thanks," he said to Jessie, who sat quietly at the table already working on his laptop.

Sipping his coffee, Aidan stared at the business card clipped with a magnet to the refrigerator. *Dr. Kathryn Engel.*

"Is this the therapist the hospital recommended?"

Jessie shook his head. "The first time I met her, I was a teenager and she was volunteering at some free clinic. I couldn't really talk to the person the hospital recommended, but I needed to talk to someone about what happened so I tracked her down and found she had a private practice. She actually remembered me. She would stop by the hospital to see me or we'd talk on the phone."

"I don't remember meeting her."

Jessie looked over at him with a soft smile. "She'd schedule her visits with me while you were in your Monday morning team meetings or she'd talk to me over the phone for a while."

Aidan nodded and took the last bite of his croissant. He washed it down with the rest of his coffee as he stared at the off-white business card with a few lines of text. "So I guess she didn't make you sit on a couch and shit."

"Nope," Jessie said, popping the "p" with his mouth as he continued to tap away at his laptop. "She's easy to talk to. She's tough if you want her to be and sensitive when needed."

Aidan nodded again. Funny how the card had miraculously appeared on the fridge *that* morning. *Yeah...right.* Jessie's way of dropping a hint without pushing. The card was there; what Aidan chose to do with it was up to him.

"I'm leaving. Let me know if you want me to pick something up for dinner." He rinsed his cup in the sink and grabbed the card before heading out the door. He definitely didn't miss the hidden smile Jessie gave him before he left.

Now, sitting at his desk, he debated picking up the damn phone. He took a deep breath and sighed heavily. He wanted nothing more than to be with Jessie, and after what had happened the night before, he needed help working through his shit. He couldn't take the chance again.

"Fuck it," he muttered, picking up his cell phone and dialing the number from the card. A few minutes later, he'd officially secured his first ever appointment with a shrink. Therapist. Exorcist. Whatever.

Too many unknowns but one screaming certainty...he couldn't do this alone. He'd already tried that and had failed miserably. Even though Jessie said they'd find a way to make it work, he had too much shit that screwed with his head. Maybe this Doc Engel could actually help. Who knew for sure?

But he had to try.

Chapter FOURTEEN

Aidan leaned against the tall window on the twentieth floor of Dr. Kathryn Engel's office, switching his focus between the slow moving clouds in the early evening sky and the traveling ants of people on the street. Almost an hour into the appointment and total talk time could be clocked at about five minutes—assuming there was a rollover term in that calculation. His second visit to the good doctor and he hadn't uttered a word since his arrival.

First visit went about the same. Outside of an introduction and a few random basic questions...*nada*. When he mentioned Jessie had referred him, Dr. Engel lit up with a huge smile and simply said, "He's wonderful." Yeah, she scored major brownie points right away with that one response and motivated his return for a second visit. Maybe he'd have one of those eureka moments and some therapeutic enlightenment would kick him in the ass. He had to make an effort. Even his captain added an *about-fucking-time* when he'd mentioned setting an appointment with a therapist. If he was going to do this, he was going to try to do it right. He refused to do anything half-assed.

Now he just needed to find a way to actually talk about what had happened and the shit-ton of crap that caused this self-imposed barrier between him and everyone else.

He glanced over his shoulder and watched the doctor update a file. She was about five feet tall and wore standard-issue red pumps that propped her up a few more inches. If he had to guess, he figured she could pass for someone in her late-forties, but he knew enough about age progression and traits to know she must have been close to reaching sixty, if not a few years more. The meticulous manicure in a matching red tone and her short, expertly-dyed hair spoke of someone who took the time to welcome the world with polish.

He shifted his focus back to the clouds and the reds and oranges painting the sky. He'd initially tried to come up with an escape plan. He'd even asked the doctor of the ethics of her having sessions with both him and Jessie. She claimed that as long as neither of them had issues with it then she didn't either since she would not speak a word about any of their discussions.

He'd flat out told the doc he couldn't discuss details of his mission during their first appointment, thinking that would nip this whole thing in the bud quickly. No dice. She seemed to have a talent for sniffing out bullshit. "I don't need to know locations or exact dates. Just time frames as a point of reference. How long ago it happened and for what span of time. Then we'll go from there."

But he didn't know where the hell to start. So he'd opted for silence.

"Time's up," Dr. Engel said.

His vision snapped back to the doctor. She walked over to her desk and looked up with a half smile as she opened her appointment book. "How about I schedule you for Friday late afternoon. How does six sound?"

He nodded, wondering when he would tire of paying someone to keep him company while he remained silent. But he was here. That should count for something. Even if it was only a baby step.

* * * *

They sat on the couch watching a late evening movie they'd already seen months ago while at the hospital. But Jessie didn't care one iota about what played on the television screen. The slow brush of fingers twisting in the short hair at the nape of his neck caught his attention far more than any TV movie. He closed his eyes and leaned back into Aidan's fingers, hoping the subtle, casual caress would become more determined.

"Sorry about that," Aidan said, withdrawing his hand and crossing his arms, focusing his attention on the movie.

Jessie groaned with the frustration thrumming through his body. Every attempt at some contact, Aidan had somehow interpreted as *stop* instead of *more*. Hinting didn't seem to work. He was trying with every ounce of energy to not push, to give Aidan the space he obviously demanded, but dammit, he couldn't take this anymore. "I didn't want you to stop."

"I thought you meant—"

Jessie abruptly turned to face him. "Kiss me."

"Um, that was subtle."

"You're obviously not picking up on the subtleties. So I'm testing a direct approach."

Aidan hid a smile he couldn't disguise in his eyes. He anchored his elbow on the back of the couch and rested his head against his palm. "I think most people would assume I'm the direct one in this relationship."

"I'm happy to play whatever role you want." Jessie reached out and ran a finger along Aidan's sleep pants. Weren't hot, studly guys supposed to be walking around naked at home, or shirtless, or…anything other than dressed with sleep pants and a T-shirt? "By the way…"

"Yeah?"

"I love that you said relationship."

Aidan scoffed, shaking his head with a smile. "You're persistent."

"When it comes to you, yes, I am. And I'm very proud of it. I get to see a special side of you that no one else sees. And it's addictive. So kiss me."

"No."

"Don't make it weird. Just kiss me."

"Not…yet." Aidan returned his focus to the television.

"Yet?"

Aidan shrugged. "You're very bossy."

"Someone has to be."

"Where the hell did the shy, quiet Jessie go?" Aidan's jaw muscles twitched, but his focus remained squarely planted on the television screen, captivated by some stupid commercial with a dog chasing after some animated dot.

"He's still here. He's just decided there are things that are really important in life worth pursuing with determination."

Aidan glanced over to him.

Jessie's lips parted on a breath as a current rippled through his body. He'd never had anyone look at him with that much desire.

"Do you know why I like you?" Jessie asked.

"Because you have masochistic tendencies?"

Jessie bit his lip to hide a smile. *Ah, he's frustrated.* Jessie had learned to decipher most of Aidan's moods, but he still needed a cheat sheet for clarification on a few of them. Aidan's sarcasm and verbal bites were especially heightened when pissed off about what people *expected* him to say, or when he really wanted to change or lighten the subject matter.

"One of the reasons is the way you look at me. It's as if nothing else exists but me and there's no other place you'd rather be." Jessie circled his fingers in a random pattern on Aidan's thigh, hoping to distract him from the television enough to draw his full attention. "Even when you're just standing there, and you're doing nothing but staring at me, it's as if you have your arm wrapped around me and pull me close to your side. You make me feel good about myself. You make me feel needed." He reached out and grabbed Aidan's hand, lacing their fingers together. He looked at Aidan's strong hand and tanned skin, a stark contrast from his lean, long fingers and fair skin. "You make me feel wanted and special. As if I matter." He returned his focus to Aidan's face. "You let me know I'm important to you."

"I do all that with a look?"

Jessie nodded. "You let me be me…and you let me know that's okay. You don't tell me I'm weak or—"

"You're one of the strongest men I know."

Jessie quietly laughed. Sometimes, Aidan said the most thoughtful and romantic things and didn't have a clue how they squeezed Jessie's heart.

Aidan turned away and lowered his brow. "I thought I had to say all that, I didn't think...I didn't think you'd know all that just by the way I looked at you." He turned back to meet Jessie's gaze. "It's not easy for me to say what I'm feeling."

"I know." Jessie nodded to himself. "You keep it all inside. You say a lot by the way you look at me, even if you don't say the words. But I know that when you do say something, when you do open up, it means so much more than when someone else says it. Because I know it comes from your soul."

"I wish I could be more open. Like the way you are." He smiled weakly. "I'm trying."

"I know. But I'm totally fine with you eye fucking me from across the room." Jessie laughed. "Now kiss me."

"Oh my God." Aidan threw his head back against the couch, smiling in obvious amusement.

"Fine, *later* then. Don't be mad. But I called my doctor today to ask her a question."

Aidan slowly turned his head toward him. "Okay," he said, enunciating each letter of the small word.

"I want to sleep with you—"

"You should buy me a drink or something first."

Jessie shoved him. "I meant *sleep*. That night we slept together on the couch, I slept the whole night through and...I liked being here with you."

Aidan quieted and subtly nodded. "Me too. But...you were worried?"

"I just wanted to make sure I wouldn't put you in a position that would be a problem for you. So I told her what happened."

"And?"

A smiled tugged at the corner of Jessie's mouth, happy to hear the intrusion of privacy hadn't been an issue. "She said it was the unexpected element that may have triggered your reaction."

Aidan straightened into a sitting position. "*May* have?"

"She said every case is different, but that was usually the reaction when the mind was hyper-aware of everything and something changed. She said it's what she typically sees in PTSD cases."

Aidan's body tensed and he released their clasped hands. "I don't doubt I have some lingering stuff to deal with but I'd never—"

Jessie quieted him with a comforting hand on his arm. "I know. And that's why I asked her about what happened. I knew you'd still be torturing yourself about it."

Aidan visibly cringed.

Something raced through Aidan's mind that alerted every nerve in Jessie's body to ease him. Jessie stroked Aidan's arm, hoping to smooth the crease between his brows. "So if we go to bed together, it should be fine. It's just not smart to startle you or sneak up on you."

"Here," Aidan said abruptly. "Not...not the bed."

"Okay," Jessie said slowly, making note of Aidan's tension and hesitation. "But only if—"

"I want to," Aidan said quickly, cutting off Jessie. "If...if I do anything... Fuck, I can't believe I'm going to say this..." He ran his fingers through his hair and exhaled heavily then pinched the bridge of his nose. "Knee me in the balls if I do anything."

A bubble of laughter escaped Jessie.

"I'm glad you find that funny."

"I promise to knee you if you do anything, then ice and stroke your balls until they're healed."

"You have a serious ball obsession." Aidan shook his head and hid a smile. "Was it Dr. Engel you spoke to?"

Jessie nodded.

Aidan rubbed his thighs repeatedly, fidgeting. "I've been seeing her. Not sure how it'll go, but...yeah, I'm trying." He looked over to Jessie with a pleading expression that speared Jessie's heart. Sometimes, even with all of Aidan's bluster and Aidanisms, a vulnerability managed to peek through his armor. Jessie wanted to be with Aidan in every way, to be the one person who knew all his hiding places, regardless of how dark they were.

"Show some mercy. Kiss me already," Jessie said, barely able to coherently assemble his thoughts.

"Later."

"You're killing me."

"Then stop mentioning it. If you keep hyping it up, you'll end up being disappointed. It's like waiting for that movie premier that's been showcasing trailers for six months, then the movie sucks because you were expecting a hell of a lot more out of it. When you don't expect it, it's usually…better," he finished with a shrug.

"You're stubborn."

"I prefer to think I'm incredibly determined."

"Nope, it's stubbornness. Kiss me."

"Later." Aidan raised an eyebrow. "We can do this all night."

"Watch the movie," Jessie grumbled, turning to face the TV again. He crossed his arms and leaned back. He couldn't deny Aidan made an effort to open up. Unfortunately, a glaring certainty lingered alongside that realization. Regardless of how patient Jessie could be, he was no match for the "determined," teasing side of Aidan who loved to win.

* * * *

Jessie tried to bury his head farther into the pillow to block the glow and flicker from the annoying, low-volume television. How the hell did Aidan get any sleep with that thing on? He turned around on the couch and met with Aidan's very-awake hazel stare. "You're awake?"

"Hard to sleep when you keep moving around so much."

Jessie shifted again on the couch, finally stilling when Aidan's hand rested on his waist. "I didn't mean to wake you. Maybe this wasn't such a good idea. I should go to bed and let you—"

All words and thoughts evaporated when Aidan's soft, full lips pressed against his. Jessie closed his eyes and inhaled sharply. He reached up and clasped the back of Aidan's neck, holding him close, not letting him escape from the gentle press of lips.

Aidan inched back slightly, just enough to break the kiss but still close enough for each strangled, controlled exhale to blow across Jessie's skin.

"Please don't leave."

Jessie slowly opened his eyes, trying to keep the simmering need from boiling over. The light from the television flickered in Aidan's eyes, revealing the uncertainty hidden in their depths. With one hand still anchored on Jessie's waist, Aidan spread his other hand across Jessie's narrow back, caging him in an embrace as they lay on the couch, staring at each other.

"Stay," Aidan repeated in a whisper Jessie would have missed had he not been mere inches away from him.

Jessie couldn't focus on a single thought, conscious only of the buzzing current and how his skin tingled under Aidan's fingertips at each contact point against his body. The beating of his heart drummed in his head, drowning out all sound except the hiss of each breath and the pounding in his ears. His focus shifted from Aidan's eyes to his full, waiting lips. Those lips. He wanted and needed those lips on him again.

Aidan leaned forward, fusing their mouths together in another kiss, slowly extracting a whimper from Jessie when his tongue outlined the seam of Jessie's mouth in a swipe that was both hesitant and tender.

Jessie parted his lips on a strangled groan, welcoming Aidan to explore, craving the slide of each intimate caress. He dug his fingers into Aidan's back, drawing him closer, begging for the warmth and weight against him to settle the storm of need brewing within. Rough fingertips ghosted over Jessie's cheek then traveled down his neck, along his shoulders then down to his waist, never breaking contact with the slow-building, mind-numbing kiss. The touch was both reverent and filled with tenderness, each graze and brush slow, as if memorizing the shape of Jessie's frame and the quiver of each muscle.

A line of fire spread across Jessie's skin and a surge of emotion tightened his chest—no one had ever touched him that way. He angled his head to bind their mouths tighter, holding Aidan in place while his heart pounded wildly, reveling in the intimacy he had craved for far too long with the one man he wanted more with each passing day. The always-present lingering want in the air was no match for the tangible need thrumming between them. He gripped Aidan's hair, clutching his fingers at the back of Aidan's scalp, refusing to let a millimeter of distance sneak into their private space. Aidan groaned into the kiss and huddled closer, digging his fingers into the cheeks of Jessie's backside, pulling him flush against his body.

Aidan broke the kiss and lazily brushed his nose and stubble against Jessie's cheek. Jessie reached up and placed his trembling palm at the side of Aidan's face, hoping to strengthen the tether of intimacy binding them in that moment. Aidan's kiss-swollen lips parted on a breath with the gentle caress. He then wrapped his fingers around Jessie's wrist, turning his face to pepper a slow trail of kisses down Jessie's palm and along the surgical scar inside Jessie's pale wrist. Aidan glanced back at him, his expression more vulnerable and open than Jessie thought possible.

And full of unmistakable love.

He twisted the fabric of Aidan's shirt in his hand, trying to ground himself. "I've waited almost two years for that."

"I've waited a lifetime."

Jessie closed his eyes as his throat tightened with emotion. He pulled Aidan closer and pressed his trembling lips against Aidan's in a slow but quick, gentle kiss.

"Stay. Please."

Jessie nodded in response, unable to speak past the knot in his throat or the overflowing emotions blurring his vision.

Aidan pulled him closer and held him snugly in an embrace. "Good night, Jess," he whispered, then buried his face at the side of Jessie's hair, eliminating any sliver of distance between them.

As Jessie lay in the one place he wanted most, trying to settle his fast-beating heart, he realized no amount of teasing, hype, or fantasy could have prepared him for finally walking through the threshold of the iron gate of Aidan's defenses. In that moment, he confirmed what he had suspected all along—he felt safe, loved, and revered inside the iron fortress and would do anything to fiercely safeguard the tender heart that had been so carefully revealed to him.

Chapter FIFTEEN

Aidan needed somewhere quiet to zone out and focus on the dozen different cases swirling in his mind, demanding his attention. He'd taken on a heavier caseload than his teammates to offset some of their time spent on Jessie's case. It was the least he could do to help since he couldn't actively work the case.

He peeked into the conference room and Travis and Sunny quieted mid-sentence. Wall extended his arm, pointing a finger at him and—in not so many words—compelled him to get the hell out of the room.

Aidan took a deep breath. He'd learned that tell weeks ago. It meant they had a supposed lead in Jessie's case but refused to let him in on it to avoid getting his hopes up. After a few letdowns early on and his reaction to the disappointment, he certainly wasn't going to argue.

He shut the door and sighed, deciding to head over to the task force file room. The relatively new team hadn't had enough time to accumulate a full room of case files, so there had to be some space available there for him to work. He turned the corner and stalked down the narrow hallway, finally arriving at the file room.

The *non-empty* file room where Manny stood with crossed arms, staring at a huge map of Florida with a series of colored circles— almost all with red Xs—and several photos of missing children pinned in the margin.

"What's this?"

Manny spun on his heel, obviously startled by the interruption. "You're not supposed to be here."

"I was looking for an empty room."

"This room's not empty."

"Your brilliance is awe-inspiring. What is this?"

Manny quieted, as if debating a thought. "I shouldn't tell you, but screw it. I'm working a different angle."

"I thought you were looking into runaways and other cases?"

Manny crossed his arms and frowned. "We had narrowed down a list of missing persons who seemed to be runaways fitting Vega's same characteristics and situation between then and now for that same area. But we haven't found a connection or lead from that angle or from reviewing any unsolved cases where the victim had been held in similar living conditions."

A shiver traveled Aidan's body as he looked at each teenager's face staring back at him from the photographs pinned to the board. He didn't want to dwell on what Jessie lived through during that time in his life, the hardship, or the loneliness.

"Since none of that panned out, I'm looking for a pattern. I've already checked out all the neighboring businesses that would coincide with the drive time Vega mentioned the asshole would take to come home." He pointed to the various markers on the map. "I've also checked local banks and gas stations, trying to find out if any of them kept any sort of documentation or log back then we could reference, or find someone who could remember a local matching the description. Something. Anything."

"That's a Hail Mary."

"Yeah. But we're running out of options to keep the case current," Manny said, tightening his lips for a moment as a thought seemed to cross his mind. "I know that's not what you want to hear, but—"

"But you can't pursue a lead that's not there," he said, parroting the words his captain always repeated when his inability to let go of a case suffocated him. He glanced up at the map, thinking over Manny's plan. "People forget or sometimes don't realize they know some important detail. How viable is the hunt?"

"Seems I poked around enough to get some attention. I got a call from a man who owns a small grocery store. He actually kept surveillance footage from prior years. Literally, the guy has years' worth of footage from different angles, transferred from VHS onto DVD stored in a home library."

Aidan crossed his arms and frowned. "Why would he keep a library of old surveillance footage?"

"It's nothing nefarious. His son was diagnosed with Asperger syndrome years ago. One day he noticed his son watching the surveillance monitor in the backroom of the shop, replaying the footage at different speeds...over and over. It seemed to calm him. Every day, he'd take another tape home and his son would catalogue them in a notebook. He'd label and tag them by date, camera angle, he'd even log a count of how many people passed that camera angle for that specific day. He managed to build up a full library of videos over the years."

Manny crossed his arms and quieted, lost in thought for a moment before he resumed speaking. He walked over to the small side table and gently placed his hand on top of a stack of aged notebooks, seemingly careful with the worn surface as if they were sacred. "His son let us borrow a few of his notes as long as we promised to return them intact, by a particular date and time. And in order," he finished with a hint of a soft smile.

Aidan planted his hands on his hips and exhaled a deep breath. "It's got to be a shit-ton of stuff to review."

"I've already got people on it. We're filtering out customers with repeat appearances. The store is on the list Vega provided of logos and names he remembered while in the house. So this asshole must have visited that shop a few times, and maybe, if we're lucky, actually did all his grocery shopping there to give us enough visual references. We can show screen shots to Jessie to identify once we've narrowed it down a bit."

Aidan quieted. "How much time did this take?" Hours, days, hell, he imagined it had taken weeks to accumulate all this information.

"Doesn't matter. It had to be done."

"Bullshit. It matters."

Manny raised a stopping hand. "I wouldn't be here right now if it hadn't been for you saving my ass." He met Aidan's gaze, quieting for a moment before he continued. "You nailed a shot most people wouldn't even bother to attempt. Some would think damn near impossible considering the time of day and conditions. But I'm guessing you didn't even hesitate before firing. So step back and let me do this. I'm good at these types of cases. You're good at shooting."

"And interrogating assholes."

Manny pursed his lips. "Fine, yes. I admit it. And interrogating assholes," he said with an eye roll.

Aidan inwardly smiled. "Give me a stack of notebooks. I'll go through them."

"I've already been going through them and I have a few analysts working on them as well. I've got the rest of the team working on a few outstanding details."

"So give me a stack and we'll speed it along."

Manny hesitated.

"What?"

Manny's lips thinned. "I was given strict order to keep you in the field. You're not even supposed to know about this, especially *if* there's a chance we might get a hit here. I can't risk it. This case is too close to home for you."

Aidan raked a hand through his hair. If there was a chance to end this nightmare for Jessie, he needed to help. He hated feeling helpless at the hands of this fucking monster. He didn't want to explore the different possibilities of what all this was doing to Jessie if he, himself, couldn't keep his cool in the midst of this storm. "If there's anything…I mean anything I can do. I don't care if you think it's menial work—"

"You don't even need to say it." Manny gave him a knowing look. The team chattered about the what-ifs of his relationship with Jessie, but at least they didn't ask or joke about it. Even the occasional homophobic jab from Manny had ceased—as if a silent truce had been made that night in the alley. He was still a hard-ass where Aidan and the other team members were concerned, but Aidan imagined that wouldn't change and could be attributed to heading up the team of hard-headed detectives who usually jumped first then asked questions. "Now I need you to get out of here and focus on all those other cases so we can work on this one."

Aidan refused to argue, especially with the one man who seemed to have uncovered a microscopic speck of hope in a field of darkness.

Son of a bitch Detective Reyes. He was starting to like the fucker.

* * * *

Aidan shut the door behind him, closing his eyes with a heavy exhale as the tension slowly evaporated from his body. He loved getting home. Correction…coming home to Jessie, especially after a long day. He threw his keys and wallet on the table by the door and shrugged out of his sport coat, walking over to the dining room area to drape his jacket on one of the chairs. He turned toward the living room and spotted the new floor lamp tucked in the corner. Simple, stylish, and refined. Just like Jessie.

A smile tugged at his lips. Details… Jess was all about the smallest of details. Over the last couple of months, Jessie had managed to add a small sprinkle of items throughout the house to make it feel more like a home—a picture frame here and there, a plant, a simple decorative sculpture.

In the back of Aidan's mind, he figured the lamp was Jessie's solution to the television white noise he found annoying but refused to complain about. He never delivered a complaint, only alternatives. If having a lamp on in lieu of the television white noise meant keeping Jessie in his arms through the night…done. Lamp could stay.

He had hoped his earlier text to alert Jessie he wouldn't be late would allow for a chilled out night of vegging out on the couch. "Jess, I'm home."

"Hey!" Jessie responded, his voice traveling from his bedroom. "Be right there."

Aidan withdrew his firearm and shoulder holster and set them on the dining room table. He twisted his neck from side to side until he heard the relaxing pop, then glanced up into the dark kitchen. He sharply turned and stilled when Jessie emerged from the hallway wearing a sharp, fitted, dark blue pinstripe suit and baby blue shirt with dark sapphire tie. The mix of blues against his fair skin and dark hair only served to accent his already alluring crystal blue eyes.

Aidan swallowed heavily, his now-hardened dick pushed against the zipper of his jeans. Jessie was dressed up and ready at this time of night. For what?

Shit.

Jessie greeted him with a wide smile. "How was work?"

Aidan shrugged, unable to swallow or respond past the knot in his throat. No sense trying to sound enthusiastic. He'd taken too damn long to make the first move. Or was it second? It had been about two weeks since that kiss on the couch, *hell*, he could count down to the number of hours and minutes with the memory so deeply etched into his brain. He should have done something. Should have made a move by now. He'd promised to try and all he'd done was sit on his ass and argue with himself and come up with a zillion different ways this whole *us* thing could fail.

He'd obviously blown his chance and Jessie now looked elsewhere.

Jessie cocked his head, his eyes narrowing, scrutinizing Aidan's features. "You're really quiet. What's on your mind?"

Aidan shrugged again, not really sure what the hell to say. He had no claim on Jessie. If he wanted to go out on a date, Aidan couldn't stop him. He cleared his throat before attempting to speak. "You look…nice."

"Thank you," Jessie said, raising an eyebrow. "But that's not what was on your mind."

Aidan looked away, clasping his hands behind his back. He pivoted back and forth on the balls of his feet, trying to think of something nice. "New lamp?"

"Yeah. I figured it was worth a try to see if it worked instead of the TV at night. It's got a backup battery inside that charges while it's connected. So it'll work even if there's an outage."

Aidan pursed his lips and nodded. *Details.*

"So why don't you tell me what's really on your mind?"

Aidan returned his focus to Jessie. Damn, he looked good in that damn suit, which brought him right back to the thought that had pissed him off. "You look like you've got a hot date." *And it's not with me.* There, he'd said it, sort of. He'd voiced the words in his head…and it stung to think of it.

"Hopefully. I guess we'll see how it turns out. Did you remember to grab something to eat?"

The doorbell chimed, sparing Aidan a need for a reply when Jessie stepped away to answer it. No, he hadn't remembered to grab something to eat for himself. All he could think about was getting home to Jess and being with him. He clenched his fist, internally cursing himself and biting back the anger that began to simmer. He wanted to twist the head off whatever smiling asshole was on the other side of that door to take Jess away from him. He turned when Jessie opened the door and spoke.

"Here you go. Thanks!"

Aidan's brow furrowed at the delivery man. Pizza? What the hell? He wasn't completely useless and could figure something out if Jessie went out on a damn date. Or…fuck it all to hell. No way would some guy come over to *their* house and—

Jessie walked over to him. "I can actually see the wheels viciously turning in your head. I think smoke's going to start coming out of your ears if you're not careful."

"I thought you had a date," he said, not even bothering to hide the bitterness in his voice. He couldn't protest, but that didn't mean he had to like it.

Jessie smiled and held up the pizza box between them. "I do. So I suggest you get your ass in the shower and get ready. Because dinner's here and I've got a movie already picked out."

Aidan blinked.

Jessie set the pizza box on the breakfast bar countertop. He reached up, cupping Aidan's face and placed a gentle kiss on his lips. "You, my wonderfully frustrating, incredibly hot man, are very stubborn. Just in case you haven't figured it out, the date is with you. The pizza has extra cheese and bacon…exactly the way you like it. And the movie is an action flick with tons of shit blowing up to get you excited."

"What about what you want?"

A slow smile spread across Jessie's features. "I want you. So get your ass in the shower already. You're cutting into our date time."

Aidan grabbed Jessie's face and smashed their mouths together for a short but heated kiss, hoping to convey a mix of relief and want. He stepped away and headed to his room, unbuttoning his shirt along the way.

"Aidan?"

He poked his head back out into the hallway, waiting for Jessie to continue.

"Can you skip the shave? I like the stubble."

Aidan nodded in acknowledgment and raced to the shower, leaving a trail of clothes in his wake.

* * * *

Jessie reached for the remote and switched off the movie as the final credits rolled. Aidan had eased into the night and had been quiet over dinner and for the better part of the movie. But he couldn't seem to take his eyes off Jessie, either with a direct stare or sneaking in a sideways glance.

Jessie made a mental note: wear more suits at home.

He straightened his rolled up sleeves and stretched his arm across the back of the couch, shifting to face Aidan. "I've been meaning to ask you something." Jessie obviously needed to take the lead and start some conversation or spend the next few weeks craving another kiss like that night on the couch.

"Yeah?"

"Do you mind if I watch some old home videos of yours?"

"No, I don't mind."

"Thanks." Jessie worried his lip, trying to find the best way to steer the topic into something personal. "Tell me something about yourself."

Aidan leaned back against the opposite side, resting his elbow on the back of the couch with his head in his hand. "I have hazel eyes."

Jessie didn't miss the slight quirk of Aidan's lips as he spoke. "Tell me something most people don't know."

Aidan looked upward as if trying to pluck a random fact. "I'm a polyglot. I can understand a dozen languages and I'm fluent in seven of them."

Jessie pursed his lips and cocked his head. "Interesting. Does that include sarcasm?"

"No. Make that eight." A playfulness passed over Aidan's features as he spoke.

"Smartass. I meant something personal," Jessie said, reaching for Aidan's hand. "I'm being serious."

"I thought it was one detail a week?"

Loopholes. Always looking for a damn loophole. He squeezed their clasped hands. "Aidan?"

Aidan quieted.

"You know I don't like to push," Jessie said, rubbing his thumb along Aidan's hand.

"You actually don't seem to have a problem being Mr. Bossy or taking the lead."

Jessie bit his lip. *And you don't seem to mind.* "I'll tease you, but I won't ever push you about the really personal stuff."

Aidan looked away then down at their joined hands, turning his body on the couch to face Jessie. "So, what do you want to know?"

"Anything you want to tell me."

"That doesn't help." Aidan chewed his lip then looked up. "Give me a starting point I can work with."

"Okay." Jessie scooted over on the couch, inching a little closer to Aidan, stopping when their knees bumped together. "Tell me about your tattoo. When did you get it?"

"After my last mission."

Jessie nodded. Give or take six years ago from what he knew. "Tell me why you got an angel. Considering you gave me the glass figurine, I know angels are important to you."

"My mom believed in angels. She believed people who died young had a special role as angels. More powerful in that life and in that role than this world could offer." Aidan quieted, as if his mind had wandered to some distant thought. "She believed they were guardians who protected and watched over us, to keep us safe and give us strength. I think that was her way of rationalizing why young people died."

Jessie touched Aidan's arm, hoping to transport him back to the here and now, not really sure if Aidan's mind had wandered to a dark place.

"Sorry. I zoned out."

"Don't apologize. Is the angel supposed to be your mom?"

Aidan shook his head. "I…had this done before my parents died. This is my guardian angel. I imagine she's tough, snarky, and wouldn't put up with any of my shit."

"So she's a female version of you."

"I hope I'm a fraction of what she is in my mind." He quieted again and his brows knit together. He reached out and ghosted his fingers over Jessie's arm as if needing the contact. "After I left the service, I was numb. I needed to disconnect from things that had happened but…I think I got too good at it. I…couldn't feel anything and didn't really want to. I questioned everything. I should have been thankful I was out of there and back home. But…I felt nothing. And that freaked me out a bit. That's when I did this."

"I bet it hurt." Jessie reached out and ran his fingers through Aidan's hair, knowing the rhythmic stroking usually eased him. It was blatantly obvious there was so much Aidan wasn't saying.

"Hurt like hell," Aidan said with a chuckle. "Definitely wasn't numb during those endless hours while I was getting it done. I think the artist was a bit of a sadist though. He'd work on it full days at a time."

Jessie softly smiled, reaching over and pulling up the edge of Aidan's shirt. "This looks different than what I'm used to seeing."

Aidan yanked the shirt up and over his head, stretching his torso, offering Jessie a better view. "Yeah. It's a black and gray style. It's mainly ink and shadows rather than harsh lines. I like it because it looks different, like a painting or pencil sketch…if that makes sense."

"And the message, 'what doesn't kill you makes you stronger'…I thought it was to remind you of your strength." Jessie grazed his fingertips along the edge of the inked scroll at the side of Aidan's torso. "I thought that was why you had done this. To see the message staring back at you in your reflection. To never give up."

"It's a phrase my mom said to me once when I was a kid. I didn't understand what she meant at the time, but I always remembered it and later realized its meaning." Aidan quieted again. "Anyways, I figured it would be something my angel would yell at me if she were at my side."

"How many people have seen it?"

"Counting you and the nurse's sneak peek while you were in the hospital?"

Jessie nodded.

"Four."

Aidan was all about the unspoken words and finding the clever ins and outs of things. "Are you counting you and the artist in that number?"

The edges of Aidan's mouth curled up into a lopsided grin. "Yes."

Emotions swelled in Jessie's chest. And he wasn't going to lie to himself, he was a bit past pissed the nurse was on the short list of people who had gotten a peek at Aidan's ink.

"I didn't do this to show it off. I'm not a peacock."

Jessie chuckled, remembering a prior conversation. "I've been told we're turtles."

"I bet I know who came up with that little nugget of wisdom," Aidan said with a hint of a grumble and a whole lot of sneer.

Jessie quietly laughed, leaning in, nuzzling the side of Aidan's neck, tracing his fingers along the ink on Aidan's skin.

Aidan sighed, reaching up and placing his hand on Jessie's back. "No one's…ever touched me like that."

Jessie kissed the corded muscle of Aidan's neck and up farther, biting the stubble of Aidan's jaw when the words finally registered in his lust-filled mind. He inched back slowly, watching every flicker of emotion pass over Aidan's face. "Ever?"

"I'm not a virgin. Far from it." Aidan's brow lowered and his jaw muscles twitched, clearly frustrated, maybe upset, but most definitely stuck somewhere in his *should-I-or-shouldn't-I-talk* headspace.

That small, pulsating vein at his temple threatened to burst with his growing frustration.

"I think we're good on the talking thing for one night," Jessie said, hoping to avoid his retreat.

Relief washed over Aidan's features. He nodded and exhaled deeply, pulling Jessie closer, flush against his still bare torso.

"Wait a second." Jessie pushed off Aidan and out of his hold, biting his lip to hide a smile at Aidan's frown. He unbuttoned his dress shirt and pitched it to the side chair, lying back down and sighing with the skin-on-skin contact. "That's better."

Strong arms caged him in an embrace and a stubbled jaw brushed against the side of his hair. "Yeah."

He closed his eyes, enjoying the gentle caress of fingers against his skin and the warmth of the embrace as sleep slowly took over.

Chapter
SIXTEEN

Jessie couldn't think straight. He closed his eyes and took a deep breath, hoping to calm the vibrating sexual tension pulsating through his body. The nearness of sitting with Aidan on the couch for another lazy weeknight, watching television in their usual routine, drove him to shake with the need for intimacy. He wanted Aidan's mouth on him again. And he didn't care where exactly said mouth landed. Those soft yet hard lips, the demanding yet gentle press of them, asking while commanding an invitation to explore.

His frustration had reached epic levels.

He wanted a hell of a lot more than a quickie kiss he'd manage to steal when Aidan had his guard down. But, for some reason, Aidan always pulled away and the iron wall came crashing down before they could take it further.

He wanted *his* Aidan, the one hidden behind that iron barrier, the one who'd turn in his sleep and wrap his arm around Jessie, pulling him snugly against his sleeping body.

The small things Aidan did meant the most, when he didn't over-think or worry about how the world interpreted his actions. He acted as if he didn't care, but in truth, he probably cared more than most.

Jessie looked over to the frustratingly beautiful man at his side, sitting with arms crossed on the couch and his bare feet propped up on the coffee table. A smile tugged at the corner of Jessie's mouth at the stark dichotomy between the usually tense Aidan Calloway and this version who seemed to capture a picture-perfect definition of peacefulness with his closed eyes, resting his head against the top backrest of the couch.

"Aidan?"

"Mmm."

"I'm going to kiss you," he announced, not wanting to incorporate the element of surprise into the mix and risk an instinctive reaction. The moment Aidan's eyes opened, Jessie swung his leg over him, straddling him. He leaned over Aidan, taking advantage of the dip in the couch and his position.

Aidan uncrossed his arms, moving his hands to grab Jessie's waist in a tight grip.

Jessie pressed his body—not so subtly—against Aidan, biting his lip to hold back a moan when his body met with equal hardness. Aidan quickly looked away, swallowing heavily, as if embarrassed by his noticeable eagerness. He kept his vision pegged on some spot on the wall to the right while his Adam's apple bobbed.

"Please…don't turn away." Jessie reached out with one hand and firmly gripped Aidan's jaw, tilting Aidan's head back as he leaned in, barely an inch between them. "I know you can feel how much I want you."

Aidan slowly closed his eyes, his lips parting with a deep intake of breath as Jessie slowly pressed their bodies together in an upsweep motion. Something settled between them, as if nothing else existed, just the softness and hardness of their bodies, pushing and pulling against each other, and the sounds of their breaths huffing in the air. Aidan's hands twisted the waistline of Jessie's sleep pants, tightening his grip and tugging him closer.

His Teasing Aidan had snark. Stubborn Detective Calloway had determination. Overprotective Guardian Aidan had a possessive yet caring side.

But Aroused Aidan was a completely different beast.

In control but…not—as if an untamed wildness lay just beneath the surface.

Aidan's lips parted and his head lolled to the side, seemingly in a trance, appearing to let his guard down and give in to the moment.

Jessie's heart pounded fiercely as he pushed into Aidan, reveling in the firm body pressing against him. Aidan bit his lower lip and arched into Jessie as a pained moan escaped him. He slowly opened his eyes, his gaze heavy-lidded. Jessie reached out with his other hand, his fingers trembling as he brushed the side of Aidan's hair in a rhythmic stroke. He pressed their foreheads together, just as spellbound and mesmerized by their closeness as Aidan. Heat flooded his body and tightened his chest. He closed his eyes in a haze of want and need, enjoying the hard prickling of the stubble against his fingers and the crackle of desire and want in the air, sparking between them.

He finally pressed his lips to Aidan's, teasing him with a tentative swipe of his tongue. A moan escaped when strong hands tugged him closer and a tongue teased his own in a seductive dance, tangling with his, inviting him to explore. His pulse sped with each tender swipe and each demanding pull. He separated from the kiss with a gasp, every nerve ending in his body acutely aware of Aidan's heat and the warm mouth gently biting his chin.

Aidan's fingers threaded through his hair at the nape of his neck, gripping tightly, holding him in place as he trailed kisses down Jessie's throat. A possessive groan escaped Aidan seconds before he swiped his tongue along the length of Jessie's neck.

Jessie lazily opened his eyes, drugged with the need coursing through his body. He forcefully held Aidan's face to still him, staring at the confusion mixed with want in those hazel eyes. He slammed his mouth against Aidan's in a fierce kiss, pouring every ounce of desire, want, and love into it, hoping his telepathic message was received loud and clear.

Strong fingers traveled up his spine, cupping the back of his neck, holding him in place while Aidan devoured his mouth with unbridled need. A moan echoed in the room. Teeth clashed and fingers dug into scalp and skin. Jessie tore himself from the kiss, gasping each breath, swallowing heavily, hoping to tame the blazing fire coursing through his veins and dampen the need vibrating through his body.

Aidan desperately wrapped his arms around Jessie and pulled him close, resting his head against Jessie's chest, his body heaving with each deep, rapid breath. The gesture surprisingly vulnerable and halting any further exploration.

The cloud of heat and need evaporated, leaving behind a fog of confusion.

An urgency to comfort Aidan overtook every ounce of his body. Jessie wrapped his arms protectively around Aidan's shoulders and pressed a tender kiss to the top of his head, then another. "What's wrong?"

Aidan silently tightened his arms around Jessie, holding him close in a strong, yet tender embrace.

Jessie stroked Aidan's hair, mixing in peppered kisses, overwhelmed by the need to soothe the sudden tension and quiver in the otherwise strong arms encasing him. They held each other for some time until the fire settled and only tenderness remained, each caressing the other with tentative strokes of their fingertips. Jessie finally pulled away and repositioned himself on the couch, slowly guiding Aidan to spoon him as he did each night they slept.

He softly smiled when Aidan immediately wrapped his arm around his waist, tugging him close. He held Aidan's hand in his and entwined their fingers, pulling their joined hands up to his lips and kissing Aidan's fingertips. He nestled into the embrace, reveling in the warm puffs of air breezing by his ear, comforting him in a cocoon of safety he could only find in Aidan's arms.

* * * *

Aidan leaned against the window frame and clenched his jaw, hearing the doctor's scribble of the pen tip against her notebook. Sometimes, she'd sit at her desk, other times—like today—she sat in the side chair doing some form of paperwork to pass the time. Maybe he'd need a padded room after this appointment. He hated the fucking silence. It gave him too much damn time to think. The kiss still lingered in his mind, and those addictive snuggling embraces, and yet, he didn't know what to do next. He wanted so much. "I don't know why I keep coming here," he said in an almost growl.

The pen stopped.

He turned sharply and shoved his hands into his pockets. "And before you ask me *why do I think I come here*, I believe I just answered that question." He bit down hard enough that his back molars started to hurt. "I. Don't. Know."

The doctor set the folder and pen on the side table and clasped her hands in her lap. "You *do* know why you're here. Because deep down inside, you know that whatever all this is, it's eating away at you and costing you your life. And you're scared of what that's doing to you because it's a loss of control. And you, my dear, love to be in control."

Aidan responded with a raised eyebrow.

"I can tell you're angry and frustrated and I'm guessing that's because you're at a stalemate in life and want to move forward but don't know how. It's obvious we're going to get to the root of the problem on your terms. So *you* need to start talking when you're ready. I'm not going to sit here, lecture you, or turn your answers into questions and ask you how you're feeling. I'm here to listen and arm you with the tools to help you cope with what's happened that's put you in this headspace and help you manage *it* rather than let it manage you so you can choose the path to the future you want, free of encumbrances." She waited and stared, her focus never flinching away from his. "I do have one question for you. And it's the important one."

Aidan continued to stare, waiting for her to resume her soapbox speech.

"Regardless of who asked you to come see me, the important thing is that you need to do this for yourself. Otherwise, it won't happen on your terms and you won't have control of moving forward," she said. She crossed her legs and stared at him intently. "So you need to ask yourself…*am I doing this for him, because he asked me to? Or, am I doing this for myself because I need to work through things so I can finally have control of my life again and work on being happy?*"

He scowled and slowly straightened, letting the doctor's words sink in. "You're not very nice. You're supposed to be comforting and tell me everything's going to be fine."

Dr. Engel slowly raised a perfectly tweezed eyebrow. "*You* don't need nice. During our first visit, you demanded I ignore your *bullshit*," she emphasized. "Remember?" She glanced up at the clock on the wall then stood. She thumbed through her appointment book. "Pick one. Late afternoon Tuesday or Thursday."

Aidan pushed his palms together and took a deep breath. *His terms.* "Both."

A slow smile spread across her face before she squiggled in the appointment book.

He finally made his way toward the door, hesitating with his hand on the knob. "Yes." He looked over his shoulder back at the doctor. "To both questions. It's not either or. He asked me to talk to you, but I'm also doing it for myself. I...I want..." He sighed. He wanted to be normal again. He wanted to be with Jess. He wanted to be happy. He wanted to be able to finish a day without feeling the weight of the daily fight wear him down.

She nodded. "Jessie is very special."

"He is."

"He cares for you."

"I know."

"And it's obvious you feel the same."

He hoped his silence said more than any mangled words could summarize.

"I'll see you Tuesday."

He walked out the door, suddenly feeling a little lighter. *Fuck being a quitter. I can do this.* He didn't have a clue how all this would play out, but one thing was certain, he had just taken a toddler-sized step in the right direction.

Chapter
SEVENTEEN

Jessie grabbed the remote and switched off the television as the closing credits scrolled. He stretched his arms above his head and yawned so hard Aidan could swear Jessie's jaw popped. "How about we try sleeping in the bed tonight?"

Aidan's body immediately tensed. Definitely a subject he had hoped to avoid. Jessie had sacrificed far too many hours of sleep just to be with him on the couch each night for over a month and couldn't disguise the hint of dark shadows under his eyes. Even through sleep deprivation, Jessie refused to abandon their nights together. He had promised to try and Jessie's patience probably ran as thin as his sleep schedule these days. Aidan caved, nodding his response.

"My bed's not that big but...um..."

"It's the only bed in the house." Aidan took a deep breath and exhaled slowly, hoping to hide the tension thrumming through his body. The master bedroom had a huge, vacant space where a king-size bed could easily fit, but he used the space for his home office, preferring the openness to pace when thinking on a case.

Jessie slipped his hand into Aidan's and led him toward the guest room. "The lamp is kind of bright in here, are you okay with the blinds being open to get the light from outside?"

Aidan nodded. Any light was better than none at all. The nod earned him a smile as Jessie walked over and opened the blinds, letting a faint gold cast of light filter in from the aging street lamp outside.

They settled onto the soft mattress and Jessie positioned himself next to Aidan. "Good night," he said with a huge yawn before reaching over and switching off the lamp light.

Aidan closed his eyes and tried to focus on the comfort of the bed and the softness of the pillows under his head.

I can do this.

He took a deep breath and exhaled slowly, concentrating on the soft head of hair resting on his shoulder and the gentle fingers wound around his arm. *I can do this.* He slowly eased into a calming peace.

Scrape, scrape.

His eyes sprang open. His heart hammered against his chest, faster with each passing millisecond. His lips parted, trying to take in a little more precious air while remaining as still as possible. He looked over, cursing the large tree that swayed in the wind and blocked out most of the light filtering in through the blinds.

Scrape, scrape.

A branch brushing against the window; he was familiar with the sound. But he looked from side to side and couldn't see it, couldn't confirm it was a branch or the sound of someone making their way through the makeshift barrier of downed trees and discarded wood just outside the door of where he'd been held captive. In an instant, a flood of snapshots flashed in his mind. The dark room, the hard bed, the musty smells, the braided material used as a rope.

Scrape, scrape.

He gripped the sheet at his side and took another deep, shaky breath, steeling himself.

I can do this.

An old metal garbage can crashed to the ground outside. He cursed under his breath at the elderly neighbors who insisted the aluminum bins were better than the city-provided ones. He stared at the ceiling, hearing the scrape of aluminum as it traveled with the wind along the paved road. The too familiar sound brought in another wave of memories, echoes of chains sliding across the floor to restrict him to the musty, dirty slip of mattress during some of his punishments.

It's not real. I can do this.

Jessie stirred beside him and tugged at the sheet covering them.

The material slid against his wrists, mirroring the slide of the material used moments before they'd string him up through the pulley. He swallowed heavily and his breathing sped.

I...I can do this.

The gentle hold caressing his arm now felt like a vise, clamping him down, limiting his movement, tying him down just as it had years ago for so many months. His throat tightened, remembering the material wrapped around his neck that further restricted him. He couldn't breathe. He screwed his eyes shut, a pointless action that didn't wipe away the series of images flipping through his mind—the blindfold, the punishments, the beatings, the blood, the screams. His fingers numbed in the death grip he had on the sheet. The faint glow of light from the window lessened, blocked by the tree blowing in the wind. The rhythmic puffs of warm breath against his arm pushed him over the edge.

Scrape, scrape.

He slipped out from under the sheet, needing to escape. He landed quietly on the floor. Instinctively, he wanted to stay in the room, but the multimedia production playing in his mind forced him to distance himself. His entire body heaved with each torturous breath he managed to pull through his constricted throat, fighting the current reality with the growingly vivid flashback that threatened to take hold of his senses.

I...can't...do this.

He crawled his way to the corner of the room, feeling the comfort of the hard wall against his back, knowing no one could surprise him from behind. He brought his knees up to his chest and rested his forehead against them. The shadows of defeat and helplessness taunted him, kicking and screaming at him, throwing him back into that hell from so many years ago.

Scrape, scrape.

He screwed his eyes shut and slapped his hands over his ears like a child, trying to will the pictures to fade and the sounds and screams to silence.

* * * *

Jessie woke to a cold, empty bed. He stilled and listened more closely at the faint sound in the room. Strangled breathing. He immediately reached over to the lamp and flipped the switch, flooding the room with bright light. He gasped when he saw Aidan in the corner of the room, rocking himself, gripping his hair.

He launched from the bed and knelt in front of Aidan, cautious to not startle him.

"Aidan, it's Jessie. Open your eyes." He reached out and hesitated. He took a deep breath. "Aidan, I'm here for you," he said and gently placed his hand on Aidan's bare foot.

Aidan immediately pulled away, folding into himself.

Jessie stood and walked over to sit cross-legged on the bed, granting Aidan some distance. He grabbed his phone from the nightstand, swiping his finger across the display until he found what he needed, then returned the phone back to its place, careful to avoid any harsh sounds or movements.

The complex melody of the piano sonata filled the room, each strike of the instrument's ivory keys bringing with it a calming mix of tones that echoed in the otherwise silent room. The rhythmic chorus of sounds accompanying a rise and fall of single notes with elegance.

Aidan's grip in his hair loosened, his body slowly relaxing. He wrapped his arms around his knees, still shielding his face.

"You're safe here. You're home. And there's no one here but you and me," Jessie said in a soft tone he hoped mirrored the smooth wave of sounds from the sonata.

Aidan's toes curled and his hands fisted. "I want to be alone," he croaked.

"I'm not leaving you when you're like this. I'll sit here until I know you're okay. Then I'll leave if you want me to."

Twenty minutes and three full sonatas later, Aidan rested his chin on his knees, his face still half hidden behind his crossed arms. "I don't understand why you stay with me."

"There isn't enough time on this earth for me to give you all the reasons why."

Aidan shook his head and sighed. He peeked over his arms, his eyes filled with a well of pain that twisted Jessie's heart. "I tried."

"I know."

"I'm sorry."

Jessie slowly rose from the bed, conscious to not make any sudden moves. He knelt in front of Aidan again and reached out, sliding his fingers in Aidan's hand.

Aidan immediately gripped onto Jessie's hand like a lifeline. "I'm sorry I scared you," he whispered.

"I wasn't scared. I was worried. I shouldn't have pushed you tonight."

"You didn't push." Aidan laced his fingers with Jessie's. He slowly slid his feet along the floor, straightening his legs and opening his arms. "C'mere."

Jessie immediately crawled into Aidan's lap and rested his head on Aidan's shoulder.

Aidan wrapped his arms around Jessie and sighed. "We can try the bed thing again another night, but give me a little time before we go for round two."

"I'm sorry. I just thought you liked the couch better. I didn't know the bed would be a problem." Jessie stroked his fingers along Aidan's skin, reveling in the warmth and safety the strong arms always provided. "You let me know whenever you're ready."

"Promise," Aidan said, placing a gentle kiss at the side of Jessie's head.

"Does this happen often?"

"No…not really."

"So the nightmare from that night and tonight are the only times this has ever happened?"

Aidan sighed. "Never used to happen this often." He paused, probably debating if he should say anything more. "I'll get an occasional flashback, but it's not usually strong. Lately, it's a little tougher. I don't know if it's the cases I'm working on or all this stupid therapy talking shit that seems to have opened some fucked up vault in my brain."

Jessie brushed his fingers along Aidan's arm, enjoying the

closeness and the rare intimacy of Aidan sharing something he most likely would have preferred to keep quiet.

"How did you know the music would help me?"

"I read that it helps to have something stimulate your senses that ties you to the present. A cold glass, a smell you associate with good memories, and sounds…like talking to yourself or playing music."

Aidan tightened his hold and buried his face in Jessie's hair. "Thanks for thinking of me."

"I'm always thinking of you."

"That's so stalkerish."

Jessie smiled, knowing a snarky Aidanism was a sign his Aidan had returned. He reached up and placed a tender kiss on Aidan's lips. He closed his eyes and rested his head on Aidan's shoulder, finally relaxing into the embrace. He focused on the up and down rhythmic stroking of the fingers against his arm and the slow, calming sounds of the sonata streaming in the room, lulling him to sleep.

Aidan gave him a sense of peace unlike anything he had ever experienced. He hoped to someday offer the same in return.

* * * *

Jessie let the consistent buzz of the chainsaw and the sway of the chair numb his senses as he wrapped up his research notes on a case. A few more paragraphs on his report and he could finally focus on the distracting eye candy drawing his attention.

He lazily swung in the chair hanging from the corner of the back porch of their home, fighting the urge to peek above the edge of his laptop. The wicker seat hung like an open birdcage from the top of the porch beam and always seemed to rock him to sleep if he closed his eyes and let the sounds of the day fill his senses. Aidan hated the hanging chair and rejected the idea of sitting in it but also refused to take it down since Jessie loved it so much. They often spent some quiet time together on weekends—Jessie in his hanging chair and Aidan on the bench at his side—simply enjoying the company of each other or stealing a short nap in the early evening.

A weekend nap was not on his to-do list today. The moment he'd seen Aidan in his worn out tank top and holed shorts, Jessie had grabbed his laptop and figured work while enjoying the view in the backyard was a far better alternative to his afternoon. He needed to finish this report and email it before the end of day—his work ethic wouldn't allow him to miss a deadline. But dammit, the very enticing and distracting view hindered his progress.

After several hours, he was thankfully close to finally wrapping up the report which would have taken him thirty minutes to complete at the dining room table. He totally had time to sneak in a rewarding peek at Aidan.

"Are you going to cut the whole thing down?" Jessie asked, shielding his eyes from the afternoon sun.

Aidan wiped the sweat from his brow and switched off the chainsaw. "What was that?"

He watched the thin sweat-drenched tank top hang off Aidan's body, wishing like hell Aidan hadn't worn the stupid thing that just blocked his view of all that ink he loved so much. "I asked if you were going to cut the whole tree down."

"Just the parts that are too close to the house."

"Why don't you take a break and drink something? It's too damn hot out here."

Jessie looked down at his laptop, trying to finish the sentence. *Dammit.* He'd lost his train of thought again. He needed to wrap up the conclusion of his report so he could focus on Aidan and every inch of visible skin in his sweaty outdoorsman performance. Screw it. He glanced up to sneak another peek.

Aidan stepped down the ladder and set the chainsaw on the ground. He walked toward Jessie with that prowl-like gait that always made Jessie's heart beat a tiny bit faster and his throat dry. The corners of Aidan's lips curled into a smile. *Tease.* He walked up to Jessie and braced his hands on the sides of the wicker birdcage chair, stilling the swinging motion. "Are you getting any of that work done you wanted to do or am I a distraction?"

"You're not a distraction." Jessie returned his focus to his laptop and pecked away at the keys.

"Really?" Aidan asked, leaning in a little more.

Jessie shook his head, trying to focus on the report from hell. No, he wasn't thinking about the trickle of sweat traveling down Aidan's neck he could see in his periphery or the strong, heated scent coming from Aidan's body. Nope, not for a second.

"Not even a little bit?"

"Nope," Jessie said, popping his lips on the "p" as he typed.

"Good." Aidan pushed off the wicker seat, resetting the slight swinging motion again. He fisted the sweaty material in the center of his back and yanked the drenched tank top up and over his head, rolling it into a ball and pitching it to the corner of the porch floorboards.

Jessie swallowed heavily, peeking over the laptop at Aidan's inked torso and the way it glistened with the beading sweat. He licked his lips, feeling the sudden urge to run his tongue along the newly exposed salty skin. His eyes met Aidan's teasing hazel stare.

"Good thing I'm not a distraction," Aidan said with a grin.

Jessie smiled and shook his head. Payback for something he had done or some teasing comment made. Oh, he could totally play that game with the playful side of Aidan that sometimes surfaced. He resumed his typing, anxiously working through the remaining few sentences of the report while Aidan returned to his tree-chopping task. Another sentence completed, another rewarding peek for his viewing pleasure. He glanced up at Aidan as he finished trimming the lower branches from the tree. His hair stuck up in all directions and his holed-jean shorts were a darker shade along the waistline.

Jessie took a deep breath. He wouldn't dare get caught dirty, sweaty, or messy. Just the thought triggered a chill to travel up his body. But damn. His inner-swine wanted nothing more than to rub itself against all that sun-kissed, sweaty, dirty, tan skin.

Finish. The. Damn. Report. He forced himself to focus and wrap up the last few sentences. Jessie mentally fist-pumped as he composed the new email, attached the file, and hit send. He closed his laptop with a sigh, now able to finally enjoy his private little show.

Aidan glanced over his shoulder toward him, scowled, then switched off the chainsaw. He stepped down the ladder and walked over to him with a seriousness that overtook his entire body. "Jess, I think you need to go inside."

"Why?" he asked with a pout.

"I think you're burning."

"But I'm under the porch." He stretched his arms out, looking at his fair skin for any redness. Damn, how long had he been sitting in the chair? The porch's pergola roof construction minimized the sun but obviously didn't block out all of it nor did the woven material of the chair. He looked up and had to squint to block out the brightness of the afternoon sun. *Shit.*

"C'mon. Let's take a break and grab something to drink." Aidan held the wicker seat as Jessie stepped out with his laptop tucked under his arm.

Even though his private little show had been cut short, he certainly wasn't going to argue. He remembered a trip he once took on a boat. The day was overcast so he hadn't given a sunburn a second thought. Until that night when he looked at himself in the mirror to see his body swollen and blistered with sun poisoning. That look definitely wouldn't work to seduce a certain hot detective.

"Is it okay if I get a little wiring work done in the house?" Jessie asked as they walked inside, setting his laptop on the breakfast bar.

"You don't have to ask. Just make sure you have someone here with you if you don't know the worker. I don't want to let our guard down until we have that bastard in custody. If it's weekend work, let me know, and I'll be here. Or we can call Bull and have him come in if you want."

Jessie nodded and sat on one of the barstools, while Aidan entered the kitchen. "I was going to ask Cole if he could get a hold of some of the guys from his old crew."

"I'm not sure I want to know what you're planning." Aidan grabbed the lemonade from the refrigerator and filled two glasses.

"It's a surprise." Jessie leaned over the countertop and gave Aidan a quick kiss before grabbing the drink. "Don't ask."

"Mmm. I think you need to do that again so I'm distracted and don't start to wonder what the hell you're up to."

Jessie smiled, leaning in to give him another quick kiss.

Aidan inched back, pulling his lower lip into his mouth as if still savoring the lingering taste of the kiss.

"So *I'm* a distraction?" Jessie teased, sipping his lemonade.

Aidan's eyes scanned Jessie's face and a frown slowly tugged at his lips. "Take your shirt off."

Jessie perked up…and so did his dick. He yanked the shirt up and over his head.

"Shit."

Sooo not the reaction I was hoping for.

"You did burn. Go jump in the shower while I pick up the stuff outside."

Jessie sighed, sliding off the barstool and making his way down the hall to the bathroom.

"Let me know when you're out of the shower so I can put some aloe gel on your back," Aidan yelled out.

Jessie slowly turned and let his gaze travel up Aidan's body. "Are you going to rub my front too?"

Aidan stifled a chuckle. "I will rub whatever skin was exposed."

"You're no fun," Jessie grumbled, turning to make his way to the shower.

Jessie sat on the couch, closing his eyes, enjoying the cool gel spread across his neck. Or maybe it was the rippling chill in his body at the rough fingertips brushing against his skin. It didn't matter. This had been a tiny excursion to heaven. First, his back, then his legs and arms with the finishing touches on his face and neck. Even though he knew this was Aidan's way of taking care of his sunburn, he just closed his eyes and enjoyed embellishing his thoughts farther than Aidan wished to take this little exploration.

"You…need to stop that."

Jessie's lips parted when one of Aidan's slick fingers worked its way down his throat. He opened his eyes when the contact vanished. "Huh?" He blinked, trying to focus his thoughts on what Aidan had said. "Stop what?"

Aidan wiped his hands and capped the bottle of aloe gel.

Jessie reached out, resting his hand on Aidan's arm, hoping to draw his attention and avoid his retreat from intimacy. "Stop what?"

"You were…moaning."

Jessie raised an eyebrow. "I was?"

Aidan swallowed heavily and nodded.

"Why's that a problem?" Jessie inched forward on the couch. "You never answered my question from before. Am I a distraction?"

Aidan's focus snapped back to him, a fierce fire staring back at him in those hazel eyes.

Jessie's lips parted on a breath. *Damn.* He wanted to know what it felt like to have that same level of passion unleashed upon him.

Aidan looked away again, trying to hide from the scrutiny.

He knew all of Aidan's hiding places. The back porch was his calming place, his place of solace—where he went when his frustration reached epic proportions and he needed to clear his mind. He'd sit on the porch bench for lengthy stretches of time without uttering a single word, staring off into nothingness until he was calm enough to return to whatever he was doing in the house. The couch was his pondering place—where he'd absently look at the television, but his mind was elsewhere. He'd cross his arms and prop his feet up on the coffee table, quiet, statue-like, with a vacant look in his eyes. It was tough to imagine there was anyone inside that shell, but it was obvious when the gears were spinning wildly in his mind. He'd also find his escape in work, sometimes burying himself in a case file spread out at the dining room table or at his office desk in his bedroom. There, his focus was obvious and laser sharp with no distractions.

Jessie had managed to find a way to reach him in each of his hiding places, like playing hide-and-go-seek, he'd give Aidan a running start to let off whatever had triggered the escape, but then he'd find him and lure him back in to try to avoid the isolation Aidan often subjected himself to. But when Aidan escaped to his dark place and slammed that iron gate, it was the only place Jessie couldn't reach.

He pulled on Aidan's chin, drawing his focus again. "Don't shut down. Talk to me."

"What do you want me to say?"

Jessie tugged on Aidan's hand. "I want you to answer my question."

"Which one?"

He looked down at their clasped hands and stroked Aidan's long fingers, hoping to ease the tension.

"What part of this is frustrating you?"

Aidan shrugged.

Jessie wanted to grab Aidan and throw him flat onto the couch and pounce on him, kissing him silly until he finally surrendered to the mix of desire and passion Jessie often saw in his eyes before he hid them away. He chewed on his bottom lip, hoping for some enlightenment. Aidan hadn't come up with some excuse to escape. Jessie might not know how to break through, but this was Aidan's way of trying. "Okay, how about we start over?"

Aidan looked up, a flash of hopefulness crossing his expression.

"I said we would work up to talking about the big stuff. Right? So I'll go first. Ask me anything." A flicker of excitement sparked when Aidan's thumb brushed against Jessie's fingers.

"I didn't know your name was Jessiah until…that night," Aidan quietly commented, staring at their clasped hands.

Jessie inched closer, wincing slightly when the cushion brushed against his sunburned skin. "I don't use it. Only for legal documents when necessary."

Aidan pulled away the small couch cushion and gave it a menacing stare. "It means 'gift.' It's…fitting," he absently said. He grabbed the softer throw blanket and folded it, positioning it carefully behind Jessie.

A hint of a smile tugged at Jessie's lips with Aidan's attentiveness, revealing that secret, tender side Aidan tried to bury deep, deep down under his harder facade.

"My father gave me that name. He was very religious. My parents had a few miscarriages before I came along. So when my mom was able to carry me to term, he thought I was a gift to them. Needless to say, he threw that in my face a few times." Jessie quieted for a moment, trying to silence the flood of memories that surfaced about his father, the yelling, and how he always ended up feeling more like a discarded item than a gift in his eyes. "Mom always called me Jessie so that's what I prefer to use."

"But you still kept your name."

Jessie stared at their hands, a welcomed distraction to the thoughts circling his mind. "I guess, in the back of my mind, I figured maybe my father might come around someday. But if I changed my name, it would be a clear sign that I wasn't open to working things out." He shrugged and pulled Aidan's hand between his palms. "I know he and I have moved past that point. Now it's just a matter of me not wanting to be some thirty-year-old guy who wants to change his name to something cuter."

"You are cute," Aidan said with a half smile.

Jessie laughed. "Sweet-talker. You know, your name means little fire. I think it became a self-fulfilling prophecy on your part."

Aidan didn't say anything in return. Instead, he just stared down at their hands as the partial smile slowly faded from his expression.

"Did I say something wrong?"

"Huh?" Aidan looked up as if Jessie had pulled him from some thought.

"You got all serious on me."

"Oh…sorry."

"What are you thinking about?" Jessie asked.

Aidan shook his head as if shaking off whatever had a hold of his mind. "Nothing."

"Please don't shut me out."

Aidan's brow lowered before he quietly spoke. "I'm not."

Jessie sighed. He could sense the tension between them and his mounting frustration at not being able to break through. Rather than risk alienating Aidan, he opted to cherish their time together for the rest of the night. He tried to position himself in his usual spot tucked under Aidan's arm. As soon as his body pressed between Aidan and the couch, he winced from the sunburn.

Aidan immediately stood and walked to the hall closet, grabbing a spare bedsheet and pillow. He threw them on the floor next to the couch and positioned himself on them.

"What are you doing?"

"Your sunburn's going to be a bitch all night and I'm not going to aggravate that. Besides, you didn't sleep much last night with my stupid bed drama."

"And I'm not going to let you sleep on the floor."

Aidan's jaw muscles twitched and his brows knit together. "Jess, I can't sleep in that small-ass chair in the corner. So it's either you on the couch and me on the floor next to you, you in your bed and me on the floor next to you, or you in your bed and me on the couch. Pick one."

"So you and me in the bed is not an option?"

Aidan's jaw muscled twitched again. "No. And I need you to please not push me on that subject."

Jessie rubbed his own arms, trying to resist the need to scratch his burned skin. He wanted to be in bed, but his desire to be near Aidan overpowered his own needs. He was becoming a petulant child and knew it was the sleep deprivation creeping up on him combined with the painful irritation of his careless sunburn. He needed a solid few hours of consecutive downtime, but if Aidan wasn't ready to give the bed a shot again, he wasn't going to push, especially without a solution or knowing what had happened to trigger his reaction. "Okay, couch," he said, finally caving.

He settled himself in a lying position but let his arm hang over the edge to rest on Aidan's chest where he lay on the floor at his side. Aidan grabbed his hand and held it tightly in his, pressing it against his chest.

"Night, Jess."

He rubbed his thumb along Aidan's fingers. He wasn't being pushed away, but deep down, he couldn't help thinking Aidan was retreating again.

* * * *

Aidan stood behind the couch as he sipped his coffee, watching

Jessie stir in his sleep. There was something peaceful about the way Jessie slept. His features relaxed and a hint of a smile touched the corners of his mouth as if a dream filled his mind and transported him to his happy place.

A place Aidan wanted to be.

He took a deep breath, going through the last few weeks in his mind. He'd promised to try, and it seemed he kept screwing things up along the way. He refused to walk away; that was a step in the right direction. At least…he hoped so. But his hyper-awareness worked overtime, conscious of everything he did and said, worried the slightest thing would push Jessie away. Any semi-questionable thought or string of words remained silent. He wouldn't take the chance. The bed thing had turned out to be an epic fail and had triggered his mission of yard work the next day. He loved that Jessie wanted to be with him while he worked, but now, seeing Jessie's sunburned shoulder as he snuggled into the pillow…maybe it hadn't been such a good idea after all. He'd let Jessie sneak in a few hours of sleep instead of waking him for their morning workout. He hoped that earned him a point.

Why the hell didn't someone publish a book on how to make this *us* thing work for people? He sighed and took another sip, leaning over to pull up the soft throw when it slipped off Jessie's body.

Jessie stirred again, turning upward on the couch to face him. "Good morning," he said, with a sleepy and sexy as all hell grin. The tousled look suited him, whether he believed it or not.

"Good morning."

Jessie stretched his arms over his head and yawned, finally sitting up on the couch.

"How'd you sleep?"

Jessie shrugged. "Good. Better if you'd have been with me."

Aidan took another sip of his coffee, hiding a smile. "How's the burn feel?"

Jessie stretched his arms again. "Better." He cocked his head and twisted his mouth as his eyes traveled along Aidan's face and arms. "It's amazing how you can't tell you were outside yesterday. You have this golden tan color but no burn at all."

Aidan chuckled. "Yeah, I don't burn…not like you do. Neither does Ty. We get that from our mom. She used to say something about olive skin coloring…whatever that means," he said with a shrug. "But Dad, he used to burn like you. Mom always teased him about looking like a lobster after our weekend barbecues."

Jessie smiled and rested the side of his head against the back of the couch. "That, right there. That's all I ask for."

"What's that? Burning like a lobster after a barbecue?" he asked, holding back a chuckle as he sipped his coffee.

"No. Telling me about you. The little things. That's what I want."

"Oh." He quieted, fidgeting with his now empty mug. He turned and walked toward the kitchen to rinse out his cup.

"Are you leaving already or do you still have a few minutes?"

"I've got about five."

"Okay," Jessie said, rising from the couch and making his way to the bathroom. "Give me a couple of minutes."

Aidan watched Jessie disappear down the hallway and into his bedroom. There's nothing he wanted more than to block every thought from his mind and just hide away with Jessie, without the worry of saying or doing something wrong that would knock him off the pedestal Jessie seemed to prop him up on.

He gathered his case files from the dining room table and stuffed them into his bag. He had to figure out what to do. Dr. Engel had nailed it—he had reached a stalemate in his life. Jessie wanted him to open up, to peel away the protective layers he used as a shield. But doing so would leave him exposed, vulnerable, weak—definitely not a state he chose to be in. And if Jessie walked away, well, he didn't want to let his mind go there. He could handle a lot of things—Lord knew he could—but Jessie leaving…definitely a what-if he wanted to avoid more than a flashback.

Jessie returned to the living room all polished and presentable as usual. Even his shirt looked as if it had been de-wrinkled. How the hell did he do that?

"Now kiss me before you go off to work."

This part, Aidan could totally do without even thinking. He snaked his arms around Jessie's waist and tugged him close as he bent to press his lips against Jessie's, hoping to convey his feelings with each swipe of his tongue and pull of his mouth.

The warm press against his body and the gentle caress at the nape of his neck was all he needed to transport his mind to Jessie's happy place—where optimism, love, happiness, and peace surrounded him.

Chapter EIGHTEEN

"You remember the home videos you mentioned a while ago?" Jessie asked Cole, thumbing through the manual of the new audio system Cole's old crew member had installed in the house a few hours earlier. He appreciated the Saturday company. Although he loved working from home, the isolation sometimes wore on him, especially on those weekends Aidan worked.

Cole stretched his legs and stifled a yawn. "The ones of Aidan and Ty? Yeah. What's up?"

"Do you think Ty would mind if I borrowed some of their old videos?"

"I'll ask him. Any particular ones you want? My-Ty's got them all sorted by date and color-coded by holidays and special events," Cole finished quietly, hiding a smile.

"Any would be fine." He set the manual aside. "You're going to have to give me a crash course on how to use this system."

"Super easy. It's what we've got at the shop. And I'll give you the most embarrassing videos."

Jessie smiled at how Cole could easily manage multiple conversations. His friend was far sharper than most people gave him credit for. "I think you enjoy pissing off Aidan." He kicked Cole's booted feet off the coffee table.

"I love getting a rise out of him. Haven't you noticed that little vein he's got at his temple?" Cole said, tapping the side of his forehead with a playful expression. "That little vein talks to me every time I'm in the room." He crossed his arms and firmly nodded. "I have a personal relationship with that vein of his. You should work on getting a rise out of him. It's fun to watch."

"I do get a rise out of him."

Cole slowly raised an eyebrow. "Well, well, well. It's about fucking time."

Jessie sighed. "Don't tease me about it. Please." He absently brushed his fingers along the couch cushion, following the lined pattern as his mind wandered. He loved Aidan, more with each passing day, and sensed the stubborn man had an immense capacity to love and believed even he would be overwhelmed if Aidan were to open the floodgates. Aidan would love intensely. He'd love hard. And he'd love forever.

"Jessie," Cole said, pulling him from his thoughts.

He looked up at an oddly serious Cole.

"Don't give up on him."

"I'd *never* give up on him," Jessie fiercely said.

"He trusts you, and that's a huge first step for him whether he admits it or not."

"I know," Jessie whispered, brushing the random pattern on the cushion.

They chatted for a while and ran through the new system basics before Cole finally left. Jessie showered and worked on preparing dinner, tinkering with the new system in between. He grabbed the other bag of items and strolled throughout the house. He walked into the master bedroom…*Aidan's* bedroom. He stood there for a moment, taking in the emptiness of the space. The far left corner of the room held a desk area where Aidan often worked on a case if he didn't want a distraction from the living room.

A warmth filled his chest, remembering how Aidan had finally admitted that Jessie was, in fact, a distraction. No teasing, no banter, just a casual truth mentioned without a second thought.

Next to the desk area was a couch that seemed more worn out than the one in the living room. Aidan swore he'd never use the couch, refused to even think about what Hunter and Cam might have done on that same couch when Hunter lived there. But Jessie secretly thought Aidan kept the furniture in the room as both a reminder of his friend and to fill the great emptiness of the space. He sighed, returning his focus to his task. He plugged in the item and walked in to the next room to follow the same process.

"Jess, I'm home," he heard Aidan yell from the living room. He wadded up the now empty bag after having plugged in everything and made his way to the living room.

"Hey, how was work today?"

"Good." Aidan spoke, but his focus wandered to the new additions in the house. He never questioned, never demanded, and always allowed Jessie ample flexibility to do whatever he wanted. "You've been busy."

Jessie grabbed the small pouch from the kitchen countertop. "Here, this is for you."

Aidan took the small cloth bag and opened it, withdrawing the earbuds. "What's this for?"

Jessie fished Aidan's phone from his pocket and swiped at the screen. "You mentioned the flashbacks were getting a little more frequent lately with some of the task force cases and your sessions with Dr. Engel, so I set something up on your phone yesterday, but you raced out before I had a chance to show you."

Aidan peeked over the phone to see what he was doing.

"The earbuds are small so they fit in your coat pocket. When you need them, fish them up your collar, then run this app"—he tapped the screen and stuck the bud into Aidan's ear—"and you've got a full library of music that should work like the other night if it ever gets tough."

Aidan looked away, listening to the music. He glanced at his phone and swiped a few items, working his way through the program and the files Jessie has set up for him. He finally looked at Jessie and leaned forward, placing a kiss on his lips. "Thanks." He scrolled through some of the songs on the playlist then withdrew the earbuds. "And what about all that?" He pointed to the wall, unable to hide his curiosity.

Jessie grabbed Aidan's hand and led him over to the panel. He pressed a few buttons and a low, soft piano sonata echoed in the room.

Aidan looked up at each of the corners of the room and spotted the speakers discreetly installed in the ceiling. "You should work surveillance. I didn't spot them when I walked in."

"One of Cole's old crew members installed them."

Aidan raised an eyebrow. "Should I be worried about what he installed?"

"No. I watched him closely," he teased, knowing Cole's former car-stripping crew of friends always kept everyone on their toes.

"How closely?" Aidan asked, snaking an arm around Jessie's waist and pulling him near.

His heart fluttered at Aidan's forwardness. Was that a hint of jealousy? He didn't dare get excited at the thought.

"So the music plays in the living room?" Aidan asked.

"It's wired for the whole house. But you can change the music in each room if you want or only run it in certain rooms. It'll play whatever you have uploaded to your cloud."

"To my what?"

Jessie smiled. "I already set it up for you. Same system as your phone. And the living room is hooked up so we can have it double as a surround system when we watch a movie."

Aidan leaned down and placed another kiss on Jessie's lips. He looked toward the outlet and cocked his head but didn't ask directly.

"Night-lights. They're rechargeable so you don't have to worry about them if we lose power. Really low wattage so they won't be too bright at night and the power usage is minimal. I have them now in every room."

Aidan quieted, staring off to the side at the night-light in the socket. His focus shifted, scanning the speakers in the room and the panel on the wall.

Jessie bit his lip. Damn. Maybe he'd push the *do-whatever-you-want-in-the-house* liberty. "We don't need to—"

Aidan silenced him with another kiss. "It's perfect. Don't change a thing."

"Are you sure?" He wrapped his arms around Aidan's neck and brushed the hair at the back of his head.

"Yeah. I just can't believe you did all this…for me."

"If you change your mind, let me know. I kinda pushed it a bit. I should have asked before I had holes opened in your walls and ceiling." The worry evaporated when Aidan tugged him closer.

"This is *our* home, Jess. You don't have to ask. If you want to change something, change it. I draw the line at a pastel couch or any heavy floral decorative shit. Other than that, you can change whatever you want."

An uncontrollable laughter escaped him. "So I guess I should cancel the painters coming over tomorrow? They're installing lilac wallpaper with decorative orchids and a gold border with a summer bouquet mix of sunflowers and daisies."

"Tell me you're kidding."

"I'm totally kidding."

Aidan exhaled heavily.

"By the way."

"Yeah?"

"I *am* changing your couch. The one in your bedroom. But don't worry. The pastel roses in the pattern are barely visible so it shouldn't be a problem."

Aidan didn't say a word but swallowed heavily. The blank stare a dead giveaway he attempted to disguise the bubbling panic.

Jessie patted his shoulder. "Still kidding."

"You're getting too good at this sarcasm thing." Aidan blew out a breath.

Jessie bit his lower lip but couldn't hide the smile. "I live with the master of sarcasm. It's only fair a tiny bit of talent rubs off on me after all this time." He leaned his head on Aidan's shoulder and placed his hand against Aidan's chest, feeling the strong heartbeat pulse against his palm. He craved this closeness, this easiness whenever they were together. The arms around him tightened and the thumping of the heartbeat quickened.

"Thanks, Jess. For all this. For always…thinking of me."

His chest tightened when lips pressed against the top of his hair—that simple gesture Aidan always did that seemed to spike his pulse each time. From anyone else, the caresses or touches would be casual.

From Aidan, the subtle, barely-there gestures were paramount and incredibly cherished.

Jessie tightened his arms in the embrace, not wanting the moment to end. He let a contented sigh escape, enjoying the fingers grazing his skin to the rhythm of the piano sonata softly echoing in the room.

* * * *

Aidan knocked on the door and shoved his hands in his pockets to stop fidgeting. He didn't usually pick up the phone and request an impromptu visit, but dammit, he had to do something. His frustration bordered on unbearable, and if anyone could guide him on what to do, he could only think of one person he trusted enough for this type of chat.

"Hey," Ty said, opening the door. "Come on in."

"Sorry it's so late." Aidan walked into his old condo, now home to Ty and Cole. The place actually looked lived in and welcoming. A far cry from the *fuck-off* vibe that had vibrated from the walls when he'd lived there.

"It's okay. Cole's wrapping up some work so he's running a little late. Do you want something to drink?"

"I'm fine," Aidan said, walking over to the window, enjoying the bird's eye view under the evening sky. He loved this side of his city, the one that blanketed all the darkness in shadows and accentuated each right angle and curve of cityscape elegance with a twinkle or transition of light. He looked over to the glass curio in the corner at the items on display. "I'm never getting my bullet collection back, am I?"

"Hell no!" Ty walked up to the glass enclosure displaying a collection of small model cars Ty had gathered over the years. He stood in front of the case and stared at the three dozen bullets showcased on a single shelf, sorted by size ranging from a .22 long rifle up to a .50 caliber machine gun round which looked like a tiny torpedo. Some were from guns Aidan had shot during his time in service, others collected because, well, bullets were cool as hell to look at, as long as the target was elsewhere.

He sighed. He should have packed them up when he moved out.

Ty turned with a shy smile. "I always think of you when I see them."

Okay, fine. He could keep the damn things. "How much time do I have before Cole gets here?"

"I'm guessing you've got about fifteen, twenty minutes tops. He wrapped up the meeting with Drayton with the contracts for the test track use so he's on his way back already."

Aidan nodded. He could keep this short and sweet and escape before Cole wormed his way into the conversation. His brother led him to the couch and encouraged him to take a seat.

"What's up?"

Aidan rubbed the back of his neck, not really sure what or how much to say. But if he wanted to have this chat and escape before Cole arrived, he had to spit it out. "How do you do it?" He exhaled heavily and kept rubbing the back of his neck. "How do you open yourself up to Cole without falling apart?"

Ty's expression softened and looked about a step away from reaching out to give him a hug. "Cole makes it easy for me." He shifted on the couch and turned his body to the side to face Aidan. He quieted for a moment and looked away, his expression transitioning into something more serious as if carefully crafting the string of words just as he meticulously worked each restoration project in his shop. He finally made eye contact again, determination burning in his gaze as if he had mentally nailed the perfect set of sentences to communicate. "You don't talk, Aidan. You need to. I knew nothing about your private life before Cole pushed. And I'm glad he did. I didn't even know you were gay. You could have told me that."

Aidan inwardly cringed. "It just always worked out better for me to keep it quiet."

"But even from me?"

"I couldn't risk my brother hating me," Aidan whispered.

"But you *knew* I was gay. I came out to Mom and Dad ages ago. Why would you think that?"

Aidan shrugged. "It's never been easy."

Ty shook his head and took a few deep breaths to level his tone again before he spoke. "I've always respected your privacy, but you're really closed off, and that's not good." He shifted again, resting his hand on the back of the couch, bringing himself even closer into Aidan's space as if the proximity would ease the tension of the candor. "You're not weak for being open or for showing your human side."

Aidan pursed his lips, not really wanting to rehash a memory or break out into some Dr. Phil moment.

"I hadn't realized how closed off you were until that night you came over here for dinner when I met Jessie. He's changed you."

"Like Dr. Jekyll and Mr. Hyde?" he asked with an arched eyebrow, leaning forward and resting his forearms on his thighs.

Ty sighed. "You always do that."

"Do what?"

"Use sarcasm or some smartass comment to lighten a moment to avoid things getting too serious. You do that when you're uncomfortable with the direction of the conversation. More so now than you ever did before. We're treading in real personal territory here and I can understand why that's unsettling you. But you're here, so I know it's important. And I'm really glad you trusted me enough to talk to me. You haven't done that in years."

Aidan looked away when Ty got that *I'm-so-going-to-hug-you-right-now* look on his face. He could only deal with one emotional element at a time.

"I see hints of the old you. You used to be happy, Aidan. I don't know what triggered the change, but you...became harder, and your smile wasn't the same. It was almost..."

"Almost what?" He glanced over at his brother, not really sure he wanted to know the answer. His brother had no idea of most of the bullshit he tried to work through. Ty had had enough to deal with in his life with the shop, the accident, and his recovery; he certainly didn't need his big brother dumping a truckload of drama on his plate as well.

"It's like a sad smile. It's as if you go through the motion because someone *expects* you to smile, but your eyes are still...hollow. It's not like a scar that's permanent, so I know it's something you're fighting.

You've changed *because* of Jessie. He brings back that old smile. I see hints of it. And I hadn't realized it was missing until I saw you guys together. It's as if you were in a dark place and he came in with a flashlight to shine a little bit of light to help you back on the path."

"You're really poetic," he said. He cursed inwardly, realizing he was doing that sarcasm/smartass thing his brother had mentioned. "So…I guess Cole is your flashlight?"

Ty smiled. "He's more like a Hollywood movie premier spotlight endlessly rotating three hundred and sixty degrees."

Aidan huffed out a laugh then quieted, holding back another smartass comment on the tip of his tongue. He pushed his palms together, trying to find the right words. "What do I do? I suck at this stuff."

"Lucy, I'm home," Cole yelled in his best Ricky Ricardo imitation as he entered then turned to relock the door behind him. He dropped his keys on the kitchen counter then chuckled when he saw them sitting on the couch. "My-Ty, we're going to start charging for our counseling services. We'd make a fortune with these two."

"What are you talking about?" Aidan said with a bit of a snarl.

"Let me guess? You're here about love advice."

Aidan reached up and pressed his thumb and middle finger against his eyes. He had hoped to be in and out of there without having to deal with the Renzo wrath. He just needed a few minutes to talk to his brother. "Shit, man. Don't you ever shut the fuck up?"

"Sure I do. But it requires Ty's dick in my mouth."

Aidan rubbed his temple and groaned at Ty's muffled chuckle. The slowly building Renzo-headache would soon blossom to a full-fledged migraine if he didn't nip this in the bud.

"You want advice?" Cole insisted, standing in the middle of the open space with his arms crossed.

"No." *Yes, but I just want you to shut the hell up.*

"Uh-huh. I'm going to give it to you anyway. Do with it whatever you choose. Listen up." Cole dramatically cleared his throat as if ready to give a speech. "Jessie loves you. Period. It's that simple so don't make it complicated. That man thinks you're the stars, the moon, and the whole damn galaxy. And you know the only way you can make that man love you *any* more than he already does?"

Aidan looked at Cole, not saying a word. He couldn't believe it, but he actually *did* want Cole to continue talking.

Cole walked toward them, leaned over, and wrapped his arms around Ty's neck. He placed a tender kiss on Ty's cheek and nuzzled him for a moment before returning his focus to Aidan. The humor completely vacant from his expression and tone when he spoke. "Let him in, Aidan. Block everyone else out if that makes you feel safe. But give him that skeleton key to get inside all your secret rooms. If you can do that, he will love you more than you ever thought possible." He kissed Ty again and released him. He stared back at Aidan with a raised eyebrow, a slow-spreading cocky grin and the usual playfulness back intact. "My-Ty, I'd say you've got about two minutes before my future brother-in-law here runs away from all this personal talk." He gave Ty another kiss on the cheek then retreated to the bedroom, taking each step as if it were part of a dance move to a song playing in his head.

Aidan exhaled heavily and ran his fingers through his hair.

Ty reached out and placed his hand on Aidan's shoulder. "You know he's right even though you won't admit it."

He clenched his jaw and took a deep breath. "How do you put up with him?"

Ty leaned back into the couch and a slow smile spread across his face at some thought. He looked up to his brother and his brown eyes sparkled with that always present happiness at the mere mention of Cole's name. "I have his skeleton key and he has mine."

Aidan rolled his eyes. "You guys are hopeless romantics. Not everything is like that outside of your love bubble."

"It's about a connection, Aidan. It's about being able to talk to one another without even saying a single word. And that can only happen when someone knows you, the *real* you. And *you* want that. You can get pissed off all you want and growl at Cole forever, but you want it, and that's why you're trying to figure out how to make that happen." Ty leaned forward, his expression a mix of compassion and concern. "Stop fighting it and just let it happen."

"It's not that easy."

"I know it's not. Believe me, I fought off Cole more than you know. I was scared out of my mind. I had something special with him when we were just co-workers, and the thought of losing that…" Ty shook his head and took a deep breath. "That's what made me slam the brakes each time there was a hint of us getting close." He quieted and looked toward their bedroom, rubbing his hands together. "He was always so happy, smiling all the time as if there was nothing in the world that could ever bring a gray cloud into his bright blue sky."

"He's happier since he's with you," Aidan added quietly. He shook his head and scoffed. "I didn't think it was possible, but that little cocky shit is more confident too."

Ty smiled. "And all I had to do was let him in." He shook his head as if hanging on a memory. "I hadn't realized I was pushing everyone away and I had managed to put myself in a corner." He looked up at Aidan, his brows arched upward with concern. "You're doing that. You've been doing that for a while. I'm worried you're going to work yourself so far into a corner you won't know how to get out of it."

And that right there was exactly why Aidan had decided to show up for this little one-on-one with his brother at the last minute. For the last few months, he'd battled with himself, trying to keep a safe distance from Jessie. The solitude he'd forced upon himself *was* a dark place. He'd lived it for too many years, thinking it was best to isolate himself and spare his soul wearing away any more. But Jessie had managed to slowly draw him out with his shy smiles and casual touches, brightening up his dark little corner.

"My-Ty, come to bed," Cole yelled from the bedroom. "Let grumpy Aidan go home to his man. I need you to come here and shut me up."

Ty bit his lip and crossed his arms as if he could somehow hold in the laughter that shook his body.

"He's a rude motherfucker."

"And he's all mine."

Aidan sighed. He ran his fingers through his hair again. He wondered what it would be like to take that chance, to close his eyes and swan dive into that crystal blue pool that always seemed to draw him in and ease him. "Just…tell me what to do."

Ty smiled. "Give him your skeleton key, then let him open that door and see just how fucking awesome my big brother is."

Chapter
NINETEEN

Aidan pulled up to the crime scene and found a spot on the side road to park. He hated this shit. He looked out his front windshield. A standard issue, plain one-story house in a residential area that seemed to have been constructed sometime in the early 1970s. "I really wish Reyes would have taken this one," he grumbled.

His partner released her seat belt. "Me too. But if he were here, the others from his department would think he's poaching. We're only here to confirm it ties to the Miller serial case."

Aidan sighed and turned off the engine.

The team had a general plan when it came to new case reviews. If the case potentially linked to a file on the task force list of assignments, the team went out to the crime scene to assess the possible connection. To avoid overstepping within their own departments, Aidan and Sunny couldn't touch the initial site visit of a homicide, Travis couldn't evaluate an organized crime case, and Reyes couldn't assess special victims. So they'd mix up the assessments to determine if the case merited a transfer over to the task force.

Which meant, Sunny, with her issues, and Aidan, with his potpourri of emotional baggage, were stuck reviewing this special victim crime scene. At least, with homicide cases, they had found a way to desensitize themselves to the human suffering side of things by focusing on a body and evidence to formulate their own theories at a controlled pace rather than rely on the rush of vivid, mental, heartbreaking images from the personal retelling of a traumatized victim.

"Let's split up so we can cover more ground and get the hell out of here," Sunny said, pulling the badge from her inside pocket.

"Sounds like a plan," he said.

They exited the vehicle and walked toward the old house, clipping their badges on their waist and slipping under the police tape blocking off the scene. They each grabbed a pair of gloves and split up. Sunny assessed the exterior and he inspected the interior. No one asked why two detectives from homicide were present at a non-homicide scene, further justifying the swap of the initial assessment.

He entered the living room and a sense of dread immediately suffocated him. The deep red and black painted walls added to the overall sinister darkness of the house, and the worn, rusted fixtures appeared as if they hadn't been used in years. The low ceiling height, which he could easily reach with the tip of his finger if he stood on his tiptoes, made the older construction even more obvious. The room, although small in size, appeared larger with the absence of furniture. He stepped over the extension cord of the large light perched on a tripod, most likely placed there by detectives to illuminate the otherwise dark space. He walked through the neighboring room and entered the cramped kitchen and what appeared to be a connected dining room. He momentarily brought up his wrist to his nose, hoping to block some of the musty smell in the air. Obvious mold resided somewhere, either in the dark and dingy carpet or the water seeping through parts of the ceiling and leaking on several spots in the flooring.

The only pieces of furniture in this area were an old piece of wood—probably the dining room table—and a single matching chair. Deep grooves sliced into the stained dark red oak wooden legs of the furniture enough to reveal the lighter, raw wood beneath the scratched surface. He looked over to the side, toward the kitchen. A stack of dirty dishes filled the sink and spilled over onto the countertop, pooling with remnant, rotting food and fluids.

He took a shallow breath and slowly exhaled, trying to ease the sudden tension coursing through his body.

Something tugged at his consciousness, alerting him of danger.

Dr. Engel's voice echoed in his mind. *Ground yourself to the present.* He never ignored his instincts. He withdrew the earbuds from his pocket and fished them up under his collar to make them less visible before pushing them into his ears and switching on the classical music. Beethoven, Mozart they all worked equally well. The steady, somber sound of a piano seemed to be the strongest tether to reality for him.

He slowly took each step along the perimeter of the wall then down the short hallway, observing the techs and detectives as they worked in each room, reveling in the absence of the sound stimuli from the quiet chatter that would linger at a scene. He'd occasionally nod or give a chin-up gesture in greeting when his focus landed on a questioning gaze. He looked around, observing the placement of objects and the spattering of blood against the wall as he walked.

He passed a pair of detectives in the hallway on his way to the room with the most foot traffic and the forensics camera flashing. He entered the room and again sensed that odd tug of his consciousness, alerting him to a memory trying to take center stage. He closed his eyes for a moment and channeled his focus on the haunting vocals accompanying Schubert's "Ellens dritter Gesang" whispering in his ear. The music not only grounded him to the present but also brought a new and very welcomed visual to the forefront of his mind—Jessie cuddled up in his arms on the couch with his never-ending smile.

He took a centering breath and walked along the edge of the rectangular room, slowly scanning the crime scene in sync with the somber vocals. The painted wall shared the same black and red color scheme as the rest of the house, and the dark, dingy, disgusting stained carpet covered the floors in what looked like—based on the other rooms in the house—possibly the master bedroom. Another portable, police-issued light fixture in the corner provided enough light to illuminate the central focus on the crime scene. He didn't need to have stellar detective skills or be psychic to sense the evil in the room. It screamed torture chamber from every square inch of the space.

A piece of old, weather-worn plywood, nailed from the inside, covered the one small window. A series of steel eye bolts in various sizes were screwed into the wall, equally spaced as if intended to follow the stud pattern of the wall's interior for greater support. He inhaled sharply when he spotted the thick, sturdy rope threaded through the last bolt in the corner, hanging loosely as if a natural wall accessory to the room.

Aidan retreated to the corner, away from the investigators processing the scene. He glanced at the only piece of furniture in the room—a single, long, narrow old table with a series of objects neatly organized on the surface of the distressed wood. He visually inspected each item from a distance, cataloguing them in his mind and comparing their relevance to the team's existing cases. Off the edge of the rough wood hung a small slip of black fabric that suddenly seemed larger than the room itself.

A blindfold.

Time suddenly warped, throwing him back into a period he had hoped to block out. He screwed his eyes shut as the images flashed before him.

The blindfold, tied tightly around his eyes, depriving him of the sunlight. Except for those rare moments when they'd rip the strip of material away and the sun would shoot a bolt of bright fire to his brain.

He forced himself to open his eyes as Beethoven struck angry piano keys in his ear, mirroring his temper and frustration at not being able to control the flashback's effect on him. Each angry strike of the ivory key cemented his connection to the here and now.

The sound. Focus on the sound. This is not real. This is not happening now. Listen to the music. Focus on a visual. Something real. Something important.

He took a deep breath, screw the musty smell in the air. He closed his eyes and a sudden peace seemed to flow through his body with the welcomed thoughts of Jessie filling his mind—his smile, the soft strands of dark hair brushing against his lips as he held him at night. The vision coated his muscles with renewed strength and determination to continue. He opened his eyes and exhaled slowly.

The semi-flashback lingered, mixing reality with the memory, yet didn't seem to take full control of his being. He focused on the narrow wooden table and the objects in *this* room. Superimposed and slightly blurred over the table was a ghost of a room with a similar worn piece of furniture and a different set of items scattered on its surface. His gaze trailed up the wall, and the faint image of a primitive pulley system in a stone ceiling, of ropes and braided fabrics running through a makeshift hook, flickered like a weakened television signal coming in and out of focus.

This is not real. This house is not made of stone and mud.

He took a deep breath to steady himself. He could do this. He could filter out the visual noise he was all too familiar with, knowing exactly which elements were there to taunt him.

Focus. You can fucking do this.

The image flickered again then dissolved, leaving him only with a piano sonata playing in his ear and the now sharp, high-definition scene before him. He took a few more calming breaths and slowly approached the narrow wooden table for a closer inspection.

He zeroed in on the objects—knives in various shapes and sizes. He took a step closer as if pulled to the table by an invisible rope and saw the kukri blade and the blood-smeared tanto knife. His attention sharply focused on the last, oddly shaped man-made weapon. "Fuck," he whispered on an exhale as the mental pieces connected, linking this case to another.

The flash of the forensics camera momentarily blinded him, weakening his guard against the flashback tugging at his consciousness. His lungs froze with a sharp inhale. Another flash. A large shadow cast against the wall of the detective holding the blindfold up in the air hurled him into another memory.

The blindfold was yanked from around his eyes. He quickly turned to look over his shoulder, and through the blindness of the bright sun, an outlined silhouette of a man haloed by the light, hovered over him like an angel of death holding a braided object, raised in the air ready to strike. The figure yelled a single word, before the object crashed down on his back.

The man's yell faded behind the piano sonata in his ear.

He swallowed heavily, fisting his hands and steeling himself. *This isn't real.*

The haloed figure from the flickering image vanished as quickly as it had appeared.

Focus.

He took a deep breath and straightened. Sunny entered the room from the side door and visually circled the scene before walking over to him. He casually pulled the earbuds out and returned them to the inside pocket of his sport coat.

She crossed her arms and rubbed her biceps. "There's a weird vibe in here. It's creepy as hell."

Aidan couldn't have agreed more.

"This isn't like the Miller case," she whispered.

"No, it's not. But look at the table. What do you see?" He glanced around the room, trying to keep their conversation from prying ears. Sunny hated it when he spoon-fed her information she could deduce on her own.

"What am I supposed to see?"

He waited. Sunny's detective skills were spot on. Her focus was intense and he could imagine her processing each item with careful detail. *C'mon. It's right there.*

He had always had an uncanny ability to disconnect from the traditional frame of thinking and connect pieces of a puzzle together. He never suffered from that out-of-place sense of disconnect people experienced from seeing the checkout person from the local grocery store in a different state and out of uniform, where it was easy to recognize the face, but placing *the where* was sometimes a little tricky. Aidan had a gift of remembering details and fluidly making connections from different places and times. It was seamless, effortless. He had an infinite stream of details, faces, places, and events. He had a memory bank of pieces he could easily assemble into coherent elements of a single puzzle. It was the only way he could explain how quickly he read between the lines or saw things others missed. And it was that same damn mental gift that caused his flashbacks to be so exhaustingly vivid at times.

"I don't see it." Sunny scowled and crossed her arms, not shifting her focus from the table.

"Look at the knives. And stop trying to frame your conclusions based on the Miller case."

Her scowl deepened as if she could focus her thoughts more intensely with her eyes. Moments later, the scowl slid off her face and her gaze snapped back to him.

"What do you see?" he asked.

"The last blade. It has the same odd curve shape of the Butterfly Killer's victims."

"Yes." He hated that fucking nickname and cursed the day he spotted the small inked insect as the case link.

A slow, wicked grin spread across Sunny's face. "Reyes is going to be super pissed he wasn't here."

"Yes," he said, fighting the smile that tugged at his lips.

Sunny's eyes rounded. "You know what this means."

Aidan nodded. "It means we finally have a lead if she's got that butterfly tattoo. We need to secure her at the hospital before the son of a bitch figures out she's escaped from this hell."

She pulled her cell phone from her pocket and started pressing keys. "I'm texting Wall to meet us there. Now, let's get the hell out of this place. It's totally creeping me out."

His sentiments exactly.

* * * *

Aidan walked through the doorway and locked the door behind him, quieting the buzz of the alarm system. He closed his eyes and inhaled the delicious scent of dinner wafting in the air.

"Hey there!" Jessie called out from the kitchen.

He needed this, needed Jessie and this bubble of safety that surrounded them here. He wanted to surrender, to rewind time and forget everything that happened in the last few hours, to give in and take Jessie in his arms, carry him away and make love to him the entire night. Hell, the entire weekend. Maybe the whole fucking week if he could manage to wipe his mind of all the damn memories that stopped him. But he couldn't. His heart and body wanted one thing, but his mind stopped him every time.

And today, his mind had taken extra effort to remind him exactly why he couldn't take that next step.

He set the alarm system and dropped his keys and wallet on the table. He screwed his eyes shut and roughly rubbed his forehead, finally raking his fingers through his hair. He needed to wrap the day up with some semblance of his sanity still intact. He needed a shower. And sleep. No, maybe not sleep. He didn't want to risk crashing so hard a nightmare would sneak up on him. Not today. He couldn't handle it after the day from hell. The crime scene had hinted at what to expect, but nothing could have prepared him for the interview with the victim that nearly broke him. It had taken every ounce of energy in his now zapped body to stand steady and strong with his fellow task force members in the room. Maybe the weekend off would give him enough time to rebuild his armor before starting over on Monday.

"I made..." Jessie trailed off once he walked out of the kitchen and into the living room, barefoot and shirtless, wearing his dark blue jeans. He immediately walked over to Aidan and reached out, placing his hand against Aidan's cheek.

Aidan released a shaky breath with the contact. Jessie's magical touch always settled the storm brewing within. He leaned into the caress, letting Jessie stroke his cheek, needing the tether of strength he always offered.

Jessie waited, a never-ending fountain of patience with him. "Dinner should be ready in a few minutes," he softly said, still stroking Aidan's cheek. "You have time for a quick shower." He reached up on his tiptoes and brushed his lips against Aidan's.

Aidan nodded and reluctantly pulled away from the touch. He willed his boots to move, one step, then the other. He managed to remove his jacket along the way and shed the rest of his clothes. How? He had no clue. He robotically switched on the water in the shower and stepped in when the steam began to rise. He closed his eyes and turned his face up toward the hot spray and let the water sluice down his body, hoping the remnants of the day would wash away and escape down the drain.

Snippets of the victim's interview from the hospital circled his mind. Her retelling of how he'd used the knives and everything he had done to her.

How he'd beat her.

Like me.

How he'd tied her up and blindfolded her.

Like me.

How he'd tied her to the hooks in the wall as he'd beat her, cut her, and found other ways to torture her.

Like me.

The memories, too vivid and her retelling much too similar for him to mentally block. Seeing her on the bed, bandaged, bruised, and swollen.

A reminder of Jessie after the attack.

A reminder of himself after another torture session.

All his effort and strength had gone to steeling himself, to ensure he appeared unaffected to his team. He had stood like a stone figure in the corner of the room without moving a single inch during the two-hour interview, performing an award-winning impersonation of Wall. He couldn't risk crumbling in front of his team.

No way would he show any form of weakness.

The interview had awakened far too many visions and taken too much strength to sustain his guard. He had barely escaped the hospital room before he began to crumble, unable to fight the demons in his head who sought vengeance, lashing out at him with repeated memories in quick succession. The yelling loud and the pictures vivid. He grabbed the lemon soap and lathered up the washcloth. He shoved his nose into the now lemon-scented material, hoping to replace the lingering smell of copper from a memory filling his senses. He rested his forearm against the shower tile wall, scarcely able to keep himself upright. The yelling voices echoed in his mind, all six of his captors screaming in unison. He barely had a chance to catch his breath when a phantom strike made contact with his back, throwing off his balance, forcing him to plant his palms against the tile to avoid falling to the floor. One strike, then another, and another. He gnashed his teeth, holding back the pain, his mind warring with the present and the past. The memory vivid, the smell in the air dank as if he were in that same room from years ago and the pain as sharp and as piercing now as it had been back then.

Is this real?

His body arched with another memory. This one more haunting than the others. He screwed his eyes shut and clawed at the tile wall, fighting the soreness of the rare, but most memorable torture they dispensed in the end when he tried to escape. He held back a growl of protest, tensing at the unbearable agony and searing burn of the phantom plunge of the truncheon-like object into his unprepared body. He shook his head vehemently as each breath sawed in and out of his lungs, trying and failing to fight the fire inside his body.

It's not real. It's not...

Or was it? He fought the memory but didn't have the energy to distinguish the now blurred line between reality and memory of a darker time. He focused his vision at the tile wall staring him down.

No. It's not real.

He was in a shower. *His* shower. Not out in the sun and mud under the spray of the ice cold water. He wasn't bound or gagged. He snarled at the tile wall, gritting his teeth and willing himself to straighten.

No. This isn't real. They can't break me.

With his remaining strength, he desperately scanned the shower for the fallen washcloth, snatching it up from the tile floor and feverishly rubbing his legs and body to wash away the lingering phantom blood and mud.

"Aidan?"

He spun quickly, almost losing his balance. A figure stood on the other side on the steam-covered glass. *Jess.* So close, yet so far away. He wanted to reach out. He needed his tether to ground him and support him and recharge his strength to battle the inescapable memories.

Aidan slowly straightened when Jessie approached. He inhaled sharply as Jessie opened the shower door and stepped in, not caring that he still wore his jeans. He reached out and grabbed Aidan by the shoulders, gently guiding him to turn his back toward the shower head, never breaking eye contact. He couldn't tear his focus away from every move Jessie made and how his lean muscles flexed with each controlled, careful shift in position.

Aidan closed his eyes when Jessie cupped his face, unable to control the strangled whimper that escaped, craving the closeness and strength his mind and body desperately needed. He reached out and snaked his arm around Jessie's waist, pulling him closer, reveling in the warmth and safety of the embrace, not caring about the harsh denim rubbing against his bare skin.

He exhaled a shaky breath, feeling a small ripple of peace begin to spread throughout his body as if a pebble had been pitched into the dark, still water of his soul. One pebble, then another, and another. Fingers stroked through his wet hair, calming his inner storm and tossing another pebble and another. He wrapped his other arm around Jessie's shoulders and held him close as Jessie placed tentative kisses along his neck, and pitched more imaginary pebbles his way, finally enough to stop the overflowing well of flashbacks.

"Dinner's going to burn," Aidan mumbled into Jessie's now wet hair.

"It'll keep. You're more important."

Aidan took a deep breath and tightened his hold on the body in his arms until the water ran cold, thankful for the endless supply of strength and peace Jessie always seemed to offer.

* * * *

All these damn flashbacks sneaking up on him were forcing Aidan to bump up his timetable to speed along his progress. For the last two weeks, he made it a point of trying harder during his therapy sessions, well, at least he thought so. He had to do something, anything to lessen all these damn memories that had suddenly awakened and messed with him. But he couldn't lock them away again. He'd been there and done that, and wouldn't go down that road again.

He hadn't been here in a while, but when the good doctor issued his first homework assignment, he figured this was a good place to start. He exited his SUV and rolled up his shirt sleeves as he worked his way along the familiar path. Another hot day but he figured he might as well do this now before he had a chance to talk himself out of it. He had sneaked away at lunchtime to be here. He had a goal and a deadline. Two things he could manage. Now he just needed to figure out all the details in between.

He ducked under an overgrown tree as he thought about his last few sessions.

"The increased frequency of your flashbacks is your mind's way of letting you know it's ready to heal," his doctor had said. Well, apparently his brain hadn't gotten the memo that a simple *I'm-ready-let's-work-on-this* would have sufficed. But in his typical style, he never did anything the easy way. "You need to talk," his doctor had said. *No shit*, he remembered thinking. "Say something to someone about something you're keeping to yourself. That will let you know it's okay to open up, to put yourself in a situation where you feel vulnerable. Pick someone. I don't care who, but it has to be someone you're close to. Someone whose opinion matters to you. Then share something you've kept closely guarded."

He finally reached his destination and sat on the ground between the two raised stones. He brought his knees up to his chest and wrapped his arms around his legs, suddenly feeling like the junior high school kid who used to cause them so many headaches. "Hi, Mom. Hi, Dad," he said with a sigh. He'd managed to nail down the *who* part of the assignment. He'd picked someone. Now he just needed to cover the *what* and the *why*—*what* he wanted to say, and *why* it needed to or should be discussed. Essentially, if it nagged his mind repeatedly, Ms. Fix-it said it merited a talkie.

Lovely.

He sat for a few minutes, trying to find the right set of words to string together to cover the other two parts of his assignment so he didn't feel like a failure. "I kinda suck at this, but my pain in the ass doctor seems to think talking will help me with stuff, so I figured I'd start with you guys since you can't push me if I don't say enough or tell me to shut up if I say too much." Leave it up to him to find a loophole in the doctor's homework assignment. Even knowing they weren't physically there, listening, he still found himself looking over his shoulder and off at a distance, avoiding the one-sided conversation.

He took a deep breath and tightened his arms around his knees. He could do this. Maybe. *Now or never.* "Dad, I know you loved me. I never questioned that. But it was really tough for me to be your kid. You were *the* Calloway. Everyone knew you, and everyone wanted to be you. And there I was, your son, heir to the car throne I didn't want. I felt as if I had failed you. And it didn't help that I suck at this whole talking thing. And when we did try, I couldn't hold an interest in a car conversation if my life depended on it." He took a few deep breaths, recovering for a moment after the rushed spill of words. "I'm sorry about that," he mumbled. "I know that was important to you." He sat for a few minutes, enjoying the sun's heat on his face and the silence. It was a different type of quiet. A place of rest and supposed tranquility. The sounds weren't muted, but there was a certain calmness in the air.

He sat for a bit more before breaking the audible stillness with his voice. "I felt like an outsider most times. When Ty came along, it's as if he just made everything perfect. You and he could do the car thing and he and I totally meshed with the sports. He was the glue that held everything together."

He quieted again. He needed to focus on what he came here to say. He had warmed up. Sorta. Kinda. Not really. He figured it was best to speak before he found some other excuse to stop.

"Dad, I'm…gay. I know I never actually told you, but I know you and Mom probably talked about it. She knew." He sighed. Had he actually just come out? Had he officially slapped a label on himself? He'd said it out loud, that should count for something. He looked over to his mother's headstone. "I know you knew. I figured that out the first time you asked me if I had met a nice young man in school." He shook his head at the memory. "Who the hell asks their son that?" he asked with a smile. "Thanks for never pushing. I'm not sure I would have been able to hold a conversation about this back then. Even after Ty came out to you guys. I guess I didn't want to risk creating any more distance. Being gay was one more thing that made me different from you both."

Why the hell is it so damn hard to say this stuff out loud?

He looked upward and sighed. "Gay. I hate that fucking word. Makes me sound as if I'm supposed to be happy 'cause I like dick." *Shit.* He cringed and ducked his head in his knees. "Sorry." He took a deep breath and glanced over his shoulder again before returning his focus to the carved stones. "I probably should have said something, especially after Ty came out. But…it's not like I had to worry about bringing home a date or something. No one ever stuck around that long. So I figured…it was best to just leave things alone…and not bring up something else that made us different. I had a million excuses…but I know now…I…just didn't want to disappoint you."

He closed his eyes and took a deep breath. "Dad, I know you're probably looking at me sideways, and Mom, I know you'd try to hug me if you were here, but that's how I felt at the time. It just never worked out for me and I always felt I was being punished for wanting to be with someone. I couldn't risk you guys turning away too." He pushed the tips of his boots into the ground and started rocking back and forth. "Ty's kinda pissed at me about it, and I know he wishes I would have told him years ago. It's just...too hard sometimes. Ty makes it look easy. He surrounds himself with others who are totally okay with him. Me?" he scoffed at himself. "Seems I can't do anything the easy way."

He swallowed heavily and rested his chin on his knees, trying to think of how best to talk about what had happened. Where to start, what to say. His mind wandered, thinking of different ways to begin the conversation. What would they say? What would they think of him once they knew? It was silly, but somehow, even in a one-sided conversation, talking about what had happened brought it all to the surface again and made it too real.

He closed his eyes and took a deep breath.

He couldn't do it.

He didn't want to bring something so ugly to a place of supposed peace and rest. Besides, he'd spoken more to them in one stretch than he thought he'd be able to manage when he'd arrived. He had officially moved on from toddler steps to a trotting stride. He could be hard on himself but wouldn't deny he'd made progress.

One point for Team Calloway.

He stretched out his legs and leaned backward, resting his weight on his hands. "So, guys. Now you know, with one-hundred-percent assurance, your Calloway legacy is two very gay sons." He couldn't resist a chuckle before quieting. "Don't worry, Ty's got Cole. Dad, I think you would have adopted him if you could. He's a total gearhead like you and Ty. It'd be great for everyone else if his mouth was taped shut, but I'm learning to pick my battles with him.

"And, Mom, now that I'm officially *out*, I know what you're going to ask me." He half smiled, swearing he could hear his mother's soft laughter before she asked the question he knew would soon follow his declaration. "Yes, I've finally met a nice young man. And I think you'd love him."

Chapter TWENTY

Jessie rested his head on Aidan's shoulder and sighed. He loved their quiet time together. They sat on the bench on the back porch and enjoyed the silence of the night, the only sound the occasional barking of a dog at a distance. He wrapped his hands around Aidan's arm and kissed him on the cheek. "You're really quiet tonight."

Aidan ran his fingers through the back of Jessie's hair. "Sorry. I've been racking my brain with a few cases and they're driving me nuts."

Nuts. Jessie snickered. "I don't mean to laugh."

Aidan shook his head and scoffed. "You need to chat with your therapist about your ball fetish." His features softened and his smile lingered. The openness in his hazel eyes made a slight appearance.

"It's not my case, is it?"

"No." Aidan's brow lowered. "The team's not letting me go anywhere near your case until there's something solid to go on." He quieted, his expression deepening as if he were lost in thought.

"I'm sure they're trying. But if Michael doesn't want to be found, that's going to make it tougher for everyone." *Including me.* "I'm not going to put my life on hold and I'm not going to let him have that much power over me."

"Can we…not talk about that asshole?" He placed a tender kiss at the side of Jessie's head. "Please."

"Okay." Jessie could only imagine the self-torture Aidan subjected himself to, not being able to solve the case and having most of his team members fight him on his involvement. And stress was certainly not something he wanted to focus on at that moment. "Tell me something about you."

Aidan turned to face him, reaching up to brush his thumb against Jessie's cheek. His expression relaxed as if a burden had been slightly lifted with the change in subject. "What do you want to know?"

Jessie inched closer, hoping Aidan would take the not-so-subtle hint. He smiled when Aidan leaned in for a kiss then slid his arm around his shoulders, pulling him into a single-armed embrace. He lay down across Aidan's lap, clasping Aidan's hand and holding it to his chest. "Tell me about the first guy you liked. And don't give me just a year, grade, or age. Tell me where you met. Tell me something about him."

"Okay." Aidan quieted for a few moments before speaking. "Sixth grade. I met him at a football game. He went to the opponent's school."

"You were a rebel even back then." Jessie laughed, slowly stroking their entwined hands. "Don't stop now. You're on a roll."

"Who's the smartass now?" Aidan ran his fingers across Jessie's forehead, brushing away a random strand. He quieted for a few seconds as if gathering his thoughts before he finally spoke. "We talked between plays, and it was…easy. After school, we'd meet up at the basketball court at the nearby park." Aidan took a deep breath. "One day, we're hanging out by the bleachers at his school, watching the visiting team scrimmage before the football game. My arm was up against his. Before I knew it, we were holding hands. It felt…nice."

Aidan's hold on their still-clasped hands tightened.

"One of the kids from the visiting school saw us. All hell broke loose after that. They beat us up so badly. After that, he hated me. He said it was all my fault because I had held his hand." He quieted and his body became rigid. He released Jessie's hand and spread his arm across the back of the bench.

"What about after him? And I swear, if you mention the quota for the week—"

Aidan glanced down at Jessie. "You should amend your requirement and make it one subject matter for the week rather than one detail."

"Consider it amended. What about after him?"

Aidan shrugged then looked away again. This would have been the perfect time for Aidan to deliver another Aidanism to steer the conversation away from revealing something personal or emotional. Instead, he remained quiet and his jaw muscles tensed.

Jessie reached up, running his hand along Aidan's neck then chest. "Tell me."

Aidan nudged him to sit up. He then leaned forward, pushed his palms together. Aidan's thinking face was not something most people experienced. He usually cloaked whatever thought crossed his mind with something snarky. But it was obvious he was struggling with the thought. Whether it was what to say, how to say it, or how much to say, Jessie wasn't sure, but he was certain Aidan was trying.

Jessie leaned forward in a sitting position, mirroring Aidan's pose, hoping to break his concentration before he strained a reveal-too-much-personal-info brain muscle.

Aidan sighed. "Sorry."

"Don't overthink. Just tell me."

He ran his fingers through his hair and clasped his hands again, almost seeming angry at himself for the nervous gesture. "I screwed around a lot in high school. Nothing steady and nothing serious and definitely nothing at my school. I'd talk to a guy, meet him at the mall or something."

"So no cheerleaders?" Jessie teased, bumping Aidan's shoulder and hoping to lighten Aidan's mood.

Aidan half smiled. "No, but the captain of the football team blew me after the championship game." He looked sideways and tried to hold back a playful grin.

"I thought you didn't do anything at the school?"

"The game was at the visitor's school."

"Do you always look for the loophole in a situation?" Jessie laughed.

"Always."

"What about after high school?"

Aidan shook his head at some thought. "I thought things might change, you know, because times are *supposed* to change and all that crap. But all that's bullshit. When I was in the service, just after boot camp, there was this guy. We clicked right away, but we kept everything on the down low for the few months we were together. One night, we're messing around... I mean, we weren't doing anything, just sitting really close, shoving each other and saying stupid shit. Two other guys from our unit walked in and started cracking jokes about how friendly we looked together. I played it off, but he couldn't." Aidan sighed heavily and shook his head again. "Rumors started spreading and it got really tough out there."

He quieted for a few moments, leaning forward, resting his forearms against his thighs. "When you're in the field, you need to know the guys in your unit have your back. And somewhere along the line, that changed. He couldn't handle that. He decided to call it quits, but I stayed. When I signed up again, I thought things would settle down, but they didn't. I got pissed and...reckless. I put myself in the line of fire and at risk more often than not just to prove I didn't fit their stereotype." He pursed his lips almost into a sneer while his eyes held a slow simmering anger beneath the surface. "We had talked about doing a tour together." He shrugged. "I guess that's the closest I ever came to a relationship."

"Did you love him?"

"No," Aidan said without hesitation. "We shared something in common and that made things a little easy, but that's it. It might have turned into something down the line, but who knows. I was pissed off he didn't even bother trying."

Jessie placed his hand at the back of Aidan's neck, rubbing the tension in the tight muscles. "What about after the service? Anyone since then?"

"No," he responded, his features devoid of any emotion.

Jessie remained quiet, processing the new bit of information— *personal* information—Aidan had provided. After all this time, he'd barely opened up about details, especially something that seemed to hold such a mix of emotions for him. Aidan often said little in his words but spoke volumes in his body language and tone. His words from the other night connected with the new personal piece of information, interlocking like two pieces of the same puzzle, finally revealing a little more of the big image. "You're worried I'm going to walk away if we get closer," he said, more as a statement than a question.

Aidan pushed his palms together and thinned his lips. "I lost the only two guys who were more than friends to me. I lost my parents. My best friend's in protective custody. I almost lost my brother. And..." He stopped himself as if fighting to finish his sentence. "I feel I've been cursed since birth to be alone."

"I'm not walking away from *us*."

"I've been through all kinds of shit and I'm still here. But losing you..." He looked over to Jessie, the mix of emotions screaming from his hazel eyes gripped Jessie's throat. "I can't lose you. I won't recover from that. I don't need you to leave for me to realize—"

"What are you afraid of?"

Aidan's jaw muscles twitched. "I wasn't expecting to ever find someone who'd understand me. Someone who'd want to be with me." He looked away and took a deep breath. "I don't ever want to lose that feeling."

"You won't." Jessie wrapped his arms around Aidan's bicep.

Aidan scoffed. "I'm a stubborn asshole who's insensitive and sarcastic and—"

"Just because you say it, doesn't mean it's true. You're a sweet man. I'm glad I'm the only one who knows that side of you."

"I know I'm not easy and I know I'm going to fuck this up—"

Jessie released Aidan's arm and firmly gripped his face, drawing his focus. "I'm not going to let you sabotage what we *can* have. I've already told you I'm not going anywhere. You joke that you're taking baby steps, and I'm fine with that because I know that means you're not giving up."

"No one is that patient," Aidan said, pulling away, sitting straight and tugging on the edge of his shirt. "And...I'm not sure I can do the hold your hand walking down the street thing. You need someone nice. Someone who'll laugh as much as you do and be as...I don't know...as perfect as you."

"First of all, I'm not perfect. Secondly, that sounds really boring," he said, ticking the items off on his fingers. "And I'm completely rejecting my invitation to this pity party you're hosting at the moment. It doesn't suit you at all."

Aidan shook his head and scoffed.

Jessie reached up and ran his thumb along Aidan's stubble. "I want someone who makes me feel special. Someone who respects me. Someone who makes me feel safe and strong. Someone who treats me like an equal in the relationship. Someone who cares enough about me to stop for a second and make sure I'm okay. Someone who I can be the real me with and lets me know that's okay." He searched Aidan's features, trying to send a telepathic message that would bypass his iron defenses. "That's you, Aidan. It's always been you. That's you without even trying."

Aidan turned toward Jessie, leaning in to keep his cheek in contact with Jessie's fingers.

Jessie's lips parted on a breath, clearly seeing every unspoken emotion aimed at him in those hazel eyes—a silent message that nothing else mattered in that moment or in the world other than Jessie. It was those intimate, candid moments Jessie craved more than anything, where Aidan shed the facade the outside world knew and exposed his soul for only Jessie to see. "I don't need someone who's going to hold my hand in public then treat me like shit in private. I'm fine going slow, and I'm fine being discreet, because it's nobody's business. This is about you and me."

Aidan turned and kissed Jessie's palm. "I'm not ashamed of us. I just don't want anyone telling me it's wrong because I know it's not." He leaned over and brushed his lips against Jessie's ear. "It feels too fucking perfect when I'm with you."

Jessie closed his eyes, knowing the words wouldn't come easily for Aidan...if they ever did. But it was always there, in his eyes, in the way he tentatively ghosted his fingers with a touch, and the way his tone softened when they were alone. Because of Aidan, he finally knew what it felt like to be loved. So if Aidan needed time or space, Jessie would grant him an eternity if he could cherish a few moments with the real Aidan—the one who showed the unfiltered, sacred, pure emotion in his soul.

He observed every fidgeting gesture in Aidan's body. He reached out, stroking Aidan's arm, hoping to ease the tension in his tight muscles. "You know I love you, Aidan. I don't say it because I don't want you to think I'm pressuring you to say it back. But it's there. It's a constant between us. Words don't come easy for you, and that's okay.

I feel it in everything you do." He brushed his fingertips along the length of Aidan's arm, hoping his words didn't spook Aidan and trigger his retreat. "Everyone you've gotten close to…leaves. So I understand why you close yourself off whenever we start to get close."

"I don't mean to," Aidan whispered.

Jessie glanced up, his chest tightening at the worry in Aidan's expression. The battling need to stay strong and the desire to open up pushed and pulled in that hazel gaze. "I know," he said, reaching out to stroke Aidan's hair at his temple. "Your heart knows I'm not like everyone else, but until your head gets with the program, you're going to fight it. But please know, every second of every day, with every breath and heartbeat, I love you."

Aidan's jaw muscles twitched.

"I can understand why you need to be a hardass at work and why you guard your privacy so fiercely. But I want you to be yourself with me and know you're in a safe place and can tell me anything."

Aidan pressed a lingering kiss to the side of Jessie's head. "I don't deserve you."

"Do you want me to kick you in the balls now or later for saying that?" The soft rumble of Aidan's chuckle vibrated throughout Jessie's body, lighting up each nerve ending.

"Promise me something," Aidan whispered.

"Anything."

Aidan kept his face hidden as he spoke. "If you… If…I take too long and you think you're going to give up on me…give me a heads up, okay?"

Jessie turned toward Aidan and brushed their lips together for a barely-there kiss.

"I'm not giving up on you. Whether you know it or not, when I was in the hospital stuck in that weird state of limbo, it was you…your voice, knowing you were there… You brought me back. You never gave up on me." He reached up and placed his palm at the side of Aidan's face, hoping to calm the worry staring back at him in those hazel eyes. "Just know, I'm here with you. However long it takes through whatever we need to work through."

Aidan leaned forward and pressed their lips together, cupping

Jessie's face to deliver a kiss fused with tenderness and need, sparking the always-present urgency for closeness while keeping it in check with a solemn vow of forever.

Jessie reached out, grabbing onto Aidan's arm, reveling in the slow slide of their tongues, triggering a surge of goose pimples to burst across his skin. He dug his fingers in the lean muscles and reached up with his other hand, tugging Aidan closer. A whimper escaped when Aidan broke the kiss, inching away slightly but staying close enough for each strangled breath to blow across Jessie's cheek.

"I promise I'm trying."

"I know you are," Jessie said, running his fingers through Aidan's hair. "But I might nudge you a bit along the way. Are you okay with that?"

Aidan nodded. "I swear there's nowhere else I'd rather be than with you."

Jessie closed his eyes and wrapped his arms around Aidan's neck, holding back the flood of emotions triggered by the promise in those few words. "Then don't you dare stop trying, or I'm kicking you in the balls."

Aidan quietly laughed, pulling Jessie close, refusing to release him from the embrace. "Deal."

* * * *

"Aidan?"

"Yeah…" he said, leaning back on the couch. He could easily do this every night. Hanging out, avoiding all the drama and stress of work and the burden of having to be on guard all the time. Being with Jessie was easy. Effortless. And definitely what he needed nearing the end of another long week at the precinct.

Jessie grabbed the remote and switched off the television then turned to face him, delivering a heated stare. That look in those piercing crystal blue eyes always shot a bolt straight to his dick. The desire, the need, the want.

All for him.

Only for him.

"I'm horny."

Aidan's heartbeat quickened. "Is this your way of nudging me?" Maybe a week of non-progress in the relationship department triggered Jessie's nudging gene to kick in.

Jessie stared at him, not saying a single word. He pulled the T-shirt up and over his head and tossed it carelessly to the side.

"Okay," he said, cautiously, not really sure what the hell to do with this side of Jessie. He would expect Jessie to be subtle, to have folded the shirt perfectly and set it on the table.

Jessie shook his head slowly. "It's definitely *not* okay." He inched toward him.

When Jessie had that determined look in his eye and decided to step it up, taking the initiative when his slow ass didn't make a move, Aidan was totally screwed and defenseless. The spontaneous element both excited him and made him nervous as hell. Aidan inched back toward the end of the couch, hoping for some safety in his corner. Apparently, exactly where Jessie wanted him to be. Cornered, unable to escape. Jessie worked his way up Aidan's torso, slowly, cautiously, inch by inch, pressing himself into Aidan.

"I know you're horny too."

Aidan swallowed heavily. "No, I'm not." *Bullshit.* Hornier than a herd of feral beasts during mating season, he willed his body to remain in check, fighting his natural reaction to Jessie's nearness.

Jessie arched into Aidan then dipped his head, kissing and nipping Aidan's earlobe. "You're lying. You have a tell."

"No, I don't." He gripped the edge of the sofa cushions, trying to level his breathing.

"Yes, you do."

"I don't."

Jessie reached down and gripped Aidan's rock-hard dick jammed between them. "Trust me. You've got a very big, unmistakable tell."

"Jess…"

Jessie stopped and backed away a few inches, granting just

enough distance between them to stop the exploration. He scanned Aidan's features, observing in that way he did that seemed to be deciphering each of Aidan's actions. "Do you…want me to stop?"

Fuck. No. Aidan wanted this closeness. Every atom in his body desperately craved a physical connection with Jess. He shook his head, unable to speak.

Jessie pulled Aidan's shirt off. "Touch me."

Aidan released a shaky breath. The weight of Jessie, the warmth of his skin, his scent, the tentative touch—all becoming familiar and addictive.

Jessie rubbed his thumb along Aidan's stubble. "Touch me."

Aidan reached out but hesitated. He clenched his fist before finally deciding to graze his fingertips against Jessie's skin. Jessie closed his eyes and pressed himself against Aidan's hard chest, burying his nose at the side of Aidan's neck and running the tip of his tongue along Aidan's bobbing Adam's apple. Anticipation thrummed through Aidan with his forwardness.

He wanted this…more than anything.

"Tell me what you want," Jessie whispered between licks and kisses along his neck.

He moaned and turned his head, granting Jessie more room to continue exploring. He reached behind Jessie's neck and gently cupped the back of his head, keeping him in place and holding him close, not wanting the contact to end.

"I don't know." *This. All of this. Any of this.*

Jessie pulled back and watched him closely. "Okay, how about you tell me what's a *hell no,* then we'll go from there."

Aidan cleared his throat, not exactly sure where or how to begin. And hell, there was no way he could think of more than one thing at a time with his fingers buried in Jessie's hair and Jessie's fingertips rubbing against his skin while he waited for Aidan to speak.

Jessie inched closer, leaning in and placing a trail of slow kisses along Aidan's jawline. "Nothing will scare me away from you."

A frustrated moan escaped him. He couldn't sort his thoughts or assemble a sentence when Jessie did that thing with his tongue and lips against Aidan's skin. Jessie reached out and clasped Aidan's wrists, pulling them up and out, bracing him as Jessie pushed his body against him.

Aidan instinctively stilled. "*Never* hold me down."

Jessie immediately released him and gazed into his eyes as if fitting another piece into the puzzle. "Okay."

Fighting his growing arousal, he couldn't focus on stringing together more words. He screwed his eyes shut and let Jessie continue with his kissing trail. He finally opened his eyes and reached out to cup Jessie's face, knowing he needed to speak and finish his thought. "That applies to me and you. I can't...I..." He took another deep breath as he stared into the crystal sea of blue in Jessie's questioning gaze, trying to connect his thoughts into a sentence. "I won't hurt you."

The edges of Jessie's lips curved upward into a soft smile. "I know."

Aidan exhaled a relieved breath.

"But you know..."

Aidan closed his eyes for a moment when Jessie's fingertips traveled down from his neck to his torso, tracing the ink at his side.

"Having your way with me over your favorite couch, on the table, or against a wall won't *hurt* me." Jessie leaned over Aidan and chased his fingertips with the warmth of his mouth.

Aidan arched up into Jessie's lips, seeking and craving every slow, long swipe of his tongue and brush of his full lips. Every millimeter of contact awakened his body, resurrecting desires and needs that had been dormant for far too long. He gripped the back of Jessie's head, encouraging him to continue as a groan escaped. He reached around with his other hand and kneaded Jessie's ass cheek, tugging him closer, flush against his already hard and ready body.

"Fuck...don't stop," Aidan said on another groan as Jessie pressed against him while licking and biting his chin and jaw. He threaded his fingers in Jessie's hair and closed his eyes, reveling in the prickling current coursing through his veins and every nerve ending of his skin.

It had been too damn long and his body was hyper-aware of even the tiniest graze and caress. "Jess..."

"Mmm," Jessie mumbled with a teasing nip against his skin, pressing his weight against Aidan.

Aidan reached under Jessie's chin with his index finger, drawing Jessie's focus. "Tell me what *you* want," he said, his voice thick with need.

Jessie ceased the teasing touches and reached up, carding his fingers through Aidan's hair. After a few gentle strokes, he tightened his grip and pulled Aidan's head to the side, leaning in and kissing along the corded muscle of Aidan's neck as he spoke. "I want to lick every inch of you. I want to know what you feel like in my mouth and how you taste."

Those words shot straight to Aidan's dick faster than a jolt of adrenaline. He screwed his eyes shut. His breath came in quick bursts and a groan escaped when Jessie pressed his hand against the rock-hard bulge in Aidan's jeans. He peered back at Jessie, mesmerized by the teasing stare and obvious want and need in his gaze.

Jessie smiled and bit his lower lip. "Are you okay with that?"

He nodded and wrapped his arms around Jessie, pulling him closer. A frenzied storm of want and need pushed him to the edge. He was close. Too damn close and probably wouldn't last long enough to free his hard-on from the ridiculously tight jeans cutting off his circulation. He had abandoned all sense of control the second Jessie's lips touched his skin. He pushed up into Jessie's body, craving friction and contact. His breath hitched at the sound of the zipper. He raised his hips when Jessie tugged at his jeans, inhaling sharply at the rush of cool air brushing past his heated skin. He gasped when Jessie's cool fingers wrapped around him and began a slow up and down sliding rhythm.

Aidan bit into his lower lip as his body arched, pushing into Jessie's grip. "I'm not gonna last."

Jessie nipped his earlobe and whispered, "Good. Then I won't have to wait much longer." He quickly lowered his body on the couch, between Aidan's legs, and swiped his tongue along Aidan's shaft from root to tip.

"Fuck!" Aidan grabbed at the cushions beneath him, writhing when Jessie's lips wrapped around him and pulled him into the wet warmth of his mouth. A current shot up Aidan's spine and rippled throughout his body, numbing his senses and igniting a fuse within. He couldn't think and couldn't breathe as fingers dug into his waist—lost to everything but Jessie, his firm touch, and the warmth of his mouth wrapped around him. His heartbeat pounded furiously as if trying to rip through his chest. He looked down at the lust-filled gaze staring back at him, unmistakable desire shone in Jessie's eyes. Jessie wanted him.

Him.

That gaze and its intensity fueled the lighted fuse traveling along every muscle in his body. "Jess…" He barely managed to warn him before the fuse reached its target and exploded in an orgasm that shifted his being, simultaneously charging and numbing every inch of his body into oblivion.

He lay weak on the couch, barely able to breathe, wondering if he'd ever come so hard in his life. He threw his forearm over his face. No. Never that hard. Never like that. And sure as shit never that fast.

"You okay?" Jessie asked, sitting up and resting his head against Aidan's shoulder.

"That was…embarrassing." He peeked under his arm, frowning when Jessie chuckled. "I'm glad I amuse you."

"*I'm* glad I can make you come that fast."

Aidan grunted a reply.

Jessie licked along the shell of Aidan's ear then nipped at his earlobe. "I'm perfectly fine practicing to improve your response time."

"Smartass." Completely under Jessie's spell, he couldn't muster an ounce of control over a millimeter of his body. He'd just lost it moments ago and his treacherous body eagerly awaited round two.

"Can we do that again?" Jessie asked quietly, stroking his fingertips against Aidan's chest, hesitating to make eye contact.

Aidan reached out and raised Jessie's chin until their eyes met. "*I'm* glad you want me enough to do that again."

A shy but teasing smile spread across Jessie's face. "I want you enough to do *a lot* of things to you."

Aidan grasped the back of Jessie's head and pulled him into a kiss. He groaned when greedy fingers wrapped around his semi hard-on, quickly bringing him to full attention with a renewed reservoir of want and need flooding his body. They kissed and moaned, grabbing and pulling each other repeatedly. He eagerly let Jessie explore every inch of exposed skin he wanted to touch, lick or kiss.

Later that evening, they both lay spent on the couch, barely able to breathe, still half-dressed. He smiled, giddy with excitement, reveling in the wonder that they hadn't scratched the surface of all the *things* Jessie wanted to do to him that he would willingly allow.

* * * *

"Good morning," Jessie said in a tone thick with sleep as he walked over to the kitchen.

"Hey," Aidan said, hiding a grin. Responding with "great fucking morning" would have been a bit much. He certainly didn't want to push his luck and say anything more than the bare essentials and risk screwing up the warm fuzzies lingering from their night on the couch. He glanced over his shoulder and his body immediately responded to the rare sight of a tousled-haired Jessie. He returned his focus to the brewing pot of coffee. He couldn't chance being late—the team would know something was up and he didn't want to screw up his good mood telling them to fuck off. He'd already extended his morning as much as possible, unable to rip himself away from Jessie's warmth.

"Staring at it won't make it brew any faster."

Aidan smiled. "Smartass." He turned to sneak a glance at Jessie leaning against the entryway and stilled. The playfulness evaporated as a wave of anger slowly took its place. He took a few deep breaths to hold off the simmering fury. In two steps, he stood by Jessie, pulling down the edge of his sleep pants. "What the fuck?"

Jessie looked down at his bruised skin. "It doesn't hurt."

Aidan gripped the waistband of Jessie's pants and twisted them in his fist. "Did I…" he began but couldn't speak through the tightness in his throat.

Jessie reached up and placed his hand against the side of Aidan's freshly-shaven face. "It doesn't hurt at all. I swear."

He closed his eyes and shook his head, stumbling as he took a step backward. The thought that he'd hurt *his* Jess.

"Look at me."

He bent his head and slumped his shoulders, folding into himself. "I'm sorry," he whispered. "I—"

"Look at me, dammit."

Aidan flinched. He took a deep breath and finally opened his eyes, making contact with the blue gaze that always weakened him.

"You would never hurt me. I know that. And *you* know that. So stop it. I bruise easily. I always have. I also don't tan when out in the sun like you do… I burn."

Aidan shook his head and looked down at the angry purple marks stamped across Jessie's hip. He looked over to the opposite side of his hips and the breath left his lungs when he saw another set of matching bruises. "Fuck." He turned away as a series of images flashed across his mind—Jessie in the hospital bed, the blood, the swollen-shut eye, the bruising…

A firm grip and pull on his arm yanked him from his spiraling thoughts. Jessie stepped forward, invading Aidan's personal space, his shoulders squared, and a fire of determination burned in his eyes. "Don't do that."

"Do what?"

"These bruises are not the same as the ones I had in the hospital."

Aidan scowled. Sometimes, he hated how transparent he was to Jessie.

"And I already told you, this doesn't hurt." Jessie wrapped his arms around Aidan and ran his hands up and down his back. "Besides, I love the fact that you let your guard down with me and lost control. It lets me know how badly you want me. So just stop it."

Aidan exhaled heavily and stepped away, turning back to the coffee pot that seemed to be taking forever to brew. "Bruises are bruises, Jess. I did that to you. Wanting you is no excuse for hurting you." He scoffed, unable to hide his contempt. Wouldn't that be the same miserable excuse that son of a bitch would use for hurting Jess and putting him in the hospital?

Jessie yanked his shoulder again to force him to face him. His lips thinned and his chest heaved with each measured breath. "I asked you to not do that. It's not the same thing."

Aidan crossed his arms. "Enlighten me. It's a bruise, Jess."

Jessie closed his eyes and took a deep breath. He looked off to the side as if gathering his thoughts, finally returning his attention back to Aidan, calmer and more in control. "I'm going to ask you a few questions. You answer yes or no."

"Jess—"

Jessie raised a stopping hand. "Humor me."

Aidan inclined his head, encouraging him to continue.

"Would you throw something at me in anger?"

Aidan straightened. "Jess, this isn't funny—"

Jessie crossed his arms and planted himself firmly in front of Aidan. "Yes or no. Which is it?"

"No."

"Would you ever hit me in anger?"

"No," he responded, the anger slowly simmering at this line of questioning, not really sure why Jessie thought he might do something like that.

"Would you ever call me useless, stupid, or tell me the world would be better off without me?"

A knot formed in Aidan's throat as the painful realization began to set in. "No," he said, barely able to voice the small word.

Jessie took a deep breath and tilted his head upward, fighting the tears that began to pool in his eyes. "If I had said 'stop' or 'no' at any point last night, would you have stopped?"

Aidan swallowed the painful knot in his throat, finally understanding the reason behind Jessie's questions. "Yes." He reached out and gently placed his hands on Jessie's waist, barely grazing his skin. "Jess…"

"I know you want everything nice and sweet with me. But it's not the same, and I need you to understand that. I'm not afraid when I'm with you and you are not malicious or hurtful." Jessie jabbed his finger at Aidan's chest. "You are not abusive. You don't scare me."

Aidan leaned in and placed a tender kiss on Jessie's lips. "I guess you didn't get the memo about me being a frightening son of a bitch."

Jessie threw his arms around Aidan's neck. "There *is* something about you that scares me."

Aidan frowned. "What's that?"

"I'm afraid you'll never really let go with me. That you'll always keep a part of yourself stashed away in that internal safe of yours. Sometimes, I see a hint of it before you catch it and hide it away. I saw it in your eyes last night. I want that. I want all of that. It doesn't scare me. What we do together, however wild it gets, it's not violent."

Aidan pressed a kiss to the side of Jessie's head, holding him close, not wanting to imagine what Jessie had been through growing up and as a teen. "I'd never hurt you, Jess."

"I know. But now, with these bruises, I'm worried you're going to pull away and hold back more than ever. And that…" Jessie paused before continuing. "That hurts me more than any bruise I've ever had."

Aidan exhaled heavily. He really wished he was a better communicator.

Jessie inched back, separating from the embrace. He looked up at Aidan, a fiery look of determination screamed from his expression. "Question for you."

Uh-oh, round two. "Go ahead."

"Do you trust me?"

"You know I do." Aidan crossed his arms and cocked his head.

"Do you think I trust you?"

He frowned and shoved his hands in his pockets. "I…I hope so."

"Then trust me enough to know my limits and to be honest with you to tell you when you get there. Because I *know* you'll listen and stop if I need you to."

Aidan sighed. *Dammit.* He hated when people made logical arguments that didn't play in his favor.

Jessie took a step forward and grabbed Aidan's waist with far more aggression than Aidan could have anticipated. But his dick definitely took notice and wanted to join in. "I'm not fragile," Jessie said. "If you want slow and sweet, soft and nice, that's fine. But if you want me any other way, don't you dare hold back. Because I sure as hell don't want you going elsewhere. Understand?"

"I wouldn't go elsewhere." Aidan's jaw hurt from clenching his teeth so hard. It took him years to finally open his heart to someone. Not just someone. *Jessie.* No one had ever had a hold of his heart the way *his* Jess did. And no one else ever would. He reached out and grabbed the back of Jessie's head and pulled him forward, slamming their lips together, telling him, without words, just how much he wanted every inch of him, all to himself, and only him. He guided Jessie exactly where he wanted him, pushing his tongue between Jessie's lips and unmistakably branding him with a kiss filled with want and need.

Jessie gripped Aidan's biceps for balance, digging his fingers into the hard muscle. They finally separated from the kiss but still remained a breath away.

A slow smile spread across Jessie's face. "That's what I'm talking about."

Aidan shook his head. He was a weak son of a bitch when it came to this man. He looked into those crystal blue eyes he loved so much and huffed out a quiet laugh at the mischief staring back at him. Without question, Jessie had him wrapped around his finger and handled every inch of his mind and body.

And for the first time in Aidan's life, he was totally fine with that.

Chapter TWENTY-ONE

They followed their routine for the rest of that week, spending some time working at the dining room table on one of the files in Cam's case then eventually retreating to the comfort of their couch. Jessie loved their lazy Sundays, especially when they did nothing but spend time together. It didn't matter if they hung out on the back porch, worked out together, or just joked around. He cherished the privacy—the peacefulness, the closeness, the slow, lazy brush of fingers against his skin in a casual caress.

"Are you off next Saturday?" Jessie asked.

"Yeah. Did you want to do something?"

"Maybe in the afternoon. I have a delivery coming in the morning so I wanted to make sure you were here."

"Delivery?"

"I ordered some furniture. Well, technically, you did, it was on your credit card. But I did transfer the money into your account."

Aidan raised an eyebrow. "So you weren't kidding? Tell me it's not pastel or flowery."

"Hot pink."

Aidan lazily chuckled. "I picked up on your sarcasm that time."

"It's for your room. I ordered a bed—"

"Jess—"

He held up a stopping hand. "Hear me out."

Aidan stiffened but nodded.

"The bed is king-size. That way, whenever you're ready, we're not squeezing into the full-size bed in the guest room. There's no deadline and I'm not pushing you to jump in the bed. But I want a new bed that will be ours for whenever you are ready."

Aidan didn't look bothered, but there was a hint of emotion shining from his hazel eyes. "Okay."

"I also bought a couch to replace the one you refuse to use. We can move the one that's there now into the workout room. That way, you still keep it, but you'll have one in there you will actually use."

Aidan continued to watch him carefully, a barely noticeable softness tweaking his features. "When did you go to the furniture store?"

"Online. A totally review-driven choice, but anything is better than the bed in the guest room, and I think we're wearing out this couch far quicker than it was intended."

"Hey, I like this couch."

Jessie laughed and patted the backrest. "I know you do that's why it'll be a cold day in hell before I even joke about doing anything to this old girl."

A teasing smile lingered on Aidan's lips.

"I know it's your bedroom—"

"It's *our* house."

A swell of emotions tightened Jessie's throat. He reached for Aidan's hand. "I know it's important for you to have your space, but I hate sleeping in the guest room on those nights you work late."

"You could sleep on the couch."

"You refuse to wake me and I refuse to have you sleeping on the damn floor and you aren't comfortable in that small side chair. So this way, if you work late, I'll sleep in the new bed in your room—"

"In *our* room."

Jessie smiled. "In *our* room. And when you get in, you can sleep on the new, extra cushioned couch in the same room. That way, we don't have walls and a hallway between us."

Aidan reached up and brushed his thumb along Jessie's cheek.

"You're such a control freak."

Jessie leaned forward, a mere inch away from Aidan's face. "And I think you like it."

"I do. But only when it's you."

Jessie leaned in for a quick kiss. "It'll be our secret."

Aidan cupped the back of Jessie's head and pulled him forward, lazily nipping and sucking on Jessie's lip then pulling away. He stood, tugging Jessie by his hand.

"Where are we going?" Jessie asked, refusing to stand, still dazed after the kiss.

"We need to move out that old couch from our room." Aidan tilted his head as if a thought had crossed his mind. "If we move over the dresser that's in there and shift the desk to the corner the way Hunter had it before, I've still got my pacing space when the bed comes in."

Jessie bit his kiss-swollen lip, trying to hold back the flutter of emotions at Aidan's enthusiasm.

"C'mon." He started walking away and stopped when Jessie didn't follow. "It was your bright idea." He returned to the couch and reached behind Jessie, wrapping one arm around his back and the other cupping his ass, effortlessly picking him up, off his feet and pulling him flush against his body. "Besides, I like seeing you work up a sweat with me."

Jessie wrapped his arms around Aidan's neck and anchored his legs around his waist. "Mmm. I like the sound of that."

"So…" Aidan brushed his lips slowly against Jessie's. "What do I need to do to convince you to help me?"

"Are you taking your shirt off?"

Aidan brushed his lips back and forth against Jessie's mouth. "If you want me to."

"Well, when you put it that way, how can I resist?"

Aidan laughed and pressed his forehead to Jessie's, still holding him in his arms as he made his way into *their* room. "You're insatiable."

"For you, always."

* * * *

Aidan entered his passcode and walked through the cage and down the hallway—his stride, lighter than normal. He couldn't seem to get Jessie or their weekend together out of his head. Jessie had turned his teasing up a notch and Aidan had been completely at his mercy. They'd spent the better part of the weekend at home, vegging out on the couch watching movies or just making out the way he figured most teenagers with raging hormones would.

He pushed through the meeting room door and pulled out the chair next to Sunny. "Good morning," he said, plopping himself in the seat.

Sunny shifted her head toward him and slowly raised an eyebrow.

"What?" Aidan said, grabbing one of the files from the center of the table.

"You're smiling."

"What?" he asked again, thumbing through the file.

"You're smiling." She reached over and closed his folder, drawing his attention.

Aidan looked up. "I heard you the first time. I *do* smile, you know."

Sunny turned in her seat to face him. "Newsflash. You only half smile or do this real twisted, evil grin thing which just freaks me out. But you're smiling. Like…really smiling. Smiling with your eyes."

"You can't smile with your eyes."

"Sure, you can. It's the difference between a genuine smile and a Calloway smile. You, my dear, are smiling like the rest of us."

Aidan lowered his brow. "Put a cork in it, Sunshine," he mumbled, pulling the file away from her grasp and reopening it.

Sunny laughed. "See, you can't even be pissed off and taken seriously right now. You're still smiling."

The door opened and both looked up to greet Travis. He set his cup down and watched them, slowly taking his seat. "What did I miss?"

"Nothing," Aidan said, thumbing through the pages.

Sunny bit her lip, but her body shook, holding back the laughter.

"Oh, come on, guys. Fess up. It's got to be fucking hysterical if Calloway's smiling."

Aidan looked up at Travis, narrowing his eyes as he spoke. "You guys are impossible. Review the file before the meeting."

Sunny and Travis laughed in unison. "Sunny, give me Vega's number. Whatever he put in his coffee, we need to mass produce that shit!"

Aidan tightened his lips, holding back a chuckle. "Shut the fuck up. You guys make it sound as if I never smile."

Sunny and Travis quieted and both stared at him, neither saying a word.

"We've known each other how long now?" Travis asked.

"Almost three years. Why?" Aidan asked.

"I don't recall you smiling. At all. In fact, I've wondered if you have teeth."

Sunny crossed her arms and sucked in her lips, stifling a chuckle. "He does. You see them when he sneers and growls," she finished, unable to hold back the laugh.

"You guys are…annoying. Stop it," he said.

"Hey, Calloway."

Aidan looked up at Travis.

"Jessie Vega."

A flood of memories from their weekend together raced through Aidan's mind in a flash—the teasing glint in Jessie's blue eyes, the softness of his dark hair, the warmth of his mouth, the sounds he made when they kissed.

Travis and Sunny both pointed their finger at him and started laughing. "Busted!"

Aidan shook his head and scoffed. He rose from his seat and closed the file, staring at his teammates who couldn't seem to stop laughing at him. "Call me back when the meeting starts."

He walked around the table just as Wall entered the room. At least he could count on Wall to not give him a hard time.

His silent teammate looked at Travis and Sunny with a frown, no doubt wondering what the hell he had missed. He glanced up at Aidan and his features relaxed, then transitioned into one of his lopsided grins. He quirked an eyebrow and crossed his arms, staring at Aidan as Travis and Sunny began another round of laughter at the silent exchange between them.

"Shut up," he said to Wall as he pushed past him out the door.

* * * *

"I can feel your heartbeat."

"That's because you have your hand on my chest." Aidan wrapped his arm around Jessie's waist, tugging him closer, reveling in the quiet intimacy of just lying together on the couch watching television as he stroked his fingers up and down Jessie's arm. He'd thought about this all day, not even caring about the jokes at work from his teammates. He sighed, closing his eyes, relaxing, enjoying Jessie's tempting touches and the series of open-mouth kisses trailing along his skin.

"Your heart's beating faster."

"Having your mouth on me does that."

Jessie licked up the side of Aidan's neck, then kiss-bit his stubbled jawline. "How about this? Does this make your heart beat harder?"

"That makes a lot of things harder."

"Mmm, and what are you going to do about that?"

Aidan arched an eyebrow, holding back a grin. Damn, he liked it when Jessie teased him. His body immediately responded to the promise in that spark in Jessie's eyes. He leaned in for a kiss, reaching up behind Jessie to hold him in place. He groaned when Jessie opened his mouth, welcoming him to explore. He swiftly undid the drawstring of Jessie's sleep pants, dipping inside to wrap his hand around him. Jessie pushed up into Aidan's hold, snaking his arms around his neck, pulling him closer as a strangled whimper escaped.

Damn, he loved that sound.

Jessie pulled away from the kiss, closing his eyes and leaning his head on Aidan's shoulder. He thrust his hips seeking more friction, twisting the hair at the back of Aidan's head, letting out a groan before spilling his release into Aidan's hand. He buried his face against Aidan's shoulder, gasping for air, still gripping Aidan's hair tightly in his fist.

Aidan placed a kiss against the side of Jessie's head. "Guess I'm not the only one who comes fast."

Jessie's breath puffed across Aidan's skin and his words slurred slightly. "I think we need a benchmark. Best two out of three."

They lay there, still for a few moments, pressing slow kisses against each other, neither one wanting to move an inch. He pushed his nose against Jessie's soft hair and sighed, reveling in the weight against his body and the warmth in his arms, enjoying the lazy caress and brush of fingertips against skin. For the first time in his life, intimacy wasn't rushed or hidden. There was nothing to be ashamed of and no one to shatter the spell that lingered in the peaceful air.

He withdrew his hand from within Jessie's sleep pants, his fisted hand still holding Jessie's release. Aidan returned Jessie's scrutinizing stare as he held his hand up to his mouth then licked every drop of Jessie's essence from his fingers until nothing remained, never breaking eye contact with the lust-filled, sea of blue staring back at him.

Jessie moaned and gripped the sides of Aidan's head before slamming their mouths together in a demanding kiss. Jessie shifted his position, now flush against Aidan's already awake and ready body. Aidan reached down and wrapped his hand around both now hardened shafts, reveling in the silky heat gliding in his fist. He screwed his eyes shut and focused on the steady up and down rhythm. Every electron in his body lit up and charged, ready to burst on command. He thrust his hips forward, seeking friction. A lifetime of stolen moments or rushed releases hadn't prepared him for the degree of desire and want coursing through his veins for every possible tender, passionate show of intimacy he could steal. Not just with anyone, with this man.

His Jess.

The one man firmly planted in Aidan's heart and securely seated in his being.

Fists tightened and fingers dug into skin as the rhythm sped. They locked their lips into an uncoordinated, messy kiss a brief moment before they each grunted and spurted their release between them.

Aidan rubbed his nose against the sweat-dampened tips of Jessie's hair curling against the edges of his face. He wondered where along the line he had given up complete and total control of himself and let Jessie lead. "What the hell are you doing to me?"

Jessie reached up and brushed away the now sweat-slicked hair from Aidan's face. "Hopefully, a lot of things."

Aidan huffed out a quiet laugh. "You're insatiable."

"For you, yes. I finally have you and I want all of you."

"Mmm," Aidan hummed before leaning in for a lazy kiss. He couldn't stop touching Jessie, holding him, kissing him.

"Are you tired?" Jessie asked when they finally separated from the kiss.

Aidan lazily shook his head, staring at Jessie as if seeing him for the first time. He loved discovering all the tiny nuances of Jessie's personality, especially the quiet, private layers no one else saw but him. Tired? Hell no. His body had been dormant for far too long and had a reserve that even surprised him.

"Good," Jessie said, diving in for another kiss.

* * * *

"So…where are we going?" Jessie asked, returning the items to the pantry and the refrigerator. He hadn't expected Aidan to arrive home early, and he definitely hadn't expected him to announce a dinner excursion, especially not after spending so much time on the couch lately, having far too much fun to want to escape the house.

"Wherever you want to go is fine. You're always cooking and you stay in the house unless you've got an appointment, so I figured a break would be nice. To get out, do something…different. As long as

I can pick a steak, I'm fine with any place you want to go."

"You choose the spot. Surprise me," Jessie said.

"Okay."

"So where are we going?"

"Uh, I thought you said to surprise you?"

Jessie bit his lip, trying to disguise the humor at seeing Aidan squirm. He figured Aidan was probably getting a little edgy lately, always giving in and letting Jessie get his way each time. "I need to know what to wear."

"A suit. Definitely a suit. A dark one. Either the blue one or the charcoal."

"So it's a date?" Jessie asked, trying to contain the flutter in his chest. He cherished their time hanging out on the couch or back porch but going out in public together? Definitely one heck of a milestone.

"Uh, okay," Aidan said with a pinched expression.

"It's not a date?"

Aidan rubbed the back of his neck. "If you want to do something else too, we can."

"We don't have to do anything else. Dinner's fine."

"Okay. So it's *not* a date?" Aidan said, scratching his stubble.

Jessie hid a grin at Aidan's confusion. "How about you tell me. Do you want it to be a date?"

"I want to take you out to dinner. I want you to wear a suit, because you look hot as hell in them. If that makes it a date, then cool. It's a date. But if I have to do something else to make it a date, like a movie or…fuck if I know…a walk on the beach or something. Let me know and we'll do that too."

Jessie wrapped his arms around Aidan's neck. "Where did you get that from?"

"Google."

"I think you better leave the research to me." Jessie chuckled.

"As long as you wear your suit." Aidan snaked his arms around Jessie's waist and leaned in for a quick kiss.

Jessie nuzzled Aidan's neck. "And you need to keep your stubble. It's hot."

"You like soft balls and hard stubble. I think you're confused regarding what you want."

"I know exactly what I want. I want all of you, soft and hard and everything in between."

"Mmm." Aidan tugged Jessie closer and kissed his temple. "By the way…"

"Yeah?"

"You're cutting into our date time."

Jessie smiled, hearing his words from their other night repeated. He inched back, easing out of the embrace. "Then get your ass in the shower so we can get going."

"This is nice," Jessie said, sipping his wine. He set his glass down and crossed his arms, leaning forward to rest them on the table. Damn, he wanted to reach out and touch Aidan. "People are staring."

"Of course they are. Look at you."

"I think they're staring at you," Jessie said.

Aidan pursed his lips and finished the last of his water. "This looks like my standard issue work clothes. Trust me, they're looking at you." He wiped his mouth and tossed the napkin to the side.

"You trimmed your stubble." Jessie rested his chin against his fist, unable to tear his eyes away from Aidan. "I like that."

Aidan delivered a wicked, teasing grin. "Yeah?"

"Oh yeah." He bit his lip when the tip of Aidan's boot brushed against his leg. His heartbeat sped at Aidan's forwardness. In. Public. *I don't care if what he's doing is hidden by the tablecloth. It's still out in public.* "Is the big tough detective playing footsie with me?"

Aidan crossed his arms on the table and leaned forward, pitching his voice low. "I want to make sure you remember I'm the one here with you while everyone's busy staring, drooling over you in that dark suit."

He quietly laughed. He slipped his socked foot out of his dress shoe and slid it up, inside Aidan's pant leg.

Aidan stilled, his focus steady.

Jessie withdrew his foot after a few seconds, not wanting to push his luck. He leaned forward in his seat, crossing his arms on the table, mirroring Aidan's pose. "Make no mistake. I know damn well who I'm here with. And I know who the hell I'm going home with too."

Aidan slowly inhaled, his lips parting on an equally measured exhale. "Where the hell have you been my whole life?"

"Waiting for you."

"Fuck," Aidan said, under his breath. "Let's get out of here."

"Did you want to wait for the dessert menu?"

"If you want to, we can…or I can pour something sweet over you at home and lick it off." Aidan's jaw muscles twitched, the gold flecks in his eyes seemed to kindle with the reflecting flicker of the candle at the center of the table.

Jessie's arm shot up, pointing toward the server walking in their direction. "Check please."

Chapter
TWENTY-TWO

Jessie dried the glasses while Aidan washed the last of the dishes. Aidan silently focused on the task, but his mind seemed to wander a million miles away. He handed Jessie the dish and rinsed out the sink. He slung the towel over his shoulder and crossed his arms, his face still showcasing the same frown for the last ten minutes. "The other day, when we were talking about names, and you said I was shutting you out," he finally said.

Jessie waited for Aidan to continue, refusing to interrupt him. The "other day" had actually been weeks ago. So he'd obviously mulled it over, chewed on the topic, and still toyed with it in his mind for a while.

"When you said my name meant little fire."

Jessie nodded, encouraging him to continue.

"Made me think back, when I was a kid."

Jessie waited.

Aidan looked down. "It's stupid."

"Not if it shuts you down like this. It's obviously important."

Aidan remained quiet for a while, long enough for him to assume Aidan had given up on whatever he was going to say, until he decided to resume the conversation. "My mom was pregnant with twins."

Jessie stilled. "When?"

"I had a sister. Nadia." He looked over to Jessie then turned away, folding the towel over the oven handle to dry. "We were fraternal twins. I guess it's like those parents who name their kids with the same first letter or dress them up in the same outfits or something. My mom thought it would be cute to have the names be the same. Just, opposite I guess because we were boy and girl twins." He shrugged, but the frown remained.

"What happened?"

"She died two weeks after we were born. She was really small and wasn't strong enough." Aidan quieted, almost to a whisper. "I've never told anyone that."

Jessie took the two steps to reach him. He tugged Aidan's hand and led him to the couch to sit. "Did your parents tell you?"

Aidan shook his head. "I found a small box of stuff one day, hidden in the back of the closet. I was a pint-sized, nosy little shit. I asked my mom about it. She said it wasn't something they talked about because they never wanted me to feel as if I wasn't enough or as if I were to blame. Here's the weird thing…and I don't really know how to explain it. I don't remember her. I mean, I was two weeks old. But I knew *something* was missing…I just never really had a clue what it was. But after that day, it all made sense."

"What about your dad? Did you talk to him about it?"

Aidan quieted again. He looked down at his hands and pushed his thumb into his palm. Jessie placed his hand in Aidan's and laced their fingers, knowing the contact often eased him.

"My dad was probably one of the most easygoing guys in the world," Aidan continued. "Always smiling, never angry, and he never raised his voice. Ever. Everyone loved him and he lived for the shop. Even when he wasn't there, he was working on a car in the garage at home. But it's as if I couldn't communicate with him. I mean, the man spoke cars and I spoke sports. Two very different languages," he said, distantly. "I mentioned Nadia once and he cut me off before I could say anything more. He refused to talk about her. The look in his eyes scared me to death. It was pure rage and pain and I swore I never wanted to see that look in his eyes again. It was so out of character and I didn't want to be the one to trigger that in him. I heard him screaming at my mom that night, wondering how I found out. That was the only time I had ever heard him scream in my life. He was so fucking mad," he said, almost in a whisper. He took Jessie's hand between his two, staring at them for some time before he continued again.

"He took the box and burned everything in it. Afterward, he couldn't stop crying and apologized to my mom for having done that. Said he wasn't thinking and now he had nothing of hers to look at or touch." Aidan quieted. "I shouldn't have said anything to him about her."

Jessie closed his eyes and leaned into Aidan. He couldn't imagine being so young, carrying the burden of such guilt and blame for the loss of a sibling.

"I always wondered if maybe Nadia would have been more like Ty, into cars and stuff." Aidan shrugged. "If she would have fit better."

He wanted to yell at Aidan for the thought Jessie was positive had crossed his mind in that moment—*would it have been better if she had survived instead*. He rubbed Aidan's shoulder and didn't say a word.

"About a year after all that happened, my mom found out she was pregnant again. My parents made this big deal about wanting me to name my new baby brother...be a part of the whole thing. I couldn't do it at first." Aidan seemed distant. "After that shitstorm I caused, I didn't want to do anything to hurt them ever again. So I focused on school, my homework, whatever I needed to get through the day and not give them any trouble. But I..." He looked up, the pain screaming from his expression. "I felt like I was a constant reminder."

He remembered something Aidan had said a while ago: *I feel as if I've been cursed since birth to be alone.* He needed to steer the conversation away from the melancholy thoughts. "How did you come up with Ty's name?"

"They kept pushing about the name, and after a while, I...really wanted a brother." Aidan looked away and blew out a heavy breath. "I figured maybe my little brother could bridge that gap between us. Somehow be the link that tied me to my family so I wouldn't feel like the odd man out. So I wouldn't feel so...alone. He turned out to be that and so much more," he said with a lopsided grin. He turned his body slightly toward Jessie. "It's as if he put a big bandage on this hole I had. You know? Like the wound was still there but somehow better and didn't hurt as much. Anyways, I figured Ty with a y was better than the i-e. Because seriously, who names their kid after a noose. He would have gotten picked on and I would have been busy kicking ass."

Jessie smiled. Those little things Aidan said sometimes meant the most. "You could have called him Link or Bridge."

"I'm not that deep. I was a troublemaker and not very creative. I spared him the future torture of a nickname. At least I thought I had until that pain in the ass future-brother-in-law of mine came along. Anyways, it's short. It was supposed to be easy."

"Does he know that's why you named him that?" Jessie asked.

"I told him it would make life easier and people wouldn't come up with stupid nicknames."

"Not that. The other part. You should tell him. I think he'd like to know how important he is to you, even before he was born."

"Why does it matter now?" Aidan looked genuinely confused. "He knows he's important to me."

"It matters. And I'm sure he'd like to know about Nadia, too."

Aidan vehemently shook his head. "Absolutely not. I won't have him hating me because I took away a chance at having a sister."

"Is that what you think?"

"It's a fact. And I'm not going to have him hate me because I survived and she didn't."

"Do you hate your brother?"

"What the fuck?" Aidan's face contorted. "Of course not! What the hell kind of question—"

"He survived the accident and your parents didn't. Do you love him any less?"

Aidan stilled. "No," he said on a gasp. He didn't move, looking off to nothing in particular as if lost in thought. His features transitioned into a pained expression, his shoulders hunched, and he screwed his eyes shut as if a sudden realization had blindsided him. He buried his head in his hands. "Oh God. Is that what he thinks?"

Jessie stroked his back, hoping to ease the building tension. "You have no idea what he thinks about the accident unless you talk to him. Tell him, Aidan. I think he'll understand how you feel, more than you can imagine. And I think it'll mean the world to him that you talk to him about stuff like this. This is something, not just about you, but about the *both* of you. Not just about your sister but your parents. You both share the same loss."

"I've never talked to Ty about the accident. I figured he didn't want to relive it. I just thought it was best to focus on his recovery," he whispered before his voice trailed off.

Jessie pulled Aidan into an embrace and stroked the back of his hair when Aidan leaned on his shoulder. "Open the door of communication and let Ty know it's okay to discuss it with you. Then leave it up to him. What if he blames himself and thinks you feel the same? He won't ever approach you about it."

Aidan's arms wrapped around Jessie. "You're like my human translator."

Jessie smiled, thankful the somber Aidan didn't linger. "I'll play any role you want."

"Perv."

"And you secretly love that."

Aidan eased back from the embrace and looked at Jessie, a hint of a smile coloring his features. "I do." He reached up and brushed his fingertips against Jessie's cheek. "I don't know how you put up with me."

"Kiss me and make me forget how insufferable you can be."

A teasing grin slowly spread across Aidan's face. He leaned in and placed a quick kiss against Jessie's lips and inched away, still grinning.

Jessie rolled his eyes dramatically. "That totally didn't help me forget anything."

Aidan, barely a breath away from him with the grin still plastered across his face, quickly kissed him again.

"Nope, still remembering everything." Jessie wrapped his arms around Aidan's neck and narrowed his eyes. "You're going to have to try much, much harder than that. You are a royal, teasing, pain in—"

Aidan latched on to Jessie's mouth with more force, reaching up and cupping the back of Jessie's head to hold him in place as he flipped them over on the couch and rested his weight on Jessie's body. Aidan replaced the teasing, barely-there kisses with a hard press of lips and forceful, never-ending surge of unmistakable desire and need. He firmly cradled Jessie's head, guiding him in place as he devoured Jessie's mouth in the heated exchange.

Jessie melted into Aidan's hold, gripping his shirt for purchase and moaning with each slide of Aidan's tongue and brush of lips.

He arched into Aidan, craving the closeness and warmth as every other thought quickly escaped his mind.

* * * *

Jessie rocked on the balls of his feet, waiting. He stole a glance at his wristwatch, relieved he had plenty of time to get to his client meeting at the courthouse.

The door swung open and Jessie's eyes widened. Cole greeted him, wearing nothing but his superheroes undies and a backward baseball cap, with a hint of his dark black hair peeking out the back.

Jessie shook his head and sighed. "You could have gotten dressed. You knew I was coming over."

"That's so boring." Cole grabbed Jessie's lapel and pulled him into the condo. "You're in my house. You're lucky I'm wearing anything at all. Besides, Ty got me these. I had to break them in." He waggled his eyebrows and made his way to the kitchen.

Ty emerged from the bedroom, a chuckle escaping him. "Morning, Jessie."

Jessie waved, trying to avoid looking at Cole who now pointed his comic book covered ass up in the air as he dug into the refrigerator.

"Sorry…I forgot to give these to Aidan last night." Ty walked over to the television cabinet and withdrew a small stack of DVDs then made his way over to Jessie. "We got a little distracted."

Distracted? Is that what the Calloway brothers called any sort of deep emotional discussion? Well, at least that was what he thought might have happened the night before. Even though Aidan usually quieted during their talks, he always listened and the thought that his brother carried any guilt for the death of their parents gnawed away at him. He hadn't been able to extract any information from Aidan when he'd arrived late in the evening and the curiosity drove him to the brink of madness.

"I want you to meet someone."

Jessie cocked his head, questioning. "Who?"

Ty extended his hands, holding the stack of DVDs. "My brother. My *real* brother. He's the one in the video with the big smile and loud laugh."

A flutter of excitement spread in Jessie's chest as he took the stack of DVDs. "Sounds like a guy I know. It's nice when he makes the occasional appearance."

"He's made more appearances since you came along." Ty shoved his hands in his jean pockets and quieted, looking down as if gathering his thoughts. He glanced up at Cole who hosted his own one-man show, singing and dancing in the kitchen as he worked his magic with breakfast. "Aidan told me about Nadia," Ty said, pitching his voice to keep the conversation between them. He looked firmly at Jessie. "He said you told him to tell me about her."

"I thought you should know."

Ty nodded, bobbing his head repeatedly as if unaware of the gesture. "I didn't know about her. I'm glad he told me." He chewed on his lips, his gaze casually traveling toward Cole. "He shouldn't carry the weight of that guilt on his shoulders. It's the kind of thing that slowly kills you a little inside." He spoke distantly, as if his words carried a deeper meaning. "We talked about…the accident. That was the first time…" He looked down at his shoes and his eyebrows twitched. He finally looked up, a mild shine appearing in his brown eyes. "It was the first time we've talked about the accident. I'm sorry I kept him here so late last night."

Jessie smiled, imagining the Calloway brothers' conversation— initial shock at the openness, quickly followed by the eagerness to reconnect on such a difficult and *personal* subject. "When he opens up, you have to totally take advantage of that tiny window."

"Yeah." Ty sighed. "I hadn't spoken to him like that in a while."

"He's trying," Jessie said, finally putting the DVDs into his messenger bag.

"He loves you."

Jessie stilled, wondering if Aidan had actually said those words to his brother.

"He's quiet about things like that, but it's obvious."

Jessie closed his bag and nodded. "He's a man of few words."

"He's got a big heart. It's a bit hidden, but I swear it's there."

Jessie chuckled, gripping the strap of his bag to busy himself. He looked over his shoulder at Cole, who now sang off-key, making up words to fill a song as he scrambled the eggs. "Not everyone is vocal about how they feel. Sometimes, you need to look beyond the words." He shifted his focus back to Ty. "I've got a meeting downtown I need to head out to before traffic really kicks in."

Ty pulled Jessie into an embrace. "Thank you." He quickly retreated, as if the gesture had been driven more by some instinctive reaction than a formal thought.

Jessie observed the subtle coloring of Ty's cheeks; seemed reveals of this nature were rare in all Calloways. "Thanks for the videos. I'll take care of them."

"I know you will," Ty said, his soft tone and the sudden warmth in his brown eyes implying far more than his words.

Jessie said his goodbyes to Cole and made his way to the parking garage. He sat in his car and sighed. He wanted to run home and binge-watch the videos, anxious to see a smiling, loud laughing Aidan come to life. He leaned his head back against the headrest, taking a deep breath. He reached for his phone and sent a quick text.

Leaving Ty's. On my way to meeting.

Aidan immediately responded. *OK. Don't be nice to people.*

A laugh escaped him. Sometimes, Aidan had the oddest ways of saying things. He typed in a quick reply. *Don't worry. I'll be careful.*

I always worry, Aidan immediately responded.

Jessie had been more than careful on the few occasions he'd left for a meeting. Maybe Aidan's paranoia had rubbed off on him, but his senses had heightened when out on his own. How Michael had managed to come back into his life and still taint the somewhat peace he had found nagged him. He was usually better at focusing on the positive things in life and pushing away the negative. But somehow, this monster still found a way to extend its claws and pierce a wound he had hoped had healed over some time ago—as best as a wound of that kind could be managed.

He drove out of the garage and stopped at the red light, tapping his thumbs on the steering wheel. He pulled out his phone again when it buzzed with a new message.

Miss you.

A swell of emotions rose in his chest. The grip on his phone tightened as he read the two small words that meant far more from Aidan than most people could imagine.

Miss U 2. :)

A short and quick response to avoid any lingering thoughts Aidan might have pondered during the extended delay before the text had arrived. The light changed and he drove to his meeting with a permanent grin etched in his face.

Chapter TWENTY-THREE

"Jess, I'm home," Aidan yelled out, smiling. He'd never get tired of saying that out loud. He shrugged out of his sport coat, waiting for Jessie's reply, ignoring the ache in his muscles from another long day. Between too many consecutive late nights with the task force and Jessie's series of client meetings, they had barely spent much time together in the evenings. Aside from missing the contact to ground him and give him inner peace, he needed Jessie's positivity and the reassurance of goodness in the world.

"Jess?"

Nothing.

He glanced toward the kitchen then to the empty dining room table.

No laptop, no scattering of folders, no music filtering throughout the house. No Jessie.

He withdrew his gun from his holster, holding his firearm in both hands as he slowly made his way through the house, listening for the slightest sound. He stepped into their room and stilled. Jessie sat cross-legged on their brand new bed, staring down at the small pillow in his lap.

"Jess?"

He didn't move. He didn't respond.

Jessie's defeated, lowered shoulders twisted his gut. Aidan took off his shoulder holster and set it on the dresser with his gun. He sat on the bed, not really sure what to do or say. "What's wrong?" He tentatively touched Jessie's chin, raising his head. His heart ached at the emptiness reflecting back from Jessie's eyes.

He leaned in for a tender kiss, gently holding Jessie's face. He inched back and saw the pool of blue begin to fill, as if the touch of lips had turned the dial on a valve.

"What happened?" he asked, stroking Jessie's cheek.

"Nothing happened. I'm okay," Jessie said, looking away.

"You're not okay." He placed a kiss on Jessie's forehead, slowly stroking his hair and drawing him near, pulling Jessie's head to his shoulder.

Jessie anchored his fingers on Aidan's arm. "It's not a good day," he whispered.

"So no inspirational posters today?"

Jessie shook his head, burying his nose at the crook of Aidan's neck.

He wrapped his arms around Jessie's waist, pulling him off the bed and onto his lap. He held him close, stroking his back and peppering kisses on his head and temple.

"I'm sorry," Jessie whispered, snuggling into the embrace, clasping his hands together and bending his knees up into Aidan's body in a fetal position.

"For what?"

"I'm supposed to be stronger than this for you." He gripped the front of Aidan's shirt tightly, burrowing himself into Aidan's body.

Aidan held him closer, pressing his lips more firmly in Jessie's hair. "I want all of you. On your good and bad days. How about you let me be the strong one in this relationship today."

Jessie looked up at him, a barely-there smile touching his lips. He reached up, ghosting his fingertips over the stubble he always sought. "I'm scared he'll come back," he barely whispered, avoiding eye contact and letting his focus follow the trail of his fingers.

"Did something happen?"

"No." Jessie buried his face under Aidan's chin, pushing his nose up against the stubble. "Sneaks up on me sometimes if I think about it too much."

Aidan rested his cheek on Jessie's head, stroking his back and holding him close. He couldn't imagine how Jessie held it together most days. He was certainly entitled to a crap day. "Are you hungry?"

Jessie shook his head.

"You want to just stay like this?"

"Can we? For a little while."

Aidan inched back, tilting Jessie's face up by the chin, and pressed his lips to Jessie's. "For however long you want." He rose from the bed, still tightly holding Jessie in his arms, and walked over to the new couch in their bedroom. He pulled the throw over them to keep Jessie warm, then leaned back, letting the weight of Jessie's body push him into the couch.

He gently ran his hand along Jessie's back, hoping to push away the bad memories with each stroke. He brushed his nose in Jessie's hair, closing his eyes as the dark strands tickled his nose and caught in the annoying, ever-present stubble he refused to shave in the evenings because Jessie loved it so much.

There was nothing he wanted more than to give Jessie the peace he deserved, to free him of this shadow that always hovered just outside of their safety bubble. He held Jessie close, offering gentle caresses as best he could until Jessie's breathing began to level off into a steady rhythm, easing them into sleep.

* * * *

"Reyes, this is all taking too fucking long," Aidan said. He looked around at his fellow team members and sensed their frustration. Each day, his fear grew. Too many months without a lead meant the case would inevitably be thrown on the backburner.

"We're close," Manny stated. "And that's all I'm telling you. You need to back the hell away from Vega's case or I'm going to request it get transferred back to the department and you know what's going to happen if that's the deal."

It would find its place at the bottom of a stack of more current cases and potentially be reclassified as a cold case. *Son of a bitch.*

"You need to get your nose out of this shit until we tell you otherwise," Manny said in a tone that brooked no argument. "Captain's orders."

"It's been months." Aidan curled his hands into fists under the table, hoping to steady the radiating anger.

Manny leaned forward, resting his elbows on the small conference table. "You know the only place shit gets resolved overnight is in the movies. This is real life. We've found breaks in cases that have sat for months."

"Aidan found the breaks in the agency cases that sat for months," Sunny corrected.

True, but definitely not the time to shine a spotlight on that bit of wisdom.

"Reyes, back off," Travis said when Manny turned to give Sunny a spiteful glare. "It's only natural for Calloway to be pissed and frustrated. Hell, *we're* pissed and frustrated, and we're not Vega's...uh..."

Wall leaned back in his chair and crossed his arms, looking at Travis. Both Manny and Sunny glanced at Aidan then back at Travis.

"We're not Vega's...what?" Manny said, undoubtedly forcing him to walk the plank and ride that elephant in the room.

Travis's focus bounced from Manny to Aidan, then to the other teammates. They all questioned his relationship with Jessie but knew better than to mention it.

"Reyes, just give me something to shut me the fuck up, please. And I don't mean give me a we're-following-up-on-leads line of crap." Aidan scrubbed a hand over his face and blew out an exasperated breath. Frustrated in so many ways, he needed some relief somewhere. And after last night, seeing, firsthand, Jessie breaking down, he couldn't handle much more of this. "Please."

Manny quieted, leaning back in his chair. He glanced at the other team members. "We have something. We're waiting on some information from one of the agencies. Once we have that, we'll need Vega to come in. I can't tell you more and I won't tell you more." He looked to the others and his focus landed squarely on Sunny for a few seconds longer than the others before returning to Aidan. "And that's all you're getting from *us* at the moment."

"So you have…something?" Aidan asked, his heartbeat drumming in his chest at a possible lead. He twisted his hands under the table, anxious for some bit of information to move the case forward.

"Something. Maybe. Yes."

Aidan rubbed his eyes. "That's vague, Reyes."

Manny sighed and tugged on the cuffs of his shirt. "I need you to keep your head in the game, Calloway."

"I can't keep my head in the game if I don't know the plays." He looked up, biting back the anger that simmered beneath the surface.

Manny scowled. "I meant the other cases. You're too close to this, Calloway. I'm surprised the captain allowed us to work on it." Manny leaned in and stared at him intently for a few moments before he spoke. "So don't fuck it up. If he pulls it away from us, you know you're screwed and so is Vega."

Aidan closed his eyes and took a few deep, calming breaths. He hated this helplessness that consumed him. He wanted to be the one to make Jessie smile, to give him the news that everything would be all right.

"Okay, let's start with the drug cases. Travis, where are we on those?" Manny addressed the team, dismissing the previous conversation.

Aidan raked a hand through his hair, trying to shift his focus to the stack of cases in front of him. He opened the file and tried to follow along with the others but couldn't. He jabbed the heel of his hand against his forehead, trying to calm the wrath twisting and taking shape into a beast filled with unquenchable rage.

He wanted to find this bastard.

He *needed* to find this bastard.

Only then could Jessie have the peace he so freely offered in return.

* * * *

Jessie tilted his head back on the couch and glanced over to Aidan still fidgeting with the towel in the kitchen. "Do you want to sit and watch with me?" he asked, extending his hand to Aidan. He smiled when Aidan tossed the towel aside then came to him, wrapping his large, warm hand around his. Aidan claimed Jessie's touch was magical, but Aidan had no clue how easily he soothed Jessie's worries with a simple caress. And after the other night, he hated admitting how much clingier he had become with Aidan, yearning for the warmth and safety of his arms. Or maybe it was territorial now that he'd finally worked his way through the tiny crack of Aidan's iron wall. He didn't want to overthink things too much, knowing Aidan could slam that door shut at any moment.

"Did you pick out a movie?" Aidan asked, finally settling into his corner spot.

"Well, not really. It's some of your home videos. Remember, I had mentioned them before? We've just been…a little busy lately."

Busy. Understatement of the year. He'd love nothing more than to return to their routine, snuggling on the couch, watching television and letting all the outside drama pass them by, but Aidan had become distant again in the last few days. Something obviously weighed heavily on his mind, but Jessie had no intention of awakening that beast.

"Yeah. I just thought they were VHS or something. I hadn't realized Ty had transferred them over to DVD." Aidan paused for a moment, lost in thought, then lowered his brow. "Did you get those from Ty or Cole?"

"Ty," Jessie responded with a smile. "Cole would have given me the embarrassing ones so I think you might be safe."

"I guess we'll see." Aidan propped his feet up on the coffee table and Jessie lay across the couch on his side, resting his head on Aidan's chest. He sighed when Aidan's arm snaked around his waist and pulled him closer, snug into their usual television-watching position. He pressed play on the remote and nestled into the warmth of Aidan's arms as the video started.

The video faded into a scene, panning across a grassy backyard.

A tall man with dark hair who looked like an older version of Ty stood behind a barbecue grill and called out over his shoulder toward the house behind him.

"What is this?" Jessie asked, peering up at Aidan.

Aidan's focus remained on the video as if trying to recall a memory. "Oh! That's my birthday. I think my thirteenth. I had this big hang up about having to control the camera since I was now 'a teenager.' That's my dad behind the grill and I'm guessing Mom's in the house."

"Ty looks a lot like your dad."

Aidan smiled warmly. "Yeah, he does."

Suddenly, the video spun almost one hundred eighty degrees then back around again. "I'm totally going to kick your ass if you keep hiding from the camera," the young voice from the video said.

Jessie laughed. "Let me guess. That's you?"

"Yeah," Aidan said with a chuckle. "Ty kept walking behind me to avoid the camera. He insisted he should have had the camera because it was my birthday, and I should be the one on the video, not him."

Suddenly, the video panned back to the house, and a tall, lean woman emerged with a platter of food. Ty may have looked like their father, but Aidan indisputably mirrored their mother. The dark hair and hazel eyes were an exact match and the inquisitive stare a dead giveaway to their hereditary link. She smiled warmly to her husband, a lopsided grin that punctuated her blood tie to Aidan.

"You look so much like her," Jessie said in awe.

"She was amazing," Aidan said, his tone wistful. He blankly looked ahead, as if watching the television, but it was obvious his mind had probably returned to that very moment in time.

A young boy ran across the video and the camera turned to follow him. "You're not escaping," young Aidan's voice said. "Ty, stop running!" he yelled, then laughed before sprinting after his brother, the video image bouncing up and down, still recording as he raced through the yard.

Aidan chuckled and leaned into Jessie. "I'd always give him a head start. Man, he was impossible when he lost so I'd let him win sometimes."

The camera finally caught up to young Ty and a hand reached out to grasp his shoulder. "Gotcha!"

Young Ty turned and smiled. His brown eyes brightened with the glare of the sun. "Gimme!" he yelled as he laughed and tugged on the camera, finally pulling it away and turning the lens to focus on a striking young version of Aidan.

Jessie's breath hitched. Young Aidan smiled wide and laughed loudly as he struggled to regain the camera. He reached out and covered the lens with his hand. "It's my birthday. Give me that thing." He flicked his head from side to side, trying to avoid his face getting caught on video. His hair blew with the summer air—the top fringing just above his eyes and the sides long enough to curl around his ears and barely touch the top of his T-shirt. Young Aidan laughed as the camera finally focused on him, capturing his playful, mischievous grin.

And unbridled happiness.

"Say something for the camera," young Ty said.

"Something."

Yeah, that's Aidan. Jessie smiled and looked up at him. His smile faded at the now stern expression on Aidan's face. Jessie returned his focus to the video playback and watched as the brothers left the camera on the ground then ran in circles until they tumbled down onto the grass. Although they were quite a distance from the camera, their laughter echoed in stereo through the video, capturing a joy which could only be described as youthful innocence and could only happen between brothers or the closest of friends. Young Ty climbed onto his big brother's back, laughing as young Aidan trotted around the yard and neighed like a horse. Ty complained when they finally approached the camera, begging for another lap around the yard. Young Aidan's face filled the screen with a huge smile, flashing every tooth in his mouth. The sweat trickled down his forehead and the now wet hair tips stuck to his face.

He neared the camera with his younger brother still arm-locked around his neck. "This birthday boy is signing out," he said, crossing his eyes and giving the camera fish lips. Young Ty peeked over his shoulder and stared into the camera and yelled "happy birthday" before young Aidan switched off the recording. The video immediately faded to black then resumed with another scene from the same day.

An oddly silent Aidan unwrapped his arm from around Jessie. "I'm going to review some of the files before the meeting tomorrow morning to try to catch something we might have missed." Aidan stood, then walk over to the door, double-checking the locks and alarm.

Jessie paused the video and waited. "Aidan?" Something seemed off, but he couldn't peg exactly what had happened to darken Aidan's mood.

Aidan returned to his side, reached down, and pressed his lips to Jessie's in a tender kiss.

Jessie wrapped his arms around him, unsure why a swell of emotions had suddenly risen within and tightened his throat.

Aidan inched back from the embrace and gave him a lopsided grin.

"Did you want to watch the rest of the video?"

Aidan looked at Jessie for a few seconds, hesitating before he spoke. "Nah. I'm going to do some work." He hesitated as if wanting to say something more. Instead, he turned away, his shoulders slumped as he retreated down the hallway to the bedroom.

Jessie sighed when the door clicked shut. He wouldn't push. Aidan would return and open up to him when he was ready…and not a moment before. He returned his focus to the television and resumed the video, lowering the volume so as not to disturb Aidan while he worked.

He sat upright on the couch and watched the young brothers continue to roughhouse and run around the yard until the recorded sessions showed the night sky and the exhaustion of the day. Each of their parents made video appearances and gushed about both of their young sons. Jessie hadn't realized how tightly he held the cushion in his hands until his fingers became numb or how the tears trickled down his cheeks until he wiped away the unexpected wetness. He rubbed at the ache in his chest as he watched the young Aidan in the video, smiling as if he didn't have a care in the world.

The smile.

An overwhelming sense of mourning overtook him as he watched young Aidan grab his young brother and rub his head, laughing hysterically as Ty protested but smiled.

Something had broken Aidan's spirit.

Jessie had come to a harsh realization each time Aidan confided a truth. It wasn't *one* thing that left a mark on Aidan's soul but a series of events, slowly adding another layer to the rising stack of heartbreaking milestones.

Jessie tightly clutched the cushion against his chest, mesmerized watching the young Calloway boys play on the screen. Their closeness, undeniable. Their happiness, indisputable. Their brotherly bond, seemingly unbreakable. Yet, something had happened to rob the joy from Aidan's soul.

Jessie absently wiped the wetness trickling down his cheeks, no longer trying to control the outlet of emotion. *This* was *his* Aidan. The Aidan with infinite mischief who teased him to no end. The same protective Aidan with an abundance of love who spent nights by his bed watching over him just to make sure he slept through the nightmares while at the hospital.

The same Aidan who lay buried under the protective layers of armor, shielding himself from prying eyes.

Jessie loosened his hold on the cushion and took a deep breath, nodding to himself as he made a decision. With resolute determination, he took another deep breath and swore he'd do anything to bring back that joy to Aidan's life and awaken that intoxicating smile again for the world to see.

* * * *

"You're regressing," Dr. Engel said.

Aidan looked over his shoulder at the good doctor from his perch at the window. She sat in her chair, patiently waiting, staring at him—her way of telling him to open his fucking mouth and speak.

"Something's driven you back into your shell. How about we talk about that?"

Aidan sighed and returned his focus to watching the people walking on the street between the tall buildings. The weight of frustration and sense of hopelessness bore on him more than usual. He was just...tired. Always trying to keep it together, putting up a good front. But last night, he'd hit an all-time low and he'd been kicked in the gut, no longer able to deny what clearly stared back at him. "I saw an old video yesterday."

"What kind of video?"

"Home video. My thirteenth birthday. Ty and me. Our parents. Small backyard barbecue thing." He shrugged. Not really sure why he couldn't lock this up in his internal vault and move on.

The doctor paused and the sound of a pen scribbling on paper echoed in the room. "Was it difficult to see your parents on screen?"

"No. That was nice."

"What part wasn't so nice?"

Aidan sighed again and crossed his arms, resting his head against the window frame. The sky's blue hue had darkened since his arrival and the deep oranges now faded into a rich red as the sun set behind the building. The colors changed, but the people racing on the street and gridlock traffic heading out of downtown remained the same.

"Aidan?"

He glanced over his shoulder again, trying to remember her question. "It was weird seeing myself in that video."

"Why?"

He turned around to face the doctor, hoping to avoid the distraction of the window. He lowered his brow, wondering what had happened to the boy in the video he used to know so well. Somehow, he had locked away the smiling, happy, playful version of himself and didn't have a clue how to reach him. And it pained him. A deep ache in his chest he hadn't experienced since the mourning of his parents. As if that inexplicable void hadn't been enough, out of the corner of his eye, he'd snuck a glance at Jessie who sat mesmerized watching the video with a hint of a smile touching his lips.

That stung even more. To know that another version of himself, one he no longer knew, could easily bring a smile to Jessie's face.

"It's as if I was looking at a different person," he said, remembering the younger version of himself running around the yard with his baby brother clinging to his back.

The doctor set her pen and notebook aside and clasped her hands together. "I'm going to ask you the dreaded doctor question. How did that make you feel?"

He refused to make eye contact. He couldn't sort through all the emotions racing through his mind to pick the correct answer. *I suck at this shit.* "I don't know," he finally said.

"Yes, you do. I'm not expecting you to say anything in particular. Just tell me what you felt. There is no right or wrong answer."

"I miss him," he whispered.

"What do you miss most about him?" Dr. Engel asked.

Aidan blew out a heavy breath, fighting a mix of pain and resentment. He pushed off the wall and sat on the couch across from the doctor. He rested his elbows on his legs and raked both hands in his hair, burying his head in his hands. "His...my smile in the video was effortless. I can't remember the last time I laughed that much." He sat up, forcing his mind to focus on stringing together his thoughts, his entire body heaving with each labored breath. He pushed his palms together and rubbed his hands, trying to ignore the ache in his chest.

"It was...strange hearing myself laugh. It's weird because I know what my brother's laugh sounds like. And I remember how much I missed it when he was recovering after the accident. And I remember the first time I heard it again. It was...like fucking magic. It sucked the air out of my lungs. But I can't...remember what my laugh sounds like anymore," he finished quietly.

Dr. Engel leaned forward. "You have this huge burden you carry on your shoulders and you don't realize how it weighs you down and affects every aspect of your life. You need to stop trying to carry this weight on your own."

Aidan looked up, his heartbeat picking up a notch. "I'm not going to broadcast my shit to the world or wear my emotions on my sleeve. That's not me. And no amount of therapy or talking or whatever the fuck you want to call it is going to change that."

She stared at him, matching his intensity. He knew better than to look away first.

"You are not a failure."

Aidan scoffed and shook his head, disgusted with himself. "You're supposed to tell me that. I pay you to listen to my bullshit."

The good doctor took a deep breath. "You're not listening to me on this because my opinion is not the one that matters to you." Dr. Engel sat back in her chair. "Okay, let's try a different approach. What's stopping you from telling Jessie what happened?"

He finally looked away.

"Aidan?"

He returned his focus to her, spearing her with a scowl he hoped would finally quiet her. "What?" he snapped, with a bit more bite than he had planned. *Well, maybe I did mean to snap. Maybe she'll finally back the hell off.*

She leaned forward again, clasping her hands. "I'm not dropping the subject so I suggest you answer the question."

Great, now she's fucking psychic too. His jaw muscles tensed as he bit back the simmering anger, staring at the doctor who refused to back down. Her persistence, both a blessing and a curse, often annoyed him. Even more so at that moment.

"Tell him."

"No."

"Why?"

"That's *my* choice to make," he said through clenched teeth.

The doctor straightened and raised an eyebrow. "You *are* learning something from our sessions. But stop trying to find the convenience in the tools you're learning."

He crossed his ankle over his knee and gripped his leg, figuring silence was a more…respectable alternative than lashing out with a few choice words.

She grabbed the pen from the side table and rolled it between her fingers. "Okay, let's look at this from a different angle."

She could sure as hell have a one-sided conversation for all he cared.

"What do you think Jessie will do when you tell him?"

He continued to silently stare. *Nothing. That's what Jessie would do because I'm. Not. Fucking. Telling. Him.*

She leaned forward. "Aidan, answer the question."

The pain in his jaw muscles began to radiate down his neck. *Why the hell doesn't she give up already?*

"Do you think he would leave?"

He turned away and tightened his grip on his leg.

"Do you think Jessie would leave?" she asked more firmly.

He scowled as he looked over to the window. Fuck the damn couch. He stood and paced the room, needing to ease some of the tension thrumming through his body. He should walk out of the damn office.

"Do you think Jessie would leave you?" she repeated.

He walked over to his spot by the window, leaning against the frame, closing his eyes with a sigh. *If she's pushing this damn much, it must be important.* He had asked her to push when he stalled. But—*hell*—she took that shit to heart like a woman on a mission to save the world.

"Aidan," she said, in a softer tone. "This is important and I believe this is a huge milestone we can't ignore. I think most of your tension stems from this. I know you have strong feelings for Jessie and I think it's a fear of him leaving you—"

"I don't think he'd leave me," he said, blurting out the words. He opened his eyes and shoved his hands in his pockets as he stared out the window. No, he didn't think Jessie would turn his back on him and walk away. "He's too supportive," he added, barely above a whisper.

After everything they'd been through, he knew—without a second of hesitation—Jessie wouldn't abandon him like everyone else had. It was the only thing he held with certainty. He sighed. The sky had darkened to a deep sapphire with splashes of gray erasing the orange from a few moments ago. Sometimes, he wished he could just as easily erase things.

"So what are you worried about?"

Aidan tried to sort the thoughts in his mind and translate them into words that actually made sense. He lowered his head, willing the words to come. "When he was in the hospital, after the attack, I was so pissed off I'd lose him. I realize now I was scared out of my mind.

There's something about him. I don't know what it is, but he keeps me balanced. Telling him this," he said, shaking his head.

He stared out the window, hoping to focus his thoughts. "He won't leave me; I'm not worried about that. But…I'm worried he'll see me differently and that will change things. He'll pity me or feel sad because of what happened. He'll see a weakness in me I don't want *anyone* to see." He glanced over his shoulder at the doctor. "Especially him," he whispered, before returning his focus to the window.

The sapphire shade of blue reminded him of how Jessie's eyes sometimes looked in the darkness of the living room, lit only by the flicker of the television screen. "He says I'm his rock. His guardian angel. Both of those things are hard and strong. That's what I always want to be for him. I know he loves me…and he loves *that* strength about me. And…I'm worried he won't see me the same once he knows." He shook his head again and blew out a frustrated breath, finally turning away from the window to face the doctor fully. "I don't think I'm making any sense."

"You think it's your strength he's drawn to and you're concerned that showing any weakness will diminish your connection with him."

"See that, Doc?" He withdrew his hands from his pockets and crossed his arms. He pursed his lips and nodded. "That's why you make the big bucks."

She cocked her head and gave him a lopsided grin. "I've known Jessie for a long time. He's stronger than many people give him credit for."

The edges of Aidan's lips curved into a smile. "And resilient."

The doctor nodded. "You know what he's been through. Did you pity him because of what happened to him with his father or Michael or when he was on his own?"

His eyes narrowed. "Hell no." For some inexplicable reason, her question really pissed him off. He straightened to his full height and squared his shoulders. "I have more respect for how strong he is. And I understand him more. I know why he needs order and control over things in his life."

A smile slowly spread across the good doctor's face.

What the fuck is so funny? Is she going to crack some stupid joke about defending Jessie's honor because I spoke up?

She crossed her arms and waited, still smiling smugly at him.

Wait a minute. The clever doctor often pulled a Mr. Miyagi on his ass, teaching him a lesson without him realizing it. *What the hell did she say? Did I pity Jessie because I knew his history? Fuck no!*

Realization came to him like a swift kick in the balls.

"Shit." *I walked right into that one.* He deflated; the fight and anger evaporating from his body almost as quickly as it had arrived.

"Now do you understand why you should tell him?"

Shit, shit, shit. "I don't think I can," he said, then turned to face the window again, shoving his hands in his pockets.

"You'd like to have an intimate relationship with him, but there's a wall you've built between the two of you. Until you break down that wall, you won't know what type of relationship you can have with him. You've kept this bottled up inside for a long time and it's managed to build resentment and an entire recipe of guilt and frustration that churns inside you. You just need to take that leap of faith. You're both problem solvers. You know that saying…when life hands you lemons. What do you do?"

He looked over his shoulder. "Throw them at people."

Dr. Engel raised an eyebrow. "You two will figure out how to make this work." She stood from her chair and walked over to him, mirroring his stance. "You make me work too hard," she teasingly said, leaning in and bumping his arm.

He chuckled, welcoming the break of the tension in the air.

"It's about honesty and trust." She raised a stopping hand when Aidan opened his mouth to interrupt her. "You haven't lied to him, but you haven't told him the complete truth. I know there's more you're not telling me because I recognize the signs. You need to tell him. If anyone will understand what you went through, it's him. Locking it up inside, silencing what you've experienced, won't help you. You're trying to define the rules on your own. Trust in the relationship you two have worked on. Be as honest and open with him as he's been with you, then work together to define the terms."

Aidan exhaled heavily, staring out the window. "You remind me of my friend, Hunter. You two should teach philosophy classes. You're both armed with logic and fancy, poetic phrases."

She tilted her head and whispered, "Works on you like a charm."

Sometimes, her snark reminded him of his mom. "Thanks....for putting up with my shit."

"That's why I'm here." She smiled and continued to stare out the window alongside Aidan. "So, would you say telling Jessie is a baby step or a toddler-sized one?"

Aidan took a deep breath. "I think we're pushing an Olympic-sized leap here."

She reached out and patted his arm in a comforting gesture. "Then go for the gold. I know how much you like to win."

Fucking smartass.

Chapter
TWENTY-FOUR

Jessie sat on the couch in their bedroom with his leg tucked under him, sneaking a glance above his e-reader. Aidan normally mulled things over in his mind, but something obviously grated on each of his nerves.

Aidan vigorously rubbed the towel through his freshly washed hair as he paced the room, barefoot with his low-slung jeans unbuttoned and half zipped. Jessie couldn't rip his gaze from the black waistband of the underwear or the strands of closely cropped hair peeking along the edge. Each pacing stride flexed Aidan's tight ab muscles, causing his ink to twist and move with each step as if the large inked scroll whipped in the wind, waving its message of strength and resilience.

He lowered his e-reader when Aidan stopped. Aidan worried his lower lip for a moment then resumed his pacing. Familiar enough with Aidan's characteristic stubbornness and need to think things over before finally voicing his thoughts, Jessie refocused on the magazine article, granting him his quiet space.

When Aidan was ready to talk, he would, and not a second before.

Aidan walked back into the bathroom, returning to the room with his hair brushed and the still lingering thinking-frown on his face. He planted his hands on his hips and finally looked over to Jessie. "I need to tell you something but I...I don't know where to start or how to say it."

Jessie set the e-reader to the side and sat up straight on the couch.

"I..." Aidan lowered his head and sighed. "I need you to just let me say it and not interrupt me at any point or I'll stop. I don't want to tell you...for a lot of reasons." He raked his fingers through his hair and blew out a frustrated breath. "But...you need to know," he finished quietly.

Jessie rose from the couch and walked over to him. He reached out, and Aidan inched back, raising his hands to avoid the contact.

"Don't. I'll...lose my nerve." Aidan's jaw muscles twitched and his frown deepened.

Jessie slid his hand in Aidan's, not letting him protest the contact as he silently led him out of their room to the back porch where they wouldn't hear a knock at the door or a ringing phone. He sat in his birdcage hanging chair and Aidan retreated to the bench. Anywhere else in the house would push them closer and Jessie wouldn't be able to resist touching him with the amount of frustration and worry vibrating off Aidan like a sonic plea for comfort.

Aidan leaned forward, resting his forearms on his thighs. He pushed his hands together, the roughness of his palms rubbing against each other the only sound in the early evening air. "Um, I don't really know where to start, so I'm..." He rubbed his palms against his thighs. "I'm just going to say it, however it comes out." He took a few deep breaths, his vision focused on a spot on the ground.

"When I served...my last mission...didn't go as planned. I can't tell you specifics, but the locations aren't relevant to what...I think you need to know." He spoke clinically, detaching himself from whatever he was preparing to say.

"We were a unit of five. I had served with all of them at some point in time prior to this assignment. We had a target and a mission. We were supposed to go in and get out. Twenty-four hours tops." He paused for a moment, pushing his palms together again. "It didn't work out that way."

His ominous tone sent a chill through Jessie's body. Jessie gripped the wicker edge of the chair, fighting the urge to reach out with a comforting touch.

"The intel we had...was wrong on a few counts. In the end, we were captured." He quieted, lowering his head. "I was the unit leader and I failed the mission."

The pain and desperation vibrated off Aidan in waves. Jessie wanted to wrap his arms around Aidan's neck and kiss him until the haunting memories evaporated, to hold him close and stroke his hair until the pain ebbed.

"They told me it was six months. I lost track of time, but Hunter…persistent son of a bitch that he is, knew something was wrong when I didn't come back within a few weeks. He gathered a rescue team and called in a lot of favors with some higher-ups." He ducked his head, rubbing his palms together harshly again, remaining silent for a few moments before he continued. "I was the only man left from my unit when he found our location."

Jessie closed his eyes, imagining the constant culpability and sorrow eating away at Aidan's soul—the failed mission, the death of the men he had been entrusted to lead, and the survivor's guilt. Jessie imagined the pain bore down Aidan's soul and supported the foundation of those inner fortress walls. He took a deep breath, slowly exhaling, hoping Aidan didn't sense the tension thrumming through Jessie's body as he usually did.

"They tried to get us to reveal our undercover agents within their group and what intel we had gathered, but we didn't. We wouldn't. They tried everything they could think of to extract information from us." Aidan looked straight ahead, narrowing his eyes as if trying to see something in the distance.

"They kept us tied up the whole time. They braided fabrics together." Aidan shook his head as if he'd gotten off track. "They stripped us after the capture, so we couldn't hide a weapon. Sometimes, they'd suspend us from this homemade pulley thing in the ceiling, using those strong as fuck braided fabrics like ropes. Thank God they never left us there long." He narrowed his eyes again and quieted for a few moments before continuing. "Just long enough to make a point. Our arms would get numb and…it was really hard to breathe. That's how Jack—" Aidan's voice cracked and he sucked in a breath. It took all of Jessie's strength not to reach for him when he saw the moisture gather in Aidan's eyes. "Usually, they kept us tied to a weird contraption with hooks in the walls using really short pieces of that fucking makeshift fabric-rope, so we'd have to stand. We'd stand for hours and couldn't move, having to stay awake for days at a time because the slack was too short and we couldn't sit. Sometimes, they'd put us on these pads...they were like really shitty mattresses, I guess...to change things up and fuck with our heads. I doubt it was a sense of mercy."

Aidan ducked his head, his eyebrows twitched as if battling with some thought. Jessie's numb fingers tingled. He released the white-knuckle grip of the chair's wicker frame. He took a slow, deep breath. Mercy? No, he imagined those monsters didn't understand the concept.

"The fabric was delicate, almost like silk, so it didn't leave a mark, but it was so damn strong when braided. How the hell could that shit be so strong?" Aidan's tone softened as if lost in the memory. "I figured it might be easier...to forget, since I don't have scars on my wrists, or anywhere else really noticeable on my body, but..." He shook his head, not finishing the thought.

But I can't forget. Jessie could hear the rest of Aidan's thought, loud and clear, screaming from every cell in Aidan's being. Jessie bit his lips, holding back words of comfort, waiting for Aidan to continue.

"We each had that same material wrapped around our necks," Aidan paused, tightening his lips for a moment before continuing. "During those times they suspended us, they wanted us to just hang there and...surrender. If we tried to break free, that makeshift noose would stop us." He quieted, his throat working as he obviously fought to speak through the emotions. "They showed us exactly what would happen if we were tempted to escape. I lost a man to their...demonstration," he finished in a bitter whisper.

He looked down and pushed his palms together again, staring at them before he continued. "They kept us blindfolded most of the time. I guess...hoping to keep us disorientated. To...make us feel helpless and weak. That whole thing about senses getting heightened..." He looked off to the side and took a deep breath. "Maybe there's some truth to that. Because I felt every brush of air that blew across my skin as if it were a fucking wind tunnel in my face." He looked down, scraping his teeth along his lower lip. "They'd take off the blindfolds when they wanted us to watch each other...witness as they...punished us. They wanted us to see every hit...hear every scream." He looked up and inhaled sharply, then exhaling a slow, shaky breath. "Fucking heightened senses. I can still hear those assholes yelling at us." He looked down, staring at his clasped hands. "And I can still hear my men screaming." He pinched the bridge of his nose then scrubbed his hand harshly across his face. "I don't know what's worse. The screams from my unit or their silence."

Jessie quickly swiped away the wetness on his cheek before Aidan noticed. His heart ached as he imagined the pain Aidan and his team had endured during those months. Understanding came crashing in and the pieces of the Calloway puzzle slowly started to fall into place. The bed, the darkness at night, the not wanting to be held down when they made out, and why he chose to lounge at home dressed. He closed his eyes, taking a deep breath fighting every instinct in his body pushing him to stand and comfort Aidan.

"We were trained to handle all kinds of shit. To...tolerate just about anything. But, we started fading as time passed. I'd talk to them, try to get them to focus on their families, something, anything positive to grab onto. But...it was too much." He rubbed his palms on his thighs and took a few deep breaths, pausing in his retelling, but his mind obviously continued to race a million miles a second. Jessie couldn't stand this, sitting idly by as Aidan struggled with so much pain. He fisted his hands and sat as still as possible. Trying...hoping to find the will to keep with Aidan's request and not interrupt.

Aidan finally spoke again, his tone barely above a whisper. "We tried to escape, but nothing worked. Toward the end, it was just two of us. Somehow, we broke free. The second we did, we took the blindfolds off and those bastards were watching us, grinning. Motherfuckers had set us up...I guess...to get our hopes up or something. Even with whatever adrenaline we had running through our body, we were too weak and dehydrated to fight them off. They...punished us for trying to escape. They found something...we weren't trained to tolerate. They..." Aidan swallowed convulsively. He clasped his hands together and his chest heaved with each forced, shaky breath. "They...violated us." He raked an unsteady hand through his hair. He closed his eyes and lowered his head. "They refused to do it themselves...they said it would be disgraceful for them to touch us that way, so they...they used what they had there instead."

Jessie couldn't breathe. Thankful to be hidden out of Aidan's line of sight in his birdcage chair, he closed his eyes and swallowed through the tightness in his throat, trying to fight the rising bile. He clasped his hands in his lap to try to steady the shake. The thought that they had violated Aidan with the intent to torture wrecked him and made his stomach churn. The fact that he had been in pain and his mind and body driven to the point of breaking and still, those monsters tried to take more from him. He knew all too well how that affected everything from that point forward. Every relationship, every interaction, and every decision and second-guess that followed...especially if Aidan had locked it up in his internal vault rather than talking to someone about it.

"I could handle just about anything, but that, I...I can't. It fucked with my head too much. I get flashbacks and the memories are there from everything else that happened. Dr. Engel says the reason the flashbacks are more frequent is partly because of the cases, but it's more of my mind finally letting all this shit out I've kept locked away for so long. But this..." Aidan shook his head repeatedly. "I can't. I just can't. There's no dealing with this. It's just...no. I didn't know it would feel like that. I can't do that to someone I'm with," Aidan said weakly, almost gasping each inhale as the strength seemingly started to evaporate from his body.

"I can deal with the couch, the bed, the crime scenes... Any of that shit. Even if I struggle with something, I'm trying to push through it. But this..." He angrily swiped at the tear that trickled down his cheek, sneering as if pissed by the show of weakness. "I can't. I don't know what this means for *us*. I know you said you wanted me any way you could have me, but...I don't think this is what you had in mind. I've been with guys where sex was all there was between us. I've never been with someone where it wasn't *the* important factor. So...I don't know how this can work. I don't expect you to be okay with this, and honestly...I'm not sure it's even possible. But I can't do that to you," he finished, almost in a whisper.

Jessie wouldn't dare deny he wanted to be with Aidan. The thought of finally being with someone who actually loved him—not because they said it with words, but because they said it with every other single detail, touch, gesture, glance, and thought—excited him with increasing anticipation the more they teased and explored each other. But the emotional connection surpassed the physical every time.

Aidan fisted his hands then wrapped his arms around his midsection, leaning forward as if he were ready to hurl. He quietly rocked himself for a few moments before he spoke again. "It was selfish of me to…let things go this far and not tell you. I know I'm an asshole for that. But…I…couldn't say no. I wanted to be with you, to…touch you."

He slowly blew out a deep breath, closing his eyes as if each word he had spoken had drawn every ounce of energy from his now drained body. "I just needed you to know. I didn't want you to ever think I pulled away because of anything you've ever done."

That's enough. Jessie stepped out of the hanging chair and walked over to the bench, taking a seat next to Aidan. He couldn't stand this anymore—the distance, the helplessness, watching Aidan struggle—and be expected to sit idly by. He clasped his hands in his lap, wanting to respect Aidan's wish to avoid contact until he had finished relieving his burden.

They stood at a fork in the road. Aidan had bared his soul and showcased—what Aidan perceived to be—his greatest dishonor on a dais for Jessie to issue judgement and determine which path they'd take in their relationship. Aidan had finally thrown open his iron doors and extended an invitation to his private fortress.

An exclusive invitation—one Jessie had patiently waited two years to receive.

Aidan had been dealt gut-wrenching punches his entire life and had survived. But now, sitting beside him, Jessie's heart squeezed when Aidan bowed his head almost in surrender, as if preparing for a final, inevitable blow that would end him.

* * * *

What have I done?

Aidan wished Jessie would push like everyone else. Maybe that way, he could push him right back and away and not have this need to connect with Jessie claw at him like a ravenous beast demanding freedom. But Jessie just let him be, as he always did. He sat silently by him like a guardian, waiting, respecting his request for no contact. But now, he wanted—*needed*—Jessie's touch and the comfort in knowing nothing would change.

He'd ripped the bandage off before he had a chance to actually think through things and realize the insanity of this all-or-nothing situation. As the seconds ticked by, the mental debate worsened. Maybe he should have kept quiet and ignored this dreaded step to move things to the next level in the personal relationship department. What next level? He'd pretty much defined a limit.

Hunter had rescued him from that hell, but even he hadn't known the extent of everything Aidan had experienced. Not even the ridiculous number of higher-ups who interviewed him or demanded statements. They knew the facts, the names, the locations, the details. But this…this was personal. Even the doctors he'd been forced to see at the military hospital before he could be discharged had been fooled. Maybe because of the minimal wounds on his body, or maybe they were more focused on his test results and ensuring the numbers fit within the acceptable standard ranges, or maybe it was simply because he told them all to fuck off and let him be. This was his nightmare and he refused to let it spread to another. Luckily, he hadn't required medical intervention for the physical aftermath, just time to heal. *Lucky. Yeah, right.*

Ms. Fix-it knew enough details to recognize something had happened to affect his ability to move into a relationship, but he refused to reveal why. The shame of being violated ate away at him, so he had buried that shit as deep as he could, locking away a part of himself and his desires along with it. If he couldn't handle it, how could he expect anyone to see past what had happened and believe in his strength? In his ability to protect them?

Now, in his greatest lapse of judgement, he had *voluntarily* spilled his darkest secret to the only man he had ever loved and truly wanted with every millimeter of his body and soul.

All or nothing. A bitter pill to swallow, one he'd forced down every fucking day since it all happened. For the first time in far too long, he'd had a spark of happiness flicker inside him, awakening a part of him he'd thought had died during his captivity. A flame that only seemed to burn with thoughts of Jessie. His stomach twisted with anxiety, waiting to hear what the truth had cost him and if Jessie would want to be with him after knowing everything.

"I want you. With all your soft and hard edges. With all your truths, regardless of how dark they may be."

Aidan sat there, having pushed that statement to the extreme. He couldn't take it one step at a time, no. He didn't do anything half-assed and had to go full force, dumping everything at once in hopes of showing his truths, of being honest. As honest as he could ever possibly be with the one person who meant everything to him.

He rubbed his arms to stave off the sudden chill on his skin. He didn't deserve Jessie, his love, his patience, his understanding. What the hell had he been thinking? He couldn't even protect him from the one monster who haunted him. Bile rose in his throat as a searing pain pierced his chest with the slow rip he sensed begin to tear through the tether that bound them.

Oh God. What have I done?

In his periphery, he could see Jessie taking a deep breath and turning to face him. "Are you finished?"

He nodded, unable to turn toward Jessie and risk catching any flicker of rejection in his eyes. He lowered his head and waited for karma to steal the one glimmer of light and hope he cherished more than life itself.

Warm fingers wrapped around the back of his neck and a gentle kiss pressed against his temple. "I love you," Jessie whispered in Aidan's ear, pulling him into an embrace, and wrapping his other arm around his shoulders. "Every second of every day, with every breath and heartbeat."

Aidan had heard those same words *before*. But at that moment, the weight of them repeated *after* everything he'd just said slammed a sledgehammer to his iron wall, demolishing his guard and lifting the heavy weight that had held him down for so many years. He had shown his true self and Jessie stood solidly at his side, rewarding him with support and unconditional love.

"I love you." Jessie tightened his arms around him. "So much."

An uncontrollable sob rose and tears streamed down his face, rendering him defenseless against the inundating wave of emotions. He reached around Jessie and fisted the material of his shirt, tugging him closer, effortlessly pulling Jessie onto his lap to sit astride him. He huddled in, burying his face in Jessie's chest. His breath hitched and another wave of emotions came crashing in when fingers gently combed through his hair and soft tender lips brushed against his temple in between comforting whispers of support and affection.

Sometime later, he took a few deep breaths, trying to cool his heated face and settle the throbbing in his head. He composed himself the best he could and finally released the death grip he had on Jessie enough to inch back from the embrace. He brushed away the wetness on his cheeks and sniffled, hiding his face. He didn't want pity, sorrow, or sympathy. He couldn't change what had happened and didn't want to dwell on it and risk retreating to that dark place again. He just needed to find a way to move on, move forward...*with* Jessie.

Aidan hesitantly glanced up, scowling at the hint of a grin playing in Jessie's expression.

Definitely *not* the reaction he expected.

Jessie ran his fingertips along Aidan's stubble. "So this is what it looks like when the dam breaks."

Aidan scoffed at the remark but breathed a sigh of relief, incredibly grateful Jessie's eyes held the same affectionate expression they always did rather than the pity he had anticipated. "Sorry," he said, sniffling again, scowling at his own weakness.

"Don't be. It's the most beautiful thing I've ever seen."

Aidan shook his head.

"Did you think I'd walk away from you?"

He exhaled heavily, trying to formulate his thoughts in the middle of the uncontrollable hurricane of emotions swirling within him. "I knew you'd stay." He looked down at his shaking hands resting on Jessie's waist. "I just didn't want you to stay for all the wrong reasons."

Jessie cupped his face, drawing his focus, forcing eye contact. "To be with you and know you...the *real* you...will always be the right reason for me to stay. We'll figure out what works and what doesn't and we'll adjust."

You. I just need you. Aidan's throat tightened. He closed his eyes and took a few deep breaths, nodding at Jessie's comment.

"Can I ask you something?"

He nodded again, gripping the waistband of Jessie's jeans, hoping to still the shake in his hands.

"What we've done so far, does any of that make you uncomfortable?"

"No."

"So me sitting on you like this—"

"I kinda grabbed you and put you here." He swallowed heavily. "Are you really okay with this?"

"I won't lie to you." Jessie firmly gripped his chin to raise his face. "I'd love to be with you and spend all night making love to you and showing you that it's different from what happened. But if you're only okay with what we do, then that works for me." Jessie ran his fingers through Aidan's hair in that way that always seemed to settle his inner chaos.

He kept his head down, staring at his still shaking hands. "I love everything we do. I can kiss and touch you all day long. And I love it when…you touch me."

"You're earning mega points today, Detective Calloway."

His heart pounded heavily, unsure of how to deal with the light-heartedness of the comment or the ease of acceptance. Things didn't go smoothly. Things never played out in his favor without exhaustively muscling his way through every stage in the process. "I…want to, but I'm sorry I can't get past what happened back then."

"Never apologize for that," Jessie said.

He closed his eyes, his lips parting with each strained breath. For some reason, a sudden weightlessness unsettled him as if he needed his armor to keep his feet firmly planted on the ground. He couldn't steady the shake in his hands or his rapid heartbeat pounding a pained staccato in his chest.

Jessie stroked Aidan's cheek. "What is it?" he prompted after a few silent moments.

Aidan clenched his hands into fists. "I can't fucking stop shaking. I…I feel like I'm falling apart."

"Then I'll hold you together." Jessie wrapped his arms around Aidan and pulled him close.

Aidan eased into the embrace, screwing his eyes shut, hoping to stave off another wave of emotions flicking along the fringes of his sanity. There, held snugly in Jessie's arms, he gasped a breath as the realization came barreling in to his mind. The smaller man with the leaner frame holding him had a strength that far exceeded his own. And without question or hesitation, *his* Jess would walk through a blazing fire to stand at his side.

* * * *

Jessie stood in the kitchen with Aidan, eating a mix of different fruits, taking a break and refueling for the next round of watching-but-not-really-watching a movie. After Aidan's reveal Friday night, it seemed Aidan couldn't stand being more than a few steps away from Jessie, regardless of what they did. A tentative touch. A lingering caress. And Jessie had lost count of the number of thank-yous whispered in his ear during their weekend, huddling close on the couch, doing nothing but spending quiet time together.

Here they were, midway into the next work week, and the need for closeness and the desire to cement the tether between them still lingered.

"You should eat a banana," he said as Aidan prepared a bowl of grapes.

Aidan raised an eyebrow. "I think you just want the phallic visual."

"Mmm." Jessie chuckled. "Marathon make-out sessions burn a lot of calories. It'll help."

Aidan tugged Jessie closer and grabbed a grape, feeding it to him. "I still think you want the phallic visual."

"I do like to watch you blow me."

Aidan coughed to clear his throat. "I swear, no one would ever guess how…forward you are in private," he absently said, mainly to himself.

"I'm comfortable around you."

"I see that," Aidan said with a grin. "I'm surprised you're not trying to steal my grapes. They look like tiny globes and they're round and juicy."

Jessie bit his lip, trying—and failing miserably—to disguise a chuckle. He stepped forward and kissed the column of Aidan's neck. He reached down and brushed his hand along the outside of the soft denim, finally cupping Aidan's balls. "I like these better." He stepped back and watched the unmistakable desire flooding Aidan's features—his eyes, his flushed complexion, his parted lips. He took another step back, needing to cool the heat between them. "I've got a question for you."

"Shoot," Aidan said, clearing his throat and popping a grape into his own mouth.

"Do you ever think you'll change your mind? That you'll ever want to—"

"Fuck?" Aidan finished the sentence for him then looked away, grabbing another grape. The desire evaporated from Aidan's features in an instant.

Jessie reached up and ran his fingers along Aidan's stubble. "It's not the same. You know that, right?"

Aidan met his stare.

He could swear Aidan's internal iron wall slowly began rising between them. "This is the part where we talk," he said, hoping to ease the sudden tension between them.

"And is this the part where you tell me fucking and making love isn't the same?" Aidan said.

Jessie treaded carefully, knowing the delicate subject could easily explode. He needed to walk that tightrope between the seriousness Aidan avoided and the banter that always drew him in. "You can call it whatever you want—sex, fuck, lovemaking, whoopee, the nasty. I don't care. I know where your heart is, so that's all that matters to me."

A playfulness reflected in Aidan's eyes. "Uh, whoopee? You don't actually call it that, do you?"

Jessie reached up, wrapping his arms around Aidan's neck. "You can call it whatever makes you comfortable. I like the thought of you making love to me all night and I'm certainly fine with a hard fuck right here in the kitchen. I don't care as long as I have you."

Aidan closed his eyes, his lips parting with each gasp of breath. "You've got a really dirty mouth."

He pulled Aidan's head down and licked the shell of his ear, reveling in the return of the desire flickering in Aidan's expression. "You have no idea."

Aidan reached behind Jessie and cupped his ass, pulling him flush against his body. He latched onto Jessie's lips, devouring his mouth as if making up for a lifetime of neglected kisses. Their tongues tangled and their grips tightened, neither wanting to pull away. They pulled away from the kiss, but remained barely a breath away, the undeniable need vibrating between them like a tangible entity.

"Aidan," he said, swallowing down the need buzzing through his entire body. "We're talking about this. Distractions won't work."

The grip on his ass cheek eased. He stroked the back of Aidan's hair, watching a million different emotions flash across his features.

Aidan closed his eyes and rested his head against Jessie. "I thought... Isn't this enough?"

"Yes, it is, if that's what you really want. But you're fighting with yourself when we're together and *I* don't want that. I will respect your limitations, but I want you to be happy. I don't want you angry or struggling with yourself whenever we're together."

"It doesn't matter what I want. I'm not doing that to you."

"It *does* matter. And you're right. You're not going to do the same. Because what they did to you was savage. It was meant to hurt you, to torture you."

Aidan quieted Jessie with a slow, quick kiss. "I don't ever want to hear you say what they did to me. Those words, coming from your mouth"—he shook his head—"it's just all kinds of wrong." He popped another grape into his mouth then retreated, leaning back against the counter and crossing his arms.

Jessie didn't want to push, but it didn't seem as if Aidan had shot down the conversation either even though his body language sent a clear *back-off* signal. Sometimes, he really did wish he owned the Calloway encyclopedia of emotions. "So...you *don't* want to talk about it?"

Aidan sighed. "*You* obviously do. So fine. Let's talk," he said with a bite of anger in his tone. He grabbed another grape and chewed on it, his face now devoid of any emotion. "You want to talk about how they shoved a fucking club up my ass and made me bleed like a stuck pig to punish me for trying to escape, how they tried to break me, fine, let's talk about that."

It took every ounce of energy to control the instinctive wince at Aidan's harsh words, but he couldn't risk his reaction being misinterpreted as a rejection. He remained still, his focus not wavering from Aidan's piercing stare.

"You wanted to talk about it. C'mon. Let's talk."

He might not be able to read all of Aidan's moods, but he did know how Aidan used his anger to distance himself—from the conversation, from what had happened, and from him. He shook his head, not understanding why Aidan continued punishing himself. "Why do you hate yourself so much?"

Aidan turned away, reaching for a grape in the now empty bowl. He stared at the empty dish, seemingly lost as if he didn't have a clue what to do next.

Jessie took the few steps forward to reach him, stopping when Aidan turned toward him. The pained expression on his face twisted Jessie's stomach and speared his heart. He pulled Aidan's hands and placed them on his waist, forcing Aidan to hold him, refusing to let him distance himself. "Answer my question."

Aidan's grip tightened, twisting the denim of Jessie's jeans in his fists. "Because I couldn't stop it," he finally said in a broken whisper. "Any of it. What they did to them. To me."

"It's not your fault." Jessie reached up and stroked his fingers gently through Aidan's hair. "There's nothing you could have done. You think you didn't fight for yourself? For them? Bullshit. You fought every damn day to stay alive. You all did."

Aidan quieted, the only sound the harsh puff of each breath. "How…" He trailed off, his eyebrows twitching as if battling with a thought.

"Ask me anything. Don't worry about how it sounds."

Aidan swallowed heavily and tugged Jessie a little closer. "How do you forget and not let all that stuff bother you?"

"I'm not going to lie to you. I can't forget it. It's always there, and some days, just when everything is fine, something triggers a memory.

Those days are the toughest and I hate them. You've seen me when that happens. But there's nothing I can do to change history. What I *can* do is not let it control me." He cupped Aidan's face. "You need to let go of this guilt you're feeling. It's eating away at you. None of this is your fault and you're not a cursed man walking. Your sister, your friend, or the guys you got close to who walked away. The men from your unit and what those monsters did to you. None of that was your fault. It's not a failure or a weakness. You have nothing to be ashamed of. You are a strong, good man who's a fighter, and nothing those bastards did can ever change that. You can't let it overtake everything in your life. You know why?"

"Why?" Aidan croaked, finally making eye contact.

"Because it gives those memories and monsters power over you, the people in your life, your relationships, and what you do and don't do. And that means they've won."

Aidan grew silent, in that way he did when he absorbed every word in their conversation.

"And I know how you love to win," Jessie said.

The edges of Aidan's mouth slowly twitched upward in a hint of a small smile. He leaned in and brushed his lips against Jessie's. "You've got this all figured out."

Jessie huffed out a quiet laugh. "Far from it. It's taken a lot of therapy to get where I am. I think I may have funded a tropical island for the doctor with my therapy expenses. But I gave you the crash course Vega special."

Aidan chuckled softly.

"Life isn't a fairy tale. And sometimes, it's mean and ugly and filled with horrible things. What matters is how you push through those times so you can enjoy the happy moments."

"I…figured it was payback for something I did."

"You're a good person, Aidan, whether you believe it or not. Your endgame is always to protect those you care about. You can't have good without evil. Otherwise, you wouldn't know the difference when you see it."

Aidan wrapped his arms around Jessie's waist and pulled him flush against his body. He pressed a kiss to the side of Jessie's head and buried his nose in Jessie's hair as he often did. "You're an eternal optimist."

"It's either that, or I risk branding myself as a victim. And I refuse to do that."

"I'm trying. I swear I am," Aidan said, running his fingers up and down Jessie's back.

"I know you are."

Aidan loosened his tight hold and inched back from the embrace. He brushed his thumb along Jessie's jaw, avoiding eye contact. His face pinched and his eyebrows knit together as he battled with a thought. "I'm sorry I snapped at you. I shouldn't have said that the way I did."

Jessie stared at Aidan in wonder at the openness and vulnerability in his expression—both heartbreaking and beautiful. He fidgeted with the button of Aidan's jeans, needing to look away from the blinding truth in the emotions on display. "Were you hoping I'd walk away after you said that?"

"I'm not sure. But I'm glad you didn't." Aidan cupped Jessie's face, leaning in for a slow, tender kiss. "I'm a difficult son of a bitch sometimes."

"Sometimes?"

Aidan's lip twitched. "And stubborn."

"*Very* stubborn," Jessie added with a grin.

"Then you know me well enough to know that I suck at letting things go, but you also know I don't give up. I might not always know what to say or how to say it, but I swear I'm trying. And I need you to know, regardless of some of the stupid shit I say…or don't say, I always want you in my life. *With* me."

Jessie placed his hand over Aidan's. "And I need you to know that I love that difficult, stubborn son of a bitch and I'm not going anywhere. Even when he tries to push me away."

Aidan crushed his mouth against Jessie's and grabbed him by the ass and the back of his head to pull him flush against his body. Jessie fisted his hands in Aidan's hair, holding on for dear life as Aidan ravished his mouth, unmistakably conveying the words he had—and hadn't—spoken with each swipe of his tongue and pull of his lips.

They finally separated from the kiss, gasping each breath between them, still gripping on to each other.

"I love you, Aidan. Every second of every day." He rested his head against Aidan's shoulder and placed his hand against Aidan's chest, closing his eyes when the strong, steady, fast beat pulsed against his palm. *With every breath and heartbeat.*

Aidan kissed the top of his head and buried his nose in Jessie's dark hair. "And I promise I'll do everything I can so you never regret that."

Chapter
TWENTY-FIVE

Jessie closed his eyes and took a deep, calming breath, fighting off the exhaustion numbing his senses. Too much had gone on in too short a period of time. He needed a little break to recharge and find his happy place. After two weeks of intense case prep work and research review with a client, he wanted to shut out the world and veg out on the couch with Aidan. Since their relationship breakthrough almost two weeks before, they hadn't had a full weekend together. And he missed their private time.

He crossed and uncrossed his legs, casually scanning the solid colored walls of the interrogation room, purposely plain, boring, and non-distracting. Detective Reyes had contacted him mid-afternoon, requesting he come by the precinct. No additional details or information. He had thankfully switched off his phone while at the courthouse, wrapping up the final summary points of his findings to a panel of a half dozen lawyers. He certainly didn't need to let his mind wander regarding the reason for the detective's call.

He looked to his left at the one-way mirror, his reflection sharp and clear, but a calming peace settled within knowing Aidan stood on the other side of the glass. He didn't need to see him to know he watched over him; he could feel his presence as if he stood directly behind him.

Detective Reyes entered the room then closed the door behind him. "Thanks for coming in. I'm sorry it took me a few minutes to get in here." He pulled out the chair across from Jessie and sat, placing a folder on the table between them. He looked different from his prior appearances, wearing tactical gear rather than the usual three-piece suit he'd worn during their prior conversations. "Camera's on while I'm in here for documentation in your case."

Jessie's heartbeat picked up its pace. "Have you found him?"

"I'm going to need you to look at some pictures." Reyes reached into the folder and removed several stacks of clipped images. "We found a few men who established a pattern that fit with the information you provided on Michael Johnson. But we need you to look at the photos to see if he's one of these men."

"Okay," Jessie said in the steadiest tone he could fake. A mix of excitement and fear squeezed his chest. Finally, after all this time, maybe the nightmare would end.

Reyes took the first stack and removed the clip, turning them toward Jessie, revealing a series of photos. "Each stack is a different person. I have twenty men I want you to see in this file. I have a few pics of each person because the footage is old, so I wanted to make sure you had at least one image as a clear reference. The angles are odd in some instances, videos are grainy at certain times of the day, and some are with different types of attire. Hopefully one of the images will jog your memory and help you identify him."

"I don't need anything to jog my memory," Jessie absently said, taking the first stack of photos for the first man. He glanced up at the detective, noticing the sudden discomfort. "Sorry, that was...rude."

"No, it wasn't." Reyes's lips thinned and his brows knit together. "I imagine you wouldn't forget his face."

Jessie shook his head. "This isn't him. This man isn't tall enough. Michael's shoulders are broader." He re-clipped the stack of photos for the first man and reached for the next, discarding the second man just as quickly.

"Take your time. We're in no rush."

Jessie rejected the third man and his stack of images, then the fourth. He took the fifth stack, unclipped the photographs, reviewed the first image then flipped to the second photo of the same man.

"Does he look familiar?" Reyes asked, almost sounding surprised.

After reviewing the second, clearer, photo, Jessie eliminated the fifth man and re-clipped his stack of photos. "No. I wasn't comfortable eliminating him based on the first photo because he had a similar build, but the baseball cap obstructed his face. Michael had one of those same hats with that team logo. The second photo was clearer." They continued to review the stacks, Jessie easily discarding each and adding a brief comment regarding the reason for his elimination. Hope began to dim as he neared the end of the pile of suspects. "I'm sorry. I know this must have taken a long time to gather."

"Don't worry about it," Detective Reyes said, subtly shaking his head. "Worth it if we can catch him."

Jessie nodded, moving another man to the discarded pile. "I really do appreciate it." He grabbed the next stack of images and automatically unclipped the stack of photos before glancing at them.

The air froze in his lungs. He stared at the familiar face and profile of the monster he could easily identify from a distance. The slight bend in his nose, the way one eyebrow appeared thicker than the other, and the number of pockmarks in each cheek. Every detail engraved in his mind surfaced. A vivid, full color image of the monster who haunted him rose in his mind in place of the grainy, poor quality surveillance image in front of him. He reached out, hoping to hide the tremble in his hand, and flipped over the first image to see the second photograph. He needed to be sure. The wrath of Calloway and every member of the team would fall upon whatever man he identified. He had to be one-hundred-percent certain.

The pounding of his heart muted all other sounds. He took a few deep breaths, unable to rip his eyes away from the man in the image, staring directly at him—the monster who haunted him far more than he admitted to anyone. He absently flipped the second photo to look at the third image. *Michael.* He couldn't stop himself from reviewing each photograph. An odd and somewhat morbid compulsion, like driving by an accident and not being able to rip your eyes away from the damage. He collected the half dozen images and stacked them neatly, needing to busy himself, hoping to disguise the uncontrollable shaking of his hands. He didn't bother attempting to clip the stack of photos together, working the binder clip would require far too much coordination than his hands could muster at that moment. He turned the stack to face the detective.

Detective Reyes straightened in the chair. "Is that him?" he asked, his tone hopeful.

Jessie nodded and clasped his hands in his lap. "Yes."

Please leave.

Reyes shoved the stacks of photos back in the folder and shot up from his chair. "Now we've officially got a face to go with the evidence we have. We'll catch him."

Jessie nodded and forced a smile.

Please leave.

Reyes's direct stare unsettled him. Oddly penetrating, as if he could inspect each of Jessie's thoughts. Behind the cool, polished demeanor, Jessie suspected this detective could easily dish out his own flavor of vengeance. "If you need a minute, that's fine."

Jessie nodded again.

Please leave.

"Thanks for going through these. I know it wasn't easy." Reyes walked over to the door and hesitated.

Jessie sat still, waiting to hear the click of the door when he exited. *Please leave.* He stared at the plain wall, willing the detective to exit the room. His lips parted on a breath when the door opened then clicked shut behind him. He took a few deep breaths, hoping to appear unaffected long enough for Aidan to leave the observation room.

Without a doubt, those hazel eyes watched him carefully, waiting for the tiniest of details to ensure he had survived the photo lineup unscathed.

He hadn't.

* * * *

Aidan stood, arms crossed, staring at Jessie through the glass. Reyes had briefed him on the team's findings before requesting Jessie arrive at the station. The tension thrumming through his body had him ready to snap.

"C'mon. What are you waiting for? Reyes sent out the text. We need to go," Sunny said.

"Not yet. Not until I know he's okay."

Sunny looked at Jessie, sitting still at the table. "He's fine."

No, he's not. Something nagged at Aidan to stay a little longer. Jessie always put up a good front, but he couldn't be as steady as he tried to appear. The way he had meticulously stacked the photos, ensuring the corners lined up perfectly—his nervous tell. In Jessie's world, high stress situations required extra caution and things needed to be excessively perfect, as if the storm within wouldn't erupt if everything else managed to remain in order.

Jessie didn't know he had set the ball in motion as soon as he had identified the man in the photograph. Manny had already run an age progression for each suspect and took it a step further, tapping the team's agency contacts to access their facial recognition technology and databases. Having an *in* with the other agencies definitely had its perks. They now had a name, a face, and a last known address. But without Jessie's official identification, their hands were tied.

Stupid fucking protocol and procedures.

If Jessie knew, Aidan suspected there would be no way he could keep it together.

"You go ahead. It's two hours away. I'll catch up." Aidan spoke to Sunny, but his focus never shifted from the man sitting at the table, in the exact same position. Aidan remained still, observing every detail of Jessie's stoic pose, resisting the urge to break through that door without some sign his presence would be welcomed. The worry ate away at him, but Jessie always needed to push through things on his own to assert his independence.

So Aidan waited.

"No way. You want this more than Reyes." She looked back over to Jessie. "What are you waiting for?"

"Not sure. I'll know when I see it."

Every bone in Aidan's body commanded he storm in there and do something—anything—to ease the obvious tension in Jessie's rigid body.

Jessie sat, unmoving, except for his bobbing Adam's apple and the slight rise and fall of his chest with each breath. His shoulders didn't move and his posture didn't waver. His gaze steady, focused straight ahead at the bare wall. He unclasped his hands, reached up to flatten the perfectly combed hair at his temple, then casually returned to his stoic pose.

But Jessie couldn't hide the tremble in his hands.

Shit. Aidan's heart violently pounded as he raced out of the observation room, leaving Sunny behind. He threw open the door to the interrogation room, spotting Jessie still sitting in the same pose. He closed the door behind him and took a step forward.

"Jess?"

Jessie lowered his head. "Aidan," he said on a whisper. "I need...you to go."

"No." He took another step closer to Jessie. "I'm not leaving you alone like this."

Jessie turned his head to the side, granting Aidan a slight view of his profile. "Please."

Please leave or please help? He walked over to the chair across from Jessie and sat. He rested his clasped hands on the table and waited.

"Detective Reyes said there was a camera in the room."

"Which he switched off as soon as he walked out."

"The...glass."

"Sunny...if she's still there. Otherwise, I'm positive she's blocking anyone from going in there until she knows we've walked out of this room."

"I need you to go," Jessie said, his voice barely above a whisper. "Please."

"I'm not leaving you."

Jessie slowly tilted his head upward.

Aidan would have dropped to his knees at the pain staring back at him had he not been sitting. Fear clouded the crystal blue eyes he loved so much, haunted like the first time they'd met so long ago.

"I'm not stupid," Jessie said. "You've told me enough about the team to guess Reyes already knew which photo I was going to pick, and I'm assuming he took liberties to find where Michael is now using that same photo and contacts the team has established. And I'm going to guess he probably had a judge on speed dial he called as soon as he walked out that door to grant him a warrant to whatever location he found for Michael." Jessie paused and swallowed heavily, staring at Aidan's vest. "And that's why he and you are in your tactical gear. You needed me to confirm it was him from the photo lineup. And now you need to go."

"I'm not leaving you."

Jessie shook his head. "I...can't do this. I need to know he's caught. So you *need* to go."

Aidan's phone chirped with a new message. He pressed the button to ignore the text. Between his pounding heart and the adrenaline coursing through his veins, Aidan couldn't focus on anything other than the pain screaming from every pore of Jessie's body. "You need me to be there. To make sure he's caught?"

Jessie lowered his head and nodded. "I can't...please...I...need this nightmare to end."

Aidan fisted his hands under the table, digging his blunt nails into his palms, hoping the sting would distract him from the anger that began to boil at Jessie's desperation.

"He tried to break me." Jessie quieted and crossed his arms tightly. "I...see that now. I...I can feel it." He looked up at Aidan, a single tear trickled down his cheek with the movement. "I think...he did," he whispered. He turned away, avoiding eye contact. He lowered his head again, his shoulders slightly shuddering.

"Jess...look at me."

Jessie shook his head. "I don't want you to see me like this."

The anger at the monster who did this to *his* Jess, the ache in his chest from the pain slowly tearing down the positivity always radiating from Jessie's spirit, the frustration at not having closed this case out months ago...all swirled inside in a tornado of vengeance, rage, and helplessness.

"If you want me to leave because you want me to be there to make sure he's caught, then I'll go once I think you're okay enough to be on your own. But if you think, for a fucking moment, I'm going to walk out this door because you don't want me to see how this monster hurt you, then you seriously don't know me after all this time."

Jessie lifted his head, his focus now squarely on Aidan. His eyes, a pool of unshed tears held back by a dam of control even Aidan wasn't sure he had. "Is this what you want to see? You want to see me broken like this!"

Aidan leaned forward and pointed a finger at Jessie. "*You* are the one who told me to not let those monsters win, to not give those monsters or memories power. Was all that bullshit?"

Jessie gasped. "No."

"Then don't you fucking dare think for a second that son of a bitch broke you. He didn't. You escaped from him and you made yourself into the man you are today. A man…" Aidan snapped his jaw shut, his nostrils flaring with each deep, forced breath. "A man who taught me what it's like to be strong. What it's like to push through shit and get out of that dark hole. So don't you crawl into that abyss, because I will fucking hunt you down and bring you back kicking and screaming."

Jessie took a deep breath and exhaled slowly, slumping his shoulders as if a mere breath took the full force of his strength.

"Now give me an inspirational poster line so I don't completely lose my shit in this room and pitch a fit."

A soft, pained chuckle escaped Jessie. "My mind…is strong and has the power to define me."

"And what's your mind telling you now?"

Jessie straightened his shoulders and took a deep breath, then another. He looked up at Aidan, this time, with a spark of determination in his eyes. "He didn't break me."

"You're damn right he didn't." Aidan didn't bother to hide the smile. He glanced at his phone when it chirped again with a new message.

"I know you need to go. And I need you to be there. Please."

Aidan cleared the message. The team was on their way, and Sunny waited for him outside the door. "I don't want to leave you alone. Would you be fine with me calling Julian?"

Jessie nodded.

Jessie needed someone quiet who offered support right now… *quiet* support, so that immediately eliminated Cole from the short list.

Aidan grabbed his phone and quickly dialed Julian's number. After a short conversation, they disconnected the call. Luckily, Julian and Matt were running errands while the guys staying at Halfway House took advantage of their weekend pass starting that Friday evening. "Matt and Julian are a few minutes away. They're coming right over."

"Thank you." Jessie rubbed his arms. "Aidan?"

"Yeah?"

"I'm…not as strong as you think I am."

"No, you're not. You're stronger. Don't let that son of a bitch get inside your head."

Jessie quietly laughed. "He can't. Not when you keep kicking him out."

Aidan smiled. "Damn right."

"Every second, Aidan." Jessie took a deep breath and stared at Aidan, his eyes still shone with fear, but it battled heavily with the sheer determination of the man who wore those dark suits that always made Aidan weak in the knees. "I swear, every second of every day."

A warmth washed over Aidan with the slow rebuilding of Jessie's strength staring back at him. Jess would pull through this as he always did.

"How do you do that? How do you manage to make me feel as if I can get through anything?"

Aidan leaned forward over the table, thankful the ray of hope and positivity slowly seemed to return to *his* Jess. "It's you, Jess. That's all you. You're the one who's taught me anything is possible."

Julian and Matt arrived fifteen minutes later and promised to stay with—a much calmer—Jessie until Aidan returned home. He met Sunny by the car and peeled out of the parking garage like a bat out of hell to race to catch up with his teammates.

"Will you slow the hell down!" Sunny said, gripping the seat belt and the center console. "You've almost caught up with them. They're only a mile up."

"Then it's a mile I still need to catch up." Aidan weaved through traffic, thankful for the highway offering ample visibility.

Sunny pointed up ahead to the right. "There they are!"

Aidan pressed on the gas pedal to catch up with his team members, speeding past them with his siren blaring. He glanced in his rearview mirror, smiling at the two cars accelerating to catch up with him.

"I swear. Men and cars. I don't get it," Sunny grumbled, slipping on her leather gloves.

"It's more a thing of wanting to catch the bad guy."

"Helps if we're alive to do it."

They turned the corner and silenced the sirens, silently pulling up a few houses away. They quickly exited their cars and stealthily made their way to Michael's address, sweeping the exterior, not seeing any activity from within the home.

"Travis, Sunny, head around back to block the rear exit," Manny said.

Manny gave them a second to position themselves then pounded on the door. "Michael Johnson, Miami PD, we have a warrant. Open the door."

The tension thrummed through Aidan's body as Manny pulled up the hem of his glove and looked at his watch…waiting. "Fuck, Reyes. Really? You want a fucking welcome basket too?"

"Ten seconds, Calloway. I'm not letting that slippery son of a bitch off on a technicality." Manny glanced up and over to Wall who looked as if he was itching to hit something. "Now! Break it the hell down."

Wall back-kicked the door and they stormed into the house from both entry points, guns raised and aimed forward, sweeping the house one room at a time until they all met in the center room.

Nothing. Literally, nothing. A few, random, dust-covered, discarded pieces of worn furniture remained in the otherwise empty house.

Aidan cursed under his breath. *This. Is. Not. Happening.* He holstered his weapon and planted his hands on his hips. He looked to the heavens, begging for patience. He took a deep breath and closed his eyes to center himself. He thought of Jessie, his smile, the way he'd tease him, hoping to calm the jackhammering heartbeat in his chest. But he couldn't erase the haunted look in those blue eyes and how, almost two hours ago, they'd held back a pool of unshed tears.

He lowered his head.

Something caught his attention in the corner.

"I swear, if this son of a bitch—"

"Wait." Aidan's word cut off the beginning of Manny's rant. He spotted faint scuffs marks on the floorboard in front of the oversized dresser, as if the furniture had been moved. "Wall, help me move this thing."

Wall instantly stood on the opposite end of the vintage piece and held the large wooden furniture. They looked over to the others to ensure they had guns drawn before lifting away the dresser. Behind it, a hidden door opened to reveal a narrow hallway. They cautiously walked the few steps in pairs, lighting the way with their tactical flashlights until they reached a door to a room. They flipped the single light switch inside and the team quieted at the sight. In the corner of the small, unoccupied room lay a single, dingy, twin-sized mattress on the floor next to a small end table. A brown moisture stain darkened part of the walls around the lone window in the room which had been plastered shut.

He couldn't let his mind dwell on what may have happened in this room or if Jessie had lived under similar conditions so many years ago. He tried to calm the pounding of his heart echoing in his ears. Wall stood by the table with his back to him. His biceps flexed, anger radiating from his large, rigid frame. "Wall, what is it?"

His teammate turned; the rage in his locked jaw and scowl instantly sent Aidan a silent warning message. Aidan took the two steps needed to reach him and yanked the tiny, ripped slip of paper from his gloved hand.

He stared down at the paper.

A few words, unmistakably meant for him, neatly written in sharp strokes.

He will always remember his first, Detective Calloway.

The beast within clawed to the surface and possessed him with a violent roar, tossing the wooden table across the room, against the other wall, shattering two of the legs into pieces. Strong, vise-like arms wrapped around him from behind, locking his movements. His internal beast fought the hold, violently fighting to free himself from the enemy who dared sneak up on him from behind.

"Calm down, Calloway. Don't play into his game," the voice whispered.

Aidan closed his eyes, fighting for each intake of breath against the crushing hold around him. Even through the red haze of rage, he'd recognize that bitch named Logic anywhere. He needed to be sharp and focused. And he needed Jessie. The arms around him unlocked, and he eased out of the hold, spinning on his heel.

Wall.

Aidan frowned. He glanced at Travis standing in the doorway and Manny and Sunny staring at him from out in the hallway. "I'm fine," he said, his voice hoarse. His teammates nodded and retreated while Wall stayed behind with his arms crossed. "Thanks."

Wall grunted and turned, picking the note up off the ground and shoving it into an evidence bag he pulled from his vest pocket before making his way out of the room with the rest of the team.

Great. Now he was hearing voices. He raked his hand through his hair, trying to block out the taunting words of the note. Son of a bitch baited him.

At least they now had a face for the bastard. He'd figure this out. Him and his team.

But right now, he needed Jessie.

* * * *

"Hey," Aidan said, closing the door behind him. It had been five hours since he'd seen Jessie and he couldn't stand another minute away from him.

"How'd it go?" Julian asked, switching off the television and rising from the couch. "Did you guys arrest him?"

Aidan winced.

"Sorry."

"How's he doing?"

This time, it was Julian's turn to wince. He rubbed his shaved head then crossed his arms, staring at Aidan without uttering a word.

"It helps if you actually say the words out loud." Aidan frowned, angry at himself for the inappropriate moment to dish out any sort of snark to the one guy who seemed to be at his side when stuff went sideways. Julian didn't deserve to be on the receiving end of his frustration. And Aidan certainly wasn't an authority on the whole talking thing. "Sorry about that."

"You're pissed. I get it. Matt's in the room with him. He's quiet now, so I'm assuming he's better."

"Quiet *now*?"

"He couldn't sleep so he took a pill. I'm guessing it knocked him out. I don't know. Matt usually handles that kind of stuff at the house."

Aidan nodded. "Thanks for staying with him. I know it took a while."

"Not a problem. I could watch TV here all night with your setup. It's cool."

Aidan nodded again, patting Julian's shoulder before he turned away. He walked down the hallway, hesitating for a moment before pushing the door the rest of the way open. Matt immediately glanced up, sitting in the desk chair, bedside to Jessie. He stood as soon as he saw Aidan, quietly lifting the chair and returning it behind the desk.

Jessie slept on the bed with his arms tightly wrapped around a pillow.

"Hey," Matt whispered, walking up to Aidan.

Aidan couldn't take his eyes off the pillow in Jessie's grip. "How's he doing?"

"He switched the music on and that seemed to help a little. He's been trying to keep it together, but...he ended up taking a pill because he was too edgy. It knocked him out." Matt crossed his arms, looking over his shoulder at Jessie on the bed, still holding the pillow in a death grip. "He was worried about you," Matt said absently.

Aidan's focus snapped back to Matt. "Me?"

"He was worried about what you'd do when you found Michael. I think that had him more worried than anything."

Aidan closed his eyes and lowered his head, the strength leaving his body with the deep exhale. After the hell Jessie had been through and all the thoughts that probably circled in his mind, the one thing that worried Jessie was *him*?

"Thanks for being here with him. I appreciate you guys doing that."

"Not a problem at all. We would have just gone back to the house, so it was a nice break. But I wish it would have been under different circumstances," Matt said, in his usual proper tone.

Aidan nodded. He walked Matt and Julian out and locked up for the night.

The one lead that had led the team to Michael after searching for him for so long was now, officially, a dead end. At least now, they had a face. And maybe the message deliberately aimed at Aidan could justify pursuing the case further or allocating more resources. He definitely didn't have enough brain cells at that moment to explore all the options.

His mission for the weekend: to make sure Jessie returned to some form of his usual optimistic spirit.

Aidan stripped out of his clothes and took a shower in record time, just enough to wash away any remnants of a place where that monster had resided. He grabbed the soft sleep pants Jessie liked him to wear and stood by the bed, still surprised by the tight hold Jessie had on the pillow.

The pillow encased in one of Aidan's T-shirts.

Jessie's grip was so tight his arms must be aching, but it didn't seem as if he had any plans on letting go during this lifetime. Aidan tugged the pillow, trying to remove it from his hold. Jessie's brow lowered and his lips thinned, yanking the pillow back into his body and letting out a grunt of protest.

A searing pain sliced through Aidan's chest as guilt gripped his throat. He should have stayed with Jessie, should have been with him during this rough time, should have caught Michael, should have ended this nightmare for the man he loved.

He couldn't breathe. Aidan looked away from the pained

expression on Jessie's sleeping face and stared down at his own hands, fisting them, willing the shake to stop. He needed Jessie, the warmth of his body and his calming spirit…something, anything to let him know the tether that bound them was still intact. That he hadn't broken the delicate thread he needed as much as he needed the air in his lungs.

"With every breath and heartbeat."

He knew the meaning of those words and felt them deep within, each and every day.

He slipped under the covers and wrapped his arm around Jessie's waist. He leaned in, placing a few kisses on Jessie's shoulder. He stroked Jessie's hair and peppered more kisses on his skin. "Jess," he whispered, barely above the forced push of each breath as he fought the suffocating grip at his throat.

Jessie released the pillow, turned, and wrapped himself around Aidan like a vine. He buried his nose at the base of Aidan's neck as a whimper escaped. "Aidan," he said in a breathless sigh.

"I'm here." Aidan stroked his back and tugged him closer, screwing his eyes shut to fight the storm of emotions threatening to erupt.

Jessie's fingers dug into Aidan's skin and his legs tightened around him. He tilted his head up, scraping his nose against the ever-present stubble, reaching up and gripping the hair at the back of Aidan's head.

Aidan leaned into the embrace, pulling Jessie flush against his body. "I'm sorry," he whispered, burying his nose in that dark hair he loved so much. He swallowed heavily, struggling with the knot in his throat as he held Jessie close, hoping to provide enough comfort to ease him into sleep.

That feels so fucking good. The rhythmic stroking in his hair always settled him. Aidan opened his eyes when warm, soft lips pressed against his mouth.

"Good morning," Jessie said, lying on his side, one hand tucked under the pillow and the other extended, stroking Aidan's hair.

He brushed his thumb along Jessie's cheek. "How're you doing?"

A warm smile spread across Jessie's face, softening his features. An emotion Aidan couldn't quite place welled in his blue eyes.

"I'm sorry, Jess."

Jessie bit the edge of his lower lip as if trying to hold back something he was going to say.

"I should have been here with you."

Jessie's brow furrowed in confusion. "I asked you to go."

"You asked me to be there…to make sure he was caught. I didn't. I…couldn't. He wasn't there," Aidan said, sounding far more defeated than he cared to admit.

Jessie placed his palm against Aidan's stubbled cheek. "And there's no way you could have known that. So stop beating yourself up."

"I should have been here for you. I should have—"

"Stop it and stop apologizing. You're like a pit bull that just won't let go. I asked you to be there to catch him. After you left, it was all I could think about. The fact that I had pushed you into a situation I knew would test every ounce of you. And that wasn't fair at all. It was very selfish of me."

"You're the most selfless person I know."

Jessie withdrew his hand, tucking them both under the pillow. He kept fighting a smile that tried to break the surface.

Aidan frowned. "I don't get it."

"Get what?"

"Yesterday was a fucked up day. I know it was hard. That was the only lead to work on the case. The only plus right now is that we've got a face to link to the other stuff we've got."

"Okay."

"Why are you smiling?"

The smile finally broke free. "You're in bed. And it looks like you were in bed for most of the night."

Aidan froze. How the hell had he not realized that huge detail? He slowly looked around at the sheets and comforter around them.

Jessie softly laughed, reaching out to stroke Aidan's chest. "It's not like the bed's going to suddenly turn into some Venus flytrap and gobble you up. Don't freak out."

Aidan swallowed heavily, still scanning every inch around him.

Jessie snuggled into his pillow. "Tell me what happened last night. When you got to the address."

He refocused on Jessie, trying to ignore the fact that he'd slept a full night in a bed for the first time in more than six years. "It was empty."

"But you're sure it was his house?"

The anger instantly surged through his body. "Yes."

Jessie's eyebrow twitched. "There's something you're not telling me."

Aidan debated what he should say and whether he should say it.

"Don't overthink. Just say it."

"He…left me a note."

Jessie sat up, frowning as he mulled over what Aidan had said. He finally glanced over to him. "He left *you* a note?"

Aidan nodded.

"What…did it say?"

"Jess—"

"Aidan," he said firmly. "I know he's a monster. I know him better than you do. And I know whatever he wrote was meant to hurt you and probably me. Maybe even…us. So—"

Aidan sat up abruptly. "So why the hell do you want to know what it said?" he asked through clenched teeth.

"Because he obviously struck a nerve with you. Just because I do my best to make it look as if this doesn't all get to me doesn't mean for a second I don't feel scared. I'm fucking terrified! I'm scared he's going to hurt me or you. I'm worried every damn day when you walk out that door until the moment you walk right back in at night. I'm always looking over my shoulder the second I leave the house. I'm jumpy when I'm outside, and it bothers me that he gets to me, that he's managed to do this to me all over again. But I'm not going to let that bastard screw up my head for another fifteen years. I won't let him. I can't—"

"It said '*He will always remember his first, Detective Calloway.*'" He quieted, carefully watching every tiny possible reaction to his words. He couldn't lie to Jessie. At least he was here with him now to help him through the aftermath.

Jessie stilled, his eyes never leaving Aidan's stare. He slowly began to bob his head as if some decision had been made in his mind. "He's right."

The breath froze in Aidan's lungs.

"I *will* always remember my first."

Aidan hung his head, not wanting to see any pain in Jessie's eyes at a memory. Jessie gripped Aidan's chin between his thumb and index finger, raising his head.

"*You* are my first. You are the first man I've ever loved. You are the first man who's ever made me feel…wanted and important as if nothing else matters in the world. You are the only man I want to be with. Just because he stole *one* first memory from me does not make him the most memorable man in my life."

Aidan pulled Jessie into his arms. "I swear, you need to start an inspirational poster company or something. You'd make zillions."

Jessie chuckled, wrapping his arms around Aidan's neck. "Zillions?"

"Zillions times two." He kissed Jessie's shoulder and rested his cheek against the side of Jessie's head. He tugged Jessie up into his lap, holding him close, not wanting to let him or this moment go.

"Please don't let him get to you. That's exactly what he wants. He…thrives on that." Jessie tightened his arms around Aidan. "Just like a monster," he whispered. "He can't even take credit for being the first monster in my life. My father gets that honor. So Michael is nothing. He's a recurring nightmare I wish would just go away."

Aidan tightened his hold on the embrace, hoping to settle the slight tremble in Jessie's body. He stroked Jessie's back, enjoying the closeness, the peace that slowly began to settle between them.

"Aidan, I need you to make me a promise."

He inched back, always cautious when Jessie used that tone. "Depends."

"No, you have to promise."

"Jess, if you're going to ask me to leave this whole Michael thing alone and back away, I can't do that. Especially not after knowing he's keeping tabs on you and knows a note like that would get to me. That means, he knows about us."

"This is exactly what that bastard wanted." Jessie sighed. "He gets inside your head. He's…good at that. But you are my rock, Aidan. You are the one who keeps me sane. You're the reason I'm able to smile every damn day and not lose it."

"I don't always make you smile." He looked away, remembering the day Jessie sat quietly on the bed, unmoving, and all the other times Aidan had shut down, resisting Jessie's request to be more open with him.

"I'm entitled to crack, make mistakes…be serious or sad on any given day. And that doesn't make me a failure."

He looked up. "Of course it doesn't—"

"And that applies to you too," Jessie said with a firm tone.

Aidan quieted.

"I know you somehow think this is all your fault or that you could have crashed through that door with your cape blowing like a damn hero to rescue me, slap some cuffs on the son of a bitch and magically resolve everything. It doesn't always happen that way. And that does *not* mean you failed in any way."

"I hate seeing you sad," he said quietly. "And I hate not being able to do something about that."

"You are always there for me when I need you. And you've been trying like hell to open up and be honest with me. And I know that's a huge thing for you. So here"—Jessie pulled Aidan's hand, pressing Aidan's palm to his chest—"where it counts. You've *never* failed me. Ever. And that's what matters to me."

Aidan tried to swallow past the knot that had suddenly lodged itself in his throat. The doorbell rang, sparing him a need to respond. He cupped Jessie's face and gave him a quick kiss. "I'll see who that is." He rose from the bed—still surprised as hell he was in a bed at all—and grabbed a T-shirt from the drawer, slipping it on before reaching the front door. He looked through the window, surprised to see his team outside, almost ready to storm in. He turned off the alarm and let them in. "What's going on?"

"We wanted to check on Vega," Travis said, entering the house and pulling out a chair at the dining room table. Both Wall and Sunny followed as if they'd all been there before—even though this was the teams' first visit to his home. Manny shoved his hands in his dress slacks, opting to stand.

"Uh, make yourselves at home."

"Thanks," they said, almost in unison with semi-matching grins on their faces.

Wonderful. They'd obviously gotten their wish and managed to find him looking as if he'd rolled out of bed.

Literally.

Jessie emerged from their bedroom wearing jeans and a pale blue polo shirt. Polished and ready to go, not a strand of hair out of place. "Good morning," he said in that soft tone he usually used around others.

Aidan had to find the secret wardrobe compartment in his house where someone could enter then exit less than five minutes later looking polished, because he sure as shit didn't know where it was, but Jessie seemed to have an elite-status membership to the place. He turned back to his team, the smiles no longer present on their faces.

Manny walked over to Jessie. "How are you holding up?"

"I'm okay." Jessie casually took a step back from Manny's nearness and ducked his head.

Aidan immediately straightened and stood at Jessie's side, glaring at Manny, thankful the man was perceptive enough to step back and grant more personal space between them.

"I'm not sure what Calloway's filled you in on—"

"He told me what happened," Jessie calmly interrupted. He raised his chin and firmly stared at Manny as if challenging him and any confidences he and Aidan might share.

Manny's focus shifted to Aidan, his eyes questioning.

"Yes, I know about the note as well," Jessie added.

Manny's gaze snapped back to Jessie. Aidan guessed the man wondered how Jessie could remain so even-tempered.

"I also know that was your only lead in the case."

"Yes, but that doesn't mean we're giving up," Manny said.

"I know you've each invested a wealth of time in finding him and I really appreciate that. I also know you are each as equally persistent as Aidan. So I don't think you will give up even if everyone else would at this point. But I do know there are limited resources and entirely too many active cases that need attention." Jessie swallowed heavily, pausing for a moment before putting on his best smile. A sign he wasn't completely unaffected, but it would be a cold day in hell before Jessie cracked in front of anyone. "Have you guys had breakfast yet?"

Each of the task force members looked at each other, perplexed.

Aidan chuckled, crossing his arms and puffing out his chest, damn proud of *his* Jess. Even though Jessie felt any show of weakness was not for public consumption in his book of order, Aidan knew it took a whole hell of a lot of self-control and strength to keep it together so well. And he wasn't going to kid himself, he loved the fact that he was on the short list of people who got to see Jessie's true vulnerabilities. "He's an eternal optimist. If he loses his shit, bend over and kiss your ass goodbye because the shitstorm's coming."

That earned a few chuckles from his team, and Jessie walked over to the kitchen, starting breakfast without waiting for their replies. Aidan casually glanced over in his direction, taking a calming breath when he saw the lingering smile on Jessie's face.

"So," Travis said, reaching over and grabbing the briefcase he had brought in. "We figured, since you weren't coming in today, we'd come over here and work out of your house."

Sunny looked at Aidan and quickly glanced over to Jessie before returning her focus back to him and giving him a sheepish smile.

Aidan crossed his arms and took a deep breath. He quieted, trying to settle the thoughts spinning in his head and the emotions swelling his chest. They were here for him, for *them*. Whether to check on him or to make sure Jessie was fine, it didn't matter. They cared. Jessie wasn't just a case to them and he wasn't just a co-worker. Fuck it all to hell. There would be major ass kicking if they made him get misty-eyed.

"At least let me put some underwear on."

"Ugh!" the team yelled in unison.

Jessie subtly glanced in his direction as he walked past the kitchen, his eyes clearly letting Aidan know he had received the same message of support from the team…loud and clear.

Aidan quickly changed, unable to get rid of the silly grin on his face. He looked over at the messy bed, his smile widening farther.

He could do this. Every baby step counted.

Maybe there *was* something to this Ms. Fix-it and all the endless talking. Who the hell knew for sure? But he certainly wasn't taking any of it for granted.

Chapter
TWENTY-SIX

"Where are we going?" Jessie asked, hiding a chuckle as a freshly-showered Aidan hurriedly walked back and forth between the bathroom and closet in their bedroom, wearing nothing but a towel wrapped around his waist.

"It's a surprise." Aidan thumbed through the clothes in his closet, pulling out then returning the piece of clothing upon further inspection. "I wasn't supposed to get here so damn late." He cursed, finally grabbing a pair of jeans and tossing them on the bed. "Just an hour, Calloway," he said, mocking Manny's tone. "Three fucking hours later..." Aidan shook his head as he continued to dig through the closet.

The entire team pulled longer hours lately to catch up on their active cases. After two weeks of intense work and many sleepless nights trying to locate Michael, the team had a somber discussion with Jessie—they had to focus their efforts on more active cases. They'd still work the case every chance they had, but they couldn't justify the number of man-hours that bastard demanded in his pursuit. That had resulted in a few more bad days for him, but Aidan was there, by his side like his guardian angel for support.

Jessie had officially proclaimed today—his birthday—a new start. He wouldn't let that monster shadow his life, again. "You won't even give me a hint?" He didn't really care what Aidan had in store for their evening together. Just knowing Aidan had planned something and seemed pissed to have the team encroach on their time, made him selfishly happy. He crossed his arms as Aidan finally pulled out a shirt from the closet.

"So it's a casual thing?"

Aidan stopped and turned. "It's a…surprise. So I want you to figure it out."

"Did you internet search this surprise?"

Aidan pulled off the towel from around his waist and flicked it on Jessie's ass, laughing when Jessie twisted his body just out of reach. "Sorta." A grin spread across Aidan's face. "I used my detective skills for this one." He waggled his eyebrows and turned, resuming his hunt for his clothes for the evening.

"At least tell me what to wear. Casual?"

"Suit. Definitely a suit."

Jessie chuckled, shaking his head. Aidan and his suit obsession. "You're in jeans, so can I lose the tie tonight? Otherwise, I might be overdressed next to you."

Aidan finally walked out of the closet with a sport coat in hand. "The tie doesn't do it for me."

Jessie wound his arms around Aidan's neck. "But everything else does?"

"Hell yeah." Aidan leaned in for a quick kiss, the smile still lingering on his lips.

That smile. That wicked, devilish smile that seemed to make an appearance with greater frequency, as if Aidan had somehow lessened the burden that usually weighed him down. He had managed to sleep in their bed through almost every night for the last two weeks. Except for one night after a day-long interview with a victim on a new task force case. That one night he retreated to the couch in their bedroom, but Aidan refused to give up and slept the day after in bed and each night since.

Aidan gave Jessie another quick kiss, pulling him from his thoughts. "We're going to be late. And we can't be late. I'm not positive about the parking situation yet. So get dressed." He gave Jessie a final quick peck on the lips before stepping away.

Jessie pouted. His. Birthday. *His*. He wanted to know where they were going, and from the level of excitement vibrating off Aidan, he imagined Aidan truly felt he had gotten this one right. He grabbed the dark blue suit from their closet and a shirt. "Are Calloway points getting earned tonight or are you guessing here?"

"No guess needed. I'm earning triple bonus points tonight," Aidan said, pulling up his jeans.

Jessie laughed. "You're really proud of yourself, aren't you?"

A rare, huge smile split Aidan's face. "I know I got this one right."

Jessie dressed in the requested suit, made sure his hair was in perfect order, and met Aidan by the front door, ready to leave in under five minutes.

Twenty minutes later, they arrived at the restaurant and checked in at the hostess stand. Jessie patiently waited with Aidan, taking in the restaurant's decor. The elegant stone walls added a medieval feel to the warm glow in the room. Wrought iron decorations, light fixtures, and fans all randomly positioned throughout the area added to the rustic, vintage feel of the place. More elegant and regal in its simplicity than dungeon-like. Jessie leaned over to whisper, "Is this the surprise?"

"No. But we need to eat first. It's going to be a couple of hours before we're back home."

The hostess returned and led them through the restaurant and the constant hum of chatting customers filling the dimly lit space. They walked through an arched hallway along the back wall, passing two doors on their right. The hostess opened the third door and welcomed them inside with a sweeping motion of her hand before closing the door on her way out of the room. Jessie stood in awe at the single table able to seat a large group of about twenty patrons. Aidan pulled out one of the high-back chairs and motioned for Jessie to sit.

"Private room?" He would definitely grant Aidan a few points on his romance scorecard. "And this isn't the surprise?" he asked, finally sitting.

Aidan chuckled and sat next to Jessie to his left. "No. I know the owner. I didn't want to risk being late so I called him up and he said he'd put us in one of the event rooms when we arrived so we wouldn't have to wait on a table. It's quiet back here."

"And *very* private," he teased.

"Don't give me a hard-on. It's still early and these jeans don't give me enough room to sport one."

"I noticed that," Jessie said, biting his lip, holding back a smile.

Aidan waggled a finger at him and laughed. "Don't start."

The server arrived through a side entrance and brought out their menus. "Sir, Mr. Capote mentioned you had a prior engagement this evening and need a speedy dinner service?" the server asked, cocking his head slightly.

"Yes, please," Aidan answered. "We need to be out of here in about an hour. Can we make that happen?"

The server straightened. "Absolutely, I'll start with the salads while you review your menu," he said, retreating as quickly and as quietly as he had arrived.

Aidan repeatedly checked his watch as he scanned the menu.

Jessie placed a calming hand on his arm. "It's fine. And if we're a little late, it's okay."

"No, it's not." Aidan closed the menu and set it aside. "I want it to be perfect."

Jessie placed his hand on Aidan's knee. "Here with you, like this, it is. You've already got a few points."

"Yeah?" Aidan immediately perked up. "How many?"

Jessie laughed as he reviewed the menu. "You're so competitive."

"Hey, being here with you is enough. The fact that I got something right and earned a point is a major plus."

Jessie sighed and closed his menu. "And that, Mr. Calloway, earned you another point."

Aidan shook his head and chuckled. "See? I don't even know what the hell I did to earn a point. I think you make this shit up as you go along to keep me on my toes."

They laughed easing in to the comfortable privacy when the server reentered the room with their salads and noted their orders with a promise for prompt service. They finished their salads a few moments later and set their dishes aside.

Aidan withdrew a small, wrapped box from his inside jacket pocket. "I figure we've got a few minutes before dinner arrives." He hesitated for a moment, then awkwardly handed the box to Jessie.

"This...uh, this is for you. Happy birthday."

Jessie's heart fluttered wildly in his chest. He took the small, flat box with shaky fingers and pulled on the bow tied around the wrapping paper. He glanced up at Aidan, then quickly focused on the box again, slowly separating the paper to avoid appearing too anxious. He slid off the box lid and unfolded the tissue paper inside.

His lips parted with a quiet gasp. He ghosted his fingers over the piece. A key. Not a normal key but a charm-like piece of jewelry. A key that would suit the restaurant's medieval setting almost perfectly—intentionally designed to appear rustic, somewhat primitive, not refined yet still elegant. He reached into the box, withdrawing the charm and the attached necklace. The weight, definitely platinum. The top of the key in the shape of a heart, threaded through a Figaro link chain in matching platinum. He tried to swallow past the knot in his throat. "A key?"

Aidan shifted uncomfortably in his seat. "When we started this whole *us* thing, I had a talk with Ty. Well, it was supposed to be a talk with Ty, but Cole jumped in. Anyway, they said something that stuck with me."

"What did they say?" Jessie asked, curious as to what made Aidan fidget so much.

"That I needed to give you a skeleton key to get inside me. So that's what that is. It's not a perfect, pretty key, but I had it done to match me. It's a little rough around the edges and looks like it would fit in that iron gate thing you're always joking about." Aidan shrugged. "Kinda stupid, now that I think about it. You're already inside so it's not like you need the key." His lips thinned and a frown made an appearance. "Fuck. I'm never going to get this shit right." He muffled a curse and frowned.

Jessie set the box on the table and cupped Aidan's face. "You just earned so many points they won't fit on your virtual scorecard." He reached into the box and retrieved the necklace and charm. He turned one of Aidan's hands and dropped the necklace in his palm. "Put it on me."

Aidan immediately grabbed the two ends of the necklace as Jessie leaned forward. He peeked over Jessie's shoulder, clicking the necklace in place. Aidan inched back and stared at the small key. An odd mix of emotions washed over Aidan's features, but a hint of a smile sparked in his eyes.

Jessie reached up and touched the key, hanging just below his Adam's apple—in the dip between his neck and collarbone. He held the key, running his finger along the top and sliding it across the chain link. He leaned in and pitched his voice low. "Later on tonight, you know what I'm going to be thinking about?"

"What's that?" Aidan asked with an unmistakable playfulness in his eyes.

"How much I love my key when it's all I'm wearing while you blow me for my birthday dessert."

A slow smile spread across Aidan's face. "Hopefully you won't be thinking of much of anything while that's happening."

Jessie lowered his head and bit his lip, still sliding the key along the necklace, unable to let go of the small key whose symbolic nature meant so much more.

The server walked in with dinner, and they quietly ate, sharing a cheesecake before finally slipping out of the restaurant and back into the car and onto the highway.

"Are we going to be late?"

Aidan glanced at his wristwatch for the hundredth time. "I think we'll be fine."

They drove on the turnpike speeding along, flying by exit after exit. "Are you still not going to tell me where we're going?"

"You'll know soon enough." Aidan exited the interstate and drove through backroads, turning onto a main street.

Jessie gasped when the spotlights flashed across the sky, highlighting the arena. "Are we…"

No way would Aidan get that many bonus points on his own.

"We are," Aidan said smugly.

"How did you get tickets? Today's show was sold out months ago." He craned his neck and lowered his head to get a peek at the tall sign, smiling with each new digital frame of the scrolling arena billboard. He'd always wanted to attend the traveling theatrical acrobatic show but couldn't overcome the awkwardness of going to one alone. He had finally decided this would be the year since the tour coincided with his birthday. He'd hunted for tickets, figuring he could somehow bribe Aidan to attend with him even though it was probably the last place on earth he'd like to be. Unfortunately, the show had sold out quickly.

After flagging a few attendants along his path and flashing his tickets like a magic wand, Aidan had worked their way into a private entrance of a parking garage.

"You can park in any space, sir. You will see another attendant by the arena entrance door. He will guide you where to go."

"Thanks," Aidan said, driving into the garage and easily finding a spot near the second waiting attendant.

"Consider yourself lucky tonight. You've got carte blanche on anything you want done to you," Jessie said.

"I'm lucky every night I'm with you," Aidan said, shifting the SUV in park and switching off the engine.

Jessie turned toward Aidan. "I don't think you have enough scorecards tonight."

A huge smile split Aidan's face. "Go Team Calloway. C'mon," Aidan said, exiting the truck.

Jessie immediately unclipped his seat belt and followed Aidan to the attendant.

"This way, sir," the man said, leading them through another door to a hallway. "Follow this hallway until you find your room. The number on the room door will match the seat number on your ticket."

They walked down the hallway and opened the door to their room. Jessie walked through the entryway and paused. The room had a small round table in the center and a bar table setup on the side with a few glasses and bottled waters in a bucket of ice. Jessie gasped at the private section with four seats at the far end of the room. The space extended slightly in the construction, as if the seating area were deliberately built farther out than the standard section, blocking the view of people from above or below. Privacy walls to the left and right of the seating area but open to the front, facing the main stage, silenced much of the noise from the chatter of the entering crowd around them. Jessie followed Aidan to the front row with only two chairs. The oversized recliner seats offered more comfortable spacing than the standard stadium seating he spotted in the distance for the crowd filing in.

"Is it just the two of us or are two other people joining us?"

"Just the two of us."

"Do I want to know what you did to get these tickets?" Jessie asked, settling next to Aidan.

Aidan grinned. "I called in a favor."

Jessie gripped the cushioned armrests and pivoted his head in every possible direction, observing every detail and watching the crowd across the arena trickle in and fill the stadium seats. He glanced over at Aidan who carefully watched him, his hazel eyes more a mix of pale green and amber tonight accented with the rich gold flecks. "How did you know?"

Aidan peeked over the front edge of their seating area at the crowd gathering below them before returning his focus to Jessie. "You left your browser window open a couple of months ago on your laptop. So I knew you were interested. I didn't see the charge come in on my card so I knew you hadn't gotten the tickets. When I looked it up, I saw it was sold out so I made a few phone calls."

Jessie looked around at the seating and chuckled when a server quietly entered the room for a moment to refill the ice bucket then left again. "VIP? Do you do anything half-assed?"

"Where's the fun in that?"

The lights dimmed in the arena and the music began to echo in the theater. Within moments, everything was pitch black and the only lights came from the stage, now filled with performers. A flutter of excitement bubbled in Jessie's chest, either from the acrobatic performers swinging across the stage or the strong hand that covered his in the dark. No one could see anything in the darkness, but it didn't matter. Aidan was with him, at a show he knew Aidan wouldn't have attended otherwise. The music boomed and the light show queued the transition to the next sequence of performers gathering on stage. A juggler joined the group, circled by dancers and gymnasts in an expertly choreographed synchronized display of art and elegance.

"Do you like the show?" Aidan whispered in his ear.

Jessie turned to him in the dark, reaching up to touch the trimmed stubble. He leaned in and placed a kiss on the lips he imagined were smiling at him. "I love the show."

"I knew you would as soon as the juggler came on stage. He had tons of balls."

Jessie buried his face at the side of Aidan's neck to disguise his laugh before returning his focus back to the show and the night he would always remember.

Chapter
TWENTY-SEVEN

Jessie fisted the bedsheet as his body arched, seeking Aidan's touch. He whimpered and canted his hips, needing friction to calm the fire coursing through his veins with each tender brush of lips and the slow, torturous trail of kisses up his neck and along his jawline. He had respected Aidan's boundaries, but that hadn't stopped Aidan from pushing those limits every night for the last month and a half, exploring, and discovering every sensitive inch of Jessie's body.

And Jessie sure as hell didn't object.

An animalistic rumble rose from deep within Aidan's chest as he gripped the back of Jessie's head and forcefully pulled him in, plundering his mouth in a searing, branding kiss. Jessie grappled for purchase, tugging Aidan's T-shirt, twisting the fabric tightly in his hand for balance as Aidan feasted on his willing mouth. They frantically dug into each other's flesh and pulled one another closer, seeking a deeper connection, craving the slide of tongues and the passionate bite and suck of swollen lips. They finally separated from the kiss, both fighting to inhale enough air between them.

"I...I want you to fuck me."

Jessie stilled. Through his lust-fogged mind, he must have heard wrong. He looked up into Aidan's eyes and gasped a deep breath at the desire, worry, frustration, and...was that fear? He reached up and brushed Aidan's stubble with his fingertips, focusing on the prickling sensation under the pads of his fingers to try to calm the stir of need swirling around them. "I'm sorry. What did you—"

"I want you to fuck me," Aidan said in a rush of words before smashing his lips to Jessie's in a desperate kiss.

Jessie's lips numbed with the force and their teeth clacked together. All his internal red flags waved, flashed, and set off sirens. He cupped Aidan's face and slowly broke away from the kiss. "Aidan?" he said, between breaths.

Aidan rose from the bed and paced. He raked his hand through his hair and his scowl deepened with each step. "You don't want to fuck?"

The alarming tension vibrating off Aidan's body and the desperation in his step and tone, a clear message something ate away at him. "Aidan, stop pacing please."

He stilled at Jessie's request, staring for a moment at him before wincing then looking away. "You don't want to," he said more as a statement than a question, tightly wrapping his arms around his midsection, folding into himself. "Shit."

"Come here," Jessie said, sitting up on the bed and patting the space beside him. Aidan obediently sat and stared at a spot on the floor. Jessie grabbed Aidan's arms, tugging them away from his body. "Of course I want to be with you. You know that. So don't think for a single moment my hesitation means I don't want you."

Aidan glanced up at him then looked away again, the vulnerability in the gesture squeezed Jessie's heart.

He stroked the back of Aidan's neck, hoping to soothe the tension in his body. "I'm not a top. I tried once, and it's just not... It's not me. So I'm worried I'm going to screw it up. Why don't you tell me what's going on and we'll figure out what to do. Because honestly, you look like you're about to bolt out of here, so I don't think this is what you really want. And I...I don't want you to hate me."

"I can't hate you," Aidan whispered, wringing his hands, refusing to make eye contact.

Jessie brushed his fingertips against Aidan's cheek. "This is the part where you tell me what's going on in your head and we talk."

Aidan's body shook with each breath. He remained silent for a few moments, rubbing his hands together.

An overwhelming need to soothe Aidan took priority, but he couldn't decipher what triggered this tension and obvious worry twisting every inch of Aidan's mind and body.

"Don't worry about making it sound right. Just say it."

Aidan ran his fingers through his hair and blew out a heavy breath. "I want you, Jess. I want you so fucking much it's all I think about. But I can't…unless…fuck," he said, closing his eyes and burying his head in his hands as he let out a frustrated growl.

"I get it."

Aidan turned to face him. "That actually made *any* sort of fucking sense?"

Jessie rested his head on Aidan's shoulder. "You want to make sure I'm going to be okay. So you figured you'd offer yourself up to spare me. Does that sound right?"

Aidan sighed deeply. "I swear. I'm going to strap you to me so you can do all my talking. Because that sure as hell made more sense than whatever the fuck I just said."

"I know you so I just filled in the blanks. It's that protector thing in you. In a prior life, you were probably that knight who taste tested the food before the king ate it to make sure it wasn't poisoned."

"I'm not a sacrificial lamb."

"Baa."

Aidan chuckled. He turned and pressed his lips to Jessie's head before leaning in and resting his cheek against Jessie's soft hair. "Jess, I don't know what to do here."

Jessie held back a smile. "Well, we can have a birds and bees discussion. Or is it birds and birds, or bees and bees? Or do you prefer schematics with slots and markers so you know what goes where and—"

"Smartass." Aidan bumped Jessie's shoulder. "I've done this before so I don't need your color-coded, highly-detailed schematics."

Jessie snickered.

"I'm freaking out a bit here." Aidan exhaled heavily.

"I know, believe me, I understand. But I think what's worrying you the most is thinking it's going to feel the same for me. It's not, Aidan. I promise. I wouldn't lie to you."

"I know you wouldn't," he whispered. He rubbed the back of his neck. "It's still different for me. I'm not used to *this*. I'm more of a...uh..."

"Quickies? Down and dirty type of guy?" Jessie asked, trying—with every ounce of self-control—to hide the bubbling excitement.

Aidan looked over at him, slowly inching back and raising an eyebrow.

"Hey, don't judge. I have no objection to quick and dirty," Jessie said.

Aidan smiled and shook his head. "My point of reference really sucks. It's always been about getting off quick to avoid getting caught. It's different with you, Jess. It's not just about me, it's about us."

Jessie sighed, letting the words and the emotion backing them flow through his senses. "The things you say sometimes, especially when you don't even think about it."

"Was that wrong?"

He looked up and smiled. "Couldn't have been more right. Very romantic."

Aidan gave him a quick peck on the lips. "Point for Calloway."

"For the record..."

"Yeah?"

"Don't you dare eliminate down and dirty from your skill set."

Aidan snorted in amusement. "If we can figure out a way to make it good for you, I'll get as dirty as you like."

"Mmm. I have a few ideas," Jessie said, biting his lower lip.

"And I've got a hard-on."

Jessie tightened his lips, holding back a smile. "That's so romantic," he said, oozing with sarcasm.

"I've got a hard-on...for you."

He laughed and shook his head.

"That didn't do it for you? I was going for bonus points."

Jessie laughed again. "Be still my heart. Your romance score is through the roof."

Aidan pursed his lips. "Sorry, that's as good as it gets."

"You're far more romantic when you don't try so hard."

"Speaking of *hard*."

Jessie couldn't control the laughter that shook his entire body.

Aidan looked at him, unable to wipe the smile from his face. "I can hear you laugh all day long. Gives me more peace than any fucking piano sonata I've ever heard."

The smile slowly slid off Jessie's face as he stared at Aidan.

"Damn. Was that wrong?"

Jessie shook his head and reached out to wrap his arms around Aidan's bicep, holding him close. "You just earned a shit-ton of bonus points with that one."

"Awesome. By the way…"

"I've still got that hard-on," they said in unison.

Jessie looked up at a smiling Aidan, thankful the tension between them had dissipated. "Are you okay with me having my way with you tonight?"

"Uh, you've always had your way with me," Aidan said with a half smile. "Why would I stop you now?"

He reached up and brushed his mouth against Aidan's as he spoke. "So many bonus points for Team Calloway right now."

Aidan leaned in, pulling Jessie into a slow, teasing kiss. He reached out and held Jessie's face, tilting him slightly as he licked and tugged at Jessie's lips. He dipped his head and peppered kisses along Jessie's jawline, then down his neck.

Jessie placed his palm against Aidan's chest, halting his exploration. Aidan wasn't the only one turned on, and he wanted to make sure to slow the pace. Jessie stood, facing Aidan, guiding his shoulders down onto the bed so he would lie on his back. Jessie reached over into the nightstand and withdrew the lube, pitching the bottle onto the mattress. He tugged the waistline of Aidan's sleep pants, observing and translating every tiny reaction staring back at him from those hazel eyes, needing to confirm there wasn't an inkling of the fear or worry he had seen moments ago. Aidan tipped his hips up, letting Jessie slide the soft material off him.

Commando. Mega bonus points.

Jessie knelt on the bed and straddled Aidan. He leaned down, curving his body to teasingly brush against the hard planes of Aidan's tight torso while he placed a few open-mouthed kisses along his neck. Aidan stretched, turning his head to grant Jessie better access to each corded muscle and twitching inch of skin. A smile tugged at Jessie's lips when strong hands gripped his hips and pulled him closer. He brushed his cheek against Aidan's stubble, reveling in the coarse hairs scraping against his skin. He licked and kissed along Aidan's neck, marking a path down to the ink he loved so much.

"Jess..." Aidan whispered, arching his hips up into Jessie.

He worked his way down Aidan's body, finally reaching his target and running his tongue along Aidan's hard shaft in one long swipe.

A groan escaped Aidan as his fingers dug into Jessie's hair, silently urging him to continue. Aidan set his legs apart and planted his feet on the bed the instant Jessie nudged him.

He drove Aidan to the edge then eased him back again, cupping and rolling his tender skin with one hand as he licked and sucked his hard length, tracing with his tongue each raised vein begging for attention. Aidan teased him about his ball fetish, but he truly had no idea. It drove Jessie insane, and he loved taking his time with the tender and enticing soft skin.

Jessie reluctantly released the tender sac and reached for the lube, slicking his fingers. Aidan's stare burned into Jessie's flesh as he bobbed up and down the heated skin. Aidan's parted lips and heaving chest enough to let Jessie know he was nervous but also aroused. Jessie ran his slick fingers down, under the tender skin as he kept his mouth wrapped around Aidan—their gazes locked, never wavering. He rubbed his finger along the ring of muscles, patiently waiting for the tightness to ease. He re-slicked his fingers and tried again.

Nothing.

"Sorry," Aidan whispered, pushing his head back on the pillow and throwing his forearm over his face. "Fuck. I don't know why I thought this might work."

Jessie released Aidan from his mouth and rested his head on Aidan's thigh. "You probably have a million what-ifs racing in your mind. Don't think about all that. Just focus on me, on us, and what you're feeling right now. Just breathe and try to relax."

Aidan blew out a heavy breath. Jessie rubbed his hand along the hair of Aidan's thigh, worried Aidan would perceive this as a failure.

"Look at me."

Aidan dropped the arm covering his face and propped himself up on his elbows to look down at Jessie, the worry and defeat battling in his gaze. No way would Jessie let Aidan's mind go there, to think that anything between them would end in anything close to disappointment. He re-slicked his fingers, more determined than ever. He wrapped his lips completely around the hard dick demanding his attention, relaxing his throat and taking every inch of Aidan into his mouth until the closely cropped hair tickled his nose.

"Shit!" Aidan yelled, pushing his head back onto the pillow, arching his body and granting Jessie that tiny distraction he needed to ease his lubed finger through the tight ring of muscles. Aidan's body stilled, his jaw slackened, and he gasped a breath, fisting the bedsheet at his sides. His toes curled and his chest heaved as his breathing sped.

Jessie slowly moved his finger and slid his mouth up and down Aidan's shaft in tandem, observing every muscle of Aidan's tight body, gauging his reaction. Jessie reached for the lube with his other hand, adding more slick, then closed his eyes for a moment when his finger eased into the heat of Aidan's body again without resistance.

Aidan gripped the back of Jessie's head, drawing his attention.

He pulled his mouth away but remained still, enjoying the slide of his finger and the heat of Aidan's skin pressed against his cheek. "Do you want me to stop?"

Aidan slowly shook his head, the need and heat reflected in his eyes shooting straight to Jessie's own hard-on.

A smile tugged at Jessie's lips. He hooked his finger, searching for that bundle of nerves that would be the deal-breaker, letting Aidan know exactly how much pleasure he could offer a partner.

"Fuck!" Aidan yelled, his body bowed and twisted off the bed.

Jessie groaned when fingers dug into his scalp and Aidan's release hit his chin. He immediately wrapped his lips around Aidan again, not wanting to miss another drop, sucking with more force as he continued to hook his finger to squeeze out every ounce of pleasure from Aidan's body.

Moments later, Aidan softened in his mouth and his body slowly eased back onto the bed. Jessie withdrew his finger and mouth, licking and kissing every inch of Aidan's now-sensitive tender stretch of skin.

Aidan hissed a breath and eased the grip on Jessie's hair.

"Did that hurt?" Jessie asked, kissing his way up Aidan's body.

An almost-quiet, relaxed chuckle escaped Aidan as his fingers gently combed through Jessie's hair.

"I should be asking you that question. I think I might have dented your scalp. Sorry about that."

Jessie lay on Aidan, smiling at the peacefulness in Aidan's expression. He reached out and ran his fingertips along the ever-present stubble. Aidan opened his eyes and smiled—an easy soft smile Jessie hadn't ever seen.

"Tell me you're okay."

"I'm okay. Better than okay." He swiped his thumb along Jessie's chin. Jessie looked over and immediately wrapped his lips around Aidan's thumb, closing his eyes and savoring the remnants of Aidan's release. "Is that what it feels like for you?"

"That's what it *can* feel like," Jessie said, releasing Aidan's thumb. "Not everyone hits the mark."

A wicked grin spread across Aidan's face and his eyes danced with mischief. "You know I don't miss."

Jessie bit his lower lip, trying to disguise a smile. He rested his head at the base of Aidan's neck, snuggling into the warmth of his favorite spot. "Whenever you're ready, I'm more than happy to be your target practice."

* * * *

Aidan grabbed the case files after their recap meeting and walked with Sunny back to their desks.

"What the hell is eating you? Is it Vega's case and that asshole? Don't let him get to you. He's obviously taunting you and enjoys the thought of driving you crazy. Don't give him the satisfaction."

For once, that Michael asshole is not what's on my mind.

"Calloway, we'll find him. It's a matter of time, and you know if we work cases slow and steady, shit always comes up. Just because it's on the backburner doesn't mean we leave it alone."

"I know," he responded, not really wanting to discuss the asshole on the one day it hadn't been front and center in his mind. "I'm more concerned about Jessie and what this is all doing to him. He's my priority." That seemed to quiet his partner, obviously sharing the same sentiment.

"We've got to talk to a few witnesses and I've lined them up so we can get them all squared away this afternoon before our weekend off. C'mon, I'm treating you to lunch."

"Raincheck. I've got to run an errand." Aidan stacked the files on his desk and grabbed his keys from the top drawer.

Sunny looked at him questioningly but didn't push the point.

He had an errand to run.

A big one.

And it took priority over everything at the moment.

Aidan stood stock-still, staring at the sea of products in front of him. He planted his hands on his hips and frowned at the row of boxes. So much had changed in the last few years—more brands, more choices, more…everything. Ribbed, natural, thin, bare-skin…flavored? His eyes scanned each box and label, trying to filter through the marketing bullshit to focus on the differences.

He had to make a decision. He refused to wait another day.

The other night, Jessie teased him to no end—exploring every millimeter of skin and not allowing him to turn the tables on him at all. That night was *all about Aidan*, and Jessie was a man on a mission to let him experience every possible ounce of pleasure he could draw from Aidan's body, as if trying to replace each negative memory with a new, exciting one. When Jessie hit that internal button, Aidan's body reacted with an instant flood of ecstasy he could never have imagined.

Every.

Fricken.

Time.

He was numb afterward, like a big noodle on the bed unable to coordinate any of his limbs—all in a good way. Definitely nothing like what those monsters had done to him in hell all those years ago. And definitely not the same as getting off with a fuck buddy then stuffing himself back into his pants in record time to avoid getting caught in some convenient location.

He'd been missing out.

Big time.

He wanted to experience that again. Correction. He wanted to know he could deliver that much pleasure to Jessie. The thought of being inside Jess as he writhed with pleasure beneath him, yeah, definitely at the top of his to-do list…all caps with bold letters and exclamation points. Underline that to-do item a dozen times. After that night, he'd needed a talkie session.

Stat.

He set aside his excuses and opened up to Ms. Fix-it. His desire to be with Jessie finally tipped the scales and superseded the power of his demons. He even went as far as doing the whole *lying-on-the-couch* bit with his boots propped up on the armrest. Maybe he had reached that point of trust with Dr. Engel or maybe staring at a spot on the ceiling did make it easier to reveal a dark truth. Regardless of the reason or the ironic ease with which he finally opened up about something he'd held silent for so long, talking about it with another person did lessen the twist in his stomach.

Thankfully, Dr. Engel didn't give him any shit about wanting to dive in with both feet. She'd simply told him to take the step if he thought he was ready. He sure as hell hadn't been seeking permission, but he refused to screw up his progress or risk anything blowing up between him and Jessie. The whole bed thing had worked out for them, but he didn't want to tempt the vindictive Lady Luck without talking to the good doctor first.

"Can I help you?" a female voice said, pulling him from his thoughts.

Aidan slowly turned to face the drugstore employee. Her long, flowing, wavy blonde hair bounced with each tilt of her head and smile. Oddly perky with a smile spreading wide across her face, he wondered what drove her to stock feminine items in the neighboring shelf instead of working retail where she could bank some commission.

"I'm fine." Because seriously, what grown man asked for help buying condoms and lube?

"You look a little lost."

Go away. I'm trying to be nice.

"I can help," she said, twisting her hands together.

Aidan sighed. He hated this shit. He hated shopping, hated being questioned, but most of all, he hated feeling stupid about something that seemed like the kind of thing someone could basically grab off the display as they walked down the aisle.

He wanted to hit something.

"What are you looking for?"

What the hell did Ms. Perky Blonde think he was here for? To buy a car? A suit? He reached for the black box—obviously the right choice for him if the condom shared a name with a handgun.

"Those are a larger size. Are you sure about that one?"

Seriously? *How about you give me a fucking ruler and we find out?* He grabbed another box to prove his point then looked down at the rack of lube. He reached for the brand Jessie always stocked at home and slowly turned his head toward Perky Blonde, wishing she would return to her job and leave him the fuck alone.

She smiled and nodded. "That one's good."

Did she think he needed her approval? He returned his focus to the rack and grabbed a second bottle. Screw it. He grabbed a third bottle.

"Hosting a…party?"

Perky Blonde was now officially Ms. Nosy.

"Nope," he said, mimicking the way Jessie said the word, popping the "p" with his lips. He couldn't survive condom shopping twice in the same week. Fuck it. He grabbed the remaining same brand of boxes and tubes in each row, emptying out their inventory.

He stood, straightening his shoulders with his arms full of condoms and lube. "Busy weekend," he said, walking away, hiding his grin at the shocked expression on Ms. Nosy's face.

Chapter
TWENTY-EIGHT

They lay in bed naked, Jessie straddling Aidan, waiting, staring at each other without saying a word.

Jessie combed his fingers through Aidan's hair, watching the trepidation mix with the want and need in his expression. "We'll stop if you want. But I promise you, it won't be the same."

Aidan nodded quickly and looked away. Jessie continued to run his fingers through Aidan's thick hair, knowing the stroking rhythm often soothed him. This was a defining step, to see and experience firsthand the distinction between what had happened to him and what would happen between them. But it could also potentially resurrect a storm of memories that would drive a wedge between them and throw Aidan back into his shell.

Aidan reached for the lube and condom, snapped open the cap, and squeezed a small amount on his fingers, rubbing them together. He paused for a moment and scowled, squeezing more into his palm until his entire large hand glistened with the slippery gel.

"Um, I think that's good," Jessie said.

"I want to make sure. I've got more tubes just in case."

Jessie pushed the loose strands away from Aidan's face. "I think we're fine with just the one for tonight."

"You're making fun of me."

"No. You're overthinking and worrying. It'll be fine." He pressed a kiss to Aidan's lips just as a slick hand traveled up and down his crease.

Aidan reached for the tube again. "I think I need more."

"Do you want me to do this part?"

Aidan threw his head back into the pillow. "No. I need to." He reached over and grabbed the tube again, pouring more lube between his fingers.

Jessie ducked his head to the crook of Aidan's neck, trying to hide his smile.

"*Now* you're making fun of me."

"I think you're being cute as hell," he said, unable to disguise the hint of laughter in his voice.

"Cute…is definitely not the word I'm hoping for tonight."

Jessie's laughter transitioned into a moan when Aidan's finger breached his entrance. Aidan reached up and pulled him down with his other hand, pressing his lips against Jessie's and swiping them with his tongue, demanding an invitation. Jessie deepened the kiss as he arched his backside in offering, begging for more with a muffled whimper. He broke the kiss with a gasp when a second finger joined the first. His head fell forward against Aidan's forehead as the burn mirrored the beginning of the licks of flames rising within.

"Say something," Aidan said in a gravelly tone, slowly withdrawing his fingers.

"Don't stop," he said in a whisper. Aidan pulled him into another kiss while twisting his fingers inside Jessie, exploring and stretching every inch of his depth. He writhed and pushed into Aidan's fingers then forward against his hard and ready body, seeking friction. "I'm ready," he said, reluctantly ripping himself away from the kiss.

"Not yet."

Jessie reached down between them and wrapped his fingers around Aidan's hard-on, sliding his fist along the silky, heated skin.

"Not. Yet," Aidan said carefully, with overwhelming control that was both surprising and arousing as he continued to stretch and prepare him.

"Please."

Aidan kiss-bit Jessie's jawline. "That's a low blow. You know I can't resist when you say that."

"Please…please…please—"

Aidan quieted him with a hard kiss, firmly gripping Jessie's head with his other hand and angling him, feasting on his mouth. Aidan broke away from the kiss, gasping for air, looking over and reaching for the towel he had set on the bed. He wiped the ridiculous amount of slick off his hand then tossed the towel to the side. He reached up with both hands and grabbed Jessie's head, inhaling sharply and fusing their lips together in a searing kiss. They pulled and tugged each other, turning on the bed until Aidan hovered over him, his larger form heaving with each breath, unmistakably dominant and powerful as if ready to pounce on command.

Jessie reached up and ran his fingertips along the side of Aidan's face, overwhelmed by the sense of peace and rightness blooming in his chest.

Aidan closed his eyes and exhaled slowly. "I want you so much," he said, his tone rich with desire but laced with worry.

Jessie reached over and grabbed the packet, ripping it open and snatching the lube before Aidan had a chance to reach it—no way would he survive a second round of over-slick rubbing and teasing torture. "Let me." He slowly readied Aidan, taking his time, hoping to dampen the desire thrumming through his body long enough to enjoy this for more than a few seconds. He glanced up and groaned at the harnessed restraint burning in Aidan's gaze and radiating from his clenched jaw. Aidan's arms were straight with the force of his muscles holding his body in a push-up position, granting Jessie the space he needed to complete his task. The control in every millimeter of muscle aroused each atom in Jessie's body. He wanted Aidan to lose control, to possess him, to brand his body and soul so the world would know they belonged to each other.

"You keep doing that and I'm not going to last."

"Doing what?" Jessie teased with a hint of a smile, slowly sliding his slick hand up and down Aidan's sheathed, straining dick.

"Looking at me like that."

"And here I thought it was what I was doing with my hand."

"That too."

Jessie grabbed the discarded towel and wiped his hands, relaxing into the mattress with a groan when the weight of Aidan's body rested on him. He wrapped his arms around Aidan's shoulders, gripping him closely, seeking the intimate slide of their tongues to deepen the kiss. A whimper escaped when Aidan rubbed his body against him, the friction welcomed but not enough.

Jessie separated from the kiss in a drunken haze of need and stilled with the fear staring back at him in those hazel eyes.

* * * *

Aidan took a few deep breaths, his chest heaving with each measured intake of air. The *what-ifs* racing through his mind definitely stalled his progress. His body screamed *Do it!* while his head forced him to stop. He reached out and clenched his hand into a fist just before his fingers grazed Jessie's cheek, steadying the shake and hoping Jessie wouldn't interpret it as hesitation. He wanted this, he *needed* this, but the worry kept him in check. The thought of hurting Jess…

He took a deep breath.

This was a decathlon Olympic-sized leap, and now, he wasn't sure he could do it.

Jessie gently wrapped his fingers around Aidan's wrist, guiding his hand back to his cheek when he began to pull away.

Aidan closed his eyes when his palm met the heat of Jessie's skin. He brushed his lips against the side of Jessie's neck, peppering tentative kisses upward to his jawline then features. He opened his eyes and his lungs seized at the desire and need staring back at him from those clear blue eyes.

Jessie locked his fingers behind Aidan's neck then brushed his thumbs along the corded tension. "I'm okay. I swear I am. I'll tell you if I'm not. Okay?"

Aidan nodded and exhaled slowly, letting the tension in his body ease with those words. He leaned in and pressed his lips to Jessie's then ran his palm along Jessie's body, pulling him closer to position himself.

Jessie moaned and wrapped his legs around Aidan's waist, holding him tightly as he deepened the kiss. Aidan ran his fingers up into Jessie's hair and gripped the strands harder than intended.

Stop fucking overthinking. This is not the same.

Aidan screwed his eyes shut and finally, slowly canted his hips and cautiously pushed into Jessie's welcoming heat.

He inched farther inside with a groan, reveling in the tightness and heat that slowly enveloped him. He bent to kiss Jessie's shoulder and inhaled a shaky breath, hoping to settle his racing heart and steady the tension and quiver of his muscles as he carefully seated himself completely inside Jessie.

No flashback. No memory.

Just Jessie and a sudden, odd sense of peace.

Something settled deep within, clicking into place. As if a part of his soul had waited for this precise moment in space and time to awaken and sing a magnum opus from every mountaintop in the universe. This was different. Tender. Breath-stealing in all the right ways.

Aidan's pulse sped with the play of emotions touching each of Jessie's features. Desire, passion, and need battled for attention over the indisputable love screaming from his blue eyes.

No pain.

He dug his arms under Jessie and tugged him closer, savoring the warmth of the full-body embrace, relishing the soul-calming peace Jessie always offered him.

For the first time in his life, everything felt right and connected—in his mind, body, and spirit. As if the reason he had struggled his entire life was simply to recognize and avoid questioning the perfection and the rightness of this one single moment. To know, without hesitation, their coming together was fated and beautiful, a union of soulmates who had finally found their way into each other's arms.

"Aidan?"

"Hmm," he mumbled against Jessie's warm skin.

"I'm okay. I swear I am. And right now, I need you to move or I'm not going to be very nice."

Aidan inched back and half smiled, trying to control the bubbling happiness that surfaced with this other side of Jessie he loved so much. The teasing, bossy, in control private side only shared with him. The one who always managed to part the chaos in his mind and clear a path with a simple touch or word. *His* Jess. Jessie tried not to push, but it was obvious his seemingly never-ending well of patience had reached its limit. Aidan rubbed his thumb along Jessie's bottom lip, softly at first then hard enough to tug the sensitive skin. Jessie snaked his tongue out and pulled Aidan's thumb into his mouth, hungrily watching him as his cheeks hollowed with the suction. Aidan's lips parted with each breath, mesmerized by the warm, wet heat caressing his thumb, mirroring the tight warmth encasing his hard length.

Jessie released Aidan's thumb and leaned in, a mere breath away from Aidan's face. "I want to feel you inside me, moving, owning me," he whispered. "Make me yours." He gripped the back of Aidan's neck tighter, slamming their mouths together and giving Aidan's tongue the same teasing pull as he had given his thumb only moments ago.

Aidan planted his fist into the mattress to steady himself against the crashing wave of emotions and the aching need for something so far beyond physical it transcended every emotional barrier he tried to erect. His body craved the soothing security, warmth, and inner peace only this man could offer. He pulled back slowly and instantly snapped his hips forward, not wanting to leave the heat that encased him. He eased into a rhythm, pushing himself into the welcoming depth of the comfort his body sought, while savoring the friction spiking his pulse with each graze of skin.

Jessie dug his heels against Aidan's back and groaned with each fevered push into his body. Aidan hooked his arm solidly around Jessie's waist, holding him in place as he sped up his rhythm and slammed his hips repeatedly, unable to hold back the possessive growl that rumbled beneath the surface to claim every promise that had been declared between them. They tugged and pulled at each other, trying to get closer until their movements were as synchronized and fluid as if they were one. Jessie dug his fingers into Aidan's skin with a strangled moan, arching his body, offering himself with each scrape and tug of skin.

"Aidan…"

Aidan leaned over Jessie, something inside him snapping,

suddenly overtaken with a possessiveness he only felt in Jessie's presence. The dam had broken and a flood of need, want, and desire came crashing through, coating every crack and crevice of his body with an urgency to claim.

"Say that again," he said in a near growl as he pistoned his hips, nailing Jessie's gland with each deep, pounding thrust. His rhythm quickened. He angled his hips and hooked Jessie's leg over his shoulder, driving himself deeper into Jessie's welcoming body, cursing the rubber barrier between them.

Jessie threw his head back and gasped for air, his body writhing in Aidan's firm grip. "Aidan," he whispered between whimpered breaths, grabbing the bedsheet in a white-knuckle grip as his body bowed, spilling his release with a strained moan.

The desire, the need…the reverence whispered in those two syllables ignited an inferno at the base of Aidan's spine and spread to every inch of his body, summoning his orgasm to come crashing in with a blazing roar. His vision blurred as his hips continued to snap forward through his climax. Another jolt of electricity bolted across his body, causing a growl to rip from his throat as he continued to thrust, hoping and begging the white, blinding bliss would never end. His muscles twitched from the aftermath as he pulled Jessie's sweat-slicked body toward him into an embrace, needing to hold him close.

He unlinked their bodies and discarded the condom. He huddled close to Jessie again, pushing a deep breath through the pressure in his chest. He placed a kiss on Jessie's shoulder, ignoring the lingering tremble in his lips and the ripple of emotions vibrating within. Jessie wrapped himself around him as if sensing the need to hold him together, taming the storm of emotions trying to shadow their union. Aidan screwed his eyes shut and leaned into the embrace, exhaling deeply and releasing the tension in his body.

"I love you," Jessie whispered as he stroked the nape of Aidan's neck and held him close with the protectiveness of a man ten times his size. "With every breath and heartbeat."

Aidan sighed and relaxed in his arms, in awe at how Jessie always seemed to right his chaotic world with a simple touch, glance, smile, or word. He placed a tender kiss at the side of Jessie's head and tightened his hold around the one man who had branded his soul, thankful for the gift he held closely that granted him the serenity he thought he'd never find.

* * * *

Jessie rubbed the sleep out of his eyes and frowned at the empty space next to him in bed. He sat up and listened, hearing Aidan rustling in the kitchen. *That's never a good thing*, he thought with a chuckle. Aidan tried, but the kitchen was not his domain. He rose from bed and stretched his arms over his head, smiling at the wonderful ache in his body. He grabbed his sleep pants and padded his way to the bathroom. He stopped mid-step and turned his face upward, narrowing his eyes and sniffing the delicious smell wafting in the air. Breakfast? No way.

After hurriedly finishing his morning routine, he walked into the kitchen and leaned against the entryway with his arms crossed, carefully observing each of Aidan's sharp motions.

"Are you…upset?"

Aidan shook his head, reaching into the cabinet above for the plates.

Jessie scratched his head and stifled a yawn. Even he couldn't decipher all of Aidan's moods at times. "Did last night magically turn you into a chef?"

"I picked it up from the diner on LeJeune." He reached into the refrigerator and grabbed the juice, pouring it into the two glasses he had set on the counter.

"Um, that place gets super busy. How long have you been up?"

"A little over an hour." He took the two glasses over to the dining room table and returned to the kitchen, grabbing the napkins and silverware.

"Why didn't you wake me?"

Aidan shook his head.

Jessie reached out and placed a stilling hand on Aidan's forearm when he walked past him. "Why didn't you wake me?"

"You looked really peaceful so I just watched you for a bit then got up to get breakfast. I figured you'd be hungry."

"You watched me?"

Aidan looked down at his boot tips and didn't say a word, his jaw muscle twitching with tension.

"After last night...no flashbacks or bad memories?'

Aidan shook his head, remaining silent.

Jessie reached up and ran his thumb along Aidan's stubble. "You didn't even shave. Should I be worried you were trying to run away?"

Aidan finally made eye contact. "I didn't shave because I know you like the stubble. And no, I wasn't running away. I was fucking horny and didn't want to jump you so I figured I'd get you breakfast instead."

Jessie rolled his bottom lip into his mouth. "You could have jumped me."

"I won't do that," Aidan said, shaking his head. "I'll always ask."

"And I'll always say yes."

A hint of a smile tugged at Aidan's lips. "Thank you." He reached down and placed a kiss on Jessie's lips. "Good morning."

"Good morning," Jessie said, returning the kiss. He took the silverware and napkins from Aidan's hand and set them on the counter, hoping to draw Aidan's full attention. "Now why don't you tell me why you're upset?"

The scowl returned. "Can we stop using those things?" Aidan mumbled, standing in front of Jessie with his arms at his side.

"Things?"

The scowl deepened. "Condoms. I mean, I always used them before, but I don't...want to use them with you," he finished in a rush of words.

"Is that why you're all growly and grumpy?"

Aidan grunted. "I don't...want anything between us."

Possessive, aroused Aidan is definitely a sight to see...and hot.

"We can get tested," Aidan added.

Jessie raised an eyebrow. "Tested?" He'd been tested for everything during his hospital stay and knew that even though Aidan hadn't been with anyone for some time, he was methodical about getting tested with his annual physical since his last deployment.

Aidan nodded, snaking his arm around Jessie's waist. "You're it for me. That's what serious couples are supposed to do. Right?"

"Right." A swell of emotions warmed Jessie. He should let Aidan ramble more often. "We'll get tested then."

"Good. I already looked up a place that's open Saturdays if you want to go today. And we'll put a fucking rush on it. I don't care how much it costs."

"I wouldn't expect anything less." Jessie brushed his thumb between Aidan's brows, wanting to wipe the crease that always made an appearance when Aidan pushed through something emotional. "You know...before we sit and have breakfast. We have a major supply of condoms we'll be giving up soon." He inched back when Aidan blankly stared at him, obviously missing his suggestion. "This is me, saying yes."

Aidan slammed his mouth against Jessie's and cupped one hand under his ass and the other at the back of his head, lifting him up off the ground and pulling him flush against his body.

A flutter of excitement spiked Jessie's heartbeat as he wrapped himself around Aidan, holding on for dear life as Aidan ravished his mouth and carried him back into the bedroom.

Chapter
TWENTY-NINE

Aidan strolled into the precinct, through the task force cage toward the meeting room. He stepped inside and looked around with a frown. "Where is everybody?"

Travis looked up from the file and shrugged. "Reyes has a depo, but he should be in within the hour and Wall got called in from SRT today for a protection detail. So he'll be back tomorrow if all goes well."

"Where's Sunny?"

"Not sure." Travis glowered and looked off to the side. "When I came in she was sitting out back. Haven't seen her since."

Aidan walked out in search of his partner. He made his way through the side door and, within a few short steps, spotted Sunny sitting on a bench. He sat next to her and leaned forward with his forearms on his knees, mirroring her pose.

"What's going on?" he asked.

Sunny silently stared ahead at the people in the park across the street, rubbing her hands together.

"What you tell me stays between us."

"I know," Sunny finally said. "I'm just not sure I want to say it out loud."

"Want to write it down?"

"Asshole."

Aidan chuckled. He leaned over and bumped her shoulder. "I'm not sure I like the quiet version of you. She worries me."

Sunny looked down at her hands, clasping and unclasping them.

"We can sit here all day, but it's hot as hell out here."

"I hate this weather."

"Inside's nice and cool. I think I heard the A/C whisper your name when it blew out that cold air. Sunny… Sunny…" he mocked in a soft tone.

"I can't do this."

"I know. Sitting out here is going to make you sweat in places you didn't think was possible."

"I can't do…the task force."

The humor evaporated. An admission of failure did not come easy for Sunny and usually weighed heavily. "Why?"

Sunny narrowed her eyes as if trying to focus on the people in the distance. "Some of these cases are…tough. We're off the Miller case now that the FBI has a viable witness and they finally caught the Butterfly Killer, but there'll be others like those, and I just can't. I ended up at a bar with a damn drink in my hand the other night." She looked away and sighed. "And every night we have to deal with shit like that."

Aidan took a deep breath. The Mooney family tree seemed to get its watering from alcohol. After witnessing generations of self-destruction, Sunny had confided that she had made a solemn vow ages ago to avoid the self-destructive liquid.

Sunny scowled. "It's these damn cases. I just can't do it. I don't know how the hell Reyes *chose* to work for the Special Victims Bureau. More power to him. It's no wonder he is the way he is."

He neared Sunny, pitching his voice lower. "Is it just these cases that are a problem or is it the whole task force thing in general?"

She looked over to him with a pained expression. "I love the task force. We give each other a hard time, but we're making a real difference." She turned away, focusing on a group of people at the park setting up a picnic area under a tree. "Whoever came up with the idea and thought we'd work well together was damn brilliant. Travis is the mediator. Wall never complains, hell, he never says anything.

And Reyes spurs you on and gets you going at full force more than I ever could."

He bumped her shoulder. "You spur me on just fine without the desire to want to beat the crap out of anyone."

Sunny scoffed. "Reyes does it on purpose. He knows how good you are, and he knows that if he pushes you and gets you to produce, it looks good on him."

Aidan quieted. *Sneaky fucker.* He was so busy trying to keep a level head he never would have thought Manny's annoying comments were intentional.

"I'm along for the ride and I'm learning more than I thought I could, and working with you guys—"

"Give yourself some credit. You're on the team because you're good. If it were a learning experience, they'd solicit newbies from the academy." Aidan rubbed his hands together. This was important to Sunny and giving up was not an option. "So you're fine with the group as long as you don't have to handle the abuse cases?"

"I love the satisfaction of taking down a perp who does that kind of damage to someone. But I can't deal with the victims and hearing them talk about what happened. I can handle the forensics, and I don't care how detailed the gore gets in the reports or crime scene pics. I can break it down and examine the facts without a problem. Pace myself and powwow with you and the team on the different scenarios. But hearing the person say it all, and the emotion…shit. I just can't." She turned to him. "How did *you* handle listening to that woman in the interview that day? The victim from that scene with the same knife as the Butterfly Killer's? In the hospital, when she was retelling every detail of what happened, you were like a damn statue. You didn't move at all or say a single word. Nothing. You were just…vacant."

He took a deep breath. "I hate these cases too."

"But you get through each day. How did you reset?"

"I had help." That was more than he would willingly admit to anyone. He couldn't have made it through the night or weekend without Jessie by his side silently offering support on those tough nights when he would have quietly let his stomach churn over a case.

She glanced back at the couple having the morning picnic. "I'll handle a dead body any day."

Aidan tightened his lips, holding back a laugh when a passerby gave Sunny an odd look, overhearing what she had said.

"Fucker. Don't laugh at me."

"C'mon. If I had said that, you'd be bustin' my balls right now." Visions of Jessie's laughing face filled his mind. Great, now he was thinking about Jessie and his ball fetish.

Sunny frowned at him and narrowed her eyes. "You've got this funny smile on your face. I know that wasn't me. What are you thinking about?"

"Let's focus on the problem here."

Sunny returned her attention to the people in the park again, her frown deepening. "Who the hell has a picnic at eight o'clock in the damn morning?"

Aidan held back a laugh but couldn't help wondering if this was how prickly he'd get when frustrated.

She rubbed her hands again and exhaled heavily. "Any suggestions? I'm open to just about anything to stay on board."

He wouldn't let her walk away from the task force. Period. He loved working with the team as well, but Sunny played a big part of that formula and screw it all to hell if they tried to fill her spot. "I've got an idea." Aidan pulled out his phone and dialed a number he had avoided for the last few months. "We've got some time before Reyes gets back from his depo. We need to run an errand."

Sunny lowered her brow but rose from the bench without an argument.

If he was going to hit Manny up to pull them off these cases, he better sure as hell have something to bargain with in that negotiation. It was the only fair thing to do.

* * * *

Aidan sat and waited, refusing to be the first to speak. His ass numbed in the chair and his arms, resting on the table, started to feel heavy. The sound of sliding metal bars echoed in the distance—maybe a fence from the yard or a distant cell door opening. Or maybe the cell door closed. He didn't care. And the guard standing on the other side of the bars, watching them silently sit, didn't faze him at all.

He had one focus.

Period.

He maintained his schooled features, thankful Sunny hadn't fought him with his request she stay in the car when they pulled up to the prison parking lot. He had to keep his poker face and couldn't afford offering any point of distraction.

He sat across the table from the master of power plays and former head of one of the largest drug and organized crime rings Aidan had ever seen during his career. Rick, aka Starman. The nickname was earned after finding a series of nickel bags stamped with a star emblem linking a series of drug cases. The smooth bastard had proven his ability to evade getting caught for over a decade and would still be free had it not been for Cam and his ability to remember where some run-down excuse of a shack resided in a hidden away location in the deep southern reach of South Florida. That one tiny memory had triggered a chain reaction of arrests.

"To what do I finally owe the honor of your presence?" Rick asked, his chilly leveled tone breaking the silence between them.

"You asked to see me."

"That was quite some time ago. There's something else that's motivated your visit today."

Aidan carefully chose his words. Every small word and gesture spoke volumes and could easily be deciphered by the conniving son of a bitch. He wondered how the bastard managed to look polished and pristine in prison garb. It seemed elite membership to the magic mystery closet extended to inmates in maximum security prisons as well. "I need something from you."

Rick clucked his tongue. "My dear Detective Calloway," he said, enunciating each syllable. "You stole my life, killed my beloved, and expect me to just 'give' you something." His laugh quietly echoed in the room. The grin slid off his face and he dropped the pitch of his tone. "I thought you knew me better than that."

Aidan shrugged, hoping to convey an air of whateverness. "I

didn't steal your life. You can blame that idiot judge for being careless and stupid. And your 'beloved'"—he mocked with an eye roll—"was a crazy sociopath who lunged at me. It was self-defense."

Rick huffed out a laugh and the edge of his lips curled up into a crude smile. He leaned forward and the guard immediately neared to open the door, stopping only when Aidan raised his hand to halt him. Rick looked over his shoulder then back at Aidan. "What do you want?"

Aidan could play this a few different ways, but a direct approach never worked with Rick. Ever. He *always* needed to believe that *he* was the one offering something. "I need your word."

"What makes you think my word means anything?"

Aidan leaned forward, matching Rick's pose. "As smooth and cool as you like to think you are, you're old school."

Rick's eyes quickly scanned Aidan's face, assessing him, and an odd look of fascination colored his expression. "Tell me."

"I need you to have your men back off Cameron Pierce."

Rick lowered his brow, suddenly speaking out of character, as if forgetting his role in the game. "The kid's in hiding. My men haven't touched him, so if—"

"If he were out of hiding."

"Ah, he's homesick." Rick's features smoothed in understanding and his calculating tone returned, quickly resuming his role in their pissing contest. He leaned over slightly and lowered his voice. "And you're worried…something…will happen as soon as the kid comes back."

"I know you have a price on his head. I want you to rescind it."

"You can't just cancel an 'alleged' request of that nature." Rick leaned back in the chair and clasped his cuffed hands on the table. He glanced over his shoulder again at the guard then returned his focus to Aidan. "I'm just an inmate doing my time."

"Bullshit. I learned how you work. How you ran your business. I'm not an idiot. I know you're still issuing orders from here."

Rick laughed and theatrically flattened his hand against his chest. "Detective Calloway, I think you are giving me far more credit than I deserve."

Aidan delivered one of his menacing glares. He wouldn't scare Rick, but he needed to convey his level of determination. "You requested to see me some time ago. So I *know* you want something."

Rick's jaw muscles twitched.

"And freedom is not an option," Aidan clarified.

"I'm king here. I'm not willing to relinquish my throne."

"I don't have all day."

"You're lucky as hell our wonderful judicial system travels at a snail's pace." Rick looked down at his cuffed hands, thumbing the loop of the chain. "My brother. He's scheduled to move." He raised a stopping hand before Aidan could speak. "No, I don't want him coming here. I don't want someone mooching off me and stirring the pot. It's taken me a while to build up the respect I've earned within these walls. I'm not going to have some little shit come in here and tear it down."

So much for family loyalty. Aidan tilted his head, urging him to continue.

"I want him sent to Strassburg."

"How did you hear about Strassburg?"

Rick raised an eyebrow. "I'm resourceful and I have my ear to the ground. Did you think I wouldn't hear about a prison just because you guys were testing some new protocols and shit and whatever the hell else you are trying to do with a new place for the superbly dysfunctional and extra wicked?"

"It's a new prison. The 'protocols' or policies haven't been firmly established." Other than the fact that they were setting up a new, privately-owned, cutting-edge technology, maximum-security facility for lifers and other select few inmates best kept out of the general population.

Rick inched closer, finally dropping his facade. "Cut the crap. I know it's being sold as the place no one wants to go. You've got a shit-ton of lifers in here cryin' at night like babies at the thought of being on that list."

"Then why do you want your brother there?"

"Because it's exactly what he needs to get his act together."

"Your version of tough love," Aidan said, subtly shaking his head.

"From what I've heard, that place won't allow shit to happen. So even if he fucks up, he won't get himself shanked, but he'll get a good enough scare to know he'll never want to go back to prison. Ever."

Aidan had saved enough people's hides in the past to merit a lifelong list of favors. At this point, he was willing to do anything in his power to get his friend back home and find a viable solution to get Sunny and him off these damn cases. But he still needed to focus on this dance with Rick until all the cards were on the table.

"Get my brother there, and I'll call the dogs off your kid. Hell, I'll put a price on the head of anyone who dares hurt him and his boy toy."

Aidan stared blankly, trying—with every fiber in his being—to contain his laughter. He couldn't wait to let Hunter know this guy had just called him a boy toy.

"Allegedly," Rick added, raising his hands and shrugging.

Aidan pursed his lips, fighting to hold back the smile that threatened to emerge. "I'll make sure to tell Hunter your pet name for him."

Rick smiled. "Go ahead. I'm safe as hell from him in here," he finished with a laugh that echoed in the room.

"I'm not sure I can pull enough strings to make that happen."

Rick quieted and looked at Aidan more carefully, resting his forearms on the table and leaning forward. "Bullshit. I know you. Do we have a deal?"

"I thought you couldn't call it off from in here?"

A wicked smile spread across Rick's face. "I guess we'll have to find out then."

Aidan inched closer, mirroring Rick's pose, speaking in an almost silent hiss. "You fuck with them and I will personally walk you into Strassburg myself and lock you in a cell with the most twisted, sadistic motherfucker we have on the roster."

Rick never shifted his focus from the standoff. The slow movement of his neck muscles when he swallowed the only indication Aidan had hit his mark. After a few moments, the corner of his mouth inched upward. "I thought you couldn't pull enough strings?"

Aidan's jaw muscle twitched. "Your brother doesn't have much time left on his term. I'm not sure he'll fit the criteria."

"He has thirty-four months left."

"And you're serving three consecutive life sentences. My odds are better at transferring your sorry ass over to Strassburg."

Rick's lips thinned and his eyes flickered a fire Aidan hadn't seen moments ago.

Aidan chose to stare instead of responding. Rick *never* showed emotion.

"You want names? Locations? What the fuck do you want, Calloway? Name it!"

Aidan remained silent for a moment, not wanting to appear too anxious. "You want to protect your street boys, that's fine. I don't want your henchmen. I want the guys who are buried along the line. Any judges, cops, corporations. And I want you to call off your dogs. No one from your camp goes near Cam or Hunter. No. One. I swear, if they, *or anyone* they know, love, work with or talk to so much as gets a paper cut, you will regret it."

Rick steadily stared. "I don't doubt that for a moment."

"Good." Aidan reached into his jacket and withdrew a few sheets of lined paper and a crayon.

Rick held up the blue crayon and inspected it, then glanced back to Aidan. "What am I? Two?"

"I know better than to give you a pen or a pencil, you moron. Start writing," he said, pointing to the sheets.

Rick paused for a few moments and slowly shook his head before speaking. "You're a manipulative son of a bitch, Calloway." He rolled the crayon between his fingers, tilting his head to stare at Aidan. "Bravo, you son of a bitch. You planned this all along and I walked right into it." He sighed dramatically then began making a list. Thirty minutes and ten pages later, he put the crayon down and stacked the papers neatly before handing them to Aidan.

Aidan scanned the front and back of each lined sheet filled with information. Names of people, businesses, addresses, bank account numbers, and locations. He glanced up at Rick.

"What? My head is the safest place to store all this information so people can't find a paper trail."

After spending almost two years working the case, Aidan had only scratched the surface. Without question, Manny would salivate at the chance to be the show pony bringing in all these cases. "Some have a secondary line. Why?"

"If I thought you wouldn't easily find the link to whatever role they played, I added a note on the next line to speed you along. I won't testify and I will deny I ever gave you names, but you should be able to gather enough evidence from what's on there to nail them yourself. Well, your little researcher boyfriend should be able to dig up the details," Rick finished with a smile in his voice. "He's quite thorough from what I understand."

Aidan slowly looked up from the sheets of paper.

Rick raised his hands in surrender, quietly chuckling. "Down boy. Your guy's not on my radar. I know messing with him is the same as screwing with you. And I know better than to play with a rabid dog."

"Is this it?" Aidan asked with a sneer.

"You want my blood and urine too? Firstborn?"

Aidan's stare never wavered.

Rick sighed. "Yes, that's it." He clasped his hands and leaned forward, an odd peacefulness seemed to wash over his features. "You have my word," he said earnestly. "Each of those names will turn on themselves to try to save their own asses. Cameron is directly linked to my case and Mackler only. And you trimmed that list down to just me. Didn't you?" he said, giving Aidan a steady, knowing look.

"I don't know what you're talking about."

Rick leaned back and half smiled. "You have a wonderful poker face."

Aidan didn't flinch.

"If you hold up your end of the bargain, I'll make sure no one lays a finger on Cameron and his boy toy. But I need at least one week to get the word out. So don't jump the trigger just yet on getting them back home. Work that list for a bit so you know I've held up my end and those leads are valid. I will get a message to you when everything's in place for them to return. Now…I would appreciate you holding up your end of the deal."

Aidan nodded curtly.

"Just so we're clear, your end of the deal is where you transfer my brother to Strassburg, not me into the arms of a kink-loving cellmate."

Aidan chuckled.

"You're twisted enough to do both, so I need to make sure we have a clear understanding," Rick said with a wicked grin.

"You have my word."

* * * *

"Nice of you to show up," Manny said, looking up from the file he was reviewing. He had a scattering of folders set out on the round table in their usual meeting room. He looked irritated, as if ready to pick a fight.

Aidan sighed, biting back the snippy comeback on the tip of his tongue. He could do nice...especially if he wanted something. "I was here earlier, but I had to leave to see someone. How did your depo go?"

Manny glanced at him suspiciously. "You want something. What is it?"

Fine, he could cut to the chase. Aidan shook his head. He damn sure couldn't deny he'd tried to be nice. He pulled out the chair next to Manny. "I want us off the special victim cases we take on. Sunny and I can stick to all the other cases but nothing having to do with shit like the Butterfly Killer."

Manny grabbed his mug and sipped his coffee, staring in that odd, dissecting way of his. "You *and* Sunny?"

Aidan nodded.

"Sunny can't handle it?"

"She's fine. I don't want to do them anymore. It takes a special set of skills and tolerance to handle those cases and I can't do it. I want to kill the bastards and that interferes with the whole *let's-bring-in-the-perp-alive* thing we're supposed to do."

Manny continued to stare.

Fuck, he hated that shit. That creepy stare was his way of assessing every word and filtering through the bullshit.

"If she's fine, then why take her off as well?"

Aidan sighed. "She's day to my night. Makes sense to keep us together. Besides, this is the longest partnership I've had. I don't want to mess with it."

"Why can't you handle it?"

Aidan took a slow, calming breath. There was no way in hell he was steering the conversation in *that* direction. "I already told you, my instincts on those cases are counterproductive to the end game."

"Bullshit," Manny said, taking another sip of his coffee and continuing to stare. Fucker had the stare down to a science.

"It takes a special breed to handle those cases. You're great at it—"

Manny set his mug down with a thunk. "Don't blow smoke up my ass. Is it because of Vega and what happened to him?"

Aidan sighed and shook his head. His teammate was persistent as hell. He looked up and gave him an equally scrutinizing stare. "It's personal. And I'm not discussing it. I'm making a request and I would appreciate you respecting that."

Manny crossed his arms and leaned forward, resting his elbows on the table. "Everyone has issues, Calloway. It's the reason I specialize in these cases. It's something *I* need to do, but I do understand it's not for everyone. Personally, I don't know how the hell you and Sunny handle homicides. At least when the victim is still alive, I feel there's some hope. But seeing so much death…" He trailed off and shook his head.

Aidan looked at Manny thoughtfully. Okay, so maybe the asshole wasn't that much of a prick and maybe it was all an act to get a rise out of him and spur him on.

"Are you guys fine still working those cases if you're off the site visits and interviews?"

"Yeah. Those are the kickers."

Manny nodded. "Good. Because I give you a lot of shit, but I know your track record. I definitely want to keep you on the team."

A grin tugged at Aidan's lips. "You want me behind you."

Manny scoffed. "Fuck you. Not behind me." He quietly chuckled and shook his head. "By my side."

"Aww. I'm feeling a little Reyes love here."

"Fuck you, Calloway," Manny said with a hint of a smile. "I'll talk to Travis and Wall and have them do the initial walk-through for those cases. As long as you guys stay on the team, we'll figure it out. By the way, I've been meaning to give this to you, and since we just had a moment, it's the best timing I've had in the last two weeks." He reached over into his briefcase on the table and withdrew an envelope.

"A moment? Reyes, seriously, I think you need to have a chat with your fiancée about who you prefer to stand *by* you."

Manny scowled and threw the envelope at Aidan. "Jerk."

Aidan laughed and picked up the envelope, opening it and reading the enclosure. He looked up, more than a little surprised. "You're inviting me to your wedding?"

"Marcela insisted you and Vega be there." He reached up and rubbed the back of his neck. "I told her about that night when I had a gun aimed at my head. She…didn't take it very well."

"Is she giving you shit about the job?"

"Not really. She's always known this is what I need to do and she knows the risks. But something like that shines a spotlight on the what-ifs and makes it real."

Aidan nodded absently.

"She thinks you're my guardian angel."

Aidan chuckled.

"I tell her you're an asshole, but she doesn't believe me. She knows about Vega, his case, all that stuff. She thinks you're…adorable," Manny said with a cringe. "The way you were always there at the hospital."

Aidan was dumbstruck—stuck somewhere between the "adorable" reference and the fact that Manny talked to his fiancée about him and his personal business.

"Her word, sure as hell not mine."

He blinked. Repeatedly.

"That was exactly my reaction when she said that. She really wants you two at the wedding." Manny reached up and rubbed the back of his neck again. "*I* want you guys there. The team is going. Wouldn't be the same if you weren't there."

Aidan flicked the edge of the invitation with his finger but couldn't think of an appropriate response. Yes or no would fit, but this was a big step…for the both of them. And he knew better than to say the wrong thing and mangle the olive branch Manny had waved between them. He reached into his jacket pocket and withdrew the stack of papers and handed them over to Manny. "I have an early wedding present for you."

Manny took the sheets and thumbed through them. He scanned each paper and turned them over, reading each line scribbled in crayon. He finally looked up; the wide-eyed shocked expression on his face couldn't disguise the excitement that vibrated off his body. "Do you have any idea what this means?"

"Yes." *It means my friends can come home.*

Manny looked down at the papers again, thumbing through each sheet as if he couldn't believe what he was seeing. "He just gave you all this?"

"Not exactly."

Manny's focus darted back to Aidan. "Did you make a deal with the devil?"

"That's one way of putting it." Aidan stood from his seat. "I want to start working the list to make sure it's valid before I make any moves on his request."

"I'll get Travis on this right away," Manny said, returning his focus to the list as if it were the Holy Grail. "I can already see a few names he's been trying to nail on other issues in his division."

"Well, while you're both salivating over the list, I'm going to let Sunny know about our chat." Aidan walked over to the door and stopped while gripping the doorknob. He looked over his shoulder. "I'm RSVPing."

Manny stopped thumbing through the sheets and glanced up.

"You can add two to your guest list," he said before escaping the room.

* * * *

"Hey, Calloway, got a minute?" Travis asked, catching up with Aidan in the hallway before he left the precinct with Sunny that afternoon.

Sunny extended her hand, palm up. "Give me the keys. I'll go grab your truck."

"Hell no. I just had lunch and want to keep it down."

Sunny gave him the stink-eye and Travis shook his head while Aidan hid a smile. He had to admit, he did enjoy spending time with his team. He looked over to Travis. "What's up?"

"Well, I looked over the list you gave Reyes this morning. And…it's…well, it's long."

"Yeah?"

"So, I had a thought."

"That's dangerous."

"Asshole," Travis said, slapping Aidan's arm with the folder he held. "The list requires a hell of a lot of research to have enough legal bite to take each of these guys down. Some of these are cases I've been after for a while in my division, so I know it's going to be tough to uncover some of this shit. Especially if he refuses to testify. So…I was thinking…"

Aidan crossed his arms, impatiently waiting. "Spill."

"How would you feel about bringing Vega in to do the legal research? To gather enough intel on these guys for a rock-solid case. Vega is thorough and fast at finding shit. He did all the research for Cam's case so far, so he's more familiar with it than any analyst we'd get to start working it. And the research he did to nail the additional charges on the counterfeit parts ring secured several arrests. He's worked for the DA's office, he knows—"

"I'm cool with that. You don't have to sell me on the idea."

"Yeah?" Sunny and Travis said in unison.

Aidan's eyebrows drew together. "Why wouldn't I be?"

"Uh, well. Because you guys—"

Aidan raised his hands to stop Travis. "He's the best at what he does. Period. You just admitted that. With that targeted list, I have no doubt he would not only be able to find shit on all those names quicker and far more thoroughly than any other person who's tasked with the job, but, with his legal background, he'd also be able to list all the possible charges, which an analyst wouldn't be able to do. As long as the rest of the team's okay with it and the captain approves it, I'm fine with it."

"Captain already approved it, and Reyes is heavily drooling at the prospect of closing out these cases quickly." Travis slapped the folder repeatedly against his hand, obviously just as anxious as Reyes to tackle the list.

"So call Jessie and ask him if he's interested. If you want to offer him a consulting job, then make him an offer."

"Would you be fine with him working from here?" Travis asked.

"Up to him. I know he does most of his legal research from home."

Travis flinched. "Yeah...but we can grant him full access to the different agency databases from here. Agencies are all on board with whatever we need on these cases, but they're a no-go regarding remote access outside of the designated terminal we have in-house."

Aidan wouldn't deny he'd be at peace with Jessie nearby rather than alone at home or off visiting a client. "The decision is his."

Travis nodded in acknowledgment and headed toward the captain's office.

Sunny stood at his side, crossing her arms and mirroring his stance, watching Travis head down the hallway. "And you know you're dying to have Vega close by with everything that's happened."

"Damn right."

"So are we," she said solemnly.

He looked over at his partner. "I had a feeling you were in on this."

"Of course." Sunny gave him a sideways glance. "He makes you happy...and tolerable." A snort of humor escaped her, evaporating all seriousness from the moment.

"That's so attractive."

"Shut up. We're going to love sitting back and watching him walk all over you. Vega's got you by the balls."

Aidan's laugh echoed through the corridor—at both the truth of Sunny's statement and imagining Jessie standing there smiling at the mention of balls.

Aidan walked through the door at the end of another long day, smiling when he spotted Jessie sitting at the dining room table with his laptop open. "Hey."

Jessie returned the smile and stood. "Hey yourself." He wrapped his arms around Aidan's neck and delivered a kiss, slow and sweet with an unmistakable undercurrent of want and need.

"Mmm." Aidan snaked his arm around Jessie's waist. "I love coming home."

Jessie bit his lower lip, ducking his head and brushing his nose along Aidan's stubble. "I lost track of time wrapping up this case file I have to finish up. Do you mind if we order in?"

"Not at all."

They separated from the embrace, Jessie returning to his work while Aidan stripped out of his sport coat and holster.

"Um..." Jessie began, turning in the seat then hesitating. "I got a call from your captain today."

"Yeah?"

Jessie nodded, draping his arm across the back of his chair. "He offered me a consulting job."

Aidan pulled the shirttails out of his pants and began unbuttoning his shirt. "I know."

"To research names from a list Rick gave you." He worried his lip. "I'm assuming he wants something in return. Is it doable without getting into trouble?"

A smile tugged at the corner of Aidan's mouth. He loved how Jessie always worried about him. "I think so."

"You'd pretty much do anything to get Hunter back home," Jessie said, resting his chin on his forearm. "If you need help, just let me know."

"You will be helping if you take the job."

"You're okay with that?" Jessie asked, unable to hide his surprise. "Me accepting the offer?"

"Why wouldn't I be?"

Jessie stood and shoved his hands in the back pockets of his jeans, taking the few steps to stand in front of Aidan. "Because I'd be working with you and your team. At your precinct," he said, as if stressing the location was a huge factor. "I can access my legal research databases from my laptop, but they'd grant me full access to all other databases I can't normally touch with a promise of expedited warrants for detailed info if I can find something basic requiring a deeper investigation. That's the deal-maker for me coming in." He was twitching with anticipation and talking a million miles a minute. It was that love for what he did that made him so damn good at his job.

Aidan reached out, placing his hands on Jessie's shoulders. "It's a huge undertaking, and so far, everyone on that list has been incredibly careful about everything they've done. And I can't imagine anyone more thorough than you to spot the tiniest of details that will take each of them down." He squeezed Jessie's shoulder, emphasizing his words. "And I know you're the best person for this job. So there's no way in hell I'd stand in your way."

"I love you so damn much." Jessie grabbed Aidan's stubbled face and pulled him in for a fiery kiss.

Aidan separated from the kiss, his eyes still closed not wanting to distance himself any more than the mere inch needed to take a breath. "Every second of every day?"

"With every breath and heartbeat," Jessie whispered, delivering a tender kiss.

"I do have a request."

"Okay."

He tugged Jessie close, flush against his body. "Can you wear a suit at least once a week for me?"

"Deal." Jessie chuckled, resting his head on Aidan's shoulder. "You and your suits. It's kinda cute."

"You and your balls. It's kinda twisted."

"And you love it," Jessie said with a smile in his voice.

Aidan tugged him closer, pushing his nose into Jessie's hair. "I do."

Chapter THIRTY

Working with Jessie for the last two weeks seemed to give Aidan a sense of peace and allowed him to focus on the case files more closely. Assuming he wasn't stealing a glance at Jessie from across the room. Today he wore a fitted, deep blue dress shirt with the shirtsleeves rolled up to his elbow and dark slacks that accentuated his fair skin and fit frame. Aidan stilled, taking a deep breath when Jessie reached for the stack of folders from the corner of his workspace. The muscles flexed in Jessie's forearms and Aidan's dick immediately hardened with the reminder flashing in his mind of Jessie during sex, gripping the headboard behind him, his biceps flexing and his ab muscles tightening as Aidan thrust into his body.

Watching him move with fluid grace and confidence, dressed in his always neat business attire, aroused every microscopic atom in Aidan's body. He loved seeing all that polish and perfection go to shit at home. It was his mission to totally ruin the pristine appearance everyone else saw, giving him kiss-swollen lips and bedhead tousled hair. The thought alone was enough to leave him rock-hard all day long until he could get back home and do it all over again.

Aidan had suspected but now confirmed Jessie was a workaholic. The man never took a break unless the team pried him away from his desk for lunch or a recap meeting. And that turned Aidan on far more than he could have imagined. Seemed a fierce and determined man spiked his blood pressure. The building tension throughout the day always exploded each night in a tangle of tongues and limbs as soon as they passed the threshold of their home.

He ignored the mild spike of jealousy when Wall left a cup of coffee on his desk and Jessie mouthed a thank-you, handing him a case file in return. If Aidan did that, the team would tease him. And he wasn't in the mood to fight them off while the evidence stood upright and at full attention in his pants.

He reached over to his chirping phone to retrieve the new text message.

You look hot in that shirt.

He tightened his lips, hiding a grin. He glanced up, spotting a subtle smile playing on Jessie's lips. Aidan grabbed his pen, opened the case file on his desk, and then casually responded to Jessie's text.

Two could play that game, and he loved to win.

* * * *

Jessie jotted down a note in the case file then reached for his phone, anxious to read Aidan's text reply that would include something equally teasing to spike the anticipation for their evening.

Come rip it off and lick my ink.

Jessie rolled his bottom lip into his mouth and bit down, holding back a groan. Aidan knew how to make his body stir. He sensed when Aidan glanced at him from across the room and when he entered the breakroom nearby. The hushed chatter and the curious glances from the detectives he passed on the way to the team work area were hard to miss, so they kept it professional while at work. Working with him every day for the last two weeks, his intensity, his confidence, it was no wonder others in the precinct both feared and respected him. The captain had pulled Jessie aside on the first day to give him a heads up that all the detectives were...curious. Seemed something—well, anything—*personal* relating to Detective Calloway piqued everyone's interest.

A secret smile tugged at his lips as he absently dipped his finger along the neck of his shirt, sighing when his fingertips touched the edges of the key and chain. He was the only one who held all the secret pieces to the Calloway puzzle.

He looked up from the case file and watched Aidan reading something on his computer screen. He casually rubbed the edge of his lower lip with his index finger, slowly, back and forth. Jessie's lips parted and his breathing sped. He crossed his legs, wincing, trying to tear his eyes away from the very familiar roughened fingertip against that soft, full lip he loved to tug between his teeth. He ripped his gaze from the teasing motion. Either that or risk coming in his pants and granting the team entirely too much ammunition to tease them with for a lifetime. He looked up again a few moments later and Aidan's posture had transformed. The teasing now replaced with a look of deep concentration.

Damn. That intensity was equally arousing. He remembered watching Aidan during one of the interrogations related to the first file he had researched. Reyes had headed up the questioning and Aidan had sat in as the secondary. He'd backed away, almost into the metaphorical shadows, watching the exchange closely between Detective Reyes and the suspect with his panel of attorneys, quietly observing everything with deep concentration—every gesture and unspoken word that transpired between everyone in the room.

In that moment, Jessie realized he had witnessed the trait most people probably found terrifying in Aidan—that measured, calculated control.

Jessie sighed. Aidan could sit, stand, run, crouch, and still look hot as hell and spur on his Calloway-hyperactive libido. Anything Aidan did shot a jolt of need throughout his body unlike anything he had experienced in his entire life. He'd always had self-control, but all bets were off when it came to Aidan. He wanted every soft and hard edge of him and cherished the private moments they shared.

He took a sip of his coffee and made a final note in the current file.

"Got anything yet?" Reyes asked, pulling him from his thoughts, as he not-so-casually circled Jessie's desk for the umpteenth time, waiting for the latest file.

Jessie closed the folder and handed it to him. "Just finished."

Reyes thumbed through the file, scanning each page and flipping to the next. "How the hell did you get this?" he absently commented, turning to the next page.

Jessie smiled. "You should have enough there to get the judge to sign off on a warrant." The people from Rick's snitch list had carefully covered their tracks after the corruption issue came to light in the last year, but Jessie had a knack for working patterns. Simply ignoring the last twelve months and focusing on behavior trends from prior years revealed those patterns with striking clarity. "If they give you any resistance, the blue highlights are non-privacy issue events which don't require the warrant, and the yellow highlighted items are the legal violations you can use for the charges."

He snuck a glance at Aidan again, the intense scowl still in place.

"Thanks, Vega," Reyes said before rushing off to his desk to grab his suit jacket and beckon Travis to follow.

Jessie stood from his desk, making his way over to Aidan's area.

Aidan's focus shifted to him as he approached and his features softened. "Hey you."

"Hey yourself." Jessie gave him a lopsided grin and sat on the corner edge of Aidan's desk. "How can I turn that frown upside down?"

Aidan quietly chuckled. He glanced to each side and leaned in to whisper. "You always do."

"Yeah, but something is bothering you."

Aidan leaned back in his chair and gave him a tired smile. "All this is based on a promise I'm not sure I can deliver."

"What do you mean?"

"Rick's list."

Jessie straightened the fold on his rolled shirtsleeves then crossed his arms. "You never really told me how you managed to get him to fork over that goldmine."

Aidan explained the details of the exchange and how Rick's sole request was to have his brother transferred. "I've already made all the phone calls I can make and tried to call in all kinds of favors."

"But nothing is working?" Jessie asked, cocking his head.

"The only way I can get someone on that roster to Strassburg is by swapping out one of the hand-picked names from the list. The problem is, the grand opening list of inmates have all been heavily screened and will be there for the next two years while they work out the kinks before opening it up to the general prison system for standard assignments."

"And Rick won't wait two years."

"I'm not going to attempt pissing him off with that discussion. This was his only request." Aidan rested his elbow on the desk and his head in his hand. "I already got a message from him earlier this week that the contract was now null and void on Cam."

Jessie tightened his crossed arms, resisting the urge to reach out to comfort Aidan and ease some of the visible tension in his body.

"Hey, guys," Sunny said, strolling by Aidan's desk in that not-so-casual way she did whenever she hoped to uncover a crumb of personal interaction between them. "We're all going out to grab an early dinner and drinks at the pub around the corner after work. You guys want to come?"

Jessie smiled politely, immediately jumping in knowing Aidan hated the clubs, bars, and whatever other dark and claustrophobic gathering places existed with too many sensory elements. "Nah, we can't, thanks."

Sunny waggled her eyebrows. "So, you guys have exciting plans?"

"I've got an appointment to a private showing of an art piece and Aidan's going to watch over me while I do what I need to do."

"Oh, okay," Sunny said with a pout, losing interest and turning away to return to her desk.

Aidan rubbed his face, trying to disguise a devilish grin. "You didn't...just say that."

"I so did. I didn't lie because *my* poker face sucks. You're going to give me a private showing of your art piece and then you're going to watch me while I lick every inch of it," he said, waggling his eyebrows.

Aidan coughed to clear his throat.

"Have you checked the inmates on the grand opening list for Strassburg?" Jessie could tease Aidan all day, but he wasn't cruel enough to push him too far in front of his team.

"The board supposedly vetted each name. But who knows for sure. That was going to be my next step." Aidan reached into his drawer and withdrew a file folder, handing it to Jessie. "Each of them is serving anywhere between twenty years and multiple life sentences. So the chances are slim to none I can get any of them out on early parole."

Jessie flipped through the criminal reports of each inmate. He'd learned long ago not to judge someone based on their report. "I'll look into them." Jessie looked up from the file. "Is that okay?"

A soft smile spread across Aidan's face. He leaned in to whisper. "I love having you here."

"I love being here."

Jessie stood, tucking the folder under his arm. He turned to walk away but remembered something, returning to Aidan's desk and leaning in to whisper. "Don't you dare send me a text telling me my ass looks good when I walk away from you."

Aidan's mouth tightened, obviously holding back a remark, but the spark of mischief screamed from his expression.

Jessie raised an eyebrow, straightened, and walked away. He arrived at his desk and dropped the new folder by his workstation. He reached for his mug and took a sip of his coffee, grabbing his now chirping phone to read the new text message.

Your ass always looks good. Feels even better.

Jessie immediately dropped into his seat and cleared his screen of the message. He took a deep breath, hoping to cool the heat now racing through his body and thickening his dick. He glanced over at Aidan, narrowing his eyes at the mischief still firmly in place.

Oh, he was so going to get it tonight.

Chapter
THIRTY-ONE

Aidan strolled back into the precinct with Manny and Travis after executing several warrants. More names checked off the list since bringing Jessie on board a month ago. They had arrested cops on the take, more dirty judges, and a shit-ton of corporations and government contractors along the line. Everyone pushed through their exhaustion and pulled extra hours with a sole goal: wrap this shit up. All this corruption made him feel entirely too dirty for his comfort.

He straightened in the seat to look at Jessie across the room. Fuck stolen glances, they'd made a few busts today and he needed a good look.

He frowned at the empty chair.

"He's with Wall," Sunny yelled over to him from her desk, a little louder than needed, thumbing through a file. She peeked up with a wicked grin as if what she had said armed a ticking time bomb ready to explode, and she had front row seats and popcorn waiting for the show to begin.

Travis looked up and Manny turned at his desk, a mix of worry and humor in their eyes.

Jessie and Wall seemed to get along, far better than the others. Jessie never felt threatened around him and that, for Aidan, was the most important ingredient—knowing Jessie was safe and that Wall would be a rock-solid backup guardian in a pinch. Aidan knew there wasn't anything between them other than friendship, but he wouldn't deny the ugly green monster tried to pull him toward the dark side. He trusted Jessie and never questioned his love.

Sunny flipped through another page, humming. She actually fucking hummed.

Aidan clasped his hands behind his head, trying to remain casual, knowing his partner was setting the stage for a massive attack with whatever bomb she waited to drop. "Since you seem to be all-knowing, care to share where they are?"

"Gun range."

Travis covered the "O" of his mouth and Manny hid his face in his hand.

Guns…were his thing. He slowly rose from the chair, ignoring the creaking under the force of his slow rise.

He refused to give in and go batshit crazy or let that hideous green monster strangle him. He would remain calm, because that was what happened in relationships. That was what good partners, boyfriends—or whatever stupid label society decided to slap on him—did.

Screw this shit.

He grabbed his keys and wallet and stormed out of the office, ignoring the chuckles in his wake. He'd played right into Sunny's tease. Fuck them. He stalked through the hallway, down the stairs, and through the walkway leading to the training gun range connected with the precinct building. During his trek and through the pounding in his ears, he realized it wasn't anger thrumming through his body like a live wire. Or hate or jealousy.

He stopped for a moment, just outside the range office entrance, closing his eyes and taking a few deep breaths.

He was scared. Terrified was probably more accurate. Jessie wouldn't cheat. But Aidan was a difficult son of a bitch to take and there were a million other better alternatives out there in the world who made things much easier. He swung open the door, nipping that thought in the bud before it had a chance to take root. It was close to quitting time for most staff. As expected, only the one desk clerk was stationed in the otherwise vacant space.

"Hi, Rafe," Aidan mumbled in greeting.

"I didn't think I'd get anyone else this late," the attendant said.

"Did you bring your own or do you need a loaner?"

"I've got mine." He withdrew his firearm and removed the magazine, clearing the chamber of any rounds for Rafe's inspection. "Anyone else here?"

"Yeah. I've got two guys in range B."

Aidan nodded, grabbing his gun. He worked his way through the series of shooting lanes to reach the rooms. He'd walk in, no big deal. If the two guys weren't Wall and Jess, he'd shrug it off as his bad and take advantage of the range time and get a few shots in. He finally reached the room and held on to the doorknob for a few seconds, taking a deep breath, hoping to settle the storm brewing within. He rubbed his chest, trying to ease the sharp ache.

He swung open the door and there were Wall and Jessie, leaning over a taken apart gun lying on a towel. In one split second, three things were pointed at him: two stares and the barrel of one gun.

Wall immediately lowered his weapon and scowled, relaxing the arm he'd swung behind himself to shield Jessie with his body.

"You're going to give me a heart attack," Jessie said, stepping out from behind Wall.

"I heard you guys were here." He entered the room and shut the door.

Jessie grabbed each piece of the gun and began assembling the parts together, completely enthralled in the task. Wall immediately stopped him if he reached for one of the incorrect pieces and pointed to the correct part. Aidan rubbed the easing tension from his chest, watching in rapt silence as Jessie swiftly assembled the gun.

"So you're learning to take apart a gun?" Aidan asked.

"Wall already taught me how to clean one and take it apart, so now I'm just putting it back together." Jessie continued piecing the parts without looking up, biting his lip and reaching at the end of the table for the next piece.

Aidan smiled at Jessie's eagerness. And in all truth, Wall had a never-ending fountain of patience to teach people how to clean and take apart a weapon. Far better than he could. He was usually most concerned with clocking his completion and beating his record every time he took one apart.

"And...just in case you're wondering," Jessie said, not shifting his focus from his metal puzzle. "No, Wall has not taught me to shoot because we both agree, that's your area." He inserted the magazine into the gun, extending the pistol to Wall for his inspection. He turned to Aidan, challenging him.

Uh-oh.

Wall gave Jessie a thumbs-up then put away the cleaning kit and rolled up the towel, stowing everything away in his bag. He stopped at the door before exiting the room, finally spinning on his heel to face Aidan. "Apologize for being a prick. If he dumps your sorry ass, we all suffer." Wall's brow furrowed and his jaw muscles twitched. He turned and exited the room, leaving Aidan in stunned silence.

"Aidan?"

Aidan looked to the ground, scuffing his boot on the concrete floor. "I liked it better when he didn't talk."

"C'mere."

Aidan looked up, the tension in his shoulders easing with the now softer expression on Jessie's face. He took the few steps needed to stand just outside of Jessie's personal zone. "I didn't think—"

Jessie crossed his arms and stared at him.

He lowered his head again and chewed his lip. "I'll admit I wasn't thrilled to hear you were here with him." He looked up, checking if he should quit before he said something really wrong. Jessie nodded, encouraging him to continue. "It's not because I questioned whether you were cheating or not. I know you wouldn't do that. It's more..." He shrugged, feeling like a horse's ass.

"Guns are important to you and you wanted to be the one to share it with me."

Aidan nodded. "When you say it like that, it makes me sound...I don't know." *Sentimental? Childish? Temperamental?*

"How would you have said it then?"

"Guns are personal and I didn't want you handling anyone else's weapon."

Jessie stifled a laugh.

Aidan rolled his eyes. Okay, his way sounded wrong. And a little perverted. And *did* make him sound jealous. *Shit.* All this talking and head sessions and crap had him over-analyzing everything.

"Is there a camera in here?" Jessie asked.

"Yeah. Video only. One is obvious and above at our right and there are two a bit more hidden at each corner of this side of the room," he responded without letting his focus stray from Jessie.

"Okay, I wouldn't want to *handle your weapon* if anyone was watching," Jessie said, oozing with a not-so-subtle suggestion.

Aidan laughed, shaking his head. He was never going to hear the end of this.

"Okay, Mr. Hotshot. Teach me," Jessie said, sliding on his protective glasses and inserting the soft foam earplugs.

He swallowed heavily. When Jessie was in teasing mode, he was a force to be reckoned with. And Aidan was a total weak son of a bitch at his mercy. He took his gun to the lane table and loaded the magazine, cocking the gun then pointing at the paper target to demonstrate how to hold the proper position. He motioned for Jessie to come over and directed him on his stance. He placed his hands on Jessie's hips, positioning his body in a side-to-side placement. He reached down, nudging the back of Jessie's knees so he'd bend them slightly. He damn sure wouldn't deny he ran his hand along the back of Jessie's thigh a hell of a lot longer than needed.

"I'm planning on shooting the load in the gun, not me. So stop that."

Aidan chuckled. He stood behind Jessie and lowered his arms slightly so Jessie's elbows weren't in a locked position. "Focus on the target," he whispered in Jessie's ear.

"I can't focus much if you keep doing that."

"You need to zone out any distractions when you shoot." Aidan lowered his hands to Jessie's waist, not caring if Rafe had pulled up a chair to take advantage of the little peep show. "The trick is balance and grip. You need to balance your weight to counteract the kick from the gun. So let's start with that."

"What do I do now?"

"Look through the sight, aim for the target, then squeeze the trigger slowly." He remained standing behind Jessie with his hands gently resting on his narrow hips.

A shot rang through the air and Jessie lost his footing, held only by Aidan's grip on his waist. Jessie straightened and looked out to the target. "I didn't even come close. Why the hell not?"

Aidan smiled at the frustrated pout on those plump lips. "Anticipation."

"Don't tease me. I'm being serious."

"Not everything has a double meaning. You anticipated the shot so you probably flinched and that forced the shot to go elsewhere."

Jessie tilted his head and nodded slowly. "Okay. Let's do it again." He stood in the same stance, but Aidan shifted his leg and adjusted his knees—copping a feel in between—to a front-to-back position for his second attempt to see if the change granted him better balance. "You keep doing that and I'm not going to be able to do this."

Aidan chuckled. "Maybe this position will help you keep your balance better. Aim and squeeze the trigger again. Slowly. I'm not going to let you fall on your ass. So don't worry."

Jessie blew out a few deep breaths then finally pulled the trigger, staying a little steadier on his feet this time around. He lowered the gun and looked at the silhouette target. "At least I hit the paper this time," he grumbled. He straightened his arms again, ready for another shot.

Aidan reached up from behind, cupping his hands around Jessie's, letting him position the gun to aim but holding it steady in his hands. "Fire when you're ready."

His third shot echoed in the room. Jessie set the gun down and flipped the switch on the lane divider, recalling the target through the electrical pulley system. He removed the sheet from the clips and inspected his work. The second shot had barely made the edge of the paper, but the last one had hit the black target fringe of the silhouette.

"Aidan, I hate to break it to you, but I have a feeling you're going to be the gun twirling one in this relationship."

His loud laugh resonated off the walls. "I don't expect you to be packing. But I would feel better knowing you're comfortable holding one in your hand and know how to use it."

Jessie nodded. "I can deal with that. I can say I was scared to hold one until today." He held up the target, inspecting it again. He looked up abruptly, staring at Aidan as if a thought had just come to mind.

"I've never seen you shoot. Show me."

A chance to show his guy something he could do without effort? *Hell yeah!* He took another paper target and set it up on the clips, flipping the switch to set the target back out into the lane.

"That's farther than where I had it." Jessie craned his neck, watching the paper get smaller as it flew farther away.

Aidan didn't say a word until the target hit the end of the lane. "How many shots would you like me to take?" he asked, cocking his gun.

Jessie looked at the target at the end of the lane then back to him. "Just one."

Aidan peeked over his shoulder for a quick second to judge the distance, then returned his focus to Jessie. One glance. That was all he needed. He straightened his arm toward the target while keeping his focus on Jessie. "You sure you just want me to shoot *one* shot?"

"Just one," Jessie said with a huge grin.

Aidan looked over to the target, aimed, and instantly pressed the trigger. He placed the gun on the table and flipped the switch to return the target back to them.

"You're really proud of yourself, aren't you?" Jessie teased. "You didn't even bother to aim."

He waited for the target to stop in front of him, pulled the paper off the clips, and turned the paper toward Jessie, proudly displaying the perfectly centered, single target shot.

Jessie held the paper target in his hand and looked up, unmistakable desire dilating his pupils.

Aidan leaned in and whispered, "That turned you the fuck on...hard. And don't even bother denying it. You're aiming your *weapon* right at me."

Jessie swallowed heavily, parting his lips on an exhale.

Aidan smiled smugly. He might not know what to say at times or how best to say it, but he damn sure knew how to use a weapon and how to press Jessie's buttons. He holstered his gun and made his way to the door, turning to watch Jessie's still stunned expression and growing hard-on. "*Now* I'm really proud of myself."

* * * *

Jessie sat on the bed with his back resting against pillows lined along the headboard. Strong arms and the head resting on his lap held him in place. He stroked Aidan's thick, dark hair, sighing each time Aidan turned to kiss his stomach then tighten his arms to snuggle closer. He enjoyed the peaceful moments like these between them, where monsters and haunting memories didn't exist.

He absently ran his fingers along Aidan's arm, smiling at the memory of them racing into the house, tearing away at each other's clothes. He couldn't deny Aidan's ability to handle a gun had made him rock-hard and kept him that way the entire drive home. His strength, his fearlessness, his confidence, his control, all combined with the secret, sweet side of his protectiveness to produce a strong aphrodisiac Jessie couldn't resist. Everything about him was attractive and beautiful. And the best part of it all, Aidan was completely oblivious to his allure when entering a room. Whether feared or admired, he never failed to captivate every person in his proximity and command attention.

"Do you realize you strut?"

"Huh?" Aidan said, lazily raising his head from Jessie's lap.

"When you walk. You strut." He smiled, brushing away the hair covering Aidan's eyes. "It's like you're walking to music."

"No, I don't." Aidan's eyes narrowed. "Do you…like that?"

"Oh yeah." Jessie bit his lower lip. "It's sexy as hell. You've got some serious swagger going on."

"Then yeah, I totally strut," he said, lowering his head again, rubbing his stubble against Jessie's stomach.

Jessie laughed, squirming under Aidan's hold. "That tickles."

"I know," he said, brushing his chin up and down Jessie's torso.

Jessie wiggled his body, laughing and pushing Aidan's shoulder. Aidan tugged him lower, flat on the bed, then pinned him down with the weight of his body. He stilled when Aidan reached out and brushed his thumb along his cheek, leaning in to press their lips together in a slow and seductive kiss.

Jessie's heart hammered against his chest, want and need rippled through his body. He arched into Aidan, enjoying the scrape of stubble and trail of kisses down his torso. "Aidan…"

Aidan wrapped his mouth around Jessie's hardened shaft, engulfing him in wet warmth that stole his breath. He dug his fingers into Aidan's shoulders and gasped a breath with each strong pull, writhing beneath him as the fire ignited in his veins and spread throughout his body. He gripped the back of Aidan's head with both hands and bent his knees, pushing his hips into Aidan as the fire traveled up his spine and threatened to explode.

"Aid—" He barely warned as Aidan hooked his arms around Jessie's thighs with a possessive growl, tugging him closer, taking him to the root and devouring every ounce of Jessie's release.

He gasped each breath as Aidan peppered tender kisses along his body, starting at the surgical scar along Jessie's leg and working his way up Jessie's torso to his neck. Aidan cupped his face and nuzzled his ear, placing a kiss just below his earlobe. Jessie groaned, as he always did whenever Aidan touched that sensitive spot. He finally opened his eyes, reaching for Aidan, resting his palm against Aidan's cheek, rubbing his thumb along the prickly stubble he loved so much. Aidan closed his eyes and took a slow, deep breath, leaning into the caress.

"I love it when you do that," Aidan said. He lazily opened his eyes and looked at Jessie with a steady gaze filled with heat and need. He kept eye contact while he turned his head and kissed Jessie's palm. He wrapped his fingers around Jessie's hand and pulled it to his mouth, peppering more tender kisses on the scar that marred Jessie's wrist.

Jessie's throat tightened with emotion. No one had ever looked at him with so much desire or touched him with so much care. He closed his eyes, hoping to calm his rapid heartbeat.

"What's wrong?" Aidan asked.

He opened his eyes and turned his head to face Aidan. He smiled, loving how peaceful Aidan looked lying on his side with his arm tucked under the pillow. He rested his hand on Jessie's waist and tugged him closer, obviously impatient, waiting for Jessie's reply.

"Nothing's wrong. Everything's perfect. You're perfect. We're perfect."

"That's too much perfection," Aidan said with a lopsided grin. "You're making it too easy for me to screw something up."

A quiet chuckle escaped him. "I don't think you could." Jessie turned on his side, tracing his fingertips along Aidan's inked torso. "It's your turn."

"Not yet. I just want to stay like this with you for a bit."

He gave him a watery smile. Aidan could deny it all he wanted, but Jessie knew he was a very sweet man.

"Then you can have at me all you want so I can sleep the rest of the night."

Jessie laughed. Aidan was sweet when he *didn't* try so hard.

"That didn't score me any points, did it?"

He laughed harder.

"Damn," Aidan said with a mischievous grin. "Give me an extra credit question to make up for it."

Jessie tucked his hand under the pillow, hopelessly staring at the playfulness in those hazel eyes. "It's going to require a multi-part question."

"Shoot. Something tells me I need all the bonus points I can get."

"Smartass." Jessie ran his fingers along Aidan's neck before tucking his hand back under the pillow. For some reason, he couldn't resist touching Aidan when he was so peaceful. "Did you know you wanted to be a detective when you left the service?"

"No. It's a little…complicated."

"Those are the best answers. Makes you talk more. You earn more points."

The corner of Aidan's lips curled into a smile. "Okay. But you have to promise you won't get upset or sad with anything I say. Otherwise, I don't give a shit about the points."

Yeah, Aidan was damn sweet when he wasn't trying. "I promise."

Aidan looked away and quieted for a moment before returning his focus to Jessie. "You can blame Hunter for me being a detective. It's all his fucking fault."

Jessie laughed, reaching out to touch his stubble again, then trailed his finger down to Aidan's chest, resting his palm over Aidan's beating heart. "You were good with that gun."

Aidan remained quiet for a few moments but held an intensity in his eyes. "Guns, knives, and bow and arrows."

"Did you leave the service because...of what happened?"

The intensity lingered in Aidan's eyes, as if trying to gauge Jessie's reaction to his carefully selected words. "Yes. One of the things about the service—you learn to give up control, take orders, and do as you're told. After those six months, there was no way in hell I could give up control again." His jaw muscles twitched. "So I knew I couldn't re-enlist." He absently rubbed his thumb along Jessie's hip. "I shocked a lot of people. Everyone figured I'd serve my entire life."

"What did you do after that?"

"I had offers from a few people as soon as they heard I hadn't re-upped. Contracts for hire mainly." He gave Jessie a knowing look, sending a clear message of exactly what types of contracts he meant.

Jessie set his hand back on Aidan's chest. "There's a lot more to you than that."

"At the time, I didn't think I had many options." He grabbed Jessie's hand and held it up to his mouth, placing a gentle kiss on his knuckles. "Hunter was the one who suggested I join the force or be a bodyguard and use my skills for something positive. I thought about it. I tried the bodyguard thing for a few months, but I was bored out of my mind watching over some useless prick who did more wrong than right then got scared when people were looking for him. I wanted to shoot the son of a bitch instead of protect him."

Jessie bit his lip, trying to hold back a chuckle.

Aidan wrapped his hand around Jessie's fingers and held it to his chest, stroking the back of Jessie's hand with his thumb. "I remember Hunter was working a case and we were talking about it one night. Different theories, strategies, stuff like that. It was the first time in a while I was excited about something. I remember him getting quiet and just staring at me with this stupid grin on his face. Fucker knew he was going to steer me toward the force. He said I had a knack for seeing stuff others missed and finding answers. He said it wasn't taking the shot I was good at, it was survival, protection, and justice." He quieted, as if remembering that moment. "I hadn't ever thought about that or seen myself that way."

He squeezed Aidan's hand, drawing his attention. "Hunter's a great friend."

"He's always been like a big brother to me." Aidan quieted again, lowering his brow at some thought. "He got me out of there and I'll always owe him for that." He took a deep breath and closed his eyes. "That's why I need to get him back home. I can't ever repay that debt to him, but this…I know it means a lot to him. It means a lot to me too. I miss having him around."

"I know. I started going through the names on the Strassburg roster. I'm sure we'll find a way."

"Thank you." Aidan tugged him flush against his body, draping his arm over Jessie and splaying his hand across Jessie's back. Aidan's lips brushed back and forth in his hair before he spoke again. "My parents and Ty never knew what happened to me. They didn't know I was held prisoner for six months. Ty still doesn't know…and it's not something I ever want him to find out. I'm here now, and that's what matters."

Jessie's heart ached, imagining how alone Aidan must have felt in the field, knowing no one had a clue what was happening to him or knew enough about the mission to be alerted that something had gone terribly wrong when he hadn't returned. He swallowed heavily, fighting back the emotions.

"Don't. You promised." Aidan inched back and held Jessie's chin. He tilted his face upward and pressed a gentle kiss to his lips. "I'm here. I'm home."

Jessie nodded quickly, wrapping his hand around Aidan's wrist.

"All those months I was there, I kept thinking of my parents and brother. If something had happened to me, they would have been given some cover-up bullshit story. They never would have known the truth." He placed a kiss on Jessie's forehead. "*That's* why I work homicide. I feel as if the families need to know what happened. The *truth* of what happened to their loved ones. And if I can bring down the bastard who killed someone in the process, well…then that's like having cake and eating it too."

Jessie smiled brightly, hoping to disguise the emotions squeezing his heart. "And I know how much you like dessert."

"Especially when it requires me to lick it off you." Aidan smiled wickedly, dipping his head to deliver a slow, torturous kiss that made Jessie's toes curl. "Can we spend the rest of the weekend in bed?" he asked, working his way down Jessie's body.

Jessie moaned, digging his fingers into Aidan's shoulders. "Anything you want."

"Good." He looked up at Jessie, the undeniable mischief sparking in his eyes. "Because I want dessert. Lots and lots of dessert."

Chapter THIRTY-TWO

Aidan sat at the dining room table Friday night, hoping to sneak in the last bit of notes on the case file before officially calling it the end of the week. He stretched his arms and rolled his shoulders, trying to ease the tightness in his muscles. After working the list for a solid month and a half with Jessie's research, they'd finally reached the last page of names. A few weeks, tops, and all the bullshit and drama should be over and each of them could add one hell of a notch to their personnel file for taking down one of the largest organized crime and drug rings the multi-agencies had ever seen. Sunny was excited, Travis relieved to finally close up some cold cases from his department, Wall didn't seem to care either way, and Peacock Manny had paraded around all week like Miss Universe doing a pageant crowning walk.

Then there was Jessie. The solved cases were a direct result of his endless hours putting all the pieces together. Even if Aidan was a talker by nature, he wouldn't know which words to use to summarize how he felt. Jessie's gentle nature and mad research skills won over the detectives in the precinct and resulted in a few job offers from several agencies. He was respected and treated as an equal. And to Jessie, that meant the world. He didn't need to accept a job offer to show his gratitude.

Aidan closed his eyes and twisted his neck, exhaling with relief once he heard the pop.

"Ouch," Jessie said, leaning up against the edge of the table.

"Hey there," Aidan said with a half smile, reaching out to rest his hand on Jessie's leg. He wasn't sure what the hell had happened to him over the course of the last few months, but he loved the contact, touching Jessie every chance he had.

"I've got something for you." Jessie set the folder on the table and crossed his arms.

"What's this?" He grabbed the file and skimmed the pages. "One of the Strassburg names? Vannguard Shaw. I remember the file, hard to forget with an odd name like that. He's in for murder and got a life sentence because of the Three Strikes law. What's special about his case?"

"You need to read it. Please work your magic to get this man off the list. I have the notes in the file and all the important parts highlighted that will help speed things along." Jessie leaned over and placed a tender kiss on his lips. "I'm going to bed. We've got Manny's wedding tomorrow and I want to make sure I'm well-rested." He pushed off the table and slowly made his way to their bedroom.

Aidan scowled. He didn't need to be a people-person to know a huge red-alert siren blasted in his ear. He set the file down and reviewed each page of Jessie's research, paying close attention to every highlighted line and handwritten sticky note. He swallowed heavily, turning to the next set of stapled pages, scanning them with equal intensity. A slow anger began to build with each new item he reviewed. He thumbed through to the next page and saw the glaring reason why the courts had overlooked obvious details that would have released Shaw years ago.

The murdered victim was the husband of a senator. The same dirty Senator Margaret Delereux on Rick's snitch list who the team had arrested last week. Without question she probably used her influence to ensure Shaw's extended sentence.

He reached for the last stack of papers. A chill slowly began to spread throughout his body. The senator had a son, Drayton Delereux.

Drayton? The name can't be a coincidence.

A memory suddenly came to mind. A photo he had spotted in Drayton's office during a visit over a year ago when they discussed his role in taking down the exotic car theft export network. Two young men wearing baseball caps, smiling at the camera.

He flipped to the next page, reading through endless highlights and notes Jessie had obviously been able to retrieve after gaining access with the warrant in her case. Aidan's stomach roiled with disgust at the extent the senator had gone through to rid her life of her son after her husband's death.

Aidan's concern shifted to the haunting memories that must have surfaced for Jessie during his review of Shaw's background. He raked his hand through his hair and shut the file. He stood and made his way to their bedroom, staring at Jessie's sleeping form in the darkened room. He slipped out of his clothes and slid under the sheet, wrapping his arm around Jessie's waist and placing a gentle kiss on his shoulder.

"A grocery store," Jessie whispered. "Shoplifting a loaf of bread."

He pulled Jessie flush against his body, knowing it must have brought back memories of Jessie's time begging in the streets hoping a stranger would gift him something to eat.

"And that second arrest, they had the wrong guy and dismissed the charges. It should never have counted in the Three Strikes law." Jessie turned abruptly in the embrace. "He did commit the murder, but it wasn't premeditated." He wrapped his arms around Aidan and tucked his head under his chin. "Did you see my note about his connection to Drayton?" he asked, barely above a whisper.

Aidan closed his eyes and ran his hand up and down Jessie's back, placing a gentle kiss in Jessie's hair. "Yes."

"She threw him away," he whispered brokenly.

Aidan screwed his eyes shut, remembering the pain in Jessie's eyes when he told him about his father kicking him out of his own home at such a young age.

Jessie inched back, his eyebrows twitching as if fighting to hold back the emotions. "Do you think..." He looked up at Aidan, the sadness in those blue eyes ripped through Aidan's soul. "Do you think Drayton would still want him after all this time?"

He cupped Jessie's face and placed a tender kiss on his lips. "Drayton still has a picture of them in his office even though Shaw was arrested ten years ago. I'd say it's a solid yes."

Jessie absently nodded. "Okay."

"We'll get him out of there. I promise. And, Jess," he said, stroking his thumb along Jessie's cheek.

"Yeah."

"Thank you."

Jessie reached up, barely touching a fingertip to Aidan's stubble. "For what?"

For loving me. For putting up with my shit. For always being there. For not throwing me *away when you had an easy out.*

"There's no way I would have been able to hold up my end of the deal without you finding this." He leaned in and pushed his face into Jessie's hair, loving the way the soft, silky strands brushed against his face. "You saved my ass."

Jessie wrapped his arms around Aidan's neck. "Good. Because I love your ass and want to make sure it's around for a very, very long time."

Aidan smiled, thankful to hear the lighter side of Jessie make an appearance. "And here I thought you liked my balls best."

Jessie quietly chuckled, tucking his head under Aidan's chin. "I also love your ink, your eyes, your stubble, you're amazing heart, your Aidanisms, and this whole tough guy thing you have going on that scares away most people at the precinct. It's all a package deal. I love everything."

"Everything?"

Aidan closed his eyes when Jessie softly stroked the back of his neck.

"I love you, my incredibly stubborn, sexy man. Every inch of you."

He sighed and pulled Jessie close, resting his cheek against the side of Jessie's head, thankful for the man he held in his arms and for the love that always surrounded him in his presence.

* * * *

Jessie tugged on the cuffs of his sleeves, sneaking a peek at his wristwatch.

"C'mon, Aidan. You said you wanted to be there early."

He took one last look in the hallway bathroom mirror before switching off the light and making his way to their bedroom, frowning at the silence. He figured using the other bathroom would speed things along, but now they risked cutting it a little close to the start of the Reyes wedding. He rounded the corner and there, on the edge of the bed, Aidan sat, his stubble perfectly trimmed and shaped, dressed from the waist down with his white dress shirt open and his head down staring at his hands.

"Aidan?"

He looked up, the pain and sadness screaming loud enough from his expression to knock the air out of Jessie's lungs. Aidan looked away as a deep scowl formed on his face. "You should go, so you're not late."

Jessie sat next to him on the bed and reached out, slowly caressing his thigh, hoping to coax him. "Why don't we back up a little and you tell me what's wrong."

Aidan looked down again. "I can't."

Jessie reached over and placed a gentle kiss on his cheek. "Can't what?"

Aidan sat, unmoving, his jaw muscles tightening with tension.

Jessie looked down and noticed Aidan's white-knuckle grip on the necktie twisted around his fist. He wrapped his arm around Aidan's shoulders. "The tie?"

Aidan nodded once, barely noticeable. "I tried." He looked over to Jessie, his eyes haunted. "I…can't."

"You don't need the tie."

"It's formal, Jess. If I don't show up with it, he'll think I'm disrespecting him…them. And I don't want to do that," he finished quietly. "You should go. Tell them I was sick or something and didn't want to fuck things up for them."

"You're coming." Jessie stood and tugged Aidan's hand, unwrapping the tie from his fist and pitching it to the side. "Do you have a black dress shirt?" he asked, already making his way to Aidan's closet.

"Yeah. Haven't worn it in a while, but I'm sure it still fits."

"What about a dark vest?" he absently asked, combing through the items in the closet.

"I don't wear those." He stood, walking over to Jessie. "Wait, would a vest from a three-piece work? I think Hunter left some of those when he moved out. There should be one in the closet of the workout room. It'll be a little loose, but it should work."

Jessie found the black dress shirt and pulled Aidan by the hand, leading him into the next room where he thumbed through the hanging suits and pulled out a black vest. "We need to throw these in the dryer for a few minutes to freshen them up." He smiled as Aidan followed him numbly along his path to the laundry room then back to their room and into the bathroom, without uttering a word of protest. "Sit."

He expected Aidan to make some crack about being a puppy, shadowing him around the house and following commands. His silence, as usual, spoke far more than his words.

Aidan sat on the closed toilet and looked up at Jessie, waiting for his next set of instructions.

"You trust me?" He smiled at Aidan's nod and grabbed his hair gel and spray to style Aidan's hair into a sleek, polished more formal but totally *metrosexual-I'm-hot* style. He took advantage of Aidan's silence as he brushed, blow-dried, and styled his hair, stilling for a moment of surprise when Aidan's hands reached up to rest on his waist. Aidan tried to see himself in the mirror, but Jessie held his face. "Nope. You see the final package when I'm finished." After the last few touches on his hair were complete, Jessie pulled Aidan back over to the laundry room and cooled the shirt and vest, flicking them each in the air back and forth, before having Aidan slip them on.

Aidan stood still as Jessie primped him, tugging sleeves and buttoning the shirt and vest. Aidan's focus was aimed at the ground and his arms hung loosely at his side, but it was the defeat on his face that twisted Jessie's stomach.

"Do I button the top?" Jessie asked, trying to steady his voice through the ache in his chest.

"Open. Please." Aidan looked away for a moment before speaking again. "I can't have anything tight around my neck."

A swell of emotions had Jessie holding his breath. It still twisted his heart whenever Aidan opened up with minimal coaxing. He placed a gentle kiss on Aidan's lips then finished with the vest, helping him shrug on the suit jacket. Jessie stepped back and inhaled sharply, trying to ignore the instant hardening in his own *can't-hide-a-thing* pants.

"Does it look okay?" Aidan asked, flattening his hands on his jacket.

Jessie nodded. "Oh yeah."

Aidan raised an eyebrow, a slow smile spreading across his face. "You're horny."

"And you're hot."

Aidan pulled him by the hand and guided them back to the mirror in their bathroom. He huffed out a chuckle, turning back and forth, looking at his hair and clothing from different angles, stopping himself before his fingers touched his now styled hair.

He looked like he'd just walked off a catwalk.

And Jessie couldn't wait to come back home and strip him out of all those layers, one by one.

Aidan turned and held Jessie's face, bending to place a slow, tender kiss to Jessie's lips. "Thank you."

"You can thank me later when we're in bed."

Aidan reached down to cup the growing bulge in Jessie's pants. He brushed a kiss just under Jessie's ear and whispered, "Not sure how you're going to make it the whole night with this hard-on in your way."

Jessie closed his eyes and swallowed heavily, trying not to focus on the warm breath skating across his skin. "We're going to be late," he croaked.

Aidan stepped away and shot him one of his cocky grins. Yeah, he was damn proud of himself.

They grabbed their wallets and the wedding invitation then made their way to the front door.

Once seated in the SUV, Jessie snapped his seat belt into the clip. "By the way…" he said with a veil of calm in his tone.

"Yeah?" Aidan prompted, pulling out of their driveway.

"When we get back home, I want you to keep that suit on while you fuck me against the wall."

"Shit," Aidan hissed under his breath.

A smug smile tugged at Jessie's lips.

At least now, he wouldn't be the only one battling a full-fledged hard-on for the next few hours.

* * * *

"Mmm." Jessie woke to a hard heat pressed against the back of his thigh and warm wetness trailing up his shoulder and along his neck. He moaned, stretching, craving more. He opened his eyes when Aidan pushed his hard-on against him again. He looked over his shoulder and his still-asleep but lust-filled brain couldn't decipher the emotion that flickered in Aidan's eyes before he looked away. He reached over his shoulder, placing his palm against the stubble he loved so much. "You okay?"

Aidan leaned in for a kiss. The softness and tenderness of the gesture not making it easy to decipher the play of emotions in those guarded, hazel eyes. "I'm sorry I woke you." He looked away, avoiding Jessie's questioning stare. "I want you," he finally said, almost in a whisper. "Is that okay?"

Heat instantly spread throughout his body at Aidan's words. "I'll always say yes."

His heartbeat sped when Aidan grabbed the lube and small fresh towel they kept on the nightstand. He closed his eyes and moaned as Aidan slowly worked to stretch and prepare him, peppering kisses on his shoulder as he thoroughly repeated the process. Aidan finally wiped his hand and pitched the towel to the ground. He slid one arm under Jessie's shoulder and the other around his side, clasping his hands together against Jessie's chest, holding him close. Jessie slowly exhaled and arched his body, welcoming the heated slide of Aidan slowly entering him until they were flush in their connection.

He leaned back into the embrace with a groan. He anchored his hands on Aidan's arms around him, reveling in the glide of their joined bodies moving as one and the warm puffs of Aidan's breath against his shoulder with each slow, deep grind of his hips. The tenderness of each caress, the gentleness of each thrust, the tightness of the arms wrapped around him…was all different. More intimate. A silent plea for a closer connection.

This was Aidan making love to him.

Aidan slowed his pace to a near stop, still buried deep within Jessie's body. "Did you…want me to stop?"

Jessie swallowed heavily and vehemently shook his head, rubbing Aidan's arms around him, trying to control the emotions tightening his chest and throat at the hesitation in Aidan's voice. This was Aidan's silent way of telling him how much he needed and wanted him, how much he cherished their private connection. He spoke tonight as he usually did—through his actions rather than words. Jessie turned and kissed the inside of Aidan's bicep then snuggled into the comfort of his strength, reveling in the safety and love that enveloped him, both in and out of his body.

He closed his eyes as the heat of Aidan's hand slid across his chest and up the side of his neck, guiding his face to turn so Aidan could kiss him with each slow thrust. Jessie reached behind him and gripped Aidan's thigh, encouraging him to continue, not wanting the silent declaration of his feelings to end so soon.

A need to breathe forced them to separate, but they remained close, neither wanting to distance themselves from the connection. Aidan tightened his arms around Jessie and deepened the thrust of his hips, huddling into the embrace. Jessie dug his fingers in Aidan's arm muscles and bit his lip as a bolt of current surged up his spine. The slow, torturous glide of Aidan's hips faltered moments before a whimper and groan simultaneously escaped them as they both came, in sync.

They held each other tightly, nestling in the warmth and comfort of their bodies. They remained joined for a few moments as Aidan placed tender kisses on Jessie's shoulder, holding him snugly against him.

Jessie held onto Aidan's arms and rested his head on Aidan's bicep, knowing his words were truer than ever as the strong cage of his arms offered a protective, warm embrace and the steady beating of Aidan's heart thumped against his back. With every beat of his own heart, he knew he'd always love Aidan…every second of every day.

Chapter
THIRTY-THREE

Between the time spent with the team at the precinct and the extra hours reviewing cases at home, it was a good thing they both loved their jobs. He'd managed to get Rick's brother on the roster for Strassburg, and wrapping up the cases from the checklist of names from his list offered one hell of a great distraction from Monster Michael and the frustrating dead-end investigation. But even Aidan recognized the need for a break from their routine.

"That was nice," Jessie said, leaning his head back against the SUV's headrest.

Aidan stared down the dark road, occasionally stealing casual glances at Jessie. "I'm getting attached to this whole date night thing. I know I don't say it as often as I should, but thanks. I really appreciate how you always...handle everything, at work and at home." *And me.* Seemed it got a little easier to speak his mind each day. Another baby step in the right direction.

He tapped his thumb on the steering wheel and rolled his hand over the leather material. Jessie was so ingrained into his life now, he couldn't—and didn't want to—imagine a life without him. Everything seemed easier and his presence always offered silent support. But it was his unwavering dependability when shit hit the fan in Aidan's mind that always seemed to showcase his strength the most. *That stupid fucking tie.* Aidan gripped the steering wheel tighter thinking about what had happened a few nights ago. Just when he'd thought he could push forward, it had all come right back again with that narrow piece of silk in his hand. He'd been numb, staring at the thing, not knowing what to do. Then Jessie had come to the rescue, fixing things and making it all better…as he always did. Damn, he loved that man. Even though the words didn't come easy for him, he hoped his actions let Jessie know how important and amazing he thought he was.

"What are you thinking about that has you smiling like that?"

Aidan glanced over at Jessie before looking back at the road. "I was smiling?"

"Yeah." Jessie turned to face him then poked him in the side when he didn't answer. "Tell me."

Aidan playfully twisted away from Jessie when he reached out to poke him again.

"C'mon. Tell me."

"I was just thinking about how good you look sitting there."

"Liar."

"We skipped dessert again, so my mind is wandering."

Jessie laughed and bit his lip. "You can do whatever you want to me when we get home." He straightened in his seat with a smile still lingering on his face. "For the record, I know that wasn't what you were thinking."

Aidan's grip tightened on the steering wheel. How the hell did Jessie always seem to know what crossed his mind? Sure, it made things easy sometimes, but hell, he couldn't get anything past him.

Jessie chuckled. "Now you're just pissed off you're easy to read."

Aidan pursed his lips and switched his focus between the road and his teasing passenger. "How the hell do you do that?"

Jessie turned in the seat toward Aidan, the wistful expression on his face clearly conveying how much he loved him. He'd never get tired of that. Even his lack of emotional decoding received that message loud and clear. Jessie reached into his collar and pulled out the small key charm hanging from his necklace. "Because I have your key. Gives me special powers."

Aidan shook his head. "I swear, if I—"

He gripped the steering wheel tightly when a loud boom echoed in the dark night and the truck began to swerve.

"Aidan?" Jessie said, gripping the armrests and holding his body rigid in the seat.

"Tire blowout." He steadied the truck and slowed their speed, working his way to the shoulder of the road. He sighed and unbuckled his seat belt, switching off his truck and exiting the vehicle. He stood by the driver's side and stared at the ripped tire. "Shit." He turned toward the rear of the truck to retrieve the spare when something pricked his neck, hard enough to cause him to misstep backward against his SUV.

"What the fuck?" he mumbled, reaching up, startled when his fingers brushed against the tip of something protruding from his neck. He pulled the item away and blinked as his vision quickly blurred.

A tranquilizer dart.

He looked up, out into the darkness and swayed, immediately trying to reach for his phone as a numbness began spreading through his body. His hands weren't working right. "Shit."

"Aidan?" Jessie's voice cut through the silence of the night as he leaned out of the SUV through the driver's side.

Everything started spinning. He glanced over to Jessie. *Jess*. The panic set in. "Get back in the truck and lock it. Now! Don't open the door for any reason!"

He tried to coordinate his fingers on the stupid screen. His breath sawed in and out of his lungs and a sharp pain burned through his chest. He screwed his eyes shut then opened again, blinking with far more effort than should have been needed. He shook his head, hoping to focus. He looked at his phone…what he hoped was his phone in his hand. The different digits on the display all seemed to swirl together. He almost lost his balance, held only by Jessie's firm grip around his waist. He shook his head, trying to clear the haze in his mind. "Get…back in the fucking truck."

Jessie held his own phone up to his ear, ignoring him.

"Get…back…in the truck." He swallowed heavily, fighting the sudden dryness in his mouth forcing his tongue to stick and make the words even harder to voice.

"Sunny! We're in trouble…"

Jessie's voice faded in the fog of his mind. He heard him saying a few more words but couldn't decipher them. His legs weakened and his knees buckled, dropping him onto the gravel. He held his body up with one hand as best he could, taking the dart and his phone in the other hand and tucking both items on the underside of his truck. His team would find them.

"Aidan!" Jessie's muffled voice pierced through his fogged brain. "They're coming. The team is coming. Hang on."

He closed his eyes and tried to focus on his breathing.

Shit, shit, shit.

He mumbled something, not really sure of the words he spoke as his body slumped to the ground.

Jessie pulled him up into a sitting position and withdrew Aidan's gun from his holster. He sat at Aidan's side, standing guard with the gun drawn and ready in the darkness of the night.

"Hang on, dammit!"

Aidan swayed, unable to coordinate any of his limbs. He closed his eyes, trying to focus on remember how to breathe when a shot rang through the air and everything faded to black.

* * * *

Everything felt…wrong. Off…yet…familiar.

The air smelled musty, rich with the scent of wood and nature. Each breath, although clear, seemed to take too much damn effort. His side hurt but hell if he could figure out why. His arms were numb and his head seemed to weigh a hell of a lot more than it was supposed to. Maybe being hard-headed did result in a heavier head after all.

"Finally," an unfamiliar, deep voice said, breaking through the haze in Aidan's mind. "Wake the hell up."

He willed his eyes to open, but his body was sluggish and slow to react. He took a few deep breaths and tried to clench his fists, opening his eyes and squinting at the brightness, slowly allowing his eyes to adjust. He clenched his fists again just as his vision sharpened.

He was shirtless and barefoot, with his hands tied above his head granting him barely enough slack to have his tiptoes touch the ground.

He looked up and saw his wrists bound with a rope wrapped around a hook. He looked down and saw the blood seeping from a cut on the lower right side of his torso.

This isn't the same. This isn't a flashback. Focus. This is real.

"What doesn't kill you…" The voice came from a corner of the space, obviously close enough to read the beginning of the inked message of his tattoo.

Aidan's breath heaved as he scanned the barn-like room, assessing each corner and object and making a mental note, begging his mind to keep up with his virtual checklist. *Jessie. Where's Jessie?*

"Makes you stronger." A figure emerged with his arms behind his back. "Those are some powerful words on your torso."

Michael.

Aidan stared, tracking each step Michael took as he neared. He was tall, broad, and his dirty blond hair touched the edge of his collar. A scar that looked a few months old split part of his face, starting at the hairline, running along the outer edge of his eye and down to his upper lip. A slow smile tugged at Aidan's lips. He had no doubt Jessie had inflicted the damage during that night of the attack.

Michael motioned toward Aidan's body with a chin-up gesture. "I had to slow you down. Even with the tranq, you still managed to put up a fight while I strung you up. I'm rather impressed. You didn't leave me much choice but to tie you up and keep your hands where I can see them."

The rage ignited within Aidan, burning his blood and fueling a curtain of vengeance to surge in his body. He clenched his fists again, gauging the give of the rope that bound him.

Where the hell is Jessie?

"Interesting ink," Michael said. "Guess we're going to have to test the merits of that little saying." He swung his arm around and revealed an electric cattle prod.

Before Aidan had a chance to react through the mental haze or prepare his mind and body for the jolt, the electrodes were jammed against the side of his bleeding torso at his wound. His body arched and stiffened while his blunt nails dug into his palms. A roar of pain ripped from his lungs with the surge of electricity coursing through his body. He hung loosely from the rope when Michael finally pulled the prod away, feeling the burn of the material cutting into his wrists and the strength draining from his muscles.

Michael took a step back and cocked his head. "Huh. Guess your theory is bullshit."

The sweat trickled into Aidan's eyes and down his neck and chest. Fresh blood began to ooze from the wound at his side. He fisted his hands, willing the strength of his body to return and sync with his mind.

"I've been trying to figure out what the hell he sees in you. But I just can't seem to put my finger on it." Michael paced in front of Aidan, closely watching each shift in movement.

Focus. This is real. This is not a flashback.

Aidan's heart pounded in his ears. His breath hissed with each forced exhale, trying to dissociate himself from the burning pain at his side and the flashback that attempted to flicker into his vision. He needed to buy some time to build up his strength. "Why Jessie?"

Michael looked off to the side and quieted for a few moments. "It's killing you, isn't it? Knowing the time he and I had." He took a step closer and his lips twitched with the beginnings of a grin.

Aidan clamped down on his teeth so hard he thought his molars would shatter. Mr. Asshole was baiting him, and he needed to preserve his strength and figure a way out of this clusterfuck.

Michael straightened and took a step back, resuming his pacing path in front of Aidan. "I spent my time grooming him to be the perfect partner. He'll need some retraining. He's apparently become rather stubborn over the years, but I welcome the challenge. We have the rest of our lives ahead of us." He stopped his pacing and his lips twitched into what he may have thought was a smile but appeared more like a sneer with the scar running down the side of his face and into his top lip. "I can thank *you* for delivering him back to me."

Aidan grimaced in confusion.

He resumed his pacing. "I searched the streets for years looking for him. He's…special. No one is exactly like him." He turned sharply toward Aidan. "Imagine my surprise when I see his photo in an online news report about a big drug ring arrest." Michael laughed, a low rumble that pierced Aidan's body and twisted his gut. "I guess I have you to thank for that—you and the state attorney's office for giving me his name and where he worked. It was relatively easy to find him after that." He switched the prod from one hand to another, looking at Aidan.

"Where's Jessie?" Aidan asked.

"He'll come around and realize he made a mistake leaving me."

"Where's. Jessie?"

Michael cocked his head. "We have plans for him, but he's having a difficult time focusing while you're still in the picture."

We? Aidan blinked, pushing his mind to process a little more quickly. Jessie was still alive. That was all that mattered. He fisted his hands and pulled at his wrists, causing his body to slightly swing back and forth.

"Ropes are tight. You're not getting out that easily." Michael closely observed him as he slowly strode from left to right and back again.

Aidan focused on each slow step the asshole took around him. He couldn't stop the grin that tugged at his lips when he noticed the bandage wrapped around Michael's bicep. "Did Jessie do that to you?"

Michael looked over at his own arm, indifferent to the bandage with the small stain of blood. "When we picked you two up. He...surprised me. I never expected he'd use a gun. He's more...resistant." He paused for a moment and pointed to the scar on his face. "There are several issues I'll need to address."

"Where. Is. He?"

Michael sighed. He extended his arm and jammed the prod against Aidan's torso again, sending another jolt of current through Aidan's body.

Aidan clenched his teeth, trying to hold back the yell as his body arched and his toes curled. Michael withdrew the prod again and Aidan's body instantly fell limp, the rope cutting more into his wrists as part of the soles of his feet now rested on the ground. He turned his head and peered through the sweat-slicked hair hanging over his eyes. "You better pray you kill me," he said gruffly.

Michael laughed. "I don't think you're in *any* position to issue threats."

"I'm going to kill you slow, you son of a bitch," he said, each exhale hissing through his teeth as his heart slammed against his chest.

"Assuming I don't kill you first." Michael reached out again with the prod.

Aidan fisted the rope in his hands and swung his legs forward, kicking the prod out of Michael's grasp.

Michael lunged forward with a roar, stopping when Aidan wrapped his legs around his neck, holding him in a neck-lock between his thighs. Aidan channeled his fury and tightened his legs, possessed by rage at the thought that this monster had held Jessie prisoner all those years ago and might have hurt him now. He squeezed and twisted his thighs together, jerking his legs tight until the body in his hold went slack. He released Michael, letting his body drop to the ground.

Aidan's focus snapped upward, assessing the rope and hook holding him in place. He took a few deep breaths, centering himself, trying to channel his strength. He looked over at Michael's body slumped on the ground. He didn't have much time. He held his legs together and pushed off the floor, grunting when the pain at his side sent a numbing jolt through his muscles. "Fuck."

He closed his eyes and focused. Jessie needed him. Period. Nothing else mattered at that moment.

He opened his eyes with renewed strength. He took a few deep breaths then pushed off again, gripping the rope and folding his body upward, wrapping his bare feet around the wood beam supporting the hook. He pulled himself higher, gaining enough slack to finally release himself from the metal hook. He hung upside down from the beam for a second before nimbly dropping to the ground on his feet in a cat-like move. He flinched at the jab of pain but slammed that thought behind a mental door and focused on the next step.

Aidan looked around for something to cut the rope and spotted a few discarded tools at the side of a worn wooden table. He grabbed the rusting coping saw from the stack and held the handle between his thighs. He ran the rope back and forth on the serrated edge, finally seeing a slight tear in the threads begin to spread.

The rip grew until it was finally halfway when an arm wrapped around his neck and pulled him back with force, swinging his body to the side and down onto the ground. He immediately rolled and righted himself, holding his bound hands in front of him, staring down Michael who mirrored his pose.

Michael inched to the side when Aidan shifted toward him, circling each other in an odd dance, each waiting for the other to make the first move. Aidan maintained his focus squarely on his opponent while twisting, turning, and pulling at the rope binding his hands, increasing the frayed edge with each shift.

"Here's a tip. When you knock me down, you should make sure I stay down," Michael said.

"And you should have killed me when you had the chance." Adrenaline pumped through Aidan's veins, recharging every tiny muscle and tendon in his body. "I'm a man of my word. Snapping your neck would have been an easy kill. I want you to suffer, you son of a bitch."

Michael reached down into the side of his boot, withdrawing a short spear-point blade. "C'mon, asshole," he taunted, folding his hand in a *come here* gesture.

"Where's Jessie?"

Michael sneered. "Safely locked away." He lowered his chin and held up his arm across his body with the blade gripped firmly in his fist, aimed at Aidan in a combat stance. "You're not the only one with formal training here." He stepped forward and swung his arm, and Aidan stepped back, bowing his body to avoid the swipe. The monster attempted a few more swings, forward and arching upward, growing impatient each time Aidan managed to avoid him. In a split second, the rope around Aidan's wrists finally broke free and Michael barreled forward with a yell, pushing his body into Aidan and throwing them both onto the ground. Michael raised his arm and brought down the knife, stopping only when Aidan held his wrist in the air in a tight grip.

They bared their teeth like enraged animals, grunting and rolling on the dirty, hay-covered ground, one trying to overpower the other.

"Get away from him!" A new voice echoed in the open space.

Michael whipped his head around, and Aidan took advantage of the momentary distraction. He broke free from the hold and jammed his thumb into the wound on Michael's arm. Michael let out a howl of pain and rolled onto his back, giving Aidan the second he needed to land a punch to his opponent's face. Aidan threw another punch, then another. Michael struggled and kneed Aidan in the torso, intentionally aiming for the freshly opened wound.

Aidan gasped from the pain and his vision blurred. He barely had a chance to focus when Michael slashed the knife across his chest. The anger thrummed through Aidan's body, numbing him to the burning new slice of his skin. He gripped Michael's shoulders as a growl-like sound emerged from his throat. He head-butted his opponent to weaken him then held down Michael's body as he pulled back his arm and began repeatedly punching Michael, channeling every ounce of rage and vengeance into his fists and his bloodied target. There was no flashback or monster from Aidan's past demanding his attention. His focus was vivid, sharp, and squarely aimed at destroying the monster who had stolen so much from Jessie.

"Get off him!" the voice yelled again, a split second before a shot rang through the air.

Aidan's body instantly bowed and his jaw slackened with the searing burn that pierced his core, each hissed breath racing in and out of his lungs like a blaze of fire. His lips curled into a sneer, biting back the sting of pain rippling through his limbs.

Michael grabbed him by the throat and thrust him to the ground, straddling him, pushing the weight of his body onto Aidan. "You're a weak son of a bitch," Michael said with a twisted, bloodstained smile. He hooked his other arm backward, taking aim at Aidan's body with the blade in hand.

Aidan gasped and gripped Michael's wrist with both hands in the air, stopping the blade before it pierced his body. He grunted and snarled as he worked to twist Michael's hand, shifting the tip of the blade to the side and slowly around, aiming it at its new target. Michael's eyes rounded as his arm shook, trying to redirect the blade away from his body.

A veil of red colored Aidan's vision. The rage, the pain, the hurt…justice and vengeance battled for control and recharged each tendon in his pained body. His blood was on fire, blazing a trail of fury in every inch of his muscles. He pushed the blade that final inch away from himself and into the hard flesh of his opponent's abdomen, seating the blade at the mark with full force and twisting the handle to eliminate any room for error. Aidan looked into the shocked eyes of the monster staring back at him, reveling in the justice of the fading life from that hollow gaze, before the weight of Michael's body fell upon him with a thump.

"I'll kill him," the voice shrieked brokenly.

Aidan glanced over the shoulder of Michael's slumped form and inhaled sharply, panic instantly flooding his body.

Jessie stood still with an arm locked around his neck. A young man—roughly an inch or two taller but just as lean and fit with dark hair and light eyes—stood behind him, pointing a gun at Aidan.

Aidan blinked a few times, trying to reconcile what he saw. He didn't care about the barrel of the gun aimed at him. He didn't care about the young man holding Jessie. All that mattered was Jessie and the haunted, vacant gaze as he stared at Aidan's body.

Aidan's focus shifted to the cut on Jessie's lip and his bruised eye and cheek. Anger exploded. He clenched his hands and bit back the rage that clawed its way to the forefront. His heart slammed against his chest and a pounding echo pulsated in his head.

Maim.

Kill.

Rip the fucker apart who dared hurt *his* Jess.

He shoved away Michael's lifeless body from above him and yanked the blade out from Michael's abdomen. He slowly stood and turned to face his new opponent, wiping the blood from the knife on his jeans-clad thigh, readying himself for his next target.

"Jess…"

Aidan took a step forward and the man stepped back, dragging Jessie against him like a shield. Aidan took another step and staggered slightly as the adrenaline slowly evaporated from his system. He shook his head to clear his vision. In the midst of the pain fogging his mind, he sought Jessie and the sea of crystal blue, needing some telepathic surge of strength. Instead, there it was, that haunted look in Jessie's eyes. The one he'd seen when they first met. The one he'd hoped to never see again. The fear and pain bore into Aidan's soul and radiated throughout his body, compounding the aches of his muscles and weakening him.

The man yanked Jessie's head back by his hair and turned the gun, digging the metal barrel against Jessie's temple. "You killed him!" the man yelled with a sob, the panic rising in his voice. "I want you to know how that feels!"

"Aidan..."

The crack from Jessie's plea nearly broke him and made him stumble.

Save Jessie. Nothing. Else. Matters.

He screwed his eyes shut and steadied his breathing as best he could past the pain that clamped down around his torso and burned in his lungs. He didn't want to think about where the damn pain was coming from anymore. He raised the blade and took a deep breath to steady his shaking hand.

What the hell was he thinking? He couldn't put Jess at risk like this. He lowered his hand and took a step forward. His step faltered. The room started spinning and each breath made a wheezing sound from his chest.

"Aidan," Jessie whispered. "Look at me."

It took too much effort to coordinate his breathing, standing, and keeping his hands steady. He stumbled back then looked up, focusing his attention on Jessie to ground him.

The man pulled back Jessie's head with force, a crazed, almost delirious expression washing over his features. He spoke, his tone, although a whisper obviously directed at Jessie, carried in the open space. "He's dying. You're going to watch him die and there's nothing you can do about it."

Aidan swallowed heavily as his body swayed, his attention drawn to the shine in Jessie's eyes. Aidan shook his head harshly from side to side with a grunt, trying to coordinate his body. *I don't ever want you to be scared again.*

"Jess..." He pleaded, his voice broken, pushing each breath through clenched teeth. He blinked slowly, his grip on the knife loosening as he begged for a shred of mercy to come into his life at that very moment—not for him, he didn't give a shit about himself. *Please don't hurt him.*

"Aidan, look at me, dammit. Look. At. Me." Jessie's tone hardened with a sudden strength that boomed across the room like a sonic message only Aidan could hear. His voice sharpened Aidan's focus and beckoned his fighting spirit to resurrect. "Every second of every day, with every breath and heartbeat. Know that I trust you just as much."

Jessie's few words awakened a surge of strength within Aidan. He narrowed his eyes, forcing his vision to sharpen further and took one deep, steadying breath. He straightened his arm with renewed determination and aimed the blade at the man threatening the life of *his* Jess a few yards away. Aidan flicked his arm back then forward with a final thrust of power before launching the blade across the room just as everything faded to black.

Chapter
THIRTY-FOUR

Beep. Beep.

He hated that fucking sound. It always seemed to surround him when shit hit the fan. Through the rhythmic high-pitched beeping that pierced his brain, he heard another sound—the peaceful melody of a piano sonata echoing in the background. A soothing rise and fall of music, offering a subtle, steady, comforting reminder he was still in the realm of the living.

Aidan opened his eyes, and a blurred scene of white filled his vision. He blinked a few times until the scene stopped warping in and out and finally sharpened. He slowly turned his head to the right, blowing out a relieved breath, never happier to see those crystal blue eyes staring back at him. "You're okay?"

Jessie nodded quickly. "How are you feeling?"

"Like I got shot, stabbed, and my ass kicked."

"Smartass," Jessie said, his hitching breath betraying his facade of casualness. "Doctor said you were lucky the bullet went clean through and didn't nick anything."

Lucky? Maybe Lady Luck wasn't pissed at him after all. "Did they take long to find us?"

Jessie shook his head and swallowed heavily. "The team tracked your phone and found the dart. It was some rare, animal-grade controlled drug that required a registration with each purchase." He looked down and rubbed his fingers together, busying his hands.

"That's how they found us. The farm was in that man's name. The team thinks that's how Michael would avoid leaving a footprint." Jessie quieted, an odd distant look filling his gaze. "Michael picked him up when he was a kid more than ten years ago. The man had a really warped view of things…that happened to him." He looked up at Aidan, an odd mix of fear and worry lingered in his eyes. "He fell in love with Michael. How could he love that monster?"

The emotion in Jessie's eyes tore at Aidan's heart. The monster had taken another person a few years after Jessie's escape, someone who shared entirely too many physical qualities for it to be a coincidence. He didn't even want to think of all the internal arguments and what-ifs racing through Jessie's mind at that moment. He reached out and threaded his fingers with Jessie's to still his hands, relieved when Jessie sighed at the contact. "Whatever you're thinking, stop. This is not your fault."

"Who's the mind reader now?"

"Hunter once told me, bad things happen sometimes for no reason and trying to make sense of it would drive someone nuts." He squeezed Jessie's hand. "It's over. Focus on that part."

Jessie pulled up their clasped hands, kissing Aidan's bandaged knuckles. "You said nuts."

Aidan gave him a lopsided grin, knowing Jessie was trying to force his mind to steer toward the positive. He scanned every inch of Jessie's features. His chest tightened at the cut on Jessie's lip and the darkened bruise on the side of his face. "Aside from the cut lip and the bruise, did they…hurt you in any other way?"

Jessie shook his head. He rested his cheek against Aidan's hand and ran his fingers along the bandage around Aidan's wrist. "Everyone's waiting for you to wake up."

"Who's *everyone*?"

"Ty, our friends, the team. Cole bought you a cape. He says you're his new superhero. Your captain's here too and several other guys from the precinct have been in and out of here for the last two days to see how you're doing." He placed a few kisses on Aidan's bandaged knuckles.

"Wait. What? Two days?"

Jessie nodded. "Your team's been here the whole time. Even

Manny flew back early from their honeymoon when he heard what happened. They all took a break to grab something from the cafeteria, but they should be back any minute," Jessie said, reluctantly releasing Aidan's hand.

"Two fucking days," he mumbled to himself. Aidan scowled and grabbed Jessie's hand again, firmly threading their fingers.

Jessie rubbed his thumb along Aidan's skin. "They'll see."

"I don't care. I came too close to losing you, and I'm not wasting another second. Besides, they've already been gossiping about us for months. Might as well give them a visual to go with all the stories."

"Is that *you* talking or the meds? They won't be able to *unsee* things if they walk in."

Aidan focused his gaze on the man who punctuated each beginning and end of his *happily ever after* dreams. "This is me talking. And I'm clearer than I've been in a long time. Whoever doesn't like it can go fuck themselves."

"That's so romantic."

"Don't give me a hard time. I'm opening up here." Aidan pulled their clasped hands to his lips and pressed a kiss to Jessie's skin. "C'mere."

Jessie pulled the chair closer to Aidan's bed.

"Closer."

Jessie leaned forward, resting his elbows on the mattress.

"Closer."

"If I get any closer, I'm going to be in the bed."

"That's the point. Please."

The corner of Jessie's mouth curled up into a weak smile. "You know I can't resist when you say that."

"Please, please, please."

Jessie slowly climbed into the hospital bed, careful of the bandages around Aidan's torso and across his chest. They lay quietly on the bed, holding each other and stroking each other's skin in random patterns.

"I thought I lost you," Jessie whispered. "When I saw you on the ground by the truck…and…when he shot you…all the blood…" He stopped when his breath hitched. He clutched the front of the hospital gown and gently rested his head against Aidan's chest.

Aidan stroked Jessie's back and placed a few tender kisses in Jessie's hair and forehead, reveling in the peace that slowly enveloped them. "I'm okay," he whispered. He'd been stabbed and shot before. Those wounds would heal. But the potential hole in his heart from losing Jessie…that would have been unrecoverable. He rested his chin at the top of Jessie's head and closed his eyes. "I'd do anything for you, Jess."

"I know. But I'd really appreciate it if you didn't get shot to prove that." Jessie buried his face snugly at the base of Aidan's neck, nestling into the spot he had claimed long ago as his own.

"We need to work on your sense of humor."

Jessie softly laughed.

Aidan closed his eyes, enjoying the joy of that quiet, subtle sound vibrating through his body, filling his spirit with a sense of peace, mending his soul stronger than any medicine ever could. "I love you, Jess. More than I ever thought was possible." He sighed at how easily the words flowed from his lips. He ghosted his fingers up Jessie's back and into his hair, pulling him closer and brushing his lips against the silky dark strands at the top of Jessie's head. "I know I don't say it, but I need you to know that you're not just important to me but essential. I don't walk around telling the air I appreciate it and need it to breathe. I just do."

Jessie inched back and looked up at Aidan, unable to hide the emotion shining in his eyes. "I was expecting an Aidanism, but I'll take that any day." He reached up and brushed his lips against Aidan's. "So many mega bonus points for Team Calloway." He absently stroked Aidan's stubble, quieting for a few moments before he spoke. "That's the second time you've told me you love me."

Aidan's brows knit together. "Second time?"

Jessie nodded and swallowed heavily, withdrawing his hand and tucking it back in between them, huddling closer. "When you fell to the ground, by the truck. You told me you loved me. I wanted to kick you in the balls so badly for waiting until that very moment to say it."

"You have a serious obsession with my balls." He remembered mumbling something before he passed out, but he hadn't realized how easily the words had spilled. Effortless, just like his love for the man in his arms. "Regardless of all my shit, I will always love you, even when you get tired of loving me back."

"I'll never get tired of loving you. Because you're essential to me too," Jessie said with a smile in his voice. "Besides, isn't there some unwritten rule…when you save someone's life, they belong to you? So I guess you're stuck with me."

Aidan kissed Jessie's forehead, thankful to have him safe in his arms. "You saved me a long time ago, Jess. I've been yours for a while."

"I like that."

"Good." Aidan closed his eyes and ghosted his fingers over Jessie's pale skin, reveling in the blanket of serenity and peace that surrounded them. "Because I'm told I have a hard time letting things go."

"I'm counting on it…every second of every day."

Epilogue

Four months later

Jessie sat under the tree in the backyard of Halfway House, enjoying the football game. Not really following who led or whichever team scored a touchdown, but the game obviously memorable regardless of who scored the winning play.

Aidan's birthday wish. A simple backyard barbecue with those he considered closest friends and family—minus Bull, who was at an undisclosed location on assignment.

Sunny, soon to be godmother to the new Reyes addition, had escaped with Manny's wife to the maternity store since Marcela's baby bump was starting to show. Sunny took her future godmother duties as seriously as she did everything else. But she confessed willingness to do just about anything to escape the testosterone overdose she knew would happen on the football field.

Hunter, Cameron, and Hunter's father, Thomas, had returned weeks ago and quickly settled into their old lives but new all the same. Thomas was immediately up to his old tricks and flirting with ladies at the nearby community center. Hunter now taught at the university and selectively consulted on cases with Jessie on legal strategies. And Cameron had a permanent grin etched on his face while working at the diner during the week and handling the occasional landscaping job in the evening and on weekends.

But none of that compared to Aidan's transformation. He had become Home-Video Aidan—vibrant and in full-color.

He talked more.

He smiled bigger.

He laughed louder.

And his love was boundless.

Jessie would willingly share *his* Aidan with the world—but only enough so they'd witness how amazing he truly was. He still saw the bristly personality at work on those occasions when they brought Jessie in to consult on another task force case. But behind every snarky comment or sharp jab at a fellow team member, hid a playful spark in his eyes hoping for banter.

Aidan had managed to find his version of inner-peace with the heartbreaking milestones in his life. He still had his moments with painful reminders that stabbed his heart more than he dared to admit, but it was part of Aidan's nature...to care more than most. But he always found the time to talk through those moments, either while they snuggled in bed or during one of his follow-up sessions with Dr. Engel.

"Second down. You're going down, Boy Toy!" Aidan yelled through his hands, cupped in a megaphone fashion.

Cameron and Cole laughed in the field as Hunter scowled. They each positioned themselves, crouching close to the ground with their fingertips in the grass.

"You're going to pay for that," Hunter said with an intense look on his face that contradicted the half smile. His prowl look. The one that let everyone know he was ready to dive in for the kill. Jessie knew that expression well after having worked alongside him for years in the state attorney's office. And Aidan knew his friend well enough to suspect the jab would hit its mark.

Matt blew the whistle and both teams lunged forward—flag football be damned. There would be bruises and cuts and spatters of blood, and tons of smiles all around. Hunter immediately headed toward Aidan who faked a step to the side to get to Cole, carrying the football.

"Hunter's going to nail Aidan," Ty said, slightly cringing in the chair beside him.

"No, he won't. Aidan's covered," Jessie said. "I'm more worried about Cole right now."

Ty straightened in his seat to get a better view. Wall circled and blocked Hunter, knocking him flat on his ass at the same moment Aidan rammed into Cole and dropped him to the ground.

Cole rose from the grass, brushing off the dirt from his shorts and straightening the tight-fitting skull cap on his head. "Fuck, man! Whatever happened to the flag?"

Aidan snatched the flag from Cole's pocket and waved it in the air, laughing so hard it became contagious, rippling laughter to his other teammates—Travis and Manny. Cole shoved Aidan playfully as Wall extended a hand to Hunter, helping him off the ground. Cole shoved Aidan again, baiting him. Julian and Wall immediately stood between them to break it up, Julian slapping the back of Cole's head while Wall stood guard at Aidan's side.

Jessie sighed, thankful his hard-headed Aidan was protected on the field—flag football and at work. Risks and worry were a package deal, but he was at peace knowing Aidan was part of a rock-solid team where each member had declined several offers for transfers and promotions simply to stay as a unit. Aidan had recovered quickly from his injuries, left with a gunshot scar hidden by the edge of his inked scroll, a permanent mark on his lower torso, and a slash across his pec from the knife.

A deep groove that served as a constant reminder—a mark Jessie's monster had etched into Aidan's body. A scar, Aidan countered, that proved how much he loved Jessie and how far he'd go to always love and protect him—one he'd proudly wear like a badge of honor. Jessie wouldn't deny he preferred that version better. Seemed after all this time, some of his positivity rubbed off on his prickly, always sexy detective.

"That's my brother," Ty said, pulling Jessie from his thoughts. He crossed his arms and smiled smugly looking out at the field as Aidan wrapped one arm around Cole's neck and tugged him close so he couldn't escape, then rubbed Cole's head with his knuckles until Cole started laughing.

"That's *my* Aidan," Jessie said, absently holding the key on his necklace, running his finger along the top and sliding it across the chain link. He rose from his chair and walked over to the barbecue, raising the cover and tending to the burgers and hot dogs.

"Hey, Cam! Set up the play we covered in the huddle," Hunter yelled out.

Cam looked over his shoulder and grinned. "I love it when you yell my name." Everyone in the group knew Cam's excitement stemmed from the use of his given name rather than the WITSEC name, but the double entendre was obvious in his heated stare.

"Please show some mercy for the heteros in the audience," Manny said, groaning loud enough to trigger a few chuckles.

Jessie switched his focus between the barbecue grill and the game, shaking his head when Cole tackled Julian in the next down. Even he knew it didn't make any sense to tackle your own team member, but Cole was Cole.

Aidan called a time-out and Matt blew the whistle. He ran over to Jessie with a lingering smile, grabbing one of the baseball caps from the table. "Here, put this on so you don't burn. The sun's kicking a bit today."

"I've still got the sunscreen you put on me earlier. I think I'll be okay," he said, flipping the burgers on the grill.

"Just in case." Aidan put the cap on Jessie's head, positioning it so it was perfectly centered, then leaned in and gave him a quick kiss on the lips. "And don't worry about the hat-head. You're still perfect."

Jessie knew he must have a silly grin on his face. He couldn't contain the happiness that always bubbled to the surface when Aidan kissed him or held his hand in public.

"Did I earn a point with that?"

Jessie nodded, still smiling.

Aidan quieted when Julian approached.

"Are the burgers ready? I'm starving," Julian said, grabbing a bun from the bag and handing it to Matt before taking another for himself. The others circled the grill, each taking a bit of food before settling at the two round patio tables.

Cole walked up to them and stood off to the side with a ridiculous grin on his face, watching them. Aidan rolled his eyes and turned his head toward Cole, refusing to distance himself from Jessie. "What's so funny, Mr. Future-brother-in-law?"

Cole's smile widened as it always did when Aidan threw back his self-proclaimed title. "You two. It's like watching turtle porn."

Jessie couldn't hide the bubbling happiness when Aidan pushed Cole, laughing as he shoved him away.

"Seriously, is *everyone* gay here?" Manny said with an eye roll.

Aidan smirked. "Asks the only man at this barbecue eating a hot dog instead of a burger."

Manny stopped the hot dog midway to his mouth, launching another round of laughter from the group before shrugging it off and taking a bite.

Aidan wrapped his arms around Jessie's waist from behind, pulling him close against his chest. "Thanks for an awesome birthday," he whispered in Jessie's ear.

Jessie anchored his hands on the strong arms wrapped around his waist, watching their friends laugh and joke with each other. "Birthday's not over yet."

"Mmm. I'm guessing there will be balls involved," Aidan whispered in Jessie's ear, pulling his earlobe between his teeth.

"Yeah. Yours." Jessie chuckled.

"You're insatiable."

Jessie turned in the embrace, reaching up to touch Aidan's stubbled jaw, smiling when Aidan leaned into the caress. "And you love that."

"I do." Aidan guided Jessie's hand from his face to his chest, pressing Jessie's palm over the scar on his pec. He covered Jessie's hand with his own and held his gaze with a solemn expression filled with unmistakable love. "With every breath and heartbeat."

~ The End ~

About the Author

Jaime Reese is the alter ego of an artist who loves the creative process of writing, just not about herself. Fiction is far more interesting. She has a weakness for broken, misunderstood heroes and feels everyone deserves a chance at love and life. An avid fan of a happy ending, she believes those endings acquired with a little difficulty are more cherished.

jr@jaimereese.com
http://www.jaimereese.com/

Facebook:
https://www.facebook.com/author.jaime.reese
Page:
https://www.facebook.com/JaimeReeseAuthor

Twitter: @Jaime_Reese

THE MEN OF
HALFWAY HOUSE
Series

A Better Man
A Hunted Man
A Restored Man
A Mended Man

...more to come...

Made in the USA
Las Vegas, NV
21 June 2025

23895667R00246